ALSO BY MAGGIE MCPHEE

SECOND CHANCES

AUTUMN IN THE DESERT, BOOK 2

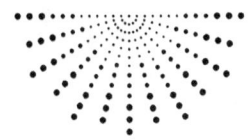

MAGGIE MCPHEE

Cover by: Zoran Petrovic/Fiverr.com name, Visual Arts

Map of Palm Lakes by: Maria Gandolfo/ Fiverr.com name, Renflowergrapx

Copyright © 2017 by Maggie & Nigel Percy

ISBN: 978-1-946014-13-9 (Ebook version)

ISBN: 978-1-946014-16-0 (Paperback version)

Sixth Sense Books

150 Buck Run E

Dahlonega, GA 30533

Email address: authormaggiemcphee@gmail.com

For everyone who wants a second chance

CONTENTS

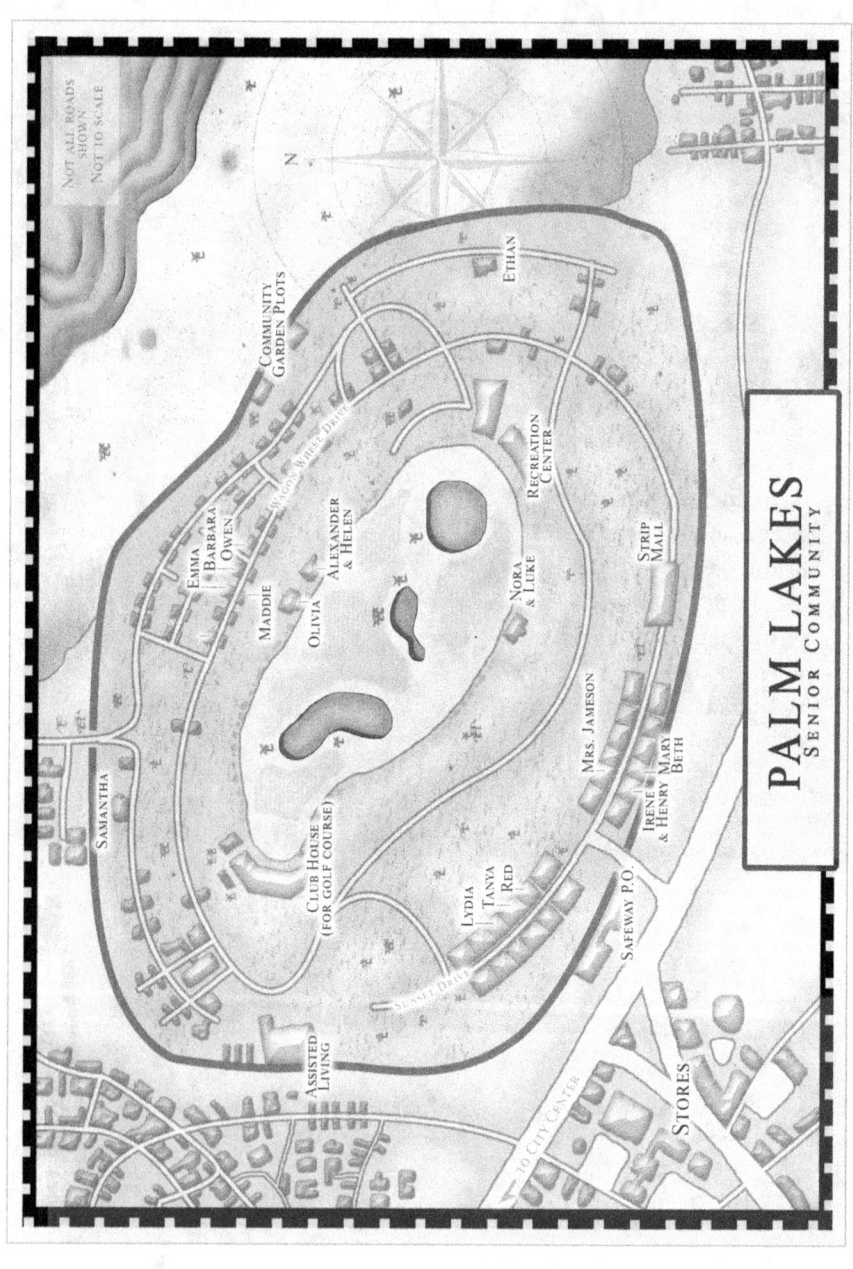

N

COMMUNITY GARDEN PLOTS

ETHAN

EMMA
BARBARA
OWEN

Willow Street Drive

MADDIE

ALEXANDER & HELEN

OLIVIA

RECREATION CENTER

NORA & LUKE

SAMANTHA

STRIP MALL

CLUB HOUSE
(FOR GOLF COURSE)

MRS. JAMESON

IRENE & HENRY
MARY BETH

LYDIA
TANYA
RED

Sunset Drive

SAFEWAY P.O.

ASSISTED LIVING

TO CITY CENTER

STORES

PALM LAKES
SENIOR COMMUNITY

CHARACTERS

Residents Of Palm Lakes
 Maddie and Stanley O'Neill and their dog Beau
 Samantha Taylor, the O'Neills' daughter, and her husband Arthur
 Alexander Stirling, recently married to Helen Mueller
 Serafina Costello, widowed
 Mary Beth Costello, daughter of Serafina, divorced & living
temporarily with Mom, in spite of being too young to legally reside there
 Ethan Westerfield, widower and volunteer with The Helpers
 Barbara Blackstone and her husband Ben and their dog Jack
 Eric 'Red' Johnson, member of The Posse
 Lydia Stern, divorcee
 Tanya Cooper, divorcee
 Owen Schmidt, serial killer
 Bernie, a neighbor who is a widower

Wagon Wheel Drive residents (single family homes)
 Maddie and Stanley O'Neill
 Barbara and Ben Blackstone and their dog Jack
 Owen Schmidt
 Emma Lightman

Sunset Drive residents (condos)
  Lydia Stern
  Tanya Cooper
  Eric 'Red' Johnson
  Serafina and Mary Beth Costello
  Mrs. Jameson
  Irene & Henry Dubois

Living along the golf course
  Alexander & Helen Stirling
  Nora & Luke Fontaine
  Olivia Deschamps, widow

Nonresidents
  Sally, Helen's daughter
  Julio, landscaping contractor

MONDAY, DECEMBER 18, 1995

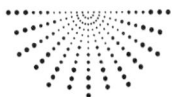

Mary Beth, 11:15am

*T*he plastic grocery bags slipped from her grasp and landed on the floor of the entryway with a thunk. Mary Beth gasped at the scene before her, deaf to the rattle of a can rolling across the tiles, then finally hitting the baseboard. Mom lay sprawled across the couch, her arms hanging over the edge as if reaching for something just beyond her grasp, the surprised look on her face hinting that her last moments had revealed something unexpected.

Recovering from momentary paralysis, Mary Beth dashed into the living room and knelt next to Mom's inert form, reaching for the neck, hoping vainly to find a pulse. Mom was gone, though her skin was still warm.

Seconds or hours later, she couldn't have said which, Mary Beth looked down as if from a great distance at her hands stroking Mom's gray hair, heard a heart-wrenching sob, and realized it was her own voice. "Mom, what happened?" she croaked. "Oh, God, why did I have to be away when you needed me?"

Desperate to do something, she stood and tried to think, but her head felt stuffed full of cotton balls. She closed her eyes to the terrible scene in front of her, pleading for it to disappear, but of course, it didn't. Then her brain finally kicked in. She needed to call 911. Not that they could fix this.

While she waited for an answer, she chastised herself. If she hadn't stopped on the way home, maybe she would have been here when it happened. Maybe she could have saved Mom.

She drummed her fingers on the countertop. *Christ, I need a cigarette!* Then it hit her that even though Mom never allowed smoking in the house, she could have one now if she wished. In typically bizarre fashion, her mind made a link between her desire to smoke and Mom's death, and her craving evaporated in a cloud of guilt. Thankfully, her call was answered quickly, and the barrage of questions distracted her from further self-punishment.

After the 911 call, she opened the front door and stepped into the brisk air to avoid looking at Mom's body. Within minutes, vehicles were pulling up with flashing lights, broadcasting that something bad had happened. Living in the Palm Lakes Senior Community made this type of occurrence fairly common, but it was different when it happened to you. She always said a quick prayer when she saw or heard an ambulance--the nuns had taught her to--but it was so personal now that prayer seemed pointless. Instead of hiding (she knew she couldn't, but the urge was almost overpowering), she steeled herself to facilitate the horrible process as uniformed people were disgorged from the Posse car, ambulance and fire engine.

A few curious neighbors appeared outside the doors of their condos or gathered on the edge of the street, held back as if by an invisible barrier, and Mary Beth swallowed the urge to shout at them for being such damn ghouls. Mom was always on her about her bad language. Then she realized it didn't matter any more what Mom thought. *Shit! Fuck! Damn!*

Across the street, short, plump Mrs. Jameson, a major busybody, stood on her front step, a surprisingly sympathetic look on her face. Funny, Mary Beth wouldn't have expected compassion from her. Mom had said she reported violations of the covenants, and Mary Beth had been avoiding the old hag for months, since she was too young to be a legal resident. In fact, all she had ever seen of Mrs. Jameson was a shadow spying from behind the curtain in her front window. It was hard to picture an elderly plump widow with bluish-silver hair and an outdated housedress as a closet Nazi. It just went to show that you couldn't judge people by how they look.

Mary Beth did her part, woodenly answering questions for emergency personnel and pointing in the direction of the living room, unwilling to go back inside. It was over quicker than she could have imagined. She stepped aside as the EMTs rolled the stretcher back through the doorway. She averted her gaze seconds too late to avoid seeing the body bag. As she listened to the metallic clanking of the stretcher being loaded into the vehicle, she realized that with her Mom dead, she was now technically homeless. Mom owned the condo, but Mary Beth was too young to legally live there or even own it. And certainly someone would notice now. How long would it take them to find out she was living there and make her sell?

The stark desert sunshine cast ugly shadows, the sun being low in the sky even near midday, and a chill breeze tugged at her jacket, reminding her of the season, though it didn't resemble winter back home. She wrapped the jacket more tightly around herself and got into her car to follow the ambulance.

ON HER RETURN HOURS LATER, street lights bathed the empty road and deserted sidewalks, illuminating the chill night. Everything looked as it always did. It was as if nothing had happened. *If only.* She pulled into the garage and walked through the silent house, wishing she could turn back time and be greeted by Mom, even to face criticism for cussing or being late.

She glanced into the living room and wondered how she'd ever be able to sit on the couch again. The condo was so small, she didn't have much choice. Well, selling the place would solve that problem.

She shook her head and went into the kitchen and poured herself a glass of wine. Thank God she had a few bottles, because it was going to be a long, sleepless night. Sitting listlessly at the breakfast table, she stared out through the sliding glass door into the darkness of the back yard and wondered what was going to become of her.

Some time later, she startled back to reality and stared at the wine glass, unaware that she had emptied it, then refilled it and wished she had someone to talk to. That was the problem with being an illegal resident. Her co-worker at Palo Verde Landscaping, Samantha Taylor, had only begun to spend a little time with Mary Beth outside of work, and it didn't feel right to ask her for help, because Samantha was awfully busy with work and caring for her aging parents, who were also residents of Palm Lakes. Helen, her former next door neighbor, had married recently and moved to another part of the community with her gorgeous new husband Alexander. They'd gone on a honeymoon to the South Pacific, and Mary Beth wasn't even sure they were home yet. She missed her visits with Helen, who'd introduced her to Maddie (to her surprise, her coworker Samantha's mother), who had become her jewelry-making mentor. Making jewelry had brought joy into Mary Beth's life, giving her an outlet for her creative energy. But she couldn't turn to Maddie; Maddie was elderly and in bad health, and it wouldn't be fair to impose on her about this. It also wouldn't do to remind her what she had to look forward to at her age. Maybe Ethan, whom she'd met at Maddie's, wouldn't mind if she called him. A volunteer with the Helpers, he came to do things the doctors said Maddie shouldn't do because of her osteoporosis, like walk their big dog or take the trash out, and since they were at Maddie's at the same time, they'd fallen into the habit of standing by their cars before leaving, just chatting. Surely Ethan wouldn't mind if she called; he was a widower and seemed to enjoy her company.

She glanced at the clock and felt guilty calling on him at this hour (anything after 9pm was ungodly late in Palm Lakes, and it was 9:10), but she couldn't stand the thought of bearing this alone for another minute. She found his number and dialed it, holding her breath.

"Hi, Ethan, it's me. Mary Beth."

"Mary Beth! It's good to hear from you. Is everything OK?"

It occurred to her she hadn't planned what to say, but there was no easy way to say it, so she blurted it out. "I came home from work today and found my Mom had died. I've just gotten back from dealing with all the formalities. I'm sitting here at the dining table wondering what to do next. It was sudden, although, I guess it wasn't completely unexpected. She had heart trouble." Mary Beth felt tears threatening for the first time.

"Can I come over? You shouldn't be alone now."

Relief flooded her. "Yes, I'd like that. But I won't be good company."

"You've never given me your address. Tell me how to find you." She cringed that she hadn't followed through on her promise of making dinner for him when he'd called to wish her a Happy Thanksgiving. If she were honest with herself, she knew she was just dreading Mom's reaction. Mom had assumed something was going on between them. Not. Well, that wasn't going to be an issue now.

She gave him directions and hung up, hoping he'd hurry. It was way too quiet and creepy being here by herself, especially after dark. She didn't believe in ghosts, but she almost felt like Mom was hanging around. Probably wanted to give her hell about something or other. When the doorbell rang several minutes later, she rushed past the living room to get to the front door, consciously avoiding looking towards the couch. Ethan stood in ragged jeans and a faded flannel shirt, backlit by a street light.

"Come in here. It's not that warm outside. You should have worn a jacket!" She pulled him into the house and shut the door.

"I was in a hurry and forgot to grab one. It's not so bad. That's one thing about winters in the desert." He stood there towering over her as if uncertain what to do next, looking around the darkened area and shifting from one foot to the other like a restless bear.

Mary Beth turned and walked back towards the light that spilled from dining room. "I can't stand to be out here for long. It was too much of a shock finding her on the couch." She pointed at the offending piece of furniture as he followed her silently past the living room.

"I was having a glass of wine. Actually, another glass of wine. Would you like one?" She indicated the other glass she'd put on the table.

"That would be fine."

She ignored his less-than-enthusiastic response and poured both of them a glass and sat down. Suddenly remembering her manners, she stood back up. "Would you like anything to eat?"

"No, I'm not hungry."

She winced at what she heard in his voice, but pushed past the tightening in her chest. "I'm sorry I didn't get around to inviting you to dinner like I said I would on Thanksgiving, and I'm sorry I never said anything about it until now. I was worried about my Mom. She had some issues with the age difference between you and me, and she could be pretty critical, and I wasn't certain I could take it if she started in on you. That's the only reason I didn't follow through. I was afraid she'd embarrass me. I know that's not much of an excuse, but--"

He reached over and patted her hand. "Don't worry about that now. I'm just so sorry you had to go through this. If I can help in any way, I will. I'd like to come to the funeral once you have it set."

So he wasn't mad at her. "Thanks, Ethan. I didn't know who else to call. I don't have any close friends here, at least not single ones. I shouldn't be so shocked, but I just don't know what to do. We had plans, and things were working out nicely. And now it's all fallen apart." She felt so numb. Where were the tears? What was the matter with her?

His gray eyes held no judgment, just compassion. She put her head in her hands. "I don't want to make this all about me, but I'm worried what to do now. I'm not legal here, and now that Mom's gone, I won't be able to stay. And I was really getting settled here and liking it. Go figure. Who would have thought I'd like living in an old fart community? Oh, shit!" She looked at him apologetically. "Sorry, no offense meant."

"None taken," said Ethan, with a grin on his face. "I'm just pleased you've been enjoying living here. Don't borrow trouble now. The wheels of the community government grind slowly. It will take time for them to discover you're here."

"You think so? That would help. I know I'll have to sell the condo, but I need time to figure out what I'm going to do. With Mom gone, I don't really have anything tying me here. I have my job, but it isn't much, and I don't have many friends. Plus I have nowhere to live." Her voice trailed off as she struggled to face how big a change this was going to be.

"I'm sorry I didn't get to meet your Mom. Tell me about her."

Mary Beth was surprised how grateful she was for the opportunity to talk about Mom. "Mom had heart trouble, but she never liked to complain about her health, so it took me a while to pry out of her that the doctor said she shouldn't be exerting herself and that living alone scared her. She had angina for a while some months back, though that was under control. But the last several weeks or so, she changed. She stopped the obsessive cleaning. She slept more. She wasn't on my case as much as usual.

"I never asked her much, because she didn't seem to want me to. Now I wish I had; it was obvious she wasn't herself. Maybe I could have helped." Mary Beth sighed and put her hands in her lap.

"Mom and I were total opposites. I took after Dad. Poor Mom could never figure me out. She hated that I smoked, cussed and wasn't a traditional woman who cooked and cleaned and raised a bunch of kids. Not that she did. I'm an only child. She couldn't have any after me, due to complications.

"My ex, Jason, and I didn't have children. Mom hated him. Like I told you before, he took up with a younger woman, whom he got pregnant, and then divorced me. I went into a funk and lost my job and ended up coming out here to start over. At first it was terrible. Mom cleaned obsessively and wouldn't let me smoke indoors and complained constantly about me being a burden. I was going batshit crazy, pardon my French. Then things changed overnight."

Mary Beth looked up to see Ethan staring at her with such sympathy, that finally, tears started to flow. She swiped a hand across her eyes. "Julio came here to do some work on the yard and offered me a job, and Helen moved in next door and we started visiting now and then, and she introduced me to Maddie, who was her former neighbor, so I could learn to make jewelry. Which led to you.

"But like I said, lately, Mom became quieter and quit cleaning as much. It was like the aliens had kidnapped her and substituted a poor version. It worried me, even though it was more peaceful, and now I can see it was a sign that she wasn't feeling well. But because I never asked, I have no idea whether she changed because she was in pain, having symptoms or just winding down."

Ethan reached over and held her hand. "Don't beat yourself up. You did the best you could." Then he squeezed it gently. "I appreciate your sharing this with me. I always wondered what caused you to end up like a fish out of water. You've been through a lot this year." He took a deep breath, then stared at her intently. "Why don't you tell me some happy or funny stories about your Mom?"

"You want to hear about my traditional Catholic upbringing and having to wear a uniform to school, or about Mom telling me not to wear patent leather shoes because they reflect up your skirt, nor pearls, because they reflect down your blouse? Stuff like that?"

Ethan sputtered in laughter. "Absolutely! Here, let me do the honors." He grabbed the bottle and refilled their half-empty glasses.

Mary Beth thought about stories she could tell that would help him picture Mom. Once she started, she couldn't stop, because recollections flooded her. Hours later, the dawn lightened her back yard. She shook her head as if waking up and looked at the empty wine bottles that littered the dining table. Her throat was scratchy from nonstop talking. Though Ethan showed signs of being up all night drinking wine, he still looked at her with a softness in his gray eyes. Suddenly, she felt guilty for imposing on him. "I'm so sorry I've been talking all night. You must be ready to keel over. You don't have to stay."

He smiled gently and squeezed her hand, which she only now noticed he had been holding. "I'm glad you called me."

"How about I make us some breakfast? That's the least I can do. We could both use coffee and something to eat after all that wine." She glanced at the empty bottles that littered the table. "I can't believe we drank that much! How about something to eat? One thing the women in my family do well is cook. What do you say? An omelet, bacon and toast?"

"If you don't mind, coffee and something to eat would be very nice." He ran his hand across the stubble on his chin, and she tangentially thought what a domestic scene this was.

It wasn't until she got up to cook that she realized she hadn't smoked a cigarette in nearly 24 hours. And she didn't feel like one. Maybe she was channeling Mom.

* * *

Samantha, 11:59am

Samantha had been putting off calling Jack for a couple weeks, and Arthur was going to become suspicious if she waited much longer. She couldn't bear to call Jack from home, where Arthur could hear her end of the conversation. Yet she couldn't call from work. The phones at Palo Verde Landscaping were not located for privacy, so she couldn't very well call a competitor about a job from there.

So on her way back to work from lunch, she pulled into the parking lot at the Recreation Center and went into the lobby where there was an old-fashioned phone booth. Hopefully she wouldn't run into anyone she knew. Too bad she didn't have one of those mobile phones, but they were just too expensive.

As she remarked to herself about the quiet inside the booth and the comfortable seat, she summoned courage, then extracted Jack's business card from her pocket. It was raggedy from being carried around for weeks and being pulled out of her pocket over and over as she looked at it and debated with herself about calling him. Weeks ago, after they had partnered on a project in a landscaping class at the local community college, Jack had offered her a job. But she still wasn't sure how much the offer was based on their obvious mutual attraction and how much was based on her qualifications. The time for procrastinating was over, though. She dialed his number, half hoping he'd be out for lunch, but he answered on the second ring.

"Temple Landscaping, Jack Temple speaking."

"Hi, Jack. It's me, Samantha."

"Samantha! It's so good to hear you. Are you going to accept my job offer? It's still open."

She was both relieved and disturbed. "I told you I couldn't take the job, but I wasn't very good about hiding my disappointment at home. I ended up having to tell Arthur, and he demanded that I give you a call and ask for full details, because he thinks I should take the job if it's better than what I have now. I still don't think I should, no matter what the offer is, and you know why. I've been putting off calling you, but I have to be able to tell Arthur I followed through. I'm sorry to put you through this, because I don't see any way I can accept your proposal."

There was a pause on his end. Maybe she'd pissed him off. Maybe that would be a good thing and end all this confusion. "Look, Samantha,

I need someone with your qualifications to help me with design and managing the planting crews. I promised I wouldn't push for anything else. And I meant it. I think we'd make a great team, and I have my hands full trying to do it all. I won't be able to expand the way I want without your help. Isn't it good that your husband is in favor of it?"

Feeling guilty and annoyed at the same time, Samantha said, "You know as well as I do that if I take the job, sooner or later, things will get personal between us, and I can't afford that. My parents need me. Arthur hasn't done anything to deserve disloyalty; not lately, anyway."

"I understand your concerns, and I respect your values. There must be some way to work this out. What can I do to make you feel safe taking the job?"

Samantha squeezed her eyes shut and rubbed her forehead with her hand. He wasn't making this easy for her. Maybe he didn't understand the power of the attraction she felt for him. Maybe he could be professional with her; she wasn't sure she could be with him. Was he just hoping to wear her down, or did he not feel as strongly? Either way would be bad for her. "Jack, do me a favor and tell me the details. I will report to Arthur. I'm not going to make any promises. I still don't think it's a good idea."

"Fair enough. How can you make a decision without knowing what I'm talking about? I know you get the use of a pickup from Palo Verde, and that they pay the gas for you, and you get to take it home as if it's your vehicle. You would get the same benefit here. I'd give you one of the trucks, a gas card and you could use it to commute. You said the commute bothered you; at least this way, it would not add expense.

"I realize you'd have to give up having lunch at home, and you wouldn't be able to drop by and see your parents during the workday like you do now. I can't do anything about that. Nor can I make the commute shorter. I know it would be a challenge to drive that round trip. The only way I could think to make it balance out was to pay you for 40 hours but only ask you to put in 35 a week. By taking a 30-minute lunch break and doing a 7 hour day, you could get back a lot of the time lost in the commute, which would allow you to spend time with your family."

Samantha was stunned. That was a sweet deal. "So what wages would you pay me?"

"You didn't tell me how much you make, but I'm guessing it isn't a lot more than minimum wage. Am I right?"

"Yeah, I think it's about two dollars over minimum wage."

"I'll pay you ten dollars an hour over minimum wage."

Samantha couldn't believe her ears. A salary like that, with added benefits of gas and car, was an incredible offer. She was wondering how she could ever say 'no' when he interrupted her train of thought. ¯

"I don't offer medical at this time, but I give all employees one week's paid vacation a year. They don't offer that at Palo Verde, do they?" She had to admit, her resolve was crumbling.

"No, they don't," she whispered. "Jack, I'll tell Arthur and phone you back with a decision soon. Thanks for such a generous offer." Her stomach clenched at the no-win situation. No matter what she chose now, she'd lose.

He sighed as if he'd used all his ammunition. "I'll wait for your call. Is there any way I can call you?"

"I don't have a mobile phone, Jack, and there isn't anywhere private you could call. It's for the best this way. I really will call you back." She paused for a second, hating to let him go, sure she was going to turn him down about the job and that she'd eventually never see him again. "I hope you have a nice Christmas."

"I wish I could see you."

"There's no point to it, Jack. And you don't have to hold that job open for me if you find someone else. But I promise I'll call and give you my final decision soon."

"OK. I'll wait to hear from you."

She reluctantly hung up the phone, cracked the door open to turn off the light and sat in the booth trying to compose herself in the shadows. She knew she'd upset him. He'd be staring intently at the phone, his face all sharp angles, his nearly black eyes smoldering. His dark good looks had a powerful effect on her, and she didn't really want him to be her boss. But the offer was way better than she could have hoped, and Arthur was going to insist she take it if she told him the truth. How could she convince him that she shouldn't? They could use the money; they had so little in savings. And the job would be rewarding for her professionally. He'd never understand why she wanted to turn it down.

11

She gritted her teeth, trying to ignore the little voice that said she should give it a chance, that she could keep it professional. *Oh, if only that were true.* Shaking her head, she headed back to work, a burning feeling in her stomach.

The high today was going to be 58, pretty typical for winter weather, but to her, it felt chilly, especially with the breeze coming from the north. As usual, she'd worn layers because it had been in the low 40s when she set off to work at 6:30. There was no heating in the office, and she spent most of her time outdoors anyway, so the weather wasn't ideal for her. She'd imagined winter in the desert would be warmer. Still, it was better than Maryland in winter, and she loved what she did.

She parked in front of the ramshackle wooden structure that was the office for Palo Verde Landscaping and went in to finish the design she'd started before lunch. The office was empty. Where was Mary Beth? Probably taking her lunch. No one stuck to rigid hours, so Samantha wasn't concerned. She sat at the desk nearest the door, still in her jacket, and bent her head to finishing the Anderson's yard design.

The door opened five minutes later and two men walked in. One was retirement age, the other, much younger. Probably father and son, as there was a marked resemblance, especially around the eyes. Both wore nothing but t-shirts and shorts. It amused Samantha, who had three layers on top and had been doing a design with fingerless gloves to fight off the chill. The father looked around the office, then at Samantha, since she was the only person there.

"So what part of North Dakota are you guys from?" Samantha asked.

Father blinked his eyes in astonishment. "How did you know that?"

Samantha smiled. "Look at how I'm dressed. Look at you. It's easy to see you don't live here. Residents feel cold this time of year. I knew you were from somewhere that would consider this summer weather. How can I help?"

He shook his head and grinned. "Lucky guess! We *are* from North Dakota, and it *is* pretty balmy today. We're wanting to look at some plants. Can you show us around?"

"Sure thing." Samantha took them on a tour of the nursery and returned to the office a half hour later to write an invoice for their purchase and put their payment in the back office. Mary Beth still hadn't returned from lunch. That was strange. She never took this long. Back at the desk, Samantha resumed the drawing of the Anderson yard.

The phone rang ten minutes later, and Samantha ran over to answer it.

"Palo Verde Landscaping, Samantha speaking."

"Samantha, it's me." Mary Beth's voice was weak and shaky.

"Mary Beth, what's wrong?"

"I came home and found my Mom dead. I won't be back today and probably not until after the funeral. Can you tell Julio or one of the brothers? I'll try to call later when I have a better idea of when I can get back."

Samantha slumped into the nearest chair. "Oh, Mary Beth, I'm so sorry. Please let me know if there's anything we can do. I'll tell Julio. You just do what you need to do. Give me a call at home when things calm down. I'd like to come to the funeral service if that's all right."

"I'll let you know once it's set. Thanks, Samantha." Mary Beth sounded forlorn.

"Just call me if I can do anything at all."

Mary Beth signed off and Samantha went to the radio to contact Julio.

It could just as easily have been her in Mary Beth's shoes. It was becoming obvious that both her parents were teetering on the edge of the precipice these days. Poor Mary Beth. She didn't have a lot of friends, living in Palm Lakes illegally. Samantha's mother spent more leisure time with Mary Beth than she did. Samantha resolved to invite Mary Beth to lunch and try to give her more support. Samantha had been so taken up with her own problems, she hadn't reached out to Mary Beth that often in recent months, even though Mary Beth was her age, making them two of the youngest residents of Palm Lakes.

BACK HOME AT the end of the work day, Samantha shared with Arthur. "Mary Beth went home for lunch and found her mother dead. What a horrible thing to have happen."

Arthur frowned. "That's for sure. Let's hope it never happens to you." His brown eyes looked squarely into Samantha's. "Did you call that Jack fellow about the job?"

"Yes, I did."

"So what's the score? Is it a good offer?"

Samantha sighed, still uncertain how to handle the subject. "It was almost too good to be true. He'll pay me significantly more. I can work 35 hours a week to compensate for the long commute, but he'll pay me for 40. He'll give me a truck and a week's vacation each year."

"So why do you seem so sad? Isn't this just what you've always wanted?" Arthur cocked his head to the side, like he was trying to figure her out. She didn't want to make him suspicious. In fact, it seemed incredible that he wasn't.

"He can't change the fact that taking this job would mean less time with you and my folks. And I'm not a kid anymore." She ignored his raised eyebrow, eloquent in expressing that to him, she was a kid. After all, she was nearly 20 years younger than he. "I'm not looking to build a career at any price. Part of me feels it's too much to ask. My parents aren't getting younger. At some point, I may need to help more, even if they don't want it. What if what happened to Mary Beth happens to me, and I'm working halfway across the city? How will I be able to care for the survivor?"

"Well, I don't see it that way. You ought to take the job. We could use the extra money. Palo Verde is pretty loose. I bet they'd take you back if you decided you wanted to return. You're a valuable employee."

"You may be right." She was galled to think how little they had in savings. It would be foolish to turn down this chance. She let out a sigh of resignation.

He finally smiled. "Of course, I'm right. This is a plum of a job. Give it a shot."

She might as well admit it. The decision was made. "I'll tell him I can start the first of the year. That allows me to give notice at work."

"Go ahead and call him now. You don't want him giving it to someone else now that you've finally decided."

Samantha started to resist, then figured it wouldn't matter. "OK." She got up and went into the kitchen to the phone, pulled out Jack's card and dialed the number, turning her back to Arthur in the other room as Jack answered the phone. "I've decided to accept your offer. I just told Arthur, and he insisted I should call you right away and accept." She hoped he understood she was unable to speak freely.

"I'm glad. When do you want to start?"

"The first of the year. That way, I can give notice at Palo Verde."

"That will be fine. I'll get a truck set up and find you office space."

"OK. See you then." Samantha hung up and turned back to Arthur. "It's done. I have the job."

"Well, I think we ought to go out and celebrate your good fortune. Where would you like to eat?"

Samantha had no appetite at all. "How about the Chinese place?"

* * *

Lydia, Noon

LYDIA DIALED the 800 number on the phone card so she could talk to her best friend Jean. She still had trouble believing Jean was in the UK now, instead of in Palm Lakes. It was currently seven hours later in the day there, making it 7pm. When she got the dial tone, she punched in Ian's phone number. "Brring-brring. Brring-brring." The typical British double ring charmed her. Jean had been expecting the call and answered right away.

"Hi, Jean. How are you doing? I know you've only been there a short while, but I really miss you." Being highly visual, Lydia desperately wished she could see her best friend, as that would tell her anything she wanted to know.

"I'm so glad you called, Lyd. Things are going great! Ian and I are getting along so well, it's like we were meant for each other. Who would have guessed that we'd be matched so well, living on different continents?"

"Well, it is pretty much what you intuitively felt, even though I know it seemed strange to trust yourself given the circumstances."

"Ya think? I meet a guy online and without hardly any facts, decide to divorce my husband and go to the UK to meet the man? It sounds crazy."

"Well, Richard's addiction to porn ended your marriage before you ever met Ian."

"I know, but it was still hard. I beat myself up about it, probably in part because Richard laid on the guilt pretty thickly." Jean sighed gustily. "Enough of that. I did what I thought was best. Best for us all."

"At least it's working out. That's what matters. So what do you two think you'll do?" Lydia held her breath, hoping Jean wasn't planning to relocate to the UK.

"Ian is willing to move to the US, since he has no family here, and he doesn't mind leaving his job. We're researching where to marry and how to get him a green card. It's more complex than I would ever have guessed. It might take a few months to get things sorted so we can come back and know he won't be thrown out by immigration."

"Will you be coming back to Palm Lakes? I could start looking for a place for you if you like. Better yet, why don't you stay with me while you both figure out what you want to do? I have a spare bedroom, and even though my condo is small, we can make it work."

"That is such a kind offer! We're still pretty vague about exactly what we intend to do and how and where to live, other than I want to live in Palm Lakes. Knowing we have temporary accommodations would make it easier, because we wouldn't have to have it all figured out. We can focus on the move, then deal with our future once we get there. I accept. Thanks!"

Lydia sighed in relief. "I'm so glad. I really miss you; you'll get tired of hearing that. It isn't the same doing things by myself. Funny, before I knew you, I was always good as a loner, but now I just can't work up the enthusiasm to do the healing work and go to classes by myself." Then she regretted saying so much, because Jean had a partner now who liked doing the same things, so Lydia was going to be a fifth wheel even if they did come back to Palm Lakes. She had never been more painfully aware of how her single status set her apart from her friends.

"I'm sorry to have deserted you. I miss you, too. It will be good to be back, though we still aren't sure exactly what we'll do. We need to find a way to support ourselves. Ian has been doing Spiritual Healing and tarot readings at a healing center here, and he suggested we consider having a business wherever we end up. I could do Reiki, and he could do Spiritual Healing, and he could do readings and I could dowse for people. It seems like a huge step to me, but I'm open to it. What about you? Why don't you think about taking your hobby to the next level? You're great at the crystal healing. Maybe we could even find a way to all work together offering complementary services."

Lydia was thrilled to be included in Jean's new life. "There may not be much of a market for such New Age stuff in Palm Lakes, but I'm open to trying. I might even do intuitive readings for people." Lydia knew this would spark questions, but it was time to share her secret with Jean. "I'm just not sure I'm ready to come out yet."

"What are you talking about, Lydia?"

Lydia blew a breath out and took the plunge. "I have this ability to read people visually. I see their energy fields, and that gives me a lot of information about them. I've been doing it since I was a kid. It would be really useful for doing readings. I don't usually tell people about it, but if we're discussing what our talents and gifts are for a business venture, I need to put it on the table."

"Damn it, Lydia, I knew you were psychic! Why didn't you tell me you could read auras?"

Lydia hadn't expected that reaction. "I don't consider it psychic. It's just another way of seeing. But it hasn't always helped me get along with people. In fact, my marriage broke up mainly because of it. It's really hard having a wife you can't lie to." She grimaced at the sad truth of it. "I guess I've been afraid to tell anyone. I don't mind being seen as eccentric, but this is beyond that. I didn't want to ruin our friendship."

"How could you ever have thought that? This is amazing! Tell me how it works and what information you get. I always knew that you could read me somehow."

"I need to see the person to do it. I can't do it with you now. In fact, I rely so much on it that phone conversations are hard for me, because I feel blind. I've been doing this my whole life. I can see colors in your aura and sense what they mean. I can see emotions as well as health problems. And if someone is going to die soon, I can see that. To tell you the truth, it can actually be as much a burden as a blessing."

"I hadn't thought of that. But you could use it to counsel people. It would be a tremendous asset to a healer, too. This makes me think Ian is right. We could set up a business together. Wouldn't that be fun?"

"I can't think of anything I'd like better. Fact is, I'm not desperate for money, so it doesn't have to pay me well. I'd just like to feel I'm doing something meaningful. Since you left, I've been lost. I can't go back to just taking classes. It isn't enough for me anymore. I guess it's time to make some big changes, though I have to admit, I'm not sure how I feel about coming out about my so-called gift."

"Well I was really scared about coming out about Richard, and then later, Ian. You helped me through it. I wish I could be there to support you. But we'll get there as soon as we can."

"It can't be fast enough to suit me," said Lydia.

"I need to ask you a question, Lyd, and please be honest with me. Putting aside the obvious attraction of having a business doing what we love, Ian and I are going to need to make decent money, because even though I got a settlement from Richard, there's no alimony, and I have no pension or other source of income, and Ian doesn't have any money put aside, plus it's a few years before he can draw his pension. Do you think we should start a business, or should we just find regular jobs?"

Lydia was touched that Jean wanted her advice. "My Dad was a successful entrepreneur, but I never had my own business, so I'm not an expert, though I do know some basics. I could check into the process for creating a business entity in this state, and I could also do a little research to see what the market is like in healing and intuitive readings. Would you like me to look into those things with the goal being to go into business together if it sounds reasonable?"

"Sure. If you're willing to do the research, we can figure out a lot before we even get back home. I feel bad putting it all on you, though."

"Jean, honey, it would be my pleasure. If we could work together, that would be a dream come true for me. I've been wondering lately what to do with myself."

"So what else is going on there?"

"Barbara's annual Christmas party is tonight. But it won't be the same without you."

"Yeah, that party in August was so great. It seems like a long time ago. Will Helen be there?"

"Yes, she and Alexander just got back from their honeymoon in Moorea. Can you believe that? I haven't seen the photos yet, but I know

I'm going to be green with envy. Helen promised to tell us more tonight. I don't have any other big news to share."

"You'll have to call me again soon. I feel so out of touch. Hardly anyone has email except you, and no one else is phoning me."

"Maybe you should give Barbara and Helen a call sometime. I know they'd like that."

"I'll have to figure out how to get a phone card to use here, like the one you have. And the time difference is a nuisance. It's hard to remember I can't just call when I think about it, or it might be the middle of night there. I'm not much of a letter-writer, and I do want to keep up on things, because I want to come back and be with you all. I want you guys to be a part of my new life."

"That sounds good to me. I'll give everyone your love when I see them. Say hi to Ian for me."

"I will. Call me again soon. Love you!"

"Love you, too!" Lydia hung up. She had lots of work to do. It felt great.

* * *

Helen, 2:35pm

HELEN STOOD in the living room of Alexander's spacious, well-decorated home and gazed out at the golf course with its pale, wintry shades of green and longed for warm tropical breezes and nothing to do all day except eat, sleep and make love. They had returned from their honeymoon a few days ago, and now she felt a chasm between them, one that she knew was of her own making. Still, she didn't know how to bridge the gap.

They'd fit together perfectly on their trip, but faced with living in his house, she was all prickly with not belonging. It was like she'd been dropped into his life to fit an empty slot, and there wasn't room for her to bring anything of herself. They were going to sell her condo, which she had just gotten comfortably decorated and newly landscaped. Her beloved cat Sheba's ashes were scattered around the tree she'd just planted there. They hadn't talked about what to do with her furniture. It

19

wouldn't fit in this house even if she wanted it to. Plus it wasn't nearly as nice as what he had, so it seemed unreasonable to consider keeping it. She'd made friends with the woman next door, Mary Beth, and she knew this move meant that she wouldn't see her often anymore. Why did she have to give up everything to make this new life, when he got to keep everything as it was before?

Then there was the issue with his cat, who was treating her like she was a wicked stepmom. She was usually so good with animals. Why was she the only one having problems adjusting? And why hadn't Alexander noticed? Did Alexander's ignorance of her inner turmoil confirm she was wrong to feel as she did, or was it part of the reason for her negativity?

She had no answers. In truth, she knew he had done nothing wrong. She felt guilty about her attitude but couldn't seem to banish it.

Unlike her, Alexander had returned from the South Pacific energized and eager to get back to writing his next food/travel book. The contract with his publisher demanded he turn in a draft soon. He had such focus and commitment, but she couldn't even decide what she wanted to write about, not that she was a professional like him. For her, writing was merely a lifelong dream. To think that some months back, writing a novel had seemed a good project for her. What colossal ego! After years of faithful daily journaling, she could barely put pen to paper anymore. And that irritated her, too, because she wasn't sure what had happened; she just seemed to have nothing to say anymore. The writing partnership she'd imagined with Alexander wasn't materializing, and it made her worry about how compatible they really were.

She didn't know how to talk with Alexander about her feelings. Big change had always disturbed her. Just as it had after Lou had died suddenly of a heart attack. She'd managed to find her footing then--after a pretty rough patch--and here she was facing a major adjustment again less than a year later. Alexander didn't seem to be aware that anything was wrong.

It occurred to her she was being harder on Alexander than she ever had been on Lou, and that unfairness made her cringe. She had never blamed Lou for not knowing how she felt. She knew he didn't care (why would he beat her if he valued her?), and she had expected nothing good from him. But with Alexander, she thought it would be different, that she'd have a soul mate. Unfortunately, since they married, his intuitive quotient seemed to have dropped to nil. She wanted him to ask her what was wrong, so she wouldn't have to complain, but he seemed unaware that anything was bothering her. The more he didn't notice, the more annoyed she got. And she knew that she was in the wrong, which only made her more upset.

Absorbed in her troubled thoughts, she didn't hear Alexander step up behind her, and when he wrapped his arms around her, she jumped.

"Sorry. I thought you heard me. I saw you weren't in your office, and I wanted to give you a hug." He held her close, and his warmth and the scent of him soothed her frazzled nerves. She held his arms around her fiercely, hoping to drive away the negative feelings. She couldn't bear to tell him. It would make her seem so ungrateful.

"You ready to make a big splash at Barbara's party tonight?" He turned her around and searched her face with his emerald eyes. She buried her face in his chest to avoid scrutiny.

"Yes, I'm ready," she mumbled against his shirt, enjoying the scent of his after-shave mixed with a fragrance that was uniquely him.

"It will be our first public appearance since the wedding. Are you nervous?" She could hear the grin in his voice.

"Why would I be nervous?"

"I know you're not big on socializing. We don't have to stay longer than you want."

"Lydia will be there, and it's always good to see her and Barbara. And Sally told me she and Red were invited."

"Really? That will cause a stir, her showing up six months pregnant with a man twice her age who isn't the father of her baby. She'll be the talk of the party."

"That might be the point. At the last party, she'd only just found out she was pregnant, but she was still noticeable."

"Of course she stood out. She was the only person there who was less than 55 years old, not to mention she's beautiful like her Mom. It should be interesting, as the Chinese say." Alexander pushed back from her and flashed his trademark sexy smile. Then he led her over to the couch and pulled her down next to him. "Maybe it's none of my business, but do you know what's going on between Sally and Red?"

21

Helen sighed and pushed her hair back from her face. "She never tells me anything. Obviously, they're dating, if that's what you call it these days. I'm worried he's going to get hurt. He just isn't her type. Not that I wouldn't be thrilled if they decided to get married. Her usual type is a young, down-on-his luck artist or musician with a drug habit. Red Johnson is the antithesis of that." Sally was her youngest and favorite child, but sometimes she couldn't figure her out. "I can't say what's motivating her."

Talking about Sally's predicament had calmed her down for some reason. She laid her head on Alexander's shoulder, the earlier storm within her having died.

He sat up straighter and her head came off his shoulder. "Well, enough gossip. I better get back to work. It's so tempting not to. But I need to learn to keep my hands off you so I can meet my deadline." He gave her a sizzling look. "We'll go to Barbara's, but you're all mine after that." He kissed her hard, got up and walked back to his office.

Slightly dazed, Helen wandered into her own little office, the converted former guest bedroom, and sat at the antique desk, the only piece of her furniture in the whole house. Her journals sat on a bookshelf across from her, and her latest one lay open on the desktop, a blank page accusing her of having nothing to say. The irritation began to well up inside her again, and she tamped it back down as she picked up the pen and twirled it in her hand, wondering what to write.

All her dreams had come true. Things she never believed or thought she'd have, she now had. She was married to a rich and talented man so beautiful he made Apollo look shabby. They were going to be writers and travel and cook fabulous gourmet meals and drink fine wines for the rest of their lives. So why was she miserable?

* * *

Red, 4:40pm

SALLY HAD JUST FINISHED SHOWERING and in typical fashion was waltzing around naked. Red suspected she did it on purpose, knowing the effect she had on him. He didn't mind at all.

22

Her long blonde hair hung loose, way below her shoulders, partly obscuring her breasts. She hadn't gained much weight with the pregnancy, but her breasts were plumper. She was still trim in spite of the expanded belly, and when she moved, she was grace personified. Or sex on a stick. Was it perverted to be turned on by a pregnant lady? He wanted her now more than ever. But lately there was a new emotion to compete with his libido, one he'd never felt before.

He looked at her stomach. "Can I feel the baby kick?"

She rolled her eyes at him, not taking his interest seriously.

"It's just so incredible. He's going to be a real football star." He placed his hand on her swollen belly.

"It's going to be a girl," she assured him stubbornly.

"What makes you so positive?" A sharp kick finally rewarded him. "Wow, that was a big one! Did you feel that?"

She looked at him with disdain. "Of course I felt it. I feel it all the time. And the baby's a girl."

He ignored her scorn and put his cheek on her belly and waited for the next kick. There was something mesmerizing about interacting with the tiny being growing inside her. He was sure it was a fine, strong boy. "I never realized what it was like to watch...I don't know what to call it...watching this baby becoming a real person! You know, I never had kids, and now I see what I was missing."

"You're lucky you dodged that bullet. Wish I had your luck."

Red couldn't believe what she was implying. "Didn't you choose to keep the baby?"

"Yeah, but sometimes I wonder if it was just hormones that made that decision."

He tried to give her the benefit of the doubt. "It can't be easy, working full time and being pregnant."

"It's not. But I manage."

Her independence impressed him, but also threw cold water on the little dream he'd been entertaining. He'd been thinking about what life would be like with a young wife and child. It shocked him to admit he rather liked the idea. He hadn't had the nerve to mention it to Sally yet, especially when she was in this kind of mood, which was most of the time lately.

He lifted his head after not getting another kick and smiled at Sally. Her gray-flecked blue eyes stared at him icily. "You are such a softie. I never would have guessed." A chill went through him. When she acted like this, he didn't know what to think. What pregnant single woman wouldn't want a man to fall in love with her and her baby? Obviously, Sally. *Great.*

He shouldn't let himself become too attached; they'd never made any promises. The red flag he occasionally saw popped up again, waving madly, and he turned mentally in another direction to avoid dealing with it. If she wanted space, he could give her space.

Sensing his withdrawal, she moved closer to him and spoke soothingly, pressing her naked body against him. "I'm sorry. I'm glad you like the baby. You're a hero for putting up with me. I'm just hormonal." Somewhat mollified, he wrapped his arms around her. It was getting harder to ignore the dire warnings from his intuition.

* * *

Lydia 6:00pm

LYDIA SCANNED the crowded great room. The annual Christmas party was obviously going to be as successful as all Barbara's events. Should they even call it a Christmas party anymore? Maybe 'holiday party' was more politically correct. She chuckled to herself at the thought.

A beautiful artificial tree filled a corner of the room, trimmed with flashing lights and southwest-inspired decorations. Mistletoe hung from the ceiling in a few doorways. Christmas-themed platters holding the sumptuous banquet were laid out on the long counter separating the great room and kitchen. Plastic plates and cups in red and green and fine paper napkins with a holly design sat in stacks at the end of the sideboard along with plastic cutlery and pitchers of water and iced tea. Barbara's husband Ben was playing bartender and greeter at the wet bar, his red and white Santa cap sitting at a jaunty angle on his head.

Barbara was making the rounds and had disappeared into the crowd again. She was wearing an ankle-length black skirt and forest green silk blouse with a wide red leather belt, her double strand of pearls providing contrast to the dark colors.

Feeling strangely lost without Jean, Lydia held back from mingling for a little while longer, taking note of the attendees while nursing the glass of exceptional red wine Ben had given her when she arrived. She didn't recognize everyone, but she'd spotted Helen and Alexander, Helen's daughter Sally on the arm of an older man she was sure was her neighbor and of course, Bernie.

She grinned when she remembered how Helen, Jean, Sally and she had struggled to evade Bernie at the last party. He was equally tipsy this time and just as socially inept. Fortunately, he hadn't yet approached her, but she'd seen him lurking under the mistletoe, hitting on various women unsuccessfully.

Information bombarded Lydia as she peered at the partygoers. Maybe theoretically it was possible to filter what came through, but she'd never found a way. A riot of colors danced around each person, the predominant shades revealing emotional state, personality traits and physical health, all through the gift of her enhanced subtle vision. It was practically automatic for her to process the information, but she did her best not to see what was before her, though it took a lot of effort to ignore. If only Jean were here, she'd be able to focus on her best friend and block out much of what was going on around her. Well, she'd just have to make the best of it, exhausting as it was. That's why she always smoked a joint after a party; she just needed to calm down and let go of all she'd seen.

She reminded herself to be an uninvolved observer no matter what she saw (it hadn't gotten easier in all these years) and rose from the chair, heading through the crowd to find her friends. She passed Bernie, who mercifully was focused on someone else, and immediately broke her resolution. The same sadness surrounded him, though his obnoxious behavior blinded most people to his loneliness. He still hadn't recovered from the death of his wife. She wondered if he ever would.

Throwing off his depressive energy, she began to wend her way over to where she'd last seen Helen and Alexander, cursing her dratted talent. Something wasn't right with Helen, and Helen was trying to hide it. If only Lydia could be unaware like everyone else. She'd just come back from a honeymoon in the South Pacific, and instead of being calm and harmonious, the energy around Helen was tinged with repressed irritation and a sort of confused desperation. Her physical appearance gave nothing away. Though her coloring was fair, she'd tanned on her vacation, and the golden tone of her skin and her reddish blonde hair glistened like sunshine in the roomful of palefaces.

Alexander, on the other hand, seemed calm and relaxed. What a godlike hunk of man he was! Tall, tanned and fit as an athlete. His thick, longish silver hair, green eyes and golden radio voice had women swooning, as usual. Maybe that was what was wrong with Helen. He seemed unfazed by the women playing up to him (his detachment would have been obvious to anyone, with or without special vision), but Helen wasn't used to being married to a man she loved, and maybe she was uncomfortable with all the female attention he drew.

As she approached them, Lydia saw that even Helen's daughter Sally was not immune to Alexander's magnetism. She and her date went up to greet Helen and Alexander, and after hugging her mother, Sally gave Alexander a full-body hug (a real feat, considering she was so pregnant). You didn't have to be psychic to notice the lust rolling off her. Red spikes of anger exploded from both Helen and Sally's date. *Well, this could be interesting.*

Helen turned her focus from Sally when she saw Lydia approaching. "Lydia! It's so good to see you!"

"I want to hear about your honeymoon, or at least the parts you're willing to share." She grinned as Helen flushed slightly. "So what's it like in paradise?"

"The water was the most amazing turquoise, and we went snorkeling and saw fish of all kinds and colors. We went horseback riding on the beach and ate the most incredible meals. I didn't want to come home." She sighed sadly.

Alexander looked at Helen as if weighing what her last statement implied, but said nothing. It was easy to see he lived too much in his head and was missing some signals.

"I'd love to see photos, if you took any."

"Are you kidding? I took a zillion. I'm putting them into a big album. I want you to see them as soon as I get them organized."

Sally dragged her date closer to Lydia. "Lydia, I'd like you to meet Red Johnson."

Yup, this was her neighbor. He was handsome, though not the movie-star type Alexander was. His short, graying blonde hair and blue eyes spoke of Nordic genes. He towered over her like a Viking and grinned at her like the neighborhood bad boy. He reached his hand forward. "I believe we're neighbors, Lydia. Don't you live two condos down from me?"

Lydia smiled and shook his hand, pleased at his powers of observation. He had a nice, firm grip. "Yes, that would be me. I'm pleased to finally meet you. Aren't you with the Posse?"

"Yes, I am." He radiated an unusual honesty and groundedness. She turned to Sally, comparing their energies. They were opposites aside from a powerful physical attraction. Amazing how sex held poorly matched people together.

Sally grabbed Red's arm, pulling him away from the group. "Let's get some of the hot crab dip while there's still some left. It's totally awesome." Red gave Lydia one last look (it almost seemed apologetic) and allowed himself to be dragged away. *That relationship isn't going to last much longer.*

Lydia turned her attention to Alexander and Helen. "I haven't bumped into Bernie, though I saw that he's here. Have you had a close encounter, Helen?" She grinned as she said it.

Helen responded with a laugh. "I think being with Alexander warned him off. I haven't had anyone grope my boobs tonight."

Alexander's eyes widened for a second, then he grinned mischievously. "The night is young, dear."

Lydia felt a rare tinge of envy and hurriedly changed the subject. "I didn't get to speak with Barbara yet. Everything has been so crazy. I think I'll go find her now. Helen, can we get together for lunch sometime now that you're back?"

"Sure, Lydia. Let's do that."

"OK. I'll tell Barbara we should set a date after Christmas. See you guys later." Lydia wove through the crowd as "Jingle Bell Rock" played in the background.

She found Barbara talking with a woman near the glass door that led to the patio. No one was outside, in spite of the cheerful fire she could see burning in the fire pit.

She caught Barbara's eye as she drew closer. "Lydia, when did you get here? How could I have missed welcoming you?" Barbara gently touched the arm of the woman she was speaking with, then turned to give Lydia a hug.

"Santa's helper welcomed me." She pointed towards Ben at the bar. "It's quite a turnout you have tonight. You must be pleased."

Barbara's brown eyes flashed warmly. "Yes, it is lovely so many were able to attend. Lydia, I don't believe you've met my new neighbor Emma Lightman. She bought Helen's house. I was just getting acquainted with her."

Emma extended her hand and shook Lydia's firmly. Her shoulder-length, straight black hair was shot through with a few silver threads. Her stunning blue eyes and ivory skin contrasted beautifully with the dark of her hair. She wore no makeup other than lipstick. Brave girl, but it worked on her. Slightly taller than Lydia (who wasn't?), she had the body of someone who was serious about yoga, willowy and trim, but she didn't dress to show off her figure, instead wearing loose blouse and slacks.

Lydia took in the colors that surrounded Emma, who seemed painfully shy and had some kind of health issue that contributed to a subdued aura. "I'm Barbara's partner-in-crime at yoga class and some other pastimes. Welcome to Palm Lakes."

"Thank you," Emma almost whispered. She seemed very uncomfortable being among strangers, and Lydia had to repress her tendency to over-empathize.

Lydia turned her attention to Barbara. "Helen was saying she's almost ready to have lunch with us and tell us all about her honeymoon. Would you like to take the lead on setting that date?"

"Sure. I'll look at my calendar and call everyone. Emma, would you like to join us for lunch next week?"

Emma's eyes widened. The skin around a two-inch-long scar on her left cheekbone flushed pink, a harsh note on her classically beautiful features. Finally she replied. "I don't know if I'm free."

"It's very casual, Emma," assured Lydia. "We just gossip and eat good food and have fun. It would be a chance to get better acquainted." Not that she thought Emma cared for that.

Emma gave a genuine smile. "Let me know, and if I can, I will." In spite of the sincerity, Lydia gave it about a 50/50 chance.

Barbara's attention strayed to the front door. "Oh, Nora and Luke just arrived. I need to go greet them. I'll bring them over to meet you, Emma." Barbara headed off towards the front door in hostess mode.

Lydia turned to Emma, who seemed to have shrunk into herself. "It's not easy being in a crowd of new people, is it? I'm pretty extroverted, but even for me, it can be tiring."

"I'm just really shy, and I don't generally go to parties, but Barbara argued convincingly that I could meet most of the neighbors while having some great food, and how could I turn that down?" A smile graced her face.

"Do you like yoga? We go to a great class. You're welcome to be part of our crew." In response to Emma's shocked look, Lydia amended, "Don't decide now. Get your feet under you and let us know. The next class doesn't start until January, anyway.

"That's very kind of you. I love yoga, but I usually just do it on my own. Maybe a class would be nice, especially if I knew someone in it." Her smile broadened to show even, white teeth.

"Have you had a chance to meet everyone?" Lydia dreaded dragging her around, but it was the least she could do.

"Oh, yes, Barbara is the consummate hostess. She introduced me to everyone. Not that I remember a single name except yours at this point."

Lydia chuckled. "We're all prone to that when meeting lots of people at one time. How about a refill? I see your glass is empty, like mine. Ben is a wizard with cocktails, and they have some terrific wines."

"Yes, that would be nice."

They drifted over to the bar, where Ben's harmless flirting caused Emma to withdraw further. It reminded Lydia of Helen when they first met. After getting refills, they went over to the counter, where Lydia piled a plate with goodies, but noticed Emma picked very few items, only nuts or bits of plain fruit. Lydia led her to an empty couch at the far side of the room, where they could sit and eat in peace. Emma seemed relieved at the choice.

29

Minutes later, Barbara came over, Nora and Luke in tow. "Lydia, you know Nora and Luke, but I wanted to introduce them to Emma." Emma blinked self-consciously and reached her free hand out to shake hands with each of them. "Emma, I met Nora in the cooking class. We often cross paths in various clubs and activities." Barbara turned to the Nora. "Emma is my new neighbor. She bought Helen's old house. You remember Helen from cooking class? She and Alexander met there--I'm pleased to say I was responsible for them partnering in the class--and they recently got married and just got back from their honeymoon in the South Pacific. Moorea, was it, Lydia?"

Lydia nodded, while Emma's eyes got wider.

"How romantic!" sighed Nora, her hazel eyes dreamy. Luke smiled as if it didn't matter one way or the other to him.

"They are just perfect for each other and so in love." Barbara smiled with satisfaction. It proved that Lydia was alone in seeing Helen's discomfort tonight. Maybe it wasn't as bad as it seemed. It was tricky interpreting what she saw.

Barbara, Nora and Luke drifted off to see other guests, and the rest of the evening passed quickly, with Barbara spending much of her time with them. Emma escaped at ten o'clock, and Lydia left shortly after. When she got home, she grabbed a joint and went out onto the patio. This time of night in winter, no one was outside. Even though Red lived two doors down, she wasn't worried. He was still at the party, and she suspected he was spending more time at Sally's place than his own.

The sky was clear and stars sparkled like diamonds on a jeweler's black velvet cloth. She savored the crisp cold air as she sat wrapped snugly in her winter coat. She started to mellow out, grateful that Digger had such good pot. It could be tricky finding a safe source of quality weed, and Digger lived in Palm Lakes, only selling to people he knew or those referred by people he knew. He got his stuff from a relative in northern California who grew it himself, so she knew it wasn't laced with anything harmful. She giggled at the thought of organic pot.

Lydia felt the cares and emotions of all the partygoers slip away from her, leaving her to contemplate the direction of her own life. The idea of 'coming out' about her 'gift' had sounded good when she was talking to Jean, who not only believed in such stuff, but relished it. The party reminded her why she'd kept it to herself her whole life. Though Barbara and Jean would probably be OK with her ability, Helen might not. She had lived her whole life hiding that her now-dead husband Lou was a wife-beater. Lydia had known the first time she looked at her. If Helen found out, would her need for privacy end their friendship? And Emma? What chance would she have for friendship with Emma, if she knew how much Lydia could 'see' just by looking at her?

She took another toke and tried to let the worried thoughts blow away on the smoke.

* * *

Helen, 11:04pm

ALEXANDER SEEMED to have enjoyed himself at the party, and that made Helen all the more irritated, because it had been an ordeal for her. Barbara and Ben had outdone themselves, as usual, but seeing her friends and having good food and drink couldn't offset the irritation she felt at all the women throwing themselves at Alexander, Sally included.

She hadn't said a word on the ride home, pretending to be tired, but she was sure he noticed she wasn't herself. Or at least, she hoped he did. Or not. She wasn't sure what she wanted.

As she dressed for bed and brushed her teeth, the frustration mounted. Was she going to have to spend the rest of her life feeling like this? She'd never been the jealous type, and she knew those women meant nothing to him. It wasn't his fault he was so incredibly handsome. She should be mad at them, not him. Why couldn't she just be happy? If only she hadn't gained five pounds since the wedding. Their love of gourmet cooking--well, eating what they cooked--was beginning to make her grow out of her clothes. Why didn't Alexander gain weight? Would he still love her if she turned into a blimp?

It had always calmed her to stroke Sheba when she was disturbed, but her dearest feline friend had died a couple months ago, so she went to pet Alexander's cat Fido, who lay in Siamese splendor on the bed (on Alexander's side, of course). The cat took a swipe at her. No claws, but clearly not interested. "Why do you hate me?" It wasn't the first time she'd asked, but it was the first time she'd said it out loud so accusingly.

Alexander stepped out of the closet. "What's wrong?"

"Your cat hates me," she complained, feeling like a spoiled child.

"Nonsense. He just doesn't know you that well yet. Give him time. He'll grow to love you."

"I miss Sheba. And now her ashes are spread in the yard at my old condo." Helen looked at Alexander accusingly.

"I'm sorry it worked out that way, but I can't think of any way to fix it." His green eyes shone with sympathy, but he just didn't get it.

"Sometimes I feel I don't belong." She knew she was opening the door to an argument, but she'd bottled her resentment up for too long.

He stepped out of the closet where he could see her in the light cast from the bathroom. "What do you mean?" His voice was calm and concerned, but he clearly had no clue how upset she was.

She rocked and held her arms wrapped tightly around her stomach. "I feel like a guest in your house. I barely found myself before we got married, and I feel I've lost myself again. Everywhere I look, I see *your* life, not mine. It's like there's no *me*. You want me to sell my condo, get rid of my furniture, and it makes sense, but I don't want to lose my life. I don't have my cat, and I miss her... Never mind, it sounds stupid."

"It's not stupid, but don't you agree it's logical to sell your place? And I didn't realize you were so attached to your furniture. I know Sheba meant the world to you, and I'm sorry she's there instead of here. What would you have me do?" Frustration had crept into his voice. He didn't understand.

Helen sighed at the impossibility of having what she wanted or even communicating it clearly. "I don't know!" She twisted a bit of nightgown distractedly. "I want a cat who loves me like Sheba did. I want to fit in and feel like I'm not just an appendage of yours. I hate all those women throwing themselves at you."

She saw his eyebrows go up. *Now he thinks it's all about jealousy. And maybe it is.*

"I'm not doing anything to encourage anyone. You're being unfair, and that's not like you."

Helen shook her head, fighting tears. "Even Sally was all over you," she whispered.

His gaze hardened. "Do you consider that *my* fault? If she weren't your daughter, I'd know exactly what to do, but you love her, and I don't want to alienate her. Are you implying I'm doing more than just putting up with her? Maybe you should talk to *her* about her behavior, not me."

Helen knew she was out of line, but now that she'd put it in words, she had to let it all out. "You allow her to rub all over you every time she comes over. That may not be encouraging her, but it isn't dis-couraging her." Helen gritted her teeth, feeling she had stepped over a line.

Alexander closed the distance between them and raised his hand, and Helen flinched and threw her hand up in defense.

His eyes widened in hurt and shock. "Do you think I'd hit you? How could you? I just wanted to reassure you." He slowly reached the rest of the way and touched her cheek, then pulled her into his chest in an awkward hug.

Helen tried to find words to explain her emotions as the tears started to flow. "I can't stand the feeling that I'm competing with every woman on earth for your attention. No, even the men. I've never felt jealous before, and knowing you have a history with both men and women makes me more insecure. Tonight I even found myself jealous of Ray and Alan, and they're a couple. I can't seem to help it. I know you're just friends with them, but I'm no good at being married to a man who is so attractive and...bisexual."

She couldn't see his face, but his voice was stony. "Look, it's late and we're both tired and we had wine at the party. This isn't going to be solved tonight. Let's try to get some sleep and we can discuss it tomorrow."

Helen knew he was right, but it was so hard to put aside the compelling need to resolve the conflicting feelings. She felt guilty, because in her previous marriage, an argument like this would have ended in her being beaten, and instead of being grateful, she was annoyed. It was like nothing he did or said could please her. "OK. Let's talk about it tomorrow. But don't make me be the one to bring it up." *God, I'm being a total bitch.*

"I promise we can sit down after breakfast, or even before, if you like, and talk about whatever is bothering you."

They got into the king size bed, and for the first time, they stayed on opposite sides, as if they were inhabiting hostile countries. Fido stayed on Alexander's side, as always. Helen felt more alone than she ever had in her life, and worse yet, she knew it was her own fault, but she didn't know how to fix it. Tears trickled down her cheeks, silently soaking the pillow.

2

WEDNESDAY, DECEMBER 20, 1995

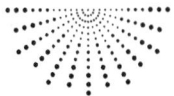

Mary Beth, 10:00am

*T*he doorbell rang, wrenching Mary Beth out of a mental fog.
Who the hell could that be? As she opened the door, the wind
peppered her with freezing rain. Mrs. Jameson stood on the porch with a
foil-wrapped dish in her hand. Mary Beth froze in the doorway, her
mouth hanging open.

An inappropriate amount of time later, Mary Beth stepped aside,
waving Mrs. Jameson in. "I'm sorry I kept you standing in the rain. You'd
think the desert would be drier, wouldn't you? This is almost as bad as
where I came from."

They stood in the small foyer, Mrs. J. dripping from the rain. "I'm
sorry to mess up your floor like this, dear, but I wanted to bring you
some food. I'm so sorry about your mother." She held the dish out for
Mary Beth, who stared at it like it was an alien artifact.

"You didn't need to do that. Here, let me put it in the fridge." She took
the dish from Mrs. J. "Why don't you come in? How about a cup of
coffee?" She headed for the kitchen without looking back.

"That would be nice, dear. I hope you don't mind me keeping my coat
on. I'm chilled right through to the bone." Mrs. J. tottered after Mary Beth

into the kitchen and sat down at the table, watching Mary Beth through thick glasses spotted with rainwater.

Mary Beth snuck a look at the casserole and discovered it was lasagna, then smiled at the unexpected kindness.

"I know you can make better lasagna than I can, but I thought you'd enjoy not having to make it yourself. You have a lot to do right now and don't need to worry about cooking." Mrs. J's voice was warm and grandmotherly.

Mary Beth brought two mugs of coffee over to the table. "Do you take cream?"

"No, thanks, black is fine." She sipped her coffee while Mary Beth tried to figure out what was going on. Mrs. Jameson was a nosy old biddy whom, according to Mom, ratted out everyone who broke the covenants. Mary Beth had spent months hiding from the old lady, because at 45 years of age, she wasn't old enough to live in Palm Lakes. Why was Mrs. Jameson being so nice? It didn't compute.

"Mrs. Jameson, you didn't have to go to this trouble, but I appreciate it."

"Please call me Catherine, dear."

Mary Beth didn't know what to say next. This woman was not acting as expected; she seemed too human.

"So when's the funeral?" The unexpected query roused Mary Beth from her speechless state.

"Day after tomorrow."

Catherine nodded her head in sympathy. "Do you have other family?"

"No, my Dad died a long time ago, and I'm an only child. Just like Mom. There won't be many people at the funeral. She didn't make a lot of friends here." Mary Beth bit her lip thinking about how small the service would be. She hoped someone else came besides her. At least Samantha and Ethan had promised.

"I know I wasn't close to your Mom, but I'd be pleased if you'd invite me."

Mary Beth blinked away what she knew must be an incredulous stare. "I always thought you didn't like the fact that I was living here illegally."

Catherine waved a small, chubby hand in dismissal. "Now why would I care about that?"

"I was told you didn't like people breaking the covenants, and that you reported infractions."

"Well that's a damn lie. I wouldn't ever." Catherine's eyes narrowed. She put her mug down and pointed at Mary Beth. "Who told you that nonsense?"

Mary Beth cleared her throat. "Well, my Mom did."

Catherine's eyes widened behind the thick lenses. "I don't know why she'd think that."

"Maybe it's because you're always looking out your front window."

"Oh, that. I don't have a lot to do, and I find it interesting to watch what's going on in the neighborhood. Of course, I'd call the Posse if I saw anything bad happen, but I don't care who plants what kind of tree or flies what kind of flag. I think most of the covenants are a bunch of crap."

Mary Beth grinned. "So do I, though I'd use a stronger word. Out of respect for my Mom, I'm trying not to cuss. She always used to nag me about my mouth."

Catherine laughed, and her slightly blue-tinted curls and double chins jiggled. "Don't hold back on my account. I'm sure I've heard worse."

Had she woken up in a parallel universe? None of this was making sense. "So do you have family nearby, Catherine?"

A shadow crossed her eyes. "No, I'm all alone these many years since my husband died, bless his soul. I never was one to socialize, and we were childless. I don't get around as well as I once did, with this damn arthritis in all my joints. Makes it hard to walk or drive."

Mary Beth felt a stab of guilt for all the times she'd felt angry at the poor woman. She was just a lonely old lady. "If there's ever anything I can do, let me know, though I don't know how long I'll be here. I'm going to have to put Mom's condo on the market and move, since I'm alone now. But while I'm here, feel free to call me anytime." Mary Beth got up and wrote her phone number on a slip of paper and handed it to Catherine.

Faded blue eyes glowed with appreciation. "That's very kind of you. I'll keep that in mind." Catherine tucked the paper into the pocket of her raincoat. "Now I know you have a lot to do, and you don't need me jawing at you. I'll go on home. But I'd love to come to the service."

"I'll let you know the details. You can go with me. It will probably be a very small service." Pausing in mid-thought, Mary Beth reached for the pad and pen again. "I'll need your phone number so I can call you." She handed them to Catherine, who dutifully wrote her phone number down in a schoolteacher's neat cursive.

As she wrote, Catherine offered, "Small services are the best kind. Only people who care will show up." Then she struggled to get to her feet and ambled towards the front door, Mary Beth tagging along behind her.

At the door, Catherine turned and impulsively gave Mary Beth a big hug, triggering the observation that she was even shorter than Mom, though considerably rounder. "Thanks for coming over and bringing the food, Catherine. I'm sorry I thought you were a spy for the HOA."

Catherine winked at her. "I think it's rather exotic, being a spy. I haven't been accused of anything that sexy in years." Then she plunged into the rain, moving as quickly as her arthritic legs would take her. Mary Beth watched to make sure she got in OK, then closed her door.

Back in the kitchen, she slumped into her chair, exhausted from sleeplessness and dealing with the unexpected. "Shit, Mom, you were wrong about that woman. And so was I. Pardon my French."

Fifteen minutes later, the doorbell rang again. *Boy, I'm getting popular.* She looked through the peephole this time and saw Helen standing in the rain, trying to close an umbrella.

"Come on in, Helen. You can lean the umbrella outside there in the corner. Let me take your coat."

"I was so shocked to hear about your Mom, and I thought you might like some company. But I don't want to impose. I know you must have a lot to do."

"Please, impose. I'd love the company. Can I get you some coffee?"

"Yes, that would be lovely." They walked back to the kitchen together, and Helen went to sit in the same chair Catherine had just vacated. Mary Beth intervened and grabbed the used mug and dried the chair with a dish towel, then prepared the new pot of coffee while talking. "Would you believe it, the old biddy across the street, Mrs. Jameson, came over with a casserole for me, and she isn't the one turning people in to the HOA. I felt like an absolute asshole for the nasty thoughts I've sent her way all this time. Sorry. I've been trying to clean up my language, but it gets away from me."

Helen giggled. "Really, Mary Beth, I don't mind. So it's good news that Mrs. Jameson isn't the one."

"Yes, it certainly is. She's coming to the service, too. She asked to be invited, which I thought was very sweet. You're welcome, too, you and Alexander. It's on Friday."

Helen frowned in regret. "I'm so sorry, but we're leaving for Wisconsin that day. I wish I could be here for you."

Mary Beth didn't want to admit how disappointed she was. "Don't worry. It's no big deal. I hope you have a nice visit with your family."

Helen's frown deepened. "One can always hope. I don't expect they will have changed their opinion of my marriage since Thanksgiving. It's going to be hard on Alexander, because they don't hide their disapproval."

"What could they possibly disapprove of? The guy's handsome, rich and talented."

"There's no explaining prejudice. I haven't really given it a lot of thought, probably because I want to avoid thinking about it. I would have dreaded the situation anyway, but the way things are going lately..." Helen began to twist the fabric of her pants leg.

"What do you mean?" Mary Beth wasn't sure she wanted any more bad news.

"You know how I told you I'd like to learn to speak my mind like you do? Well, I've been trying and doing a really crappy job of it. I think Alexander is annoyed with me, and I don't really blame him."

Mary Beth couldn't believe her ears. "What...?"

"Well, it's probably all my fault. The things he wants to do all seem so logical that I feel annoyed that I disagree. I don't want to give up my condo or my furniture, but his place is fully decorated and why should we keep paying for two places? Sheba's ashes are at my condo, and it was the first place that was all mine in my whole life, and I feel like a displaced person in his house. I feel like such an ingrate. Oh, and his cat hates me. I miss having my own place, my own cat and my own things around me. I feel like I don't belong, as if any moment, he's going to ask me to leave. I can't figure out how I fit in to his life. And though I seem to be finding the words to tell you, I'm terrible at explaining to him. The minute I try, I get tied up in knots and get emotional." She sighed deeply.

Mary Beth couldn't believe it. Helen and Alexander were made for each other. "I'm so sorry you're going through this. But I kinda know how you feel. I was beginning to feel I belonged here and had a life, and now it's gone. I don't know where I fit in, either. I have to put this condo on the market, and I need to find a place to live pronto. I don't even know a realtor. How was that woman you used?"

Helen brightened up. "Shari Lopez is great. I might have her card in my purse." She reached for her bag and dug through her wallet until she found it. Handing it to Mary Beth, she paused as if contemplating something. "I just got an idea."

Mary Beth leaned closer. "You've got my attention."

"I've been reluctant to sell my place. I know I will have to at some point. But for now, I just don't want to. What if I rent my condo to you? It's fully furnished. You can put this place on the market, maybe even sell it furnished. Shari could probably find a good buyer. I don't know how long I'll keep the condo, but if I can offset the expenses of maintaining it, I'm sure Alexander will agree to postponing the sale for a while. Do you think you could afford to do that? It wouldn't have to be a lot. We don't need the money. I just need to show him we aren't paying for an extra home we aren't using. You could pay utilities and give me a bit of rent each month. What do you think?"

Mary Beth felt tears coming to her eyes. "Damn, girl, that would be so great. I could stay here and figure out what I want to do with my life...again. It would mean a lot to me, and I understand it isn't long term. I just need time to think." She clapped her hands together. "I can keep doing jewelry with Maddie this way. Oh, this is such a gift."

Helen grinned. "You'll be doing me a favor. It will buy me time to get used to my new circumstances. I really don't want to mess up this relationship. I love Alexander, and I know he loves me. I hate feeling so irritated and angry." She glanced down at her hands clasped together in her lap, and her look turned grim. "You know, it's hard for me to admit this, but we went to a party a couple nights ago, and I was so jealous I couldn't see straight. Women were throwing themselves at him, including my own daughter, for God's sake, and I'm not used to dealing with that. I wanted to scratch their eyes out, and he was so laid back about it, it annoyed me. I've never been jealous, and I don't like how it makes me feel, but I can't seem to control it." She slumped down in her chair.

"Helen, you've made some remarkable changes in your life this year. You're my role model for sure. Don't be so hard on yourself. It isn't easy to adapt to a whole new way of being. Maybe you're just not used to being happy."

Helen shot her a bemused look, then Mary Beth saw the wheels turning. "I never thought of it that way. You're right. I have never been happy for long, and this is way more than I could ever have hoped for. It's almost like I'm trying to make my life miserable because that's all I know how to be."

"You haven't been married that long. Give yourself time."

Helen nodded. "I think it started when we returned from the honeymoon. That's when things began to get all out of proportion for me; until then it all felt like a dream. Now I'm having to deal with reality. I can't thank you enough for saying that. I'm going to try to focus on allowing myself to finally be loved and happy with my life."

"You go, girl!"

Helen's departure 20 minutes later left Mary Beth feeling better than she had in a few days. What a relief to have a place to stay here in Palm Lakes. To be able to move next door. What more could she ask for?

As if in answer, the phone rang.

"Hi, Mary Beth, it's Ethan."

Mary Beth felt a wave of guilt squash her newfound happiness. She hadn't yet called Ethan about the service or even thanked him for staying up all night with her the day Mom died. Why did she treat him that way? "I'm sorry I haven't called. It's been crazy here. I've had two visitors this morning already. But I do have a date and time for the service, and I wanted to invite you to come."

"I'd be honored." Only someone like him would consider it an honor to attend the funeral of someone he'd never met.

"You're too nice to me. I haven't even thanked you for holding my hand the other night. I don't know what I would have done if you hadn't been here. Probably drunk myself into a stupor."

"It was no trouble. I know it's only been a couple days, and you're probably busy, but I was actually calling to see if you might want some company tonight. I know you probably haven't been sleeping that well, so I wouldn't keep you up too late. But if you'd like someone to talk to, I could take you to dinner and give you a bit of time away from the condo."

Mary Beth had a brainstorm. "My neighbor just brought me a casserole. How about you come over for dinner? I can't promise it will be good, but all we have to do is heat it up. And it's lasagna, and you said you like Italian."

"I can't think of anything I'd rather do. What time do you want me to come?"

"How's 5:30 work for you?"

"Great! I'll bring a bottle of wine."

"Make it two."

* * *

Julio, 1:20pm

JULIO STOOD on the patio evaluating the progress on the block wall his crew was building around the back yard at Mrs. Lightman's. The footings were done, but that was all. Neatly stacked piles of block stood waiting to be laid, and the sides of the trench were filling with muddy water, but it would soon soak into the ground.

Propelled by the harsh wind, cold drops blew under the patio cover and stung his face, reflecting his mood. He was irritated. This weather irritated him. Not being able to finish the job irritated him. Dealing with suspicious people who expected Mexicans to rip them off irritated him. But mostly he was fed up with the relentless, boring sameness of his life.

Shaking off the mood, he turned to go back into the house. Mrs. Lightman stood at the far side of the living room as if her preference was to keep distance between them. Her straight, shoulder-length, coal black hair was shot through with a few silver threads, so it must be her natural color, he thought. The darkness of her hair contrasted beautifully with her ivory skin and stunning blue eyes. She wore no makeup, a rarity in Palm Lakes, and her clothes were expensive-looking, if not flattering to her figure. She appeared too young to be a resident, but she must be at least 55 to own a home here. He knew she was a widow, because she'd told him in a quiet voice that showed she didn't like to share about herself. He'd even noticed the urn on the table in the corner of the room, so she must have valued her late husband.

She was watching him apprehensively, like a wary prey animal eyeing a wolf. He wasn't used to seeing fear in the eyes of the women in Palm Lakes. He was far more used to admiration or lust. Though she was alone in the room with a near-stranger, it was the 90s, and he couldn't imagine being alone with a man was so threatening to her. He'd never faced this reaction before, and it flustered him. Was it possible she was picking up on his irritable mood, or was she always like this? He cleared his throat.

"Mrs. Lightman, the rain is not going to last that long, but it will delay us in finishing the wall."

She seemed to relax at the mundane announcement. "It takes what it takes."

"We will be back to work the first dry day we get, but we need the ground solid for the footings. I will come and make sure there is progress." People in Palm Lakes had the impression they couldn't trust Mexicans, and he went out of his way to show how professional Palo Verde Landscaping was.

She drew herself up as if to find courage to speak, and when she did, her voice was warmer and more confident. "Thanks for taking charge and letting me know. You know, I wanted to speak with you about another project for my yard. I was hoping to get an estimate from you."

"I would love to hear about it."

She didn't smile much, but as she thought about this subject, one blossomed on her face. It made her even more beautiful. The only flaw was the scar on her left cheek. He began to feel captivated in spite of himself.

"I came from the state of Oregon. I know it's different here. But I really would like to have a Japanese garden. Is there any way we can turn part of the yard into that?" She was so lit up with enthusiasm, he wished he could say 'yes'.

"Honestly, the types of plants used in a Japanese garden do not do well here. What purpose did you have in mind?"

"I wanted a place of contemplation and peace." She screwed her face up in thought. After a moment's silence, she said, "How about a labyrinth? Can I have one of them?"

"What is a labyrinth? Is it like a maze?" Julio had only a sketchy idea of what she meant.

"Let me show you a picture." She ran to the bookshelf and pulled off a book. Carrying it over to Julio, she thumbed through the pages, standing close enough so that he could see the picture. She smelled of soap and lavender. "Here's a picture of a labyrinth like the one I want."

It was a simple circular-looking maze laid out in tile. "We could maybe do something like that." He paused, mentally calculating the labor and materials. It would be expensive. And very labor-intensive. Normally, he would not give an affordable bid on something like this. He'd bid so high the homeowner would reject his offer. That way he didn't have to say 'no' to a request. He preferred to do plant work or maybe walls. It was hard to profit from this artistic stuff. His brothers might be annoyed if he took the job, but it was the slow season, and he was intrigued. "I am thinking we could use contrasting gravel or maybe some kind of border out of brick or something. Could I borrow this picture? I need to think about it and talk with my brothers before I can give you an estimate."

She handed over the book, taking care not to touch him. "When can you tell me?"

"I will come back tomorrow."

She smiled. "I'll be here. It's nice of you to be available so close to Christmas. It's a family time."

"My family is my brothers and their wives and girlfriends. I am not married, and my parents are dead. We do not do a lot of celebrating."

She looked down at her hands. "I'm new in town, and I don't have family, either. Sometimes a quiet Christmas is nice. My husband and I never did a whole lot to celebrate. We didn't have children or extended family."

"So you do not have anyone to spend Christmas with?"

"No, I've made a few acquaintances, but I wouldn't want to impose on them." She seemed agitated and eager to change the subject. "Thanks for coming over. I hope you can find a way to do the labyrinth."

"It is raining. Can I have a bag or something to put this book in? I do not want to damage it."

She nodded and went to the kitchen, returning with a plastic grocery bag that was nearly big enough to do the job. He slipped the book into it and shoved it under his jacket.

"So is it all right if I come by tomorrow?"

"Yes, I'll be here."

Once inside his truck, he wiped his wet face on a hand towel and wondered what was so special about this quiet woman. He tended to go for blonde, married women who were attracted to him, and Mrs. Lightman was anything but that. Yet he was inexplicably drawn to her. It wasn't only that she was a challenge or that he had become restless with life of late, though both were true. The thought of winning her trust was somehow bright and shiny and mysterious, like a country he'd never visited.

He was going to find a way to persuade his brothers to do her labyrinth so he could explore this strange, new feeling. And even though it was unprofessional, he was going to make a point of stopping by her house on Christmas. He could see she was lonely, though she tried to hide it. Maybe he could brighten her day.

* * *

Emma, 2:30pm

EMMA SAT in the living room with a cup of chamomile tea, looking towards the urn that held her husband's ashes. "Leo, I sure wish you were here. Christmas won't be the same without you."

She half expected him to reply. It was what kept her going, being able to talk to him as if he were still with her. He'd been her best and only friend, and his support lingered, giving her strength through the shared connection that hadn't disappeared when he left the earth for another

45

realm. She wasn't the religious type, but she was spiritual, and she knew he was still close by.

She got up and walked over to the urn on the corner table. Then she looked out into the yard at the beginnings of her wall. "You know, I'll be glad to have the wall finished. It will give me more privacy. And maybe Julio can come up with a way to do a labyrinth. I would have liked a Japanese garden, but he said it wouldn't work here." Julio seemed to know what he was talking about, so she'd have to trust him.

The gray day and cold rain colored her mood, dragging her deeper into melancholy as she thought about the holiday. "Christmas is a time for family, and I don't have anyone. If we had had children, they'd come visit. Do you remember when we tried to make a baby, Leo?" She laughed at the memory. "If we'd have succeeded, I wouldn't be alone now. It wasn't funny at the time, you trying so hard to get me pregnant, and me trying to let you, neither of us succeeding. It didn't seem so important then, but I feel so alone now. We were quite a pair, weren't we? If only people knew..."

She could almost hear him chuckling. His sense of humor had been one of his greatest gifts. He'd always been able to shake her out of a bad mood. Now she was alone and had to do it herself, and most of the time, she wasn't up to the task.

Leo had been older than she. And gay. She'd been surprised when he proposed; they were only friends, but it made such sense, she gave in. And never regretted it. He was just what she needed. She didn't want a lover, and marrying him benefited both of them. She got a protector and helpmate, and he didn't have to worry about rumors of his homosexuality harming his career. He was kind, thoughtful and a good partner. And she never had to worry about sex.

"Leo, Julio is very handsome and full of himself. I can't imagine what it must be like to feel that way about life, to be so confident, to dive into any experience without fear.

"He seemed bemused by me. But he tries to do a good job, and he is very businesslike. I'm not comfortable around him, but I was pretty good, even though we were alone. Maybe I'm getting over my past." She drained the mug. "Or maybe I'm just getting lonely. I'm lost without you, especially at this time of year."

She stepped out onto the lanai and let the cold wind lash at her, spraying her with raindrops. When she was chilled through, she went back inside.

Picking up the phone, she called Barbara.

"Hi, Barbara. It's Emma."

"Oh, Emma! How are you? I see the rain has stopped work on your wall."

Emma was unnerved that she was under such scrutiny. "I called to let you know I won't be coming over for Christmas, though I really appreciate your invitation. I just feel like staying at home. Thanks anyway."

"You know Lydia is coming over, so it isn't only family, but you do what feels best to you. Maybe you can come to lunch with us next week after Helen gets back?"

She didn't really want to, but maybe she could handle it. She didn't like to tell people about her food allergies. It led to too many complications. "Yes, I can do that. Thank you."

"It's our pleasure. We'd like to get to know you better."

Emma couldn't understand why anyone would want to get to know her. "Let me know a date and time."

"I will. Merry Christmas, Emma."

"Merry Christmas to you."

Maybe now that she'd gotten past that, she could relax. She sat on the couch and picked up the novel she'd started last night. Pure escapism was just what the doctor ordered.

Maddie, 6:30pm

MADDIE CURSED under her breath when the phone rang. It never seemed that the handset was nearby when someone called. She rose painfully from her chair and moved as fast as her old legs would carry her to silence the annoying ring.

"Hello?" she barked.

"Maddie, it's me, Mary Beth."

Maddie immediately felt guilty. Samantha had told her Mary Beth's mother died two days ago. Never adept socially, she was unable to think of something appropriate to say.

Mary Beth saved her the trouble. "Maddie, I just needed to call and tell you that I won't be able to make our jewelry session this Saturday. My Mom died suddenly two days ago, and I have a lot of things I need to do."

Still, Maddie found herself unable to say anything. She liked Mary Beth, but she couldn't imagine how she could help her. Finally, she responded, "Don't worry about Saturday. But I hope you'll be able to come back again, maybe the next Saturday?" It hurt to realize how much Mary Beth's visits meant to her, and how bad she'd feel if they stopped.

"Of course. I just can't make it this Saturday. The funeral service is Friday. Would you like to come?" Mary Beth sounded tentative, which wasn't at all like her.

"I don't go to funerals, Mary Beth. I'm sorry. I just can't."

"That's OK. I just wanted you to know you were welcome. My Mom loved your jewelry, and she really appreciated how much you've taught me and how generous you've been.

"Oh, and a bit of good news. Even though this means I have to sell Mom's condo, since I'm too young to own it, Helen has offered to rent me her condo, so I'll have a place to live, at least for the near future. That means I can keep doing jewelry with you."

"Helen's such a thoughtful person, I miss having her across the street. I'm glad that damn HOA isn't making you homeless."

Mary Beth laughed. "You and me both. Well, I just wanted to touch base. I'll miss you this weekend, but I'll come back next Saturday, if that's OK."

"I don't do a lot during the holidays. It will be a treat for me." Maddie had come to value Mary Beth, her talent and passion for making jewelry and her outspoken nature.

After they said their goodbyes, Maddie worried that Mary Beth would be offended that she didn't come to the funeral. Ever since they'd made her kiss the corpse of Aunt Madeline at a wake when she was five years old, she hadn't been able to bear anything to do with dead bodies.

Mary Beth had sounded sad at her declining the invitation, but there was just no way she could do it.

Even thinking about the death of Mary Beth's mother gave her a shiver of fear. Sometimes the spirit world didn't seem so far away to Maddie. On occasion, she'd seen ghosts, which was one reason she wasn't going anywhere near a funeral. She thought about the time she'd bought a gardening book for Samantha at a garage sale some years back, and that night, as the book sat on a chair near her bed, she awoke to see the specter of a man sitting in the chair, and she knew it was the book's former owner. Though nothing more had happened, the next morning she threw out the book. No need to pass something like that on to Samantha. Samantha had laughed it off when she told her, but at least she'd told her that she believed her.

She wandered out to the kitchen and noticed the pile of dinner dishes waiting to be loaded into the dishwasher and pots and pans littering the stovetop. It seemed all she did was prepare meals. Lunch was barely finished and cleanup done before she had to start on dinner. Stanley emptied the dishwasher each morning, but that was the extent of help she got from him in the kitchen. And lately, she was more tired than usual. She always had to push through the exhaustion to get things done. Now, she also had to also push through pain, as her bones hurt so bad.

She made up her mind. She'd do the dishes later. Now, she was going to have a glass of wine to take her mind off all this talk of death.

3

CHRISTMAS DAY 1995

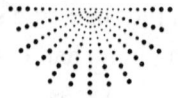

Alexander, 10:00am

Only 24 hours left before they could go home. Alexander wasn't sure he was going to make it without tearing the head off Helen's son Warren. Not that her daughter Lena was any better. She was a calculating, materialistic bitch. He'd thought Sally was a challenge, with her strange, oversexed attitude, but all she did was make him uncomfortable because he knew it upset Helen. These two, however, made him see red.

Speaking of which, as he brushed his teeth, he noticed how bloodshot his eyes were. The stress of dealing with Helen's kids had driven him to drink more than he usually would, and he was feeling the effects. He spat out the toothpaste and rinsed his mouth. He just had to get through another day without punching Warren or telling Lena to go to hell. Surely he could do that?

At least the grandkids were fun. They didn't seem to be aware of the cold shoulder Alexander and Helen were getting from their parents. Which was just as well. Christmas was for kids, and they should have a good time.

Funny that in spite of the strange events of the past few days, Helen was seeming more relaxed than she had since they returned from their honeymoon. Maybe not selling the condo took a load off her mind. He didn't understand her reluctance, but as long as Mary Beth could cover utilities and pay a little of rent, it didn't matter to him.

Helen came into the bathroom and stood at the other sink, putting on makeup. He didn't think she needed it, but she was unwilling to face her kids without what she called her 'war paint.' In deference to the arctic weather, she was wearing dark slacks and a thick sweater she had never worn in Palm Lakes. It would have been too hot to wear on the worst desert winter day.

"That's a nice sweater for Christmas day."

"It's old, but I like it. I got it at a secondhand store practically new, and it's in my colors."

He looked at the caramel tones of the pattern and the turquoise snowflakes that decorated it and wondered what difference the colors made, but didn't ask. "I like it."

She turned to him and smiled warmly. "Thanks." Then a shadow swept across her face and stole the smile away. "I'm so sorry about the kids."

"Dammit, quit blaming yourself. It's them, not you."

"I'm so glad we didn't tell them our exact date of arrival. Staying in a hotel is much better than staying with one of them. We have our privacy, and we can retire to it to escape their judgment."

He bit back his words, but they slipped out anyway. "Why do you let them disrespect you?"

She frowned and looked dismayed. "Maybe they just treat me the way Lou did. I pampered them, wanting them to love me, but in the end, they seem to see me the way he did: as worthless."

His anger flared. "I don't mind what they do to me, but it makes my blood boil when they disrespect you. You're the most wonderful person I know."

She shrugged her shoulders. "Maybe I overstated it. Maybe they're just spoiled. I had hoped they would come around about us."

"Clearly, that is not going to happen. I think it sends the wrong message to allow them to treat us like outcasts."

"I want access to my grandchildren. Should I give them up?"

Alexander sighed. "Do you find it easy to submit to this treatment? No offer of hospitality. When we go over for a meal, thinly veiled insults are thrown at us. Do you expect me to put up with that? Because I'm not sure I can. It's a challenge, and I'm tired of ignoring it. I only do so because of you."

She wilted visibly. "If I had to, I could give up Warren and Lena. They've made it clear that I don't count with them. But I hate to give up the chance to be a part of my grandchildren's lives. Are you asking me to choose between them and you?"

He heaved a sigh. "No, of course not. But I'm going nuts trying not to punch your son or tell your daughter off. I don't find it as easy as you do to accept insult after insult when I've done nothing to deserve it. I wish you'd stand up to them. What kind of example do we set by allowing others to bully us?"

"I know they've been awful, and if it continues, I'm willing to consider not visiting anymore. I don't think they'd refuse my cards or gifts to the children or block my access. Maybe they *want* us to withdraw." She looked at him, her green-tinted blue eyes shiny with tears. "You're asking me to do something irrevocable. If when we leave tomorrow, they haven't come around, I will back off from trying to make things work with them. Let them come to us. Our marriage comes first."

He knew how hard this was on her, but still he felt resentful and frustrated that he couldn't help her, and that she wasn't able to stand up for him. "Being here is not exactly my idea of a happy Christmas."

"I'm glad we came early and didn't tell them. It gave us some time to go to the bank and check out Lou's safe deposit box."

The change of subject was a relief. "You're quite the detective. You should be proud of your success."

She brushed off his compliment. "It was just luck that I found the key when I was going through Lou's stuff after he died. I wasted a lot of time back home going from bank to bank, trying to find where he'd rented a box. I'd probably still be spinning my wheels if Warren hadn't mentioned the bank statement at Thanksgiving dinner."

"Dear Warren. If only he knew he was instrumental in making you a rich woman."

She laughed. "I might have figured it out eventually on my own. I was a little distracted at the time, due to a certain man who took my fancy."

"Oh, so I'm to blame for it taking so long to solve the mystery." The mood had taken a decidedly lighter turn, and Alexander enjoyed the banter.

"Well, one mystery is solved. We found his cache, but the other stuff...I just don't know what to think." A hurt look snuck in, and Alexander decided he needed to crush it before it grew.

"Helen, Lou was an asshole. I'm glad he's dead. He beat you regularly and lied to you all the time. We now have ample proof of the lying. He made you live in near-poverty while he had piles of cash, probably used for his own secret activities. The stones we found are probably diamonds. Even though they're small, they're probably worth a fortune. We can have them looked at when we get home."

She visibly curled in on herself, as if his anger upset her instead of encouraging her. "That's not what's bothering me the most," she whispered.

"I know what's bothering you. Even after looking through all the letters and photos, it's not clear who exactly that woman is."

"I can only think of one explanation. Lou was older than I am. I told you he was in the war? He was just a young man when he went to France. Those letters are from a French woman. They're love letters, even if they are in fractured English. There's a baby she claims is his. It all happened before we met, but he never said anything to me. What does it mean? Did he get her pregnant and leave her to fend for herself in a country devastated by war? It looks like it. The letters from her are dated past the time he married me, too. No wonder he hid them. Did he love her? And if he did, why didn't he marry her? My children might have a half-brother or -sister they don't know about."

"They don't need to know. And they probably wouldn't care. I'll say it again. Lou was a jerk. Consider how he treated you. Remember what you told me about him trying to get Sally aborted? He didn't want responsibility. He didn't care for you and the kids. He probably ran screaming from that woman in France."

She looked up with damp eyes. "Then why did he keep the letters?"

"Perhaps it suited his ego to have someone say nice things about him even though he was a jerk. Maybe she thought if she sent photos of the child and kept on him, he'd change his mind. Who knows, maybe he sent her money, and that's why she kept writing. It probably gave him a boost to have her fawning over him and keeping it a secret from you."

Helen looked shocked. "I hadn't considered that possibility."

"Since he kept you out of the finances, it would have been easy to do."

"Maybe. What do you think the diamonds are about?"

"Could they be war booty? Did he ever tell you anything about the war?"

"Not a word."

"They could be his way of having liquid assets that don't take up much space in case of a need to leave suddenly. Or if they are war booty, they could have sentimental value. Bullies like Lou look on their time in the war as their glory days, though I can't imagine why."

He followed as she left the bathroom and sat on the bed. Her hands were bunched into fists. "I just want to go home. I'm tired of people treating us bad." She paused for a minute, and her face scrunched up. "I just realized I never said that out loud before now. And I'm going to say something else, something that's even harder for me to say: I was jealous at Barbara's party. I don't like women coming on to you. Even Sally was doing it. I felt like you should do something to tell them to stop. When you didn't, I felt it meant you didn't love me enough to tell them to quit. But now I can see. I'm not doing anything to stop Warren and Lena from being insulting to you, and I should. But I just keep hoping it will change. I don't want to fight. I just want peace. Does that make me a coward? Do you think I don't love you enough?" She looked at him pleadingly.

"Maybe we both need to learn to tell people off. We don't need the approval of others."

She smiled at him weakly. "Are you able to face Christmas dinner?"

"I think we did good at the Christmas eve dinner and present-opening last night. I'm sure we can handle this."

"I guess if you can put up with a present like you got, you can handle anything."

He grinned. "I always wanted a power tie."

She laughed at his sarcasm. "Let's get this over with and go home tomorrow."

* * *

Lydia, 10:00am

LYDIA RAN to the ringing phone, knowing Jean was calling. "Hello!"

"Merry Christmas! It's me, Jean!"

"I knew it was you. Merry Christmas back at ya! It's great to hear your voice. How are things going?"

"Well, the weather is pretty much what you'd think. We have gray days with cold rain, gray days with snow and occasional clear days with penetratingly cold, damp weather. I'm missing the warmth and dryness of the desert. Aside from that, it's terrific. Ian doesn't have family here, so we just had a quiet day together and made a nice roast for dinner with all the trimmings. We haven't decorated his apartment, nor got a tree, and we decided not to exchange presents. We're saving money, and frankly, we haven't known each other long enough to get good ideas for gifts. Which sounds kind of strange, when you consider it feels like we've known each other forever."

"What matters the most on holidays is who you're with. I'm glad you went to the UK. Not to be judgmental, but Richard didn't seem to have much in common with you, and he didn't seem to love you. I'm glad you had the strength to leave."

"It would have been a pretty miserable Christmas if I hadn't. We'd gotten to the point where we had nothing to say to each other. It wasn't that we fought, but there was such tension, me judging him for the porn and him thinking I was an airhead for my interests. I feel like I've been given a second chance at happiness, and I'm feeling pretty high. But enough about me. How are you doing?"

"Just fine. The weather here is lovely. A bit chilly and rainy recently, but today they're predicting sunshine and a high of almost 70."

"Don't make me envious."

"Ha! I have to have something to counter the Ian factor."

"We need to find you someone special, Lydia. Don't you wish you could find your soul mate?"

"I used to believe in soul mates. I'm not so sure anymore. Or maybe it's just that it's harder when you've been saddled with special vision like me. But I don't want to be a downer. I guess my answer is I'd love to find someone special, but I'm not sure it's going to happen for me. Let's face it. I've been a freak my whole life, and that makes it hard to find a partner."

Jean gasped. "What an awful thing to say! Take it back. Right now. You are not a freak. You're gifted. I can see how it's been hard on you, but certainly there is someone for you. Promise me you won't give up."

Lydia sighed. "I haven't given up. I'm sorry. Being alone on holidays can be depressing. I'm so grateful to Barbara for inviting me to dinner. If not for her, I'd be sitting at home tonight drinking wine and eating a TV dinner, feeling sorry for myself. I am very blessed in my friends. I am going to be so happy to have you back here. How's that going?"

"Getting him back there is turning into a bit of a nightmare. He has to get all kinds of records together, shots, proof that he isn't a felon and all kinds of other garbage so we can apply for his green card. One bit of good news: we'll be getting married here soon. It will help smooth the process. It means having a civil ceremony, but that works for me. I'm just sorry you won't be able to be here."

"Do you have a date for it yet? I might come if you invited me," teased Lydia.

"Really? We were planning to do it next month. We would work around a date that's good for you if you could come. That would be so wonderful! We need a couple witnesses, and it would be super to have you here. Could you come next month?"

"That should be fine. Why don't you email details to me about the date of the wedding and where you are living. I can find a hotel nearby."

"I'm sorry we don't have a guest bedroom. You'd be welcome to sleep on the couch."

"No need for that. I'll get a room nearby. My only problem is I don't want to drive on the wrong side of the road, so I won't rent a car. I'll just take a taxi to your place from the airport. Maybe you can research options for me and let me know what is best."

"Of course! Oh, Lyd, this is so wonderful. It's like having my family at my wedding."

"We're soul sisters, so we have to stick together. Are you planning a honeymoon?"

"We're going to Paris and then to Chartres. We'll visit the Louvre and tour around Paris and then drive to Chartres and stay near the cathedral. There's so much to do and see, it will be magical."

"Sounds like it. So then the last hurdle will be getting through all the red tape to get his green card?"

"Yes, he has everything they've asked for, but we're moving forward at a glacial pace. We need to get married so we can submit the request for a green card. It's just lucky Richard bought out my half of the house. I'm required to have an ungodly amount in the bank to prove he won't become a ward of the state, and I have just enough. Go figure."

Lydia chuckled. "There are no coincidences. So when do you think you'll be coming back?"

"As soon as we can get the paperwork submitted, we will, and then we have to wait for approval. I think it could take a few months."

Lydia bit back the disappointment. "I'll have your room ready when you return."

"That's going to make things so much easier for us. You're a lifesaver." Jean paused for a minute. "So did you tell everyone what you told me?"

"Nah, not yet. Helen has been a bit frazzled since she returned from her honeymoon, and then they've gone to Wisconsin for Christmas, which she wasn't really all that excited about, and Alexander was positively dreading it. Trouble with her kids. I didn't want to add anything to the mix. Barbara is doing fine, and I'm having dinner there today, but I'm not going to announce something like that on Christmas day. Plus the woman who bought Helen's old house, Emma, has agreed to have lunch with us next week. I think it's too soon to tell her, so I'll have to find a time just with Barbara, then bring Helen on board when she returns. I have to admit I'm not eager. It sounded so easy when you and I last spoke, but not everyone is like you, Jean. I'm afraid Helen won't want to be friends anymore. She's very private and might feel my abilities are intrusive. Emma seems even more reserved than Helen. I just don't know."

"Don't underestimate your friends. I think anyone who is a real friend isn't going to hold it against you. Besides, if we're going to set up a business, you'll need to at least admit to some level of psychic ability."

Lydia sighed in frustration. "You know I hate calling it that. It's an establishment way of making people like me feel like we're part of the lunatic fringe. I personally think anyone could learn to do what I do if they worked at it. I think most people ignore the messages they get from their intuitive senses instead of paying attention to them. They just can't be bothered." Lydia was feeling prickly about the whole subject and wanted it to go away.

"Well, I just want you to know I think you're great, and I hope you have a great Christmas dinner with Barbara and Ben. Give them my love."

"I will. Tell Ian I said hi and don't forget to email me details so I can come to the wedding."

"OK. Talk to you later. Love ya!"

"Love you, too."

Lydia hung up the phone feeling strangely lonely and disturbed. It was so easy to share with Jean, but she wasn't looking forward to telling anyone else.

AN HOUR LATER, Lydia poured a cup of coffee and went out to her patio, which was bathed in the pale light from the winter sun. The sky was a faded blue, not a cloud in sight, and the air was surprisingly warm, though still crisp. She sat wrapped in a thick sweater as she soaked in the rays, intending to enjoy this day as best she could, still feeling adrift and alone. The coffee warmed her inside as the sunshine warmed her outside, and she began to unwind.

Her next door neighbors came out on their patio to take advantage of the unusual weather. She could hear their voices as clearly as if they were sitting next to her. Sound sure carried in the desert. The woman was going on about making dinner, and the man was doing a 'yes, dear' impression. Curious, Lydia peered around the edge of the house to see what, if anything, was visible. The patio on the condo next door extended beyond the house itself, unlike hers. There was a cover over the extended area, the whole thing surrounded by a knee wall. The man and woman sat at a table drinking wine.

The woman was facing Lydia's way but didn't see her. Lydia suddenly recognized her as Barbara's neighbor Tanya, whom she'd been introduced to at the party in August. Her aura wasn't quite as alcohol-damaged as it had been then, but she obviously had a buzz on. The man's back was to her, and she could see he had thinning brown hair and a muscular build. But that wasn't what made her gasp. He was surrounded by black waves of energy. Tendrils of red tore through the black. But the anger was not what upset her. Black was a color she almost never saw. She'd seen it only a few times, and she believed it indicated someone with murderous energy. She had no way to prove that, but she just knew it in her gut. That man was dangerous. She ought to tell someone.

But tell someone what? That she sees colors around people and that reveals things about them, and that man ought to be locked up? Like anyone would believe that.

At least she could find out about Tanya from Barbara today. It might help her decide what to do.

Shook up from seeing 'killer' energy so close, she went back inside and poured the rest of her coffee down the drain. She needed something stronger. She dug a bottle of white wine out of the refrigerator and poured a glass with a shaking hand. Sitting in the living room, she pondered what options she had, and concluded she didn't have any. She'd see what Barbara said today. She wished she had listened more to the gossip about Tanya. She knew Barbara had told her some things, but she hadn't filed them away. Well, she'd figure it out. She wasn't going to tell Barbara about her ability to see auras, not yet anyway, but she would mine some details about Tanya and figure out what to do next.

She sipped her wine and wondered what the heck she was going to do with this information. Her experience told her that people tended to express whatever their energy was, and if this guy did, someone was likely to die.

* * *

Owen, 10:30am

OWEN PACED IN HIS BEDROOM, confused about the mess he had gotten himself into. He felt like a predator trapped in a cage. He didn't like holidays, never had. And Tanya was getting annoying with her not-so-subtle hints about what she expected of him.

She hated her new place. She found it too small, as if it were a type of demotion in life. He'd only lately begun to see how critical she was of everything.

She still turned him on. She had gorgeous tits and a good body for her age, and most of all, she knew what to do with it. But lately she'd begun to whine and wheedle, and he found it irritating. "Owen, what are you getting me for Christmas? Big man, am I getting a ring? Do you really love me?"

He shivered with distaste. He couldn't remember telling her he loved her. Maybe he had in a moment of passion. But really? He'd never made any promises. Why couldn't she go back to being like she was last month? Was *this* the real Tanya? Again he was reminded how much Tanya was like Mother, who'd been a drunken whore.

He couldn't put off going to Tanya's much longer. She had insisted he show up before 11am. She wanted him to help cook a Christmas dinner. She wasn't much of a cook if you asked him.

He stepped out onto his back patio to see how the weather was. The front that had hammered the area with cold rain for days had passed, replaced by warm sunshine. The high today was supposed to be an unseasonable 70 degrees. The mild weather raised his spirits. Maybe they could sit outside and enjoy it. He ducked back inside and grabbed a light jacket from the closet in the foyer, and then stopped and went back into the living room to pick up the present he'd gotten for Tanya--at her insistence, of course. She wanted jewelry. It wasn't going to be a ring like she asked for. He wondered how upset she'd be, but he wasn't going to propose. He didn't even want to live with her, let alone get saddled with her drunk ass for life. He just wanted things to go on as they had. Why couldn't she be satisfied?

Walking a fine line between doing as he was bid and what he wanted, he'd spent more money on her present than he liked. The jewelry store clerk had been very enthusiastic about the necklace, and he thought it would look nice on Tanya. It was well proportioned for a woman with big tits; it wouldn't disappear next to them. The turquoise and silver of the Indian design (he hated that "Native American" bullshit) would look good against her tanned skin.

HOURS LATER, after a meal that was filling and surprisingly almost worthy of compliments, they sat in Tanya's living room by her miniature Christmas tree, a short glass affair that had integral twinkling lights. Two wrapped presents sat next to it. Two drinks into his self-imposed three-drink limit (he didn't like to feel out of control), Owen began to sweat. He really didn't want a fight. He just wanted to feel mellow.

Tanya went over to the table and brought the presents back, sitting down next to him. She smelled of vodka and perfume, a combination he always associated with Mother. She peered at him intently with barely focused eyes. "I'll open mine first."

He welcomed the chance to get this scene behind him. She ripped the wrapping off that the jewelry store had painstakingly and artistically done for a few extra bucks. She must have known it wasn't a ring based on the shape and size of the box, but she didn't show any sign of being upset. Not yet. When she opened the hinged box and saw the necklace, she gasped. "Owen! It's the most beautiful thing I've ever seen!" Pleasantly surprised at her reaction, he relaxed as she threw her arms around him in an impulsive hug.

She snagged his present out of his lap. "I have to do something. You stay here. I'll be back shortly. I have a better way of showing you your present." She stood unsteadily on her 4-inch heels and almost fell back onto the couch, but he propped her up. She launched herself towards the bedroom, throwing another admonition behind her about staying put. Like he was going to challenge that.

Several minutes later, she stepped back into the living room. His eyes popped wide and his jaw hung open at the magnificent site. She was wearing his necklace, and he'd been right. It was just the right size for her big chest. The only other thing she had on was a red silky negligee

61

that was a little bit of lace and a whole lot of nothing else. He felt a familiar throb in response.

"How do you like your present, Owen?" She still had on her spiked heels, and the effect was astonishing and stimulated the expected response in his groin.

Nearly speechless, all he could do was nod and mumble. "Nice."

That seemed to please her sufficiently. She beckoned him with her index finger. "How about we celebrate?"

She didn't have to ask him twice.

* * *

Emma, 3:15pm

THE CHIME of the doorbell yanked Emma out of the story she was reading. She looked up, surprised that the sun had gotten so low. How long had she been reading, anyway? The clock said 3:15. Christmas day was slipping by. Good riddance. She didn't need to be reminded she was alone.

Peering through the peephole on her front door, she saw Julio standing outside holding something. Concern stabbed at her. What was he doing dropping by on Christmas? Oh, damn, she'd told him she would be here alone. Alone. An instinctive reaction based on past trauma caused her to go rigid with fear.

Forcing herself to shrug it off, she opened the door. His warm smile flashed even, white teeth. "Mrs. Lightman. Merry Christmas. I am sorry to interrupt your holiday. I failed to come back with your estimate because other demands took my time. Would it be inconvenient to return your book and talk now?"

Her mind couldn't comprehend such an obvious breach of etiquette. Surely he wouldn't visit clients' homes on Christmas? Should she turn him away? It was a tempting thought, but to be honest, she had found the day terribly lonely. She hadn't even been able to summon the energy to make a decent meal or eat. Pushing aside her lingering anxiety, she opened the door and waved him in. He held a five-gallon plant bucket with a blooming Christmas cactus in it. Decorated with a wide red ribbon to match the showy flowers, it was obviously a present from the nursery. She raised her eyebrows but said nothing.

He followed her into the living room. "I think it would be better if I put this on your patio. It is not dripping water, but, just in case"...he waited for her nod, and then let himself out the sliding glass door and placed the plant in a corner. She restrained herself from asking what the plant was for.

She pointed to the couch, and he sat down, laying the book she'd loaned him on the table. "First, I want to apologize for the delay in your wall. We will be back to work tomorrow, weather permitting. And I am sorry I did not return as promised. The Christmas cactus is a peace offering. I had a lot going on, and your labyrinth project required more time than I expected. I had to talk to my brothers. I wanted to make sure they were open to doing it. This is a good time of year for such a thing, because our schedule is more open in winter. So we can take the project on. Depending on the design you choose, the materials and labor will cost different amounts. Would you like me to tell you what the choices are?"

She dropped into the chair across from him, curious about his proposal. "Why not?" She wasn't doing anything else right now.

He took time to explain what they could offer and what it would cost, and she found herself caught up in envisioning her labyrinth completed in the walled back yard, an oasis of peace in her life. It was a compelling image. "I like the idea of the gravel with the border you suggested. Using a finer gravel of the same color I already have is ingenious; it will be different, but not a maintenance nuisance, because we won't have to worry about colors mixing. How long would it take to complete?"

"We can get started by the first of the year, give or take a few days. Completion might take a week or so. Would you like me to put it on the schedule?"

"Certainly. Do you want payment in advance, or a deposit?"

He grinned. "Not necessary. You can pay when we finish. We will need to pick the exact spot, but we can do that when I come back with the crew."

An awkward silence filled the air. Finally, Julio spoke again, this time in a gentler tone. "Are you having a nice day?" His looked around the room, obviously taking in the lack of Christmas decorations--no tree, no nothing--and the fact that it didn't smell like she'd cooked. His eyes seemed filled with something. God, she hoped it wasn't pity.

"I've been relaxing and reading a book."

"Did you have a traditional Christmas dinner?"

"No, I let the time get away from me and forgot all about it. It's not too exciting to cook for one." And it was no fun trying to eat at someone else's house when you had so many food allergies, but she didn't feel like telling him that.

"Would you like to go out somewhere to get a meal? I am not doing anything right now."

She cringed at the offer. Restaurants were almost as difficult as eating at a friend's house. You couldn't control everything. She didn't fancy being awake for two hours at 3am with a stomach ache. But she couldn't bear to have his sympathy, so she couldn't tell him that. "No, I'm not much for eating out. And I doubt anywhere is open on Christmas."

He nodded as if he had expected her to refuse. Standing up, he held his hand out. "I will wish you a Merry Christmas and be on my way, then."

She scrambled awkwardly to her feet and gingerly took his big hand and shook it. He preceded her to the front door, turned and promised to be back the next day if the weather held.

"Thanks, Julio. The plant is nice, and I love the plans. See you tomorrow." She watched him walk out to his truck and drive away. Somewhere in the course of the last conversation, she'd lost her fear of him. He was acting different, though she didn't understand what had changed. Instead of swaggering and preening, he was showing a soft side. Maybe that's why she no longer felt hunted.

She walked over to the urn on the corner table. "Leo, if only you were here. At least he isn't scaring me anymore. I think he's feeling out on a limb, though I have no idea why."

She heard his voice, laden with humor. *Cara mia, don't be so blind.*

"What do you mean? What's there to see?"

He obviously fancies you.

She knew Leo wasn't really answering her, but she was equally sure this was exactly what he would have told her. He was always so good about pointing out when she went into avoidance mode, and yet, he never judged her for it.

"Well, I'm not interested," she said flatly. And that was a fact. She shrugged and picked up her book, uncertain what the intrusion had meant, not wanting to dwell on it, afraid that if she did, she might become fearful that she was being stalked--like that was a possibility. He was way too young for her, and she'd done nothing to encourage him. Such thoughts were ridiculous. She opened the book and began reading, but her mind wasn't totally engaged with the story.

* * *

Red, 5:30pm

RED STARED at Sally's stony gaze, which was locked on the contents of the package she'd just unwrapped. He'd packed the ring in a much larger box so she wouldn't guess what it was. She turned the ring back and forth in the light, the small diamond reflecting it beautifully, but her face was devoid of any emotion. She didn't like it. Why had he ignored his intuition?

He tried to fill the awkward silence. "I know you may not be ready for marriage, but I wanted to offer. I love you and the baby, and I know I'm not much of a catch, but I'd take good care of you both." Somehow, the words sounded ludicrous, in part because they were bouncing off Sally.

A pained look crossed her face, and she held the ring away from her as if it were infected. "I didn't mean to give you any false impressions."

He'd never felt so adrift. "What has all this meant to you, then? I thought you cared for me." He thought women wanted this, but clearly, Sally did not. How could he have been so blind?

"I'm just not the white picket fence, little-home-with-a-walk-in-closet type, Red. I thought you knew that." Her cold-blooded response made him defensive. "Are you just playing around? Is this all you want? Don't you want a father for your child?" He couldn't comprehend her attitude. It made him painfully aware of their nearly 30-year age difference. His hopes deflated, he reached over and took the ring from her, eager to get it out of sight.

She said nothing but had the good grace to look guilty. Even at that, her pose reminded him of a madonna, so serene and beautiful, and he felt the familiar temptation to push aside his common sense and stay in spite of her rejection of his proposal. He knew she'd let him stay on as her lover, but a line had finally been crossed, and that was no longer enough for him.

He shoved the ring box in his pocket. Embarrassment and humiliation chased him to the front door. He paused long enough for one last try. "I'm ready to make this relationship work. I know I'm a lot older than you."

Her head shot up, and her eyes flashed with anger. "Don't go playing the age card on me. There's nothing wrong with you, and age has nothing to do with what I'm saying. I'm just not ready for marriage to anyone."

Surprised at his own reaction, he countered. "Well, I am, and if this is going nowhere, I'm out. For me, it's all about age. People my age rarely get a second chance. I don't blame you if you don't want me, but I want more than what we have now." He reached for the doorknob as he slipped on his jacket, hoping she'd stop him, knowing she wouldn't. If he were honest with himself, he had known all along it would come to this. The red flags had been waving forever; he had just refused to acknowledge them.

She didn't call him back as he left, so he drove home and poured himself two fingers of scotch, neat, and sat in his recliner, wondering how he'd managed to make such a fool of himself. Why would he ever think a beautiful 30-year-old woman would want to be saddled with a three-time loser like him, even if she were pregnant with another man's child? He chugged the scotch and poured another.

He had no target for his anger but himself. He couldn't blame her; he should have known better. He already missed the baby, the son he never had and never would have. At least she didn't live in Palm Lakes. Then he remembered he'd have to face Helen and Alexander when they returned from Wisconsin. He cringed at the thought. He was going to look like such an idiot.

Two scotches weren't going to be enough. He was pouring his second drink when the doorbell rang. An irrational wish that it was Sally popped into his head. Knowing he must be wrong, but hoping he wasn't, he went to the door and peered through the spy hole. It was his neighbor Lydia. She had an agitated look on her face.

He opened the door, scotch still in hand. "Can I help you, Lydia?"

She looked back towards her house, or was it to the condo next to him?, a look of anxiety on her face. "I shouldn't bother you on Christmas, but it occurred to me that maybe you could help me with something..." Her voice trailed off, then gave him a penetrating look with her dark brown eyes and shook her head. "You're busy. Besides, you're going to think I'm crazy. I shouldn't be here." She turned as if to leave.

"Wait. Come on in. At least tell me what this is about. I'm not doing anything right now. Would you like a drink? I have a good single malt scotch. Or I could make coffee."

Her face brightened up at the invitation. She had a beautiful smile. "Thank you. I could really use a scotch, to be honest." She stepped inside and glanced around his living room. "My, you keep your place nice."

He smiled at the compliment. "I'm a bit of a neat freak. Everything in its place, you know. But it's small. Well, you know that. Your place is probably the same. Come on in and sit down. I'll get you a drink."

He went for a glass as she sat on the couch. She was dressed as usual, in a flowing, colorful skirt, a blouse with a scooped neck and a necklace with big green stones. Her lush, dark hair rippled to her shoulders. It was a good look for her. She was the antithesis of Sally, a sensuous, mature earth mother to Sally's young ice queen. "Ice or water?"

"Neat is fine."

"You're my kind of drinker." It popped out before he even thought how she'd take it, but she seemed sanguine. He carried the glass over to her and sat across from her in the recliner. "Sometimes in summer, I'm so hot, I add ice, but I prefer it neat, too." He smiled encouragingly.

She sipped the scotch nervously. "I'm so sorry to disturb you on Christmas day. This is really gauche of me. But I happened to see you drive in, and you were alone, and I've been so torn all day about what to do. I'm going in circles and getting nowhere."

He didn't bother to point out that he didn't drive by her house to get home. "So what's this about?"

She looked around as if reluctant to share her story. "I don't know where to start."

"The beginning's a good place."

"It's going to sound crazy."

Now he was getting interested. He could use some distraction after the day he'd had.

"I won't think you're crazy."

"I'm an aging hippie type. You're a cop. You've got to think I'm weird."

He grinned at her assumption. "I might surprise you."

She looked at him intently, as if for the first time. It was almost like she was seeing into him. Her nervousness vanished, only to return some seconds later. "Well, I can't keep you waiting forever. I'm going to tell you something, and I probably will regret it. But I need to tell someone, and for some reason, I felt guided to tell you. I hope you can have an open mind."

Now she had his full attention. "Please, I'm all ears. I've had a bad day, and I could use some distraction."

She smiled knowingly at him. "I am sorry your day has been disappointing. I'm only going to make things worse, I'm afraid. I got back from dinner at Barbara's about an hour ago--they eat early on holidays--and I've just been getting more agitated by the minute, and I hoped maybe since you're with the Posse, you could help me. You see, there's a man I'm worried about, but the reason I'm worried isn't going to make sense to you. You're going to have to take a lot on faith. But I promise that I haven't been drinking. Well, not much. And that what I'm saying is true."

He put his glass down, leaned forward and gave her his full attention.

She took a deep breath and let it out slowly. "Well, I don't know if you've noticed, but we have a new neighbor living in the condo between us." She cocked her head in that direction.

"Yes, I knew the place was sold. I heard it was a lone woman. For some reason, she parks her car on the street. I'm assuming she's using the garage for storage for the time being. I spend a lot of time away, so I've never even seen her."

Lydia warmed up to the story. "Well, she's a former neighbor of Barbara's, you know, the woman whose party you went to a few days ago with Helen's daughter Sally?"

He flinched when Sally's name was mentioned, and he saw that she noticed. Damn, she was observant. "Was this woman at the party?"

"No, her name's Tanya, and she did live on Barbara's street, but she divorced and moved, so she wasn't invited. I haven't seen much of her, either. This morning at about 11:30, I went out on my patio to have a cup of coffee and I saw her and a friend on her patio, which extends out from her condo, as you've probably noticed."

He nodded his agreement, and she went on. "Well, it's the guy I'm here about. I'm pretty sure he parks his car in her garage when he comes over, and that's why her car is on the street. Of course, there's no law against that. I'm guessing that she doesn't want anyone to know she's dating. It might impact her alimony. And that's not what I'm here about, either."

This was interesting news. Tanya had divorced and a guy was visiting? Could it be...? He looked at Lydia, stunned at the coincidence and unable to speak. She appeared to sense the wheels turning in his head and stopped, and her lively brown gaze seemed to be reading him. Finally, he found his voice. "In August, I interviewed a lot of Barbara's neighbors about her missing cat. Tanya was one of them." He wondered how much to share. It was all speculation. Better to see what she had. "So tell me more."

She sipped some scotch as if fortifying herself. "I see things most people don't see. I can read people in ways that are beyond body language or keen observation. I can tell how people are feeling; I get a lot about their personality; I can see health problems."

This sounded pretty far out. "How do you do that?"

"I've been doing it my whole life, and I can't tell you exactly how. But people's physical bodies are only part of who they are. Each person has an energy field that to my eyes is filled with colors, and the colors tell me things about them, because it's a part of them, a part they can't hide, lie or fake about. Only when people are about to die do the colors go away."

Red felt suddenly naked. Then he realized with shock that he had accepted what she said as true. "OK, so go ahead and convince me. What do you see about me?" He cringed at the thought of her knowing what he was going through, but he needed proof.

She looked at him in sympathy and something else. "Thank you for not throwing me out on my ear. I came to you because of what I see in you. You are a man with integrity. You are honest. You try to do right by people." She paused, as if she knew this wasn't going to be enough. "You've been hurt badly today, which only shows that you are a kind person who is willing to take a chance on life and love. I guess you found out that Sally isn't interested in a permanent relationship."

He closed his eyes in embarrassment. "So it's that obvious?"

"It wouldn't be to anyone but me. I see what everyone feels. I've learned to ignore it for the most part. I don't want to intrude; your personal life is none of my business. But I hope it helps you believe what I'm going to say next. You probably know Tanya is a drinker, but I don't have to smell it on her or see her stagger; I can tell from the color of her aura. She appears to be less toxic than when I first saw her in August. Barbara told me today Tanya went into rehab in October after an alcohol-related car accident. Her husband divorced her around Thanksgiving. And there's a man visiting her, and today I got a clear look at him, if only from the back, and what I saw terrified me." She looked at him to see what he'd say.

"Why are you terrified?" Red felt he was on a stage acting a part. Karma or the gods were pulling all the strings, and now the threads of the plot were coming together. He knew what Lydia was going to say, and she was going to be shocked that he totally accepted it.

"He's got 'killer' energy. I almost never see black, and never this much. He had red for anger, too, but it was minor compared to the midnight black that cloaked his aura. He either has killed or will kill, or both." Lydia's gaze didn't waver.

"Owen Schmidt."

She looked at him quizzically. "Who is that? And how would you know who it is? Have you seen him? I only saw him from the back. He's short with thinning brown hair and a muscular build."

"That's him. I haven't seen him here. He's a bachelor who lives next door to Barbara. I interviewed him about Barbara's missing cat. I was suspicious he killed the cat--he'd complained about it messing his yard--but there was no way to prove it. I also had strong suspicions he and Tanya were carrying on behind her husband's back. I could never figure a way to prove anything. I tried to dig up some facts by cruising the neighborhood, but never found anything concrete, and then got distracted when I started seeing Sally." Strange, saying her name that time didn't hurt as much.

Lydia looked at him with respect. "So you think the guy is this Owen Schmidt, and you know where he lives?"

"Yup. I'd bet on it. And I think he could be a killer. He doesn't have a record, but his mother died in mysterious circumstances. Don't tell anyone I told you that, but it corroborates what we're both feeling."

She smiled conspiratorially. "I won't say a word. So what made you think he killed the cat?"

"Cop-ly intuition." He grinned at her and she lit up.

"You believe in intuition?"

"I'd be dead several times over without it. I learned long ago to listen to it."

Her smile widened. "I'm glad to hear that. So you don't think I'm crazy?"

"Hell, no. You just gave me a way out of this pity party I was going to throw for myself. I have no idea what to do with this, but it's important in some way. We'll have to think how best to use this information."

"We?" She seemed tickled at the prospect.

"Well, I'm probably going to have to use you as an advisor in some capacity, since you have these skills I don't have. But promise me you won't go all Nancy Drew on me. Stay away from both of them. OK?"

If Schmidt was as dangerous as he thought, she could get herself killed if she went snooping. "I'm serious, Lydia. You have to promise me not to do anything without telling me first. I shouldn't have shared this with you, and I won't have you endangering yourself."

Looking grateful and relieved, she lifted her glass. "Whatever you say. This gives me a chance to help. I'm worried someone's going to end up dead."

He frowned and gulped the rest of his scotch. "I don't know that we can prevent that, but we'll do what we can. How about a refill?"

"You're on!"

* * *

Mary Beth, 6:20pm

MARY BETH WAS SITTING in a stupor in Samantha's living room after gorging on a roast turkey dinner with all the trimmings and a spectacular dessert of homemade pies, one pumpkin and one pecan. Maddie had a coffee at hand, and everyone else but Stanley was nursing a glass of wine.

Samantha had let Mary Beth bring a broccoli casserole, and everyone liked it except for Stanley, who preferred his veggies plain instead of with cheese and mushrooms. They'd been very nice to her, even Arthur, who hadn't met her before today. Still, she felt like a gate crasher. A depressed gate crasher at that. No one let on that they noticed, though.

It hadn't occurred to Mary Beth that there would be an exchange of presents. *Duh!* Maddie and Stanley had arrived with bags full, and wrapped presents lay on the table in front of her. She shrank down, trying not to inject herself into a family event. She hadn't thought to bring any presents, and she was embarrassed, but no way could she excuse herself and leave without appearing rude.

She had to give credit to Samantha for being an incredibly competent hostess. The meal had proceeded smoothly, and most of it was homemade, so that was no small feat. Arthur helped some, but she didn't seem to need a lot of assistance. It all seemed to flow so effortlessly.

That led to memories of Thanksgiving, when she and Mom had created a feast for just the two of them and had to eat leftovers for a week. She almost laughed out loud, then immediately felt like crying. Pushing her emotions out of sight, she composed her face and focused on the positive things about today.

It had been a very agreeable meal, and Mary Beth was grateful for the invitation. Helen and Alexander were in Wisconsin, and Ethan was visiting one of his kids over the holiday, so it would have been a lonely holiday if not for Samantha. Knowing both Maddie and Samantha made Mary Beth feel more comfortable about being here. And maybe if she were lucky, Ethan would call her later, like he did on Thanksgiving.

Samantha threaded her way to the pile of gifts, then looked at everyone. "Shall I start?"

Maddie and Stanley murmured assent. Arthur nodded. Mary Beth tried to be small and nonexistent. Samantha looked at the labels and handed Maddie and Stanley each a gift. She picked up a small package, read the label and turned to Mary Beth. "This one's for you."

Mary Beth felt breathless as she reached her hand out. The little tag said 'To Mary Beth, From Maddie and Stanley'. It was the right size for jewelry. *Goody!* She stole a glance at the other people. Stanley was meticulously unwrapping his package, making sure not to rip the paper, as was Maddie with hers. Samantha had torn the paper off her gift, exposing a book of some type, and Arthur was looking at his gift, some kind of shell necklace Maddie had made. Mary Beth wondered if he wore jewelry. He didn't seem the type, but he didn't look offended.

Mary Beth ripped the wrapping paper off her box and opened it. A lovely cloisonné poinsettia pendant hung on a thick braided gold chain. Nestled next to it were matching dangle earrings shaped like small poinsettia blossoms. "Oh, Maddie, this is so exquisite!" She pulled the necklace out and put it on immediately, then replaced her earrings with the matching ones. "I need to go look in a mirror." She stood up and went to the powder room and admired them. They complimented her dark hair and green eyes. She just wished she had something for Maddie. It was hard to go back to the living room, knowing she had nothing to give her.

When she returned, there were small piles in front of each person. Books and practical things like fancy wool socks sat alongside Maddie's jewelry, which she apparently gave to everyone for every occasion. Samantha was holding a tourmaline chip necklace up to her chest and letting everyone ooh and aah. It really complemented her coloring. Mary Beth felt herself relax. No one was looking at her like she had committed a faux pas. Her mother would have given her hell for not thinking of bringing presents, but she was so bone tired, it hadn't occurred to her.

Mary Beth sipped her wine for a while, then thanked Samantha and

Arthur for inviting her and promised Maddie she'd see her Saturday to make jewelry. Samantha walked her out to her car in the now-chilly air. "Mary Beth, thanks for joining us today. I'm so sorry about your Mom. It's a terrible time of year for this to happen, not that there ever is a good time."

Mary Beth nodded. "I'm so very grateful for your hospitality. And thanks so much for coming to the funeral service."

Samantha reached out and touched her arm. "My Mom can't go to funerals, or I know she would have come along. She really values you as a friend, and she told me she was embarrassed she couldn't make herself go. I hope you know it wasn't due to lack of affection or support. She has a phobia."

"I understand. Maddie's been so good to me, how could I hold it against her? Not to change the subject, but when is your last day at Palo Verde?"

Samantha lowered her gaze. "I start at Temple Landscaping the first week of January."

"I'm really going to miss you. I was hoping we could get to know each other better, and now you're leaving. It sucks. I don't have any friends my own age." Mary Beth chided herself for whining at her colleague's good fortune. "I don't mean to make you feel bad. Maybe we could get together now and then, even though you're taking a new job?"

"I'd like that, Mary Beth. I don't have any friends my age, either. It seems all I do is work and take care of my family. Not that I mind. But I'd like to have a friend."

Mary Beth impulsively hugged Samantha. "Then let's just do it. I know it will be hard to find the time, so let's decide to make time. The way I'm doing jewelry with your Mom every Saturday, I feel almost like part of the family."

"Whoa! Be careful of that. We're a weird family."

"I haven't got any other family at this point. I'll take weird over nothing." Mary Beth grinned at Samantha and got a smile in return. "What about having lunch one day next week?"

"I'd like that."

Mary Beth went back 'home' to Helen's condo and rattled around, unable to sit still. At exactly 8pm, the phone rang. She ran to pick it up.

"Hello, Mary Beth? It's me, Ethan."

She felt herself unwind as she dropped onto the couch. "It's so nice of you to call."

"How was your Christmas dinner with Maddie's family?"

"They were so kind to me. The food was great, and I didn't have to do hardly anything. I even got a present."

"That sounds pretty good. Things are crazy here. Kids running wild all over the place. We've had lots of good food, too. Too much, in fact. I always gain weight this time of year, with all the big meals and less exercise."

"Me, too."

Ethan made a hmmm noise, and she could picture his eyebrows wrinkling. She half expected him to finally say something about his feelings for her. If he had any. Instead, all he said was, "Are you settling in to your new place OK?"

She wasn't sure whether she was annoyed or relieved at the banality. "Yeah, Helen saved my ass big time. Pardon my French. This way I will have my house on the market in no time. The realtor suggested I sell the place furnished, so that's what I'm going to do, except for a few antiques I'm keeping. She seems hopeful that it will sell fast and for a good price."

"We'll keep our fingers crossed. I'll be home day after tomorrow. I'm sorry I wasn't there to keep you company through the holiday."

"I'm doing fine, Ethan. I'm busy getting the house on the market and doing all the necessary stuff for Mom's estate. I haven't really even had a chance to think long-term yet. I can't stay here forever. But it's perfect for a while." She immediately regretted her words. They sounded like she was fishing. It really was on her mind a lot, but she didn't want him to think she was asking him to solve her problem.

"I'm glad you have a good place to stay. You aren't going to have to worry about being out on the street. If you have to leave there, let me know. I'll do what I can to help."

"That's so kind of you, Ethan. It's good to have friends at a time like this. I appreciate all you've done to help me." He did way more for her than a friend would. Yet it was so odd and not at all like dating. He had never even kissed her and only ever touched her in platonic ways. She wasn't sure what was going on, but right now, all that mattered was that he was her friend. She had no family left. Being on her own wasn't all that liberating.

"Would you like to get together for a meal after I get back? You don't have to cook for me. I just thought you might like some company."

"That would be very nice, Ethan. Call me when you get back. And I like to cook. So why don't you plan on coming over to my new place? It has a nice big kitchen. I'll make Italian."

"You won't get any argument from me. I'll bring the wine and tiramisu for dessert. Not that I cook. They make a nice tiramisu at Safeway."

She smiled at his honesty. "Great! I look forward to it."

"See you later. Merry Christmas, Mary Beth."

"Same to you, Ethan. Have fun with your family."

She hung up the phone. The silence taunted her. She'd never felt so alone. She hadn't gotten the cable hooked up yet, but soon she'd have lots of channels to watch, instead of flipping through 'Gilligan's Island' and 'I Love Lucy' reruns like she had at Mom's. For now, though, there was nothing to do. Belatedly, she remembered that Mrs. J. didn't have family. She should have made sure she had something to do or someone to be with today. *Damn it all!* Catherine was so kind to her, and she was only now thinking about how lonely she might be. Maybe if she called her and invited her for coffee tomorrow or a glass of wine tonight...she grabbed the phone and found the number in her book. Mrs. J's phone rang several times before she picked up.

"Hello?" Catherine's wary tone made Mary Beth more annoyed at herself for not doing this sooner.

"Hi, it's me, Mary Beth. I'm sorry I didn't call sooner. I hope I didn't interrupt anything. I wanted to wish you a Merry Christmas."

"How nice of you to think of me. I've just been relaxing and enjoying a quiet day. I don't do much for the holidays."

"Would you like to come over for a glass of wine or cup of coffee?"

"I'd hate to trouble you. You don't need to entertain an old woman like me."

"Catherine, I'm here all alone on Christmas and feeling sorry for myself, and I'd rather not be. So if you'd like to visit, I'm up for a while and intend to have some wine. Just come on over and I'll pour you a glass or make some coffee."

It only took a few seconds. "I'll be over. I think a glass of wine would be nice. Give me just a minute."

"OK. I'll be ready when you arrive. The door's unlocked."

Mary Beth hung up, unlocked the front door and went to scour the kitchen for snacks. Fortunately, she had some crackers and a block of nice cheese, so she set them out on a platter and put some glasses and the wine bottle on the table. Catherine came through the front door minutes later, limping slightly.

She tossed her coat onto the couch and joined Mary Beth in the kitchen, easing herself into a chair gingerly. Mary Beth noticed. "Is your arthritis acting up?"

She shrugged it off. "No more than usual. It's not worth talking about." She looked around the room owlishly. "I like your new place."

Mary Beth smiled. "I haven't brought all my stuff over yet, but I'm getting there. This is mostly how Helen left it. She didn't take much to Alexander's, so I benefit."

Catherine reached for her glass and raised it for a toast. "I want to toast my new friend Mary Beth. Thanks for inviting me over. It's been a pretty boring day."

Once again, Mary Beth cringed that she hadn't thought of this sooner. "I'm sorry to be so late inviting you over. I accepted a dinner invitation from a co-worker. Her Mom teaches me to make jewelry. Do you like jewelry?"

"Who doesn't? But I don't buy it for myself." Her faded blue eyes looked wistfully at some point above Mary Beth's head. A brainstorm caused Mary Beth to shoot up out of her seat. "Just a minute. I'll be right back."

She rushed to her bedroom and looked on the desk, where her latest jewelry projects were sitting. The present she'd made for her mother, a necklace of graded onyx beads with gold findings and matching earrings, was in a gift box. She'd meant to wrap it for her Mom for Christmas, but everything went to shit and she never had a chance, nor gave any thought to what she'd do with it. Now she knew. She grabbed the gift box, lifted the lid to inspect the contents, then closed it and returned to the dining room.

She put the box in front of Catherine. "I have a present for you. I have to confess I made it for my Mom, but I'd like you to have it. It's my first complete set."

Catherine's eyes widened and filled with tears. Her mouth moved as if she would say something, but then shut. Her wrinkled hand reached for the box and drew it to her, opening the lid. She gasped when she saw the jewelry. "You made this yourself? It's absolutely beautiful!"

Mary Beth beamed at her reaction. "Yes, Maddie helped me a lot, but I did it myself. I even designed it mostly by myself after watching Maddie design a few necklaces. It will go with anything, being black."

Catherine picked up the necklace and undid the clasp. Her fingers clumsily tried to fix it around her neck. Mary Beth got up and did the clasp for her. "I can change the clasp if this one's too hard to do. You just let me know." She glanced at Catherine's earlobes. "I'm so glad you have pierced ears. Not everyone does."

"I'm glad, too. This is such a wonderful gift. Thank you." Catherine wiped a tear from behind her thick glasses. "I can't remember the last time I got such a nice Christmas present. I don't have one for you, though."

"When I went to Samantha's today, I didn't have one for anyone, and I got an unexpected gift. So I'm paying it forward."

"You have a lot of talent. You're going to keep making jewelry, I hope?"

"Yes, Maddie will work with me as long as I stay in the area. Which I plan to do."

Catherine reached over and patted Mary Beth's hand. "I'm glad you got to stay here, and I'm glad we got to know each other better."

Mary Beth fought tears. "Me, too."

* * *

Nora, 7:00pm

NORA STARED at her wine glass, struggling to find something positive to say. She knew Luke was terribly disturbed (not that she wasn't), and she was afraid he felt responsible for the situation they found themselves in. If she didn't steer him away from it, he'd fall into depression. It had happened before when the stress was too much for him.

The flashing lights on the tree served to emphasize the gap between where they were a few days ago and where they were now. Holiday spirit had gone out the window when they received the letter yesterday.

She glanced at Luke, who was lost in thought, a frown tugging at the corners of his mouth. "Honey, it isn't your fault the company pension fund collapsed. Who could have predicted that?"

He shook his head and grimaced. "I should never have taken it for granted. We're way overextended. Without the pension payments, we can't support living in this house. It isn't even paid for." He sighed and downed the rest of his gin and tonic, setting the glass down gently on the coaster.

Nora had no idea what to say. She didn't keep the books, but she knew about the mortgage and credit card debt. Oh, why had she been so cavalier about spending money for Christmas? She should have been more conservative. Now what were they going to do? "Luke, if one of us is responsible for this, both of us are. I spent money I probably shouldn't have. I took it for granted we'd always have your pension. We'd been keeping up on payments, so I thought we were doing OK. This is *not* your fault. It's an act of God."

His blue eyes glittered. "It doesn't matter whom we blame it on. We can't afford to live this way anymore. And I doubt God is going to pay our bills. I'll need to get a job. But who's going to want a retired accountant with stale skills? Around here, I'll be lucky to get any job at my age. And an hourly wage job isn't going to support us." He looked close to tears.

"Luke, we can both get jobs. That will make up for the low salary. And if we have to, we can sell this place and get a smaller one, even a condo. That way we can still have the amenities but less overhead." It pained her to think of leaving their beautiful home on the golf course, but she wanted to sound willing to do whatever it took.

"We have very little equity in this home, Nora. Selling it might cut expenses, but it won't give us much cash flow. We may have to declare bankruptcy. I can't believe I've gotten myself in this situation."

"You mean *we've* gotten ourselves in it. And it's not like we could have predicted this event. We're not going to solve this problem by lashing ourselves with blame." She put her glass down and went to sit beside him on the sofa. "Let's just relax tonight, and tomorrow we can start looking for jobs and create a budget and cut expenses and even look at real estate options. But tonight, let's not dwell on this. It's Christmas! Let's just be together and do something mindless. We need to decompress."

He looked blankly at her. She reached over and gave him a hug and kissed his cheek. Stroking his soft hair, she willed him to be OK. Smiling in response to her ministrations, he seemed to pull out of the downward spiral. "You're right. We can't solve this tonight. Let's try to have some fun."

Nora felt the worry ratchet down a notch. "Would you like some of those cookies I baked? And we could watch a movie or something. Or would you prefer to read?"

He pulled her into a bear hug. "What would I do without you?"

"Probably drink too many gin and tonics." She grinned. "Though I'm up for another glass of wine, so who am I to talk? Care to join me?"

"Why not? It is Christmas, after all."

She took his hand, stood and pulled him up beside her. "Come on and have a look at what we have and pick what you'd like. I'll get some nuts. They'll go better with wine than cookies would."

They walked slowly into the spacious kitchen, then into the pantry beyond. The wine cooler was filled with bottles, and Luke selected a Chardonnay and began to open it. Nora bumped hips with him as she grabbed a can of mixed nuts off the shelf and opened it. "I'm not going to put this in a dish. We can eat right out of the can."

A genuine smile graced his face. "We're just going to let it all go to pieces, then? Soon we'll be swigging wine out of the bottle."

A laugh bubbled out of her, bleeding off more anxiety. Her shoulders began to loosen and drop. As she relaxed, she began to feel guilty for not staying tense. She felt wrong for sloughing off the guilt. It was like walking a tightrope, trying not to fall one way or the other.

Back in the living room, they sat close together on the couch, unconsciously seeking support in body warmth. The moment of good humor evaporated as they sat in silence, munching nuts and sipping wine. Nora looked at the unopened packages under the tree, wondering if she should return them for the cash she could get, resentful that this disaster made her feel she shouldn't give or accept any gifts. Not wanting to express it, knowing he felt the same, she went for distraction. "How about we watch a movie? I taped one that you might enjoy."

He didn't even ask what it was, a sure sign that he was wandering off into depression. "OK, whatever you want to do."

Unsatisfied with his response, but having nothing better to offer, she got up and put the tape in the VCR and returned to sit by him and huddle for comfort. The sound of the show invaded their space, but didn't dispel the dark, heavy feelings that had gathered again.

* * *

Samantha, 7:50pm

ARTHUR WAS SITTING in the living room watching TV. Samantha was cleaning the kitchen while the dishwasher ran. It pleased her to know that the dinner had gone well. She was so gratified when everyone seemed to enjoy the food and went home happy. It made her feel like she had brought some joy into their lives.

Mary Beth needed some joy. Samantha felt guilty for not spending more time with her. Her own mother had befriended Mary Beth, yet she had been too busy with work and the job offer from Temple Landscaping to even think about reaching out to the poor girl. She was living illegally in Palm Lakes, and now that her Mom was gone, what was she going to do? Samantha promised herself she'd ask her to go to lunch one day next week.

That reminded her that soon she'd be starting her new job at Jack's nursery. She was excited at the prospect of getting to do more of what she liked, being able to really contribute to an operation. But she dreaded being around Jack. She hoped they wouldn't see much of each other. After all, she was going to be in charge of plantings and design so he could concentrate on other things. Maybe it would work out after all. But warning bells were still going off.

She stuck her head out into the living room. "Arthur, do you want a beer or something?"

"Yeah, that would be great," he tossed the answer back at her without taking his eyes off the tube.

She got a beer out of the fridge and opened it. Then she looked at her empty wine glass. She'd only had one glass of wine all day, trying to stay clear for serving the meal and making sure everyone was happy. She deserved another. She poured a glass of pinot grigio and grabbed the beer.

She arrived in the living room to see that Arthur was watching "Miracle on 34th Street. "This seems like a girly kind of movie to me," she teased him.

"It ran every year at Christmas for so long, and I have to admit I enjoy it."

She sat on the couch next to him and watched the movie, not really paying attention to it, she'd seen it so often. It made a great cover for the turmoil in her head. She wanted to call Jack and wish him a Merry Christmas. He was alone for the holiday, and she felt unreasonably bad about that. She knew she shouldn't--couldn't--call him from home.

For a minute she fantasized about going out and calling him from a pay phone, but she knew she couldn't come up with a good reason for going out this late on Christmas. She'd just have to give it up. She sighed, wishing things were different. It didn't occur to her that change is a constant in life.

4
THURSDAY, DECEMBER 28, 1995

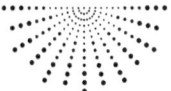

Helen, 9:00am

*W*orking with Alexander in the kitchen after breakfast gave Helen time to ponder what they'd discovered on their trip to Wisconsin and all it had revealed about Lou's secret past. She didn't have enough information to reach closure about what he'd done, and it was irritating her like an insect bite she couldn't scratch.

As she dried a pan, she wondered if telling Alexander how she felt would be a good idea. She knew he wasn't as consumed by what they'd discovered as she was; why would he be? It was *her* dead husband who had lied to her all these years, after all. She hadn't thought her feelings about Lou could get any worse. And why couldn't she let it go? That was her old life, and she didn't want it poisoning this one. But what he'd done was like a festering wound inside her. As if she needed another challenge at this point.

Not feeling certain she could share appropriately after past disasters, she bit her tongue. She didn't realize her confusion had stopped her in her tracks until Alexander spoke. "You look deep in thought." He held a freshly washed pot towards her, his green eyes examining her with concern, but she wasn't sure she wanted to talk yet.

"I'm OK." She put the dried pan down and took the wet pot from him, but she'd said it too quickly and immediately saw that he wasn't fooled. *Damn.*

"You don't have to tell me what's wrong, but I hope if it's about me, you will." His soft, understanding voice only made her feel more to blame for recent problems. Which irritated her more. She knew she should be grateful for his kindness, but instead, she felt it highlighted the vast difference between his equanimity and her roller-coaster of emotions.

Things had been up and down for a couple weeks despite her best efforts. She was still stinging from trying so hard to fit into his life. She didn't want him to feel bad. She was scared of losing him. But she couldn't have him thinking he'd done something wrong. "I'm sorry. I was just thinking about what we found in Wisconsin. I can't seem to get it out of my head. I know I should let it go, but--"

He stepped in close and pulled her into his arms, pot and all. "Shh. It's OK. I know it's hard for you to process what we found. What do you want to do?"

She wasn't used to being asked her opinion. She could hardly find her voice. "I'm not sure. I just need closure." She looked up at him with tear-filled eyes. "Part of me wants to know the whole story about that woman; another part wants to pretend I never found out. My kids are already at odds with us. If I share this with them, they'll think I'm trying to blacken their father's name. But what if there was a child that was his, half-sibling to my kids, and he or she needs help? It couldn't have been easy raising a kid alone after the war. And all those diamonds. They're worth a fortune. How do we know where they came from? If they're war booty, maybe this woman should have been given a share. What if he used her to get the gems and then deserted her? I wouldn't put anything past Lou."

He held her closer and whispered soothingly. "Or maybe the gems are something he accumulated over the years as a stash that would be small enough to fit in a box, but give him the ability to disappear at any time. Maybe it had nothing to do with the war."

"You're right. Even if I could find this woman, which is unlikely given that the most recent letter is over twenty years old, how could we be sure she'd know anything, and what good could it do to stir up the past? I just don't know, but the not knowing is tearing me up."

"Seems to me you have two choices. You can write a letter to that woman or not. If you do, it may never reach her. She may have moved or died. But maybe she'd get it and answer. We don't know how she'd respond to you. Did he tell her he married? Maybe, maybe not. Would it give her closure to hear from his widow? Possibly. Would it potentially do harm to us or your kids? I don't see how she can harm us or them, but we may need to carefully consider what we share with your kids."

Putting the pot and towel down, she took his hand and led him out into the living room and slumped onto the couch. "You're right. Thanks for laying it out so clearly. I think I'd like to try and contact her. Would you mind if I did that?"

He squeezed her hand. "Whatever it takes to give you closure is fine with me. We have enough money we could fly to France if you insist. You've never seen Paris, have you?"

She giggled. "You know I've never been anywhere except with you. I'd love to see Paris."

"Then maybe it was destined to be. Write her today."

"At least that would be one thing I'm writing."

His gaze skewered her. "I won't have you talking like that. You aren't going to ever accomplish anything as a writer if all you do is put yourself down. It's not easy getting back to work after such big changes. Trust me. I'm an old hand, and I'm having trouble applying myself. You were just getting started with the writing. So it's going to take a bit of time and effort."

His encouragement didn't remove her doubts, but it did make her feel better. "I'll write her today."

"She may not answer. You may never know."

"But if I try, maybe I can let it all go, knowing I did my best."

"Works for me." He smiled and stood up. "Don't you have lunch with the girls today?"

"Yes, I do. I'm sorry to leave you all alone."

"No problem. I need to apply myself to my book. I'll make great progress, and we'll have a delicious dinner tonight. I have just the thing in mind."

She loved how they enjoyed cooking together. "Thanks. It's a date." She kissed him and suddenly became aware that the dog next door had been barking for quite some time. "Do you hear that?"

"It's just Olivia's dog."

"Who's Olivia?"

"She's the widow next door. Must be at least 80. She has a little fluffy dog. It doesn't usually bark this much. Maybe it saw a coyote."

"A coyote? A coyote could kill a little dog." She went to the glass door and opened it, leaning out and peering anxiously in the direction of the tiny barks. Visions of how she was the last one to see Barbara's cat alive last summer came back to torment her. She wasn't going to stand by and let someone else's pet die. This time, she would take action that might create a better outcome.

She couldn't see the dog, but the barks came from the patio, which had a knee wall around it with a gate on one side. The constant stream of insistent barking worried her. "Have you ever heard her dog bark like that before?"

Alexander shook his head. "Never."

"Maybe I better go over and take a look at what has him so upset."

"I think it's a her."

"I'm going over. Want to come with me?"

"Just holler if you need me. I don't want Olivia to feel invaded. We aren't that close, and I don't know how she'll feel about people coming into her yard without invitation."

Helen grinned at him. "Wimp."

He grinned back and shrugged his shoulders. "I'll stay here. Shout if you need me."

She crunched across the graveled back yard, bracing herself against the chill, opened the gate to Olivia's yard and walked towards the patio, looking for signs of coyotes or even forced entry. She didn't see anything suspicious. The strident barking continued as she arrived at the walled patio and peered over the edge. The cutest little Pomeranian stared back at her, tail upright, little legs stiff and black eyes twinkling with intelligence. A fluffy ball of butterscotch, it paused in its barking only for a few seconds, then began again in earnest, almost as if her appearance were triggering an emotional reaction. It seemed to be urging her to do something. The patio door was closed. The dog must have exited the house via the small dog door.

"What's up, little one? Where's your Mom?" The dog perked its head to the side at the question, then began to bark sharply again as if answering. "Olivia! Are you home? It's your neighbor, Helen." Helen wasn't sure what to do next. Then she thought she heard something. Like a muffled voice.

Looking down at the dog, Helen calculated her chances of getting in without being bitten, then yelled, "Alexander! You better come over here. I think something's wrong."

She waited to hear his assent, then opened the small gate to the patio and barged in like she belonged, closing it carefully behind her. The dog continued to bark, but backed up. So far, so good.

She went over to the glass door and peered. "Olivia! Are you home?" The muffled voice was louder this time. Helen tried the glass door and found it was open, thankfully. Once she opened it enough to poke her head in, she called again, "Olivia?"

"Over here!" a frail voice said.

Helen quickly stepped inside, followed by the fluffy dog, who had stopped barking the minute Helen had opened the patio door.

She rushed over and bent down by Olivia, who was lying supine on the floor. "What happened?"

"I fell down and I can't get up. I've been here for a while, I think." Olivia's white hair was in disarray, and her brown eyes radiated pain. She reached over to pet the dog, who was obviously agitated that she was lying on the floor.

"Your dog let us know something was wrong. Otherwise, we wouldn't have thought to come over."

"She's so smart." Olivia tried to heave her bulky body up without success. The dog jumped up and barked once.

Helen reached out to stop Olivia. "You should lay still, or you might hurt yourself more. Does it feel like anything's broken?"

"I don't know. I hurt." There was a grumpy edge in her voice.

Helen took that as a good sign; at least she could feel. "We'll call an ambulance and get you to the hospital. You stay there. Where's the phone?" Helen followed Olivia's pointed finger, found the phone and dialed 911. After giving them the address, she returned to Olivia and squatted down next to her. The dog now lay next to the elderly woman, watching Helen's every move. Helen smoothed Olivia's hair and assessed her housedress and slippers. They would have to do for the trip to the hospital. Alexander joined them and checked Olivia's neck before putting a small pillow from the couch under her head. "Try to hold on, Olivia. They're on their way."

"What's going to happen to Spot?"

"Who's Spot? You don't mean the dog?" asked Helen, laughing in spite of herself. The animal in question sat up and looked at her.

Alexander chuckled. "What a great name!"

"She's my pride and joy, and she doesn't like me to leave her alone. What's going to happen to her?" Olivia was clearly more distressed about the dog than about her own health.

Helen's heart went out to her. "She can stay with us for a while, can't she, Alexander?" She looked at him hopefully.

Alexander looked at the dog. "We have a cat."

Olivia said, "We used to have a cat, and Spot loved him. She'll be OK with your cat. Please can she stay with you? If I can't get back quick, I'll make arrangements for boarding."

Helen looked pleadingly at Alexander. She would love to have an animal of her own to spoil, if only for a while. Double-teamed, he shrugged his shoulders. "Why not?"

Helen felt guilty to be so thrilled, considering the circumstances. "Olivia, does Spot have a special bed or bowls?"

"Her bed is in the master bedroom, and her bowls are in the kitchen. Get the spare house key out of the drawer by the refrigerator. Her food is in the pantry. Oh, I'm so confused, I'm sure I'll forget something. My hip hurts."

Helen looked at Alexander meaningfully. "The ambulance should be here soon. We won't leave until they get you loaded. Would you like one of us to come with you?"

"Oh, that would be so kind. My purse has my insurance card and everything you'll need for forms. It's over on that table." She waved in the direction of the kitchen, and Helen retrieved the large purse.

Helen tried to think of other details. "Do you have a leash for Spot?"

"It's hanging in the front closet, along with a little sweater for her."

"I'll go get them. Alexander, would you like to go with her to the hospital or stay home and take care of the dog?" She really wanted to stay with the dog, but it made more sense for her to go to the hospital with Olivia.

"I think Olivia would be more comfortable with you at the hospital, Helen. I'll introduce Fido to Spot and if they don't get along, I'll put Spot in the guest bedroom for now." He strode into the kitchen and got the house key. "I'm going to go get a sack to put Spot's things in. I'll be right back." And out the door he went.

"He's such a handsome man!"

Helen rolled her eyes. "I get that all the time."

"Well, I imagine you would. He could be a movie star." She sighed like a love-stricken teenager in spite of her pain.

A knock on the door saved Helen the trouble of trying to find a pleasant response. The EMTs were all business, bustling in with their equipment. Helen picked up Spot while they loaded Olivia onto the stretcher. "I'm going with her, but I'll follow you to the hospital in my car so I have transportation back."

"We'll deliver her to Emergency. You can meet her there." And they were out the door.

Helen walked home with Spot in one arm, Olivia's purse on the other, passing Alexander on his way back for Spot's things. "Don't forget her bed, leash, dishes and food."

"Sounds like she's going to be with us for a while."

"She's cute. She won't be any trouble. I'll get my car keys and wait for you to return before I head out to the hospital."

Back inside the house, Helen put Spot on the floor and let her sniff around. She was obviously curious about the new scents, especially Fido's, Helen guessed. "We have a cat. You'll need to be nice to him."

Spot looked at her intelligently and then resumed sniffing. Helen followed her as she went back to the master bedroom, where Fido lay snoozing on the bed. She saw Spot 'spot' Fido, as her head and ears perked up. She stopped sniffing the floor and scampered over to the large bed. It seemed to be too big a leap for her, because she sat down and barked once, as if telling Helen she wanted to go up and see Fido.

Fido's head shot up, and his blue eyes glanced around the room looking for the source of the tiny bark.

Helen leaned over and picked up Spot. She held her where Fido could see her, but a safe distance away, just in case. "This is Spot, Fido. She's come to visit for a little while. I hope you'll be nice to her."

Spot, who was actually smaller than Fido, was struggling to touch noses with the cat, and Fido didn't seem disturbed, so Helen brought Spot closer...and closer. Their noses touched, and nothing bad happened. Helen went to the other side of the bed with Spot and sat down, putting Spot on the covers next to her and holding her in one place. "You don't want to rush Fido. He's not used to dogs. Be patient with him or you might get scratched."

Fido showed no interest in coming over, but Spot was eager to say hi again. Just then, Alexander appeared in the doorway. "So they've already met? How's it going?"

"Fido is unimpressed, but Spot wants to be friends. I think it's a good sign. Do you think I should let her go?"

"If you don't mind Fido swatting her. I'm not sure what he'll do with a dog. He never had one."

Helen didn't want Olivia's dog to get hurt, but Fido wasn't acting threatening, so she took her hands off Spot. "Go slowly, Spot. Give Fido time to get to know you."

Without a pause, Spot walked across the big bed and stopped a few inches from Fido. Her head and tail were relaxed, and she didn't bark. She also didn't make eye contact. Fido stared for several seconds, then turned away and put his head down on the bed. Spot looked bemused and came back to Helen. "I think that was very good. Let's get you sorted so I can go to the hospital and see your Mom." She picked up Spot and noticed that the dog's soft bed was now in their bedroom. She paused long enough to show Spot. "Here's where you're going to sleep." Then she carried her into the kitchen and put her down by her bowls. "Here's your water and food dishes."

Alexander followed them. "I put her food in the pantry. You'll need to find out when and how much to feed her.

"I'll ask Olivia. I'd better get going." She handed Spot to Alexander, who was taking it more in stride than she would have expected. "It was nice of you to let us keep Spot. A kennel is an awful place."

"We'll have to see how long Olivia will be gone. I don't mind Spot visiting, but we need to be practical."

Helen frowned, but didn't feel like arguing. "Did you get the leash?"

"Yes, it's hanging in the front closet. We can't let her go out unattended. I never got to tell you what happened to Fido when we first came here. I almost lost him to a coyote. I let him out to wander. He never went far. But one day I looked out towards the golf course and saw him tearing hell-for-leather towards the house with a coyote on his tail, gaining with every step. I wasn't sure he would make it, so I opened the sliding glass door and went out to meet him. He streaked past me into the house, and the coyote skidded to a halt nearly at my feet. I never let him out loose again. We'll have to walk Spot on the leash, and that will get old fast."

"I'll do it. I like Spot. I miss having Sheba. Fido has never taken to me, and having Spot will give me an animal to spoil."

"I know you've missed her a lot. You better go now. Don't you have lunch today with the girls?"

"Oh, my God! I totally forgot! Yes, I better get going so I can get back in time. I'll call you from the hospital if I get held up. Keep an eye on Spot. Maybe you ought to give her a quick walk. Too much excitement and such a big change might cause her to break training."

His eyes narrowed. "And so it begins..."

She laughed. "I'll take care of her from now on after I get back. Just do it, OK?"

He put on a henpecked look. "Whatever you say, dear."

She smacked him lightly on the shoulder. "Don't be silly."

He pulled her into a hug, the dog between them, and kissed her soundly. "I love you."

"I love you, too. Thanks for doing this."

* * *

Nora, 9:30am

NORA BROUGHT Luke a second cup of coffee and sat with him at the dining room table. He swept his hand through his slightly shaggy silver hair, then pushed his wire-rimmed glasses up on his nose. Only then did his blue eyes meet hers. "It's a terrible time to be job-hunting."

Nora reached over and patted his hand. "We can only do what we can do."

A grimace creased his face. "We need to figure out something fast. We'll start falling behind quickly if we don't. People don't understand the danger of compound interest. We have some pretty hefty credit card balances, and I don't know how we're going to make the minimum payments if we don't find work."

Her whole body tensed in response to his worry. Could it really be that bad? She'd never involved herself in their finances, and she just didn't know. "You know, I did some checking, and even though I taught for years, I'm not certified to teach in this state. I could go to school to get certified, but it would take time and money, and they don't pay teachers much at all, so I just don't feel that's my best choice."

"You got that right. Teachers work long hours for practically nothing. I think it's worse stress than minimum wage jobs."

Relieved that he agreed, she pressed on. "I was talking with my cousin Ellen yesterday about how I'm looking for work. She has a very successful home business, and she invited me to join her. I didn't commit, because I wanted to talk with you first."

Luke's face pinched. "Not one of those MLMs. God, those are just pyramid schemes."

Nora's heart started pounding. "Because we aren't in a position to judge, I let her do a phone presentation for me. Like you, I expected to turn her down--I don't like MLMs, either--but I was very impressed with the company. Botanica makes cleaning products that are safe for the environment and other things that health-conscious people want. It isn't an MLM. I would be a rep who enrolled people as members of their shopping club, and they would shop directly from the company, not from me. I would be paid a commission when they joined and on everything they purchased for as long as they stay in the club. Even though I got excited at the prospect, I told her I wanted to talk with you before joining, and before you say no, she tells me she's bringing in a five-figure check almost every month."

Luke was still frowning, but the size of the check seemed to have given him pause. "Yeah, she wouldn't lie to you, but how many years did she have to work to build a business that big?"

"She told me she often spent 60 hours a week in the first year, but she started less than three years ago. She seems to love it, and as you were saying, minimum wage jobs aren't going to dig us out of this hole. She'd be my sponsor and help me advance as fast as possible. I know I've never done any selling, but you know me, I like to talk to people and I have lots of friends. I'd like to give it a try."

His gaze fell to his hands, wrapped around his mug. "It's unlikely I can find anything that will pay well. I called a few old friends, and they had no suggestions. They're all retired, too. They said the market is flooded with fresh, young accountants who will work cheap, and my skill set is old. I avoided getting involved in computers and software when I was working, because I was so close to retirement, and now it's pretty much mandatory. I'm going to look at minimum wage jobs starting this week." His voice was heavy with resignation. "Do whatever you want, but you need to promise that if it isn't working after a fair period of time, you'll find something that really pays."

Nora sighed in relief. "It takes time to build a business, and if I can bring in any money at all in a couple months, you have to promise to give me more time. Ellen pointed out something I hadn't thought of. It's true that at first, a minimum wage job or even a teaching job would bring in more reliable income, but as you said, that isn't going to be enough. The sky's the limit with Botanica. I can make however much I want. And I am highly motivated. This could save our home. It could actually become a substitute for your lost pension. We not only need to pay our bills; we need to put money aside. How could we do that on minimum wage jobs?"

"That's true enough." He looked down as if unwilling to meet her eyes. She could feel depressive energy seeping from him, and it was contagious. His next words proved he was stuck in blame mode. "I should have been more conservative about our finances. I acted like the money would always be there. I of all people should have known better.

I let us accumulate debt, and now we can't pay it. Even if we get jobs, we'll still have to struggle to get by."

She wanted to go beyond worry and speculation. "Why don't we look at what our options are? We don't have to decide now, but what's the worst case scenario? Let's just face it and see how bad it can be."

He perked up and began to list what he had obviously given a great deal of thought to. "Well, worst case, we declare bankruptcy, lose the house and move into a condo (not necessarily in that order). We have no relatives we can tap for funds, and our debt is pretty high and the house only has a little equity in it. But selling it and moving would lower our overhead considerably. We could also sell one car, which would save us a nice chunk of change; but that's only if we don't have two different jobs we must commute to. I can work out a budget for us, too." He locked eyes with her, embarrassment flowing off him. "I'm so sorry about this. I should have done better."

She sighed. "I don't know why you're taking on all the responsibility. I spent as much or more than you did. I went along blindly, never asking about our finances, always assuming things would continue as they were. If you blame yourself, you have to blame me, too." She picked up her mug and sipped the lukewarm coffee, then frowned and set the mug down. "We're not going to solve this by placing blame. We need to just do what we have to in order to fix it. And you know, I'll miss this house, but frankly, it's too big for us, and I can see how a change might not be so bad." She squeezed his hand encouragingly. "You know what I think? The worst case scenario isn't all that bad. Sure, it's embarrassing to go bankrupt, but it happens. In the old days, people were sent to prison or got transported for having debts they couldn't pay. We don't have to worry about anything really bad happening. Possessions don't matter. Our health matters. Our marriage matters. As long as we stay focused on what matters, the rest will work out."

Tears were shining in his eyes, but she didn't acknowledge them. He got depressed too easily, and she couldn't do this alone. She needed him to be strong. Or he needed her to be strong. She'd never been in charge of anything, but she wasn't going to take this lying down. "We're going to be all right. As long as we have each other and our health, we have what we need to be happy."

Luke stared at his mug, blinking back the tears.

She plunged on. "We can return the gifts we got each other. I saved the receipts. You always do, too. What else can we do that will help?"

"I can look at all our subscriptions and memberships and cancel most, if not all, of them. That is a substantial amount, especially the golf. We can also stop charitable contributions outside of what we give at church, but that's only a pittance. I guess every dollar helps."

"Great idea! What else can you think of?" He was so good when he got into constructive mode.

"We can look at our assets and possessions and see if there's anything we can sell that would bring decent money. All too often, you don't make much that way, but perhaps there is something. It would need to be high end. A yard sale isn't worth the effort."

"We have some art and I have some jewelry."

"They may not be worth much for cash. But we can look into it."

"Could we turn in our cars for cheaper models?"

"Yes, that is worth doing, as it will save on payments and insurance. Maybe liquidate assets and buy secondhand cars to replace the ones we're leasing. We may need two cars to commute to work."

"I have a couple of gold coins I got from my Dad."

"I'd forgotten all about them. Let me see how gold prices are."

"Do you really think we're going to need to move?"

"That's worst case scenario. Everything depends on us getting income soon. The longer it takes, the more likely we are to have to sell out and move, even declare bankruptcy. At least bankruptcy will wipe out the debt. But I don't want to go that route."

She was relieved to hear strength in his voice. "Let's see how things go. I'll make sure we spend less on food. We'll quit eating out. And I won't buy clothes except as needed for work. It will add up."

"You're taking this better than I am." He looked at her sheepishly.

Good! He's snapping out of it. "There's nothing to be upset about. No one's to blame. We just need to adapt, and you and I can do that. Like I said, we have each other and our health. That's what matters." She stood up and shook the kinks out of her shoulders, ready to commit to whatever she needed to do.

Picking up the empty mugs, she decided to set a positive tone to the rest of the day. "We'll take the presents back, but I have some fantastic food we can't return. How about I make us a really nice meal for tonight, and we just relax and watch a movie? I have shrimp or a rib roast."

"Thanks, Nora. I don't know what I'd do without you. What did you have in mind for the shrimp?"

"I'll surprise you. I promise you'll like it."

* * *

Samantha, 11:30am

SAMANTHA PUT the finishing touches on a design she'd been working on all morning. The office was quiet. Mary Beth was obviously bored. The phone hadn't rung once, nor had anyone come to the nursery to buy plants. "The week between Christmas and New Year's is always slow. Maybe you should bring a book or magazine so you don't go stir-crazy."

Mary Beth's green eyes lit up. "You think they wouldn't mind? I'm not a big reader, but anything would be better than this. I'm going batshit crazy, pardon my French. I almost feel like taking up smoking again, and I don't really want to do that."

"The brothers won't mind if you occupy yourself. If there isn't work to be done, sit quietly and read. You're lucky. Things never get that slow for me, and I like to read."

Mary Beth flashed her a smile. "What do you say we go to lunch now?"

"Sounds like a plan." Samantha swept her clipboard, books, pencil and eraser into her carry bag, along with the design, and stood up and stretched. The chairs weren't comfortable, and she was glad she didn't have to sit in one all day like Mary Beth.

"These chairs are crap. How's your back been lately?"

"It's as good as new now," she gushed. "I can't thank you enough for introducing me to that chiropractor. I have to go once a month, because these chairs are so awful, but I threw out the pain pills and only get a twinge now and then."

"I'm so glad it helped. It was great for me. Those of us with a history of car crashes can really benefit."

"I'm a convert." Mary Beth followed Samantha out the door and down the steps.

Samantha paused and looked at the cerulean blue of the cloudless sky, grateful as always for her job allowing her to spend so much time outside to enjoy Nature.

Mary Beth noticed her looking. "I used to be so amazed at how big the sky is here, but I've gotten blasé. It's gorgeous, isn't it?"

"I've never lived anywhere so beautiful. I know not everyone likes the desert, but I love it. I wish it were warmer in winter, but I won't complain, because it's way better than anywhere else I ever lived."

"I'm not sure I'm in love with the desert yet, but there are certain aspects that I've grown fond of. Shall we just take one car?"

Samantha pointed at her truck. "Let's go in mine. The brothers pay for the gas; it a nice perk."

Mary Beth nodded and climbed in. "Where shall we go? I rarely eat out."

"I usually go home, so this is a treat for me, too. The Italian place probably won't ring your chimes, because you have higher standards than me, but maybe the Chinese?"

"Yeah, let's do Chinese today. And lunch is on me. I want to congratulate you for getting a new job. You can tell me the details. You're going to be missed here."

Samantha suppressed her embarrassment. She knew Mary Beth was being sincere, but it wasn't easy to accept praise. "Julio said I could come back anytime. That meant a lot to me. He didn't try to negotiate or anything, but you know, it means more to me that he said I could come back, because I think he meant it. They don't hold grudges. He knows I have to do what's best for me and my family." She felt hypocritical putting it that way, but stuffed the guilt.

LATER, as they sipped egg drop soup, Samantha tried to steer the conversation away from herself. "How's the house sale and your new place?"

Mary Beth's eyes lit up. "Helen was so kind to let me live in her condo. It's not costing me much at all. But it's temporary, so I need to make more permanent plans. But I'm not sure what to do. Mom's condo is on the market. We're going to sell it furnished. Shari is certain it will go fast. I've set a seductive price on it." She grinned, then doubt crossed her face. "I just wish I knew what to do with the rest of my life. The only reason I came here was to be with Mom when my life fell apart. Now that she's gone, I don't know what to do. I like it here. I've made some friends, but everything feels so temporary." She shrugged her shoulders and then attacked her soup.

Samantha empathized with Mary Beth and went to the heart of the matter, at least for her. "I don't mean to pry, but does it ever bother you being so much younger than everyone else in Palm Lakes?"

Mary Beth glanced up from her soup and grinned. "Yeah, that's the hardest part. I'm not sure I'll ever fit in, even if I could find a way to be legal. You're the only person my age that I spend any time with. I see your Mom for jewelry every Saturday. And I have a guy friend who's a widower. He's a good bit older than I am. Not sure what's going on with that." Her voice trailed off, and she went back to the soup.

Samantha was touched at Mary Beth's openness. "I've lived in Palm Lakes longer than you, and I know what you mean. I work, and most of the other residents are retired. I'm a lot younger than most of them. Wives don't mind me as a landscaper, but there aren't many willing to be friends. There's one who has reached out to me lately. I'm hoping we can be friends. Most of them don't seem to want me around their husbands, not that I'm interested. Arthur doesn't realize how isolated I am; he's just happy to be able to play tennis whenever he wants. Getting this new job would help me. It's the first selfish thing I've done in years, maybe in my whole life. I've been feeling like I'm on a hamster wheel. All I do is work. This new job would be challenging, as I'd have more responsibility than at Palo Verde. My opinion would be valued more, and I would be treated like a manager or partner. I would be rewarded for my work for the first time in ages. Did I tell you he's going to pay me ten dollars an hour over minimum wage?"

"You're shitting me!" Mary Beth's mouth hung open. Then she recovered. "That's great! The pay at Palo Verde sucks. It's one reason I'm tempted to leave the area. I won't be able to support myself on what they pay me. Not for long. I'll have to live off the profits from the house sale."

Samantha shook her head. "The brothers do their best, but they can't seem to see women as breadwinners or as supporting themselves. So they pay us less than the men. This job opportunity is great for me in part because we don't have any savings, and if something happened to Arthur, I'd be in a pinch."

"You sure work hard. Your Mom is always telling me you do too much for her, but anyone can see she needs the help. She's got a bit of dementia now, doesn't she?"

Samantha cringed at how direct Mary Beth was. "Not too bad, but enough that I'm worried. She doesn't take direction well and she hates doctors, not without reason. I don't know what can be done to help her. She's fiercely independent."

"My Mom was like that, too. She didn't tell me for a long time how serious her heart condition was. Like it wasn't my business. Parents can be a real pain in the ass."

Samantha chuckled in agreement. "So tell me about this guy friend."

"There's not much to say. I met Ethan at your Mom's. He's with The Helpers. You must have met him? He's a retired engineer. Really sweet and shy, but smart, a big teddy bear of a guy. We get along fine. He's been very supportive lately." Her look became more withdrawn.

"Yeah, I was the one to arrange with The Helpers for someone to come. He seems nice, but I haven't spent much time with him. Maybe he's interested in you."

"Nah, I don't think so. He's never done anything to show interest. Just being kind, like he is to your Mom. Maybe he misses his wife. He certainly never hits on me."

"Maybe he's interested, but thinks he's too old for you."

Mary Beth sputtered in laughter. "Are you serious? I thought guys always went for younger women."

"What if he doesn't feel confident? Maybe he thinks you could do better."

"That's a friggin' joke. I'm no catch. Besides, where am I going to meet a man? I'm living like a nun. My Mom would be proud." She chortled.

"Life doesn't always turn out the way we expect."

Mary Beth looked up suddenly, pinning her with a curious stare.

99

Maybe she'd said too much. She began to scoop up the last few swallows. After a short silence, Mary Beth spoke.

"Are you happy here?"

Yup, she'd revealed too much. "Well, I like being able to help my parents as they get older. I like the weather here better than anywhere I've lived." She paused, wondering how much to say. "But sometimes I wonder if this is all there is. All I do is work, work, work. I try to take pleasure in doing a good job, but it seems hollow sometimes. I guess that's why I was open to the job offer, in spite of the drawbacks."

"What drawbacks? The commute? I hear Temple Landscaping is a bit of a drive." Mary Beth looked at her as if she knew there was more to it.

The truth had been weighing Samantha down for weeks, and she longed to share the burden with someone else. Was Mary Beth likely to keep her secret? Why not? She didn't have anyone to tell. Well, she knew Samantha's mother, and it would be a disaster if Mom found out, and Mary Beth did tend to speak freely. Then she felt irritated. Why did she feel like a criminal? She hadn't done anything wrong. Yet.

Mary Beth looked at her as if she were reading the struggle. She raised an eyebrow, but said nothing. Finally, Samantha decided to take a chance.

"I'll tell you more, but you have to promise never, ever to tell anyone, especially my Mom or anyone at work."

Mary Beth's eyes widened and she made a zipping motion across her lips. "Of course I won't tell."

Samantha felt the guilt weighing on her and didn't know how to start. There was no way she'd come out looking good if she confessed. But part of her wanted someone to judge her or yell at her, anything to stop her carrying the burden alone. "I haven't told anyone the whole story. I met the owner of Temple Landscaping at a class. You remember. The one I took in October?"

A light shone in Mary Beth's eyes as if she knew this was going to be juicy. "Sure, I remember that. It only lasted about a week, right?"

"Yeah. Jack Temple sat next to me, and we ended up partnering in the lab and eventually shared about our interests and dreams. He runs his business the way I wish the brothers ran Palo Verde, and he needed someone to take over the field work and design so he could concentrate on expanding at a safe pace while preserving quality. It was a perfect job for me, but...the commute would take me away from caring for my parents and having time with Arthur, and..." She stopped, uncertain how to characterize her feelings for Jack. They'd never done anything wrong. Was it a mistake to share with Mary Beth?

"Tell me about Jack."

Samantha looked at her, feeling helpless and vulnerable. "He's our age, tall, dark and handsome, unmarried and we were attracted to each other. We never did anything about it. When he offered me the job, I refused, over and over. But I did go see his operation without telling Arthur, and it was impressive. That was when he made the job offer. He promised he'd behave professionally if I accepted the position, and I think he means it, but even if he does, I'm not sure I can, but I got pushed into taking the job by Arthur, of all people. He could see by Thanksgiving that I wasn't happy, and when he found out why, he insisted I check the job out and take it if terms were favorable. Of course they were, and so I took it. But I have reservations."

"Are you and Arthur having problems? If you don't mind my asking."

"Not major ones. He had an affair some years back, and it's never been the same between us. I would never want to do to him what he did to me, but I'm scared. I've become more aware of our differences as we age. I guess it's OK that he's content with things as they are, but for me, things aren't as rewarding as I'd like, not in any area of my life, if I'm honest. I'm not blaming him, but we're so different and not growing any closer.

"Jack is amazingly attractive. We think alike. We both love the plants and have similar ideas about doing business. Even being around him for a few days made me realize how sterile my life is, how little Arthur and I have in common and how much I rely on work to distract me from a bone-deep restlessness." Samantha sighed.

The server brought their main course, and Samantha looked at it listlessly. "I'm spoiling lunch. Let's talk about something else." She picked up her chopsticks and fiddled with them.

"You're not spoiling my appetite at all. I'm sorry you're feeling worried, but at least you have choices. I can see you're caught in a bad situation, but there's something to be said for having options. I wish my life were that clear.

"If you ever need someone to talk to, I'm here. Call me anytime. You're such a good person, and you've changed my life forever, you and your Mom. I owe you." Mary Beth stopped and became pensive. Samantha hung on her words, wishing some magical wisdom would come through to guide her.

Mary Beth smiled gently. "You and I don't give ourselves enough credit for all we do--did--for our families. You make sacrifices that no one sees. With me, I even got criticized all the time, for my smoking, my cussing. It wasn't until Mom was near the end that she seemed to appreciate me. I saw myself through her eyes, and I felt I wasn't good enough, but all along, I was the same person. I *was* good enough. Maybe you're doing the same. Your Mom is great, but she doesn't *see* you, the real you. Like my Mom didn't see me."

She paused and practiced holding her chopsticks, clicking them together, then looked up at Samantha. "I believe we both deserve to be happy. Maybe Jack is your happiness, or maybe that new job is. Or maybe both. I wish I had so many choices." She grinned and dug into her moo shu pork, leaving Samantha to ponder how having choices made anything better.

* * *

Emma, Noon

THE CHINESE RESTAURANT was obviously a local favorite, as it was buzzing with lunch customers. Emma was charmed by the decor. She followed the other women across a tiny footbridge that spanned a 'river' full of carp and green plants that wound through the large dining area, pausing to look at the fish and wondering if maybe she could have a water feature with carp in her yard. She should ask Julio. Hurrying to catch up, she arrived at the table indicated by the hostess and sat down, hanging her purse over the chair back.

Menus were handed out, and a relaxed stream of chatter began among the women while Emma just watched. Helen waved to two youngish women at another table. "Hi, Samantha! How are you? Mary Beth! Happy New Year!" The two ladies, one dark and exotic-looking, the other fair and serious, acknowledged Helen with smiles and waves.

Helen saw Emma's curious stare. "That's Mary Beth Costello, the dark-haired one. She lives in my old condo and works at Palo Verde Landscaping. I hear they're doing a wall and some other work for you. And that's Samantha, who does design at Palo Verde. Do you know her?"

Emma shook her head. "The only one I know is Julio."

"Julio the hottie?" Helen giggled. "That's what Mary Beth calls him. I still haven't met him. Is he as good-looking as Mary Beth says?"

Emma blushed. "Yes."

Helen didn't seem to notice her coloring. Thank heaven. Barbara plunged into the conversation. "So how is the yard work coming along? I can't see now that the wall is up."

All eyes turned to Emma, and she felt she was being interrogated. This was why she wasn't into social things. "The wall is pretty much done, but they have a good bit of work left to do on the labyrinth."

Lydia's eyes widened and she jumped into the conversation. "You have a labyrinth? Cool! What type?"

Emma warmed to the subject. "It's a simple 7-circuit labyrinth. Nothing fancy. I really wanted a Japanese garden, but Julio advised against it, saying those types of plants don't like our summers. I had to go with what he said; he's the expert. I don't regret it. The labyrinth is shaping up nicely. He's doing it with gravel that is a different size but the same color as that in my yard, so maintenance will be easy, yet there's a contrast." She paused a second, then hesitantly asked, "Would you like to see it when it's finished?"

Lydia clapped her hands together. "Are you kidding? I'd love to! Just let me know when. I'll bring something to help us celebrate christening it."

Helen smiled. "I'd love to see what you've done with the yard. I pretty much ignored it while I lived there; I don't know a thing about desert landscaping, though Samantha designed a lovely yard for my condo. I've never seen a labyrinth."

Barbara chimed in. "I'll bring some snacks or something to drink, too. It sounds exotic. Your own labyrinth!"

Oh, dear, it sounded like it would turn into a party. She smiled weakly, wondering what she'd gotten into. "That sounds nice. You're all welcome to come. I'll let you know when it's finished."

Just then, the server appeared and asked what everyone wanted to order. Emma perused the menu, concerned about her allergies, and asked, "Is there MSG in anything?" The server shook her head, "Absolutely not. We guarantee no added MSG." Emma sighed in relief. "Thanks. Then I'll have the moo goo gai pan."

Everyone else placed their orders, and then the conversation began in earnest. They wanted to hear more details about Helen's trip to Wisconsin and honeymoon in the South Pacific, then Helen had to tell about her neighbor's fall and her trip to the ER today, and Emma didn't have to contribute much at all, which was pleasant. It was fascinating to watch Helen talk. She obviously was in love with her husband. Barbara spoke of her Ben with a similar depth of affection. Lydia was single, like Emma, but she seemed perfectly OK being on her own. Emma wondered where she'd fit in to this group.

Barbara drew her back into the conversation. "Emma, you said you do yoga. How about joining us in the next class here? We have a lot of fun with it."

All eyes were on Emma once again, and she shrank within herself, unsure what to say. She hated going out in crowds, but these women were so nice to her. She didn't want to appear snobbish. "If you don't mind that I'm not very talkative, I'd be happy to join you. When is the class?"

"Great!" said Lydia enthusiastically. Helen nodded more sedately, "It will be wonderful to have you join us." Barbara smiled. "It starts in the new year. I'll bring over the information about how to sign up for the class. I promise you're going to love it."

Emma hoped she would. It was a new experience, doing things with other people. Leo would be proud of her courage. By the time her moo goo gai pan arrived, she was ravenous and dug in, with only slight reservations about how she might pay for eating something with so many unknown ingredients. The company was wonderful, and she was beginning to feel that maybe she could make friends here. She'd be willing to have a stomach ache tonight if that was the price.

As they ate, Helen shared a secret with them about her trip to Wisconsin. Her late husband Lou had kept a safe deposit box there that she'd never known about until she found the key to it while going through his clothes and things. On their Christmas visit, they'd checked it out and found letters and a picture of a woman in France from the time of World War II.

Lydia, the most extroverted of the group, didn't hesitate to ask questions that would have caused Emma to cringe. "So do you think he had a love child in France somewhere?"

Helen shrugged her shoulders. "The letters lasted for some years, but the most recent is still very old. He didn't appear to have any communication with her in the past 20 years or more. Having examined it all carefully, I'd say there was a child, probably his, though knowing Lou, he would have told himself it could be anyone's. That's how he was about accepting responsibility. He didn't even want our kids." She paused as if embarrassed. Emma reflected that maybe she wasn't the only one with secrets in her past.

Barbara broke in. "You don't need to relive that part of your life. Do you think diving into this mystery is a good idea? Is it stirring up bad feelings from the past?"

Helen had tears in her eyes. "Yes and no. It makes me realize how lucky I am to be married to Alexander. He's so unlike Lou in every way. And it's seductive to have a real mystery in my life. I've gotten drawn in, and I'm not sure if it's for the best or not. Neither is Alexander. I think he wishes I'd drop it, but for the time being, I just can't. I feel so bad for that poor woman, alone in a war-torn country with no help and support from the father of her child. I thought I had it bad being with Lou, but she faced worse things alone than I did with him. At least it would seem that way. I don't know what to do."

Everyone expressed support for whatever Helen chose to do, and it seemed to calm her. Emma could see the benefits of having friends to share with, but would she ever be able to share her secrets?

Fortune cookies arrived to signal the end of the meal, and Emma realized she'd had fun. She couldn't eat wheat, so she offered her cookie to Helen, who accepted it graciously and said she'd take it to Alexander, without asking why Emma didn't want it. *I think I could get used to this.*

* * *

Lydia, 1: 40pm

LYDIA LINGERED in the parking lot, making small talk with Barbara while Helen and Emma drove off. "I was wondering if you have a few minutes and we could talk."

Barbara's eyebrows raised slightly. "Do you want to follow me home, or do you prefer that I come home with you? I'm not sure whether Ben's home or not."

Barbara's aura showed nothing more than a reasonable amount of curiosity. "I'll stop at your house for a few minutes. I don't mind if Ben's there. This isn't something you have to keep secret from him," said Lydia.

"OK, I'll see you there."

Lydia nodded and hopped in her car, steeling herself for the reaction she feared might come. As she drove to Barbara's house, she gave herself a pep talk. Barbara was always so kind, supportive and wonderful. Surely she wouldn't dump Lydia over her weird visual talent. But the lemon chicken churned in her stomach anyway. Right after lunch wasn't the best time to divulge such a secret, but there wasn't going to be a time guaranteed to be favorable.

She pulled up to the curb in front of Barbara's and belatedly realized Emma lived next door. She hoped Emma didn't notice her stopping here right after lunch. Emma was holding her secrets close and might wonder if she were the subject of conversation. Too late to worry about that now.

Once inside Barbara's house, they sat in the living room. Ben wasn't around, which calmed Lydia more than she would have thought. Having to tell only one person was easier for some reason. Barbara sat patiently waiting for Lydia to start, but she couldn't hide her curiosity.

"I don't mean to be so secretive about this, but it's something I didn't want to bring up in front of Emma. She's new to our group, and I want her to have a chance to feel comfortable, and I didn't think my revelation would have a positive effect."

Barbara's intelligent brown gaze said nothing, and there was no appreciable change in her aura. *Good.* "Well, the other day I talked to Jean, and I confessed to her that I have this ability I don't generally talk about. It's caused problems for me in the past, and I preferred not to share, but while we were chatting, she suggested we might put a business together offering healing and intuitive readings for a local clientele, and I felt I ought to tell her about it. When I did, she was very encouraging and said I should tell you and Helen, too. So here I am."

Lydia paused, unsure how to proceed in spite of all the obsessing she'd done. "You see, I've always had this ability to read people. It's a visual thing. Now that I've studied metaphysics and learned about the subtle energy body, I realize that's what I'm seeing. It's a layer around the body, and it pulsates with colors. Over time, I've learned to decipher what the colors and patterns mean. It's like a type of X-ray vision. I can read people's health, their emotions, all kinds of things just by looking at them. I can also tell when people are lying or if they're about to die." She stopped for a moment to see if Barbara wanted to say anything, but Barbara just nodded encouragingly. There wasn't much change in her energy field. "When Jean suggested I join her and Ian in a healing business combined with intuitive readings, I felt I ought to share with her that I have tools beyond the crystal healing, and they might be of use in such a business. I'm not sure the business will happen, but if I'm contemplating advertising intuitive readings, I need to come out of the closet. I want you to know I haven't said anything before because it's cost me relationships in the past, and you mean a lot to me. In fact, my marriage fell apart because of my visual talent. Most men aren't too happy about not being able to hide things from their wives."

She knew a bitter note had crept into her narrative, and she chided herself for being negative. "I guess I'm just scared of losing what I have. I love living here, but it's the people that are the most important to me. I just don't want to lose my friends."

Barbara reached over and touched her hand. Green with rose tints had taken over her aura. The color of unconditional love. "That must have taken a lot of courage. I respect you for sharing this with me. Of course, I don't mind. You have a gift, and it sounds wonderful, but I suspect it comes with a down side, and I don't blame you for trying to protect yourself. Can I share this with Ben?"

"Oh, sure. Will he think I'm a nut job?"

Barbara laughed. "He's somewhat conventional, but not judgmental.

He'll probably want you to demonstrate for him. He has a scientific mind, so he'll want to understand more about it. In fact, so do I. Could you give me more details?"

"As I said, I can tell if people are lying. I can see certain health issues. And if they have no colors, that means they are very close to death. Closet alcoholics, serial adulterers and liars can't keep their secrets from me. Everyone has secrets and deserves privacy, so I try to ignore what I see, but it takes a toll on me. I tend to take on the pain and suffering of others and worry a lot when I see something potentially bad in someone's energetic field, especially if I have to keep quiet about it. It's as much a curse as a blessing."

"So what do you see in me?" Barbara seemed a little less confident than usual, and the lightest bit of pink had crept in to her field, indicating fear. It was the question everyone asked, but with Barbara, it was easy to answer.

"You're one of the most balanced people I know. You are compassionate and intelligent and fun to be around, and being with you is easier on me than being with just about anyone else. I don't handle people's personal dramas that well. You don't seem to have any, at least not at the moment."

Barbara smiled in relief. "You're too kind. There's nothing special about me, and we all have secrets, but I guess mine are mostly old news that I've filed away. Are you going to tell Helen?"

"I was thinking about calling her now and going over there if she isn't busy. I just didn't want to blab in front of Emma. She's shy and new to our group, and I felt she wasn't ready for something this weird."

"I think that's a good assessment. Emma needs to develop trust in us, and knowing you can read her might scare her off. I think she's a really sweet person who could use a support system."

"My thoughts exactly. Of course, I'll want to tell her if she stays with us. You can help me decide when it's a good time."

Barbara grinned. "Glad to help out. Let's call Helen and send you on the next leg of this journey."

Grateful that Barbara didn't want to drill her about her talent, Lydia used her phone to call Helen, who was at home with Alexander. That gave Lydia pause, but she knew Helen didn't keep secrets from

Alexander, and he seemed like a decent man, so why not get it over with? Hugging Barbara, she left and headed out to Alexander and Helen's palatial house on the golf course.

When she pressed the doorbell, a small dog started yapping. Helen answered the door shortly after, urging Lydia inside past the whirling ball of fluff. "Is this your neighbor's dog?"

"Yes, this is Spot. We're getting along quite well. Even Fido doesn't seem to mind her." Helen took Lydia's arm and escorted her to the living room, where she perched on the edge of the couch. "Can I get you a drink?"

"No, thanks, I'm still full from lunch."

"Alexander's writing in his office. He said to say hi, and if you want, I can bring him out." Helen cocked her head, waiting for a response.

"No, that's OK. But you can share this with him. I just needed to tell you something, and I didn't want to do it in front of Emma. She's so new to our group, and what I'm going to share might not be well received by someone who doesn't know and trust me. I've lost friends over this in the past."

Helen looked a bit alarmed as a fair amount of pink invaded her aura, and she began to twist the fabric of her slacks nervously, but said nothing.

"Well, I might as well get it over with. You've been so open-minded about my interests, letting me do healing work on Sheba in spite of how weird it must have seemed to you, and I appreciate that."

Helen's eyes filled with tears, and Lydia saw the pain of grief and loss was still quite sharp to Helen by the grayish green that spread around her. "I know how much Sheba meant to you, and I wish the outcome could have been different."

"You did all that you could, and I will always believe that what you did helped her to have a peaceful passing, and I didn't have to take her to the vet to have her put down. I was really dreading that. You know, you never can be sure whether it's time or not." She swiped her eyes with a hand to get rid of the tears.

"Actually, there *are* ways to tell. And that relates to what I'm here to talk about. I value your friendship, and I hope that what I'm sharing won't cause problems, but I've decided it's time to come out of the closet, so to speak, about an ability I have." She paused, gathering her words carefully. More pink shot through Helen's aura, but not a whole lot. "Ever since I can remember, I see things about people that most others don't. There's an energy field around every person, even around animals and plants, but it's invisible to most people. It's been demonstrated to exist, but it's a New Age concept, so it's considered--she used her index fingers to form quotation marks--out there.

"Anyway, in this energy field, I see colors and patterns that over the years I learned to read. People say or act one way, but often, they are feeling things they don't share, or they are hiding the truth or maybe they have health problems they aren't aware of. It all shows in their energy fields. For example, when we came to work on Sheba, I could tell she was seriously ill, because I could see it in her aura. I was pretty sure our session wouldn't fix her, but after the session, I could tell it had really calmed and harmonized her. Had I been around her all weekend, I would have at one point seen that her aura went blank, and then I would have known she was leaving this life."

Helen's mouth hung open slightly, but no words came out. A deep blue had infiltrated her aura, showing she was thinking very hard about what Lydia had said. There was no anger, no sense of betrayal. Maybe it would be all right. Then she spoke. "I can't imagine what that must be like. To see all that. I confess I'm scared you might see something I didn't want to share, but I trust you, Lydia. You've always been supportive, and it isn't your fault you see these things."

"You believe me?"

"Sure I do! Why would you make something like that up? It can't be all that wonderful to know so much about anyone, let alone everyone. How do you manage?"

Lydia was relieved by Helen's empathy. "I don't always manage well. I don't like being in crowds for long. I tend to take things on. Between you and me, sometimes I smoke a joint just to mellow out and get away from what I've picked up. It cost me my husband. Not the pot smoking...He couldn't stand not to have secrets from me. That's one reason I'm not shopping for a replacement. It's hard to be in a relationship with someone who can read you so well. Most men aren't up for it."

"I don't think it's just men. Most women wouldn't like being an open book, either. I'm sure it's had its unpleasantness, but it probably has also saved you a lot of heartache. I think about my daughter Sally and Red Johnson. If only he'd been more aware of her real feelings. He's so hurt by her rejection."

"I know. I've seen him. We aren't close, but it's all over him how disappointed he is, and he's mad at himself for not listening to his intuition. We all have intuition, but it's too easy to ignore it. I don't get to ignore mine. It's so visual and striking."

They sat quietly together as Lydia marveled at how easy it had been to tell her best friends about her strange talent. She wondered why her next thought was that she couldn't wait to share with Red how well it had gone.

* * *

Emma, 2:00pm

EMMA BREWED herself a cup of chamomile tea while Julio spoke with the workers in her back yard about their progress on the wall, which was nearly done. Her stomach had already started to protest about lunch, but she wasn't going to give in to regrets. She'd enjoyed herself immensely, and she was determined to find a way to continue socializing with these ladies, because being with them made the day seem brighter. It was trite, but it was true.

She just needed to find a way to improve her digestion. She'd tried so many things, but none seemed to help. The doctors had given up on her long ago, saying she was allergic to a lot of things and should just take antihistamines, but she didn't like taking pills, so she kept looking for other answers that might actually restore her health. She didn't see herself as that old. She wanted to enjoy life, and now that Leo was gone, if she wanted any friends, she needed to be able to be with other people, which meant sometimes eating with them. Today had convinced her it was worth fighting for.

The back door slid open, and Julio stepped through. As he did, he cast a glance at the Christmas cactus in its new ceramic pot on the patio and suppressed a smile. She sipped her tea, knowing he wouldn't say a word about the change, but that he was pleased she had treated his gift so well.

"Mrs. Lightman," he began.

She interrupted him. "Emma."

His chocolate eyes sparkled with pleasure. "Emma," he said, testing her name. "It is a beautiful name for a beautiful lady." He said it with such conviction, she didn't have her usual reaction to flattery, which was to deny or cringe.

"We still have a few more days of work. Do you like how it is coming along?" He gave her his usual stare. She was getting used to having 100% of his attention. It was intense, but rather charming when you got used to it.

"I love it. I can't wait for it to be finished."

A look crossed his face. Could it be sadness? Impossible. "We should be finished soon after New Year's day, depending on the weather, as always." So businesslike, so honest. "Then I'll get started on the labyrinth."

"I appreciate how much trouble you've gone to in that project. You said it wasn't the type you usually do, and I am grateful you took the job."

He smiled and waved a hand. "Things are slow now. It worked out for both of us. Perhaps you have another project in mind for the future?" She thought there was hope in his voice.

"Actually, I always have projects floating around in my head. Just today, we were eating at the Chinese restaurant, the one with the river of fish flowing through it? I found myself wondering if I could have a water feature with koi in it. You'll think I'm silly asking for all these strange things."

He shook his head. "A pond is possible, but it needs to be done right. If you want something like that, we can work up an estimate. Water features are something we do a lot of. We do a good job. Many installers do not make the pond deep enough, and that becomes a problem in our climate. And you need to be careful what you plant nearby. We could discuss designs and options if you are sure you want to have one."

She laughed. "I'm not sure I'm ready to commit yet, but I am seriously thinking about it. I want this yard to be my sanctuary, a place of peace and beauty." She felt stupid saying it, but it was true.

He didn't laugh. "Of course you do. And we will help you with that."

An awkward pause ensued, and she noticed again that her stomach was aching a bit. Sipping her tea, she tried to make small talk, something she wasn't adept with. "Are you very busy now with jobs around town?"

"Not really. Things are quiet. They will pick up in January."

"The holidays have everyone focusing on doing family things."

"Not everyone has family," he said meaningfully.

"No. I don't."

"I get free meals from my brothers' wives and girlfriends during the holidays, but I do not like to intrude too much. I enjoy doing things with them, but I value my time doing things I like, as well. What do you do in your free time?"

"I like to read. I read a lot."

He frowned. "I am not much of a reader. I read a little. I like to do things outdoors. I like to hike. My family like to go to church on Sundays, but I prefer to be outside. It is more like church should be, at least to me." He seemed a little embarrassed admitting this, and she was touched that he would share.

"I always liked to hike, too, but I haven't taken the time to learn about any trails since I moved here. I don't like to hike alone. Leo used to hike with me. I haven't found anyone else who enjoys hiking." She suddenly realized he was going to think she was fishing for an invitation. It was the last thing she intended.

He brightened up. "Then you must let me show you some nice trails. Would you like to hike on Sunday with me?"

"I don't want to hold you back. You are younger than I am and probably hike a lot faster. You're obviously in good physical condition." Crap, couldn't she stop saying things that could be misinterpreted?

He grinned. "I would be pleased to have you hike with me. I am not in a race. I like to look at the flowers and the views. I know a wonderful 1 mile hike...well, it is 2 miles round trip, but mostly flat. It would be a great introduction to the area. It is popular with locals. If the weather is fine, we will see a lot of people. People even bring their dogs." He waited for her response, and he genuinely seemed to want a positive reply.

She didn't want to hurt his feelings. He'd been so nice to her. And it didn't feel like he was coming on to her. Plus, they'd be out in public, so it would be perfectly safe. "OK. If the weather is nice."

"Excellent. Would 10am be too early for me to pick you up?"

"No, that would be fine."

"Be sure to wear good hiking shoes and carry water and a hat. Even though it is winter, you will probably need water. I always carry extra, so a small bottle will do."

"OK."

"I will go now, but I will see you Sunday morning. I have your phone number and will call if the weather looks bad."

Her stomach tensed up. It was suddenly seeming like he was getting too much access to her private life. But she tamped her fear down. "I will look forward to it. I miss hiking, and I think it will be fun to see the area with someone who knows it so well. Thanks for asking me."

He reached out to shake her hand, and she laughed, because it seemed so formal. He didn't seem to mind. In fact, he appeared to be very happy.

It was only after he left that she realized him showing up at her house on Sunday was going to be noticed by the neighbors as something out of the ordinary, especially if she got in his truck and rode off with him.

Rubbing her stomach, she decided not to worry about it. She wasn't doing anything wrong. In fact, she really was looking forward to going on a hike. She sat on the sofa and looked in the direction of the urn in the corner. "Don't you dare say a word, Leo."

* * *

Maddie, 4:30pm

MADDIE SLAVED AWAY in the kitchen preparing the evening meal. Stanley always wanted dinner to be served as close to 5pm as possible, and although pleasing him wasn't her highest priority, it contributed to the brittle harmony of the house when she kept meals on track.

Stanley's food preferences had always dictated the menus, and his poor digestion meant no greasy or spicy food, while his natural

114

thriftiness meant meals were never extravagant. Which meant what they ate was always tasteless and boring. But Maddie had resigned herself to that years ago. She just wished she didn't have to spend so much time in the kitchen.

She stood with the refrigerator door open, looking for the broccoli she thought she'd asked Stanley to buy when he did the grocery shopping. Seconds ticked by, and none of the drawers or shelves revealed broccoli. For a second, she almost forgot what she was looking for. She pushed aside the aluminum-foil- and paper-towel-wrapped-celery, several baking potatoes and some zucchini. Another drawer held iceberg lettuce and a few tomatoes. Had she already used the broccoli? Or did Stanley forget to get it?

Lately, she found herself feeling confused about things too often. Finally giving up, she closed the refrigerator door and went to find Stanley so she could ask him if he'd bought the broccoli and if she'd just forgotten she'd already used it. For some reason, in spite of his being significantly older, Stanley was sharp as a tack. She knew she was asking for trouble, because he'd have no problem telling her she was becoming forgetful, but she suddenly felt a strong need to find out whether her mind was letting her down, and she was willing to take the risk of being criticized to find out. She was morally certain she hadn't served broccoli in the past week.

Rounding the corner to his office, she stopped in shock. Stanley's head was laying on his desk, but she instantly knew he hadn't fallen asleep. He never fell asleep at his desk, though sometimes he drifted off while sitting on the sofa. Forcing herself in spite of her fear, she went over and looked at Stanley, loath to touch him in case he were cold. "Dammit, Stanley, wake up! You're scaring me."

His head was turned towards her, his eyes shut. He appeared to be sleeping. Maybe he hadn't heard her. He was deaf as a post but wouldn't wear a hearing aid; he was too vain. She gingerly touched his neck and was relieved to find that his paper-thin skin was warm. She let out a breath she hadn't been aware she was holding. She shook his shoulder, gently at first, saying his name, then more strenuously, trying to awaken him. He didn't respond. She became frightened again. Something was wrong.

Her mind was a chaotic mess of fears and seemed unwilling to guide her, so she stood there looking at Stanley, as if she were trapped in a science fiction-type force field and couldn't move. It seemed like minutes passed as she tried to get control of her renegade thought processes. Eventually, she succeeded. Reaching for the phone on his desk, she dialed 911 and asked for an ambulance.

She wondered what she should do next, but rational thought seemed to have gone on vacation. With great effort, she realized she should call Samantha. She didn't really want to defer to her daughter, who had a tendency to barge in and take over, but she'd hear about it later if she didn't inform her. The phone rang twice before Samantha answered (Arthur never answered their phone unless he was alone).

"Samantha, your father had an episode, and the ambulance is on the way."

She heard a sharp intake of breath on the other end of the line. "What kind of episode?"

"I don't know. I'm not a doctor. I came to ask him something and found him asleep on his desk, but I don't think he's asleep, because I can't wake him up. They're coming to get him. They said not to try and move him, as if I could." She suddenly felt defensive about her powerlessness.

"I'm coming right over. I should be there no later than the ambulance. I'll help you get him admitted. Why don't you sit down and wait for me."

"I think I will," said Maddie, surprised that it felt good to have help on the way.

Samantha hung up, and Maddie went out to the dining room table which was piled high with her many jewelry projects. She sat, unsure what to do. Looking at her unfinished creations brought a measure of calm to her troubled mind. She wasn't thinking about Stanley as much as wondering what all this meant and how it would change her life, but instead of traveling in a straight or even wavy line, her thoughts jumped all over the place, meaning she got no resolution for her worries.

As she stared across to the living room, she saw a pattern on the white wall. It was a complex repeating pattern and changed over time. It alarmed her, because she knew the wall was plain white, but the pattern looked so real. She shut her eyes so she wouldn't see it, but when she opened them, it was still there. Too often lately, she'd seen complex patterns dancing on the wall, but it seemed to be more common when she was tired or stressed. What was happening to her? She didn't dare tell anyone. They'd lock her up for sure.

Sooner than she would have expected, Samantha used her key to come through the locked front door. "Where's Dad?" She rushed over to Maddie, looking at her intently with blue-gray eyes.

"I thought I told you he was at his desk." Everyone thought she was forgetful, but she wasn't the only one.

Samantha didn't linger. After a few minutes with Stanley, she returned to Maddie just as the ambulance was pulling up at the curb. "He may have had a stroke. At least he's still alive." She ran to the front door to let the EMTs in and led them to Stanley's office, gently pushing Beau to the side and telling him to sit and stay. Maddie continued to sit at the table, overwhelmed into inaction.

Samantha came over and leaned close to her, speaking a bit louder than usual to be heard over the hubbub in the office. "Mom, where's Dad's insurance card? Let's get whatever they need to admit him and you can drive with me to the hospital."

Maddie blinked her eyes and tried to focus on the question. She'd heard words, but they didn't make any sense to her. They were more like random sounds. She waited, hoping the words would link themselves together in meaningful fashion--that worked sometimes--but no such luck. "What?" She hated sounding stupid, but she had no idea what her daughter had just said.

The EMTs rolled the stretcher with Stanley on it through the house and out the front door, stopping briefly to get Samantha's attention. "Are you following us or are one of you riding with us?"

Waving them on, Samantha answered, "We'll follow."

Samantha looked hard at Maddie and repeated her question slowly and carefully, as if Maddie were a child. Finally it got through. Maddie pointed across the living room. "Look in the drawer of that table by the sofa."

Patting Maddie on the shoulder, Samantha rushed over to the table and sifted through its contents, finding what she wanted. She returned to Maddie. "You need to put on a jacket and bring your house keys. And put on some sturdier shoes. Those slippers won't work. Wait, tell me what coat and shoes you want, and I'll bring them here for you."

That got through fine. Maddie didn't like being waited on, but for now she'd allow it. "The blue jacket and my sneakers in my bedroom." Samantha ran off for the shoes and came back via the closet where jackets hung and snagged the blue winter jacket Maddie had bought at the thrift store.

Rousing herself to change into street shoes and put on her jacket, Maddie slowly got ready for the journey to the hospital. She hated hospitals. You always sat around for hours doing nothing. They had rotten coffee and lots of sick people and uncomfortable chairs. They smelled awful and gave her the creeps. She wished she could stay home but knew that wasn't an option.

While she dressed, Samantha asked, "Were you cooking when this happened? You haven't had dinner yet, have you?"

Maddie tried to think what exactly she'd been doing when the shit hit the fan. It was something about dinner. "I was in the kitchen..." Her voice trailed off as she sought a clear answer.

Samantha didn't wait. She went into the kitchen and Maddie could hear her putting things into the refrigerator. When she returned, Maddie was nearly ready to go. "I put the food away and checked the stove. Everything will be fine until we return."

Maddie followed Samantha out the front door, petting Beau on the way and telling him she'd be back as soon as possible. It didn't occur to her to let Beau out to pee in case they were gone a long time.

A few minutes later, Samantha dropped Maddie off at the hospital's Emergency Room door. "Just go in and sit somewhere near the door until I can get parked, and then we'll sort this out."

Maddie didn't like being told what to do, but she was too confused and tired to fight Samantha's bossy attitude. On entering the building, she was surprised at how quiet it was. Maybe people didn't have as many accidents on the days after Christmas. Or the fact that most of the patients were retirees made for calmer evenings. A few nurses bustled about, obviously focused on their tasks. She couldn't see how many patients were in the waiting rooms, as the drapes were all pulled. But it was as quiet as a church, except for the occasional squawk of the loudspeaker.

Samantha charged through the door, looking left and right, then saw Maddie and came over. "You didn't get any dinner, and this is probably going to take time. I'm sorry. Maybe after we get Daddy admitted, we can get some food."

Maddie smiled weakly. She had to admit she was getting hungry.

Samantha didn't wait for a reply. "I'm going to talk to the admissions person. You can stay here. I'll let you know what I find out."

Maddie sat in a fog, uncomfortable in the plastic chair. It reminded her of airport seating. She briefly wondered why that thought had come to mind--she hadn't been to an airport in forever. Dismissing it, she closed her eyes and found herself drifting off in spite of her discomfort.

Samantha touched her shoulder gently, but it still startled her into exclaiming. "What?"

"It's OK, Mom. You drifted off. They're going to admit Dad right away. He's not responding, and they suggested we go home and wait to hear from them. I gave them both our numbers. Why don't you come home with me and stay in our guest room tonight? I can go let Beau out, or even bring him to our house if you like. You shouldn't be alone."

Maddie really didn't want to be alone, but she also didn't want to stay at Samantha's. She wanted to be in her own house where she could do whatever she liked. She was an insomniac and liked to watch TV and do jewelry and drink wine at odd hours, and she'd be expected to lie in bed at Samantha's while everyone else slept. "No, I think I'll just go home. They said they'd call us both?"

"Yes, Mom. They'll call. But I think it would be better if you were with us."

"I'll feel better in my own home. Beau will keep me company."

Samantha sighed. "What about dinner? You didn't get any. Would you like to eat with us or have me make dinner for you? Or shall we stop and pick up something on the way home?"

Maddie's felt excitement stir in her. "I'd like some Kentucky Fried Chicken. Can we do that?"

"Of course. You'll have to eat it alone, because I have dinner in the oven for me and Arthur."

Samantha obviously wanted her to change her mind. But she rarely got to do what she wanted, and she was going to stick to her guns. "If you don't mind running by Kentucky Fried, that's what I'd like to do. It will save me cooking and cleaning up." That would certainly appeal to Samantha's desire to help.

"OK, Mom. You win. Let's go."

Pleased at her success, Maddie struggled to stand up, let Samantha link arms with her, and they marched out the door, which opened automatically for them as if they were royalty. Fried chicken! A real treat. She never got food like that when Stanley was around. The freedom to eat whatever she liked reminded her of the several times Stanley had gone on travel when he was working. She would go to the Italian delicatessen and get fixings for subs and pizza, and she and Samantha would have a ball.

Suddenly, she remembered that Stanley was in a coma in the hospital, not on a trip for work. Her excitement abated as guilt swept in. She should not forget that Stanley was seriously ill, but she couldn't summon any emotion except concern about how it was going to affect her future.

5
NEW YEAR'S EVE

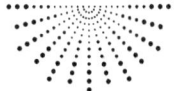

Emma, 9:50am

*E*mma paced from one end of the living room to the other, glancing at the wall clock, wondering why time was standing still. She paused and looked at herself in the reflection on the sliding glass door. Dressed in hiking boots, jeans, long-sleeved shirt and fleecy vest, she looked ready to take on any hike. Far from it. All morning, she'd been asking herself how she'd got into this mess, wishing she had gotten Julio's number so she could call and cancel. The only number she had was Palo Verde, and no one would be there on a Sunday.

The sun shone gloriously in a cloudless blue sky, and the day promised to be delightful, with no wind and a high of nearly 68. Unseasonably warm and perfect for a hike. If only it had rained. The weather gods were obviously not on her side. Julio was going to show up in ten minutes, and she was panicking about how she could possibly spend a couple hours alone with him. At the time of the invitation, she'd been so certain his interest was merely friendly. How could he be interested in anything else, considering the age difference? But now she was second guessing why a handsome young man like him would want to waste a morning with someone her age. And she couldn't come up with an answer that made any sense.

As she was dressing this morning, it had also occurred to her that they'd be finishing the hike around lunch time, and under normal circumstances, it would seem appropriate for her to either bring a picnic lunch (*oh, my God, how would that look?*), offer to treat him to lunch at a restaurant (another night of pain so soon after the Chinese outing) or make him lunch here. Making lunch here suited her stomach just fine, but of the three options it seemed most open to misinterpretation and altogether too intimate. She wasn't sure she could be comfortable with him eating here, though it was the most likely choice.

Since she hadn't planned on feeding him, she'd have to offer him something from among the provisions she already had. Fortunately, she had enough to do a nice Sunday brunch or a salad. But the thought of inviting him to lunch on top of being with him a couple hours for the hike made her cringe in fear. She'd end up monopolizing his entire Sunday. He might think she was romancing him. In spite of her reservations, she felt obliged to do something nice to thank him for the hike, and making a meal seemed most reasonable.

She went over to the kitchen counter where her small pack lay. She put her water bottle into the dedicated pocket, checked that she had her wallet and identification and a bit of cash plus a few other items, from Kleenex to sunglasses. She'd put her digital camera in, too, but was loath to use it, because it would probably lead to having a picture of him, or of him and her. This was getting too complicated.

She hadn't had time to start worrying about them being seen by the neighbors when the doorbell rang. She flung the door open and waved him inside, forgoing shaking his hand in a bid to get him off her porch fast.

He stepped in, dressed much as always in a slightly stained, straw cowboy hat, clean black jeans and a long-sleeved dark blue t-shirt with no design. The only change to his normal attire was a pair of well-used hiking boots. He flashed his usual smile, dazzling her with his white teeth. "Are you ready to hike?"

He seemed so open and guileless that all she could do was weakly say, "Yes." She grabbed her pack, made sure she had her house keys and followed him out the door. He proceeded to the truck while she locked up, and they were quickly on the road, not having seen anyone on the street.

She breathed more easily as they drove farther from the neighborhood, and after leaving Palm Lakes, she actually began to feel excited about the outing. He hadn't said a word the whole time, almost as if he knew she was teetering on the edge of hysteria. Even though she'd become less manic, she felt compelled to straighten things out with him. She couldn't picture spending all this time with him, not being clear on what it was all about. She plunged in clumsily. "Julio, it's really nice of you to invite me on this hike...but I just want to be sure you understand this isn't a date." She felt mortified the minute she said it, as if she were implying he could possibly be interested in her that way. Struggling to compensate, she blurted, "Not that you would think that, since I'm so much older than you are, but I just want to make sure there's no confusion." That was hardly adequate, but she prayed it would do the trick.

Julio stared at the road. He said nothing for a few seconds, as if considering his answer. She started to sweat. She had probably insulted him. Why couldn't she get anything right? She should never have agreed to go on this hike.

Finally, he spoke in a gentle voice. "I only wanted to help you get to know some of the nice hiking trails we have. It is not a date unless you want it to be." Then he turned and flashed his 1000 watt smile at her, and she felt herself blush clear to her toes. "Please do not refer to yourself as old. You are a beautiful woman. We can have a really nice hike today." He turned his attention back to the road.

Shamed by his kindness, she was unsure how to respond. Mentioning lunch seemed a good peace offering. "I was thinking if you're hungry after the hike, I can make us something to eat."

She saw his near eyebrow shoot up. So she had surprised him. She just hoped he wasn't going to infer more than it meant. "I didn't think to offer you a meal until this morning, so it would have to be something I have in the fridge, but I could make brunch or a salad."

"That would be very nice, thank you. I think we will be hungry when we finish the hike." He cycled back into silent mode and kept his eyes on the road as they wended their way to the trailhead. She relaxed into the natural peace that came with not having to fill every moment with words.

THE TRAILHEAD LAY at the foot of mountains that in the distance had looked purple, but up close were natural shades of brown and a bit of pale green where new growth was popping out in creases that had channeled water during winter rains. Several cars were parked in the dirt lot near the board that had a large, faded map of the trails in the area. The Waterfall Trail, only a mile long, was relatively smooth but uphill as it wound its way in the direction of some cliffs, and although there were a few other hikers, much of the time they had it to themselves. It was serene, better even than the peace she felt in her own back yard.

Julio set a gentle pace she thought must have been in consideration of her age and gender, though he seemed to enjoy stopping periodically to point out a view or tell her about a plant. She had overdressed, having forgotten how warm you can get on a hike, and was grateful for the cooling breeze.

Just then, Julio turned and pointed her to a bush at the edge of the trail. It was kind of scraggly. The leaves were small and an oily, dark greenish color. It had no flowers.

"This is a creosote bush. I want to show you something." He pulled his canteen out of the pack and poured water on the leaves at the end of one branch as she watched in confusion. He put the canteen away. "Smell the wet leaves. This is the smell of the desert after a rain. You will sometimes smell it if you live on the edge of town."

She took the sparsely-leaved, still dripping branch in her hand and leaned over and inhaled. She had to practically touch the leaves to her nose to smell it, but once she got it, the fragrance was unique and strong. And it was somehow mesmerizing, as if it transported her to a different time and place. "This is wonderful!"

"Imagine being in the desert and all the creosote bushes are damp after a summer rain. There are still clouds, but the sun has come out, making rainbows, and this scent fills the air, like the promise of life."

She did. It was heavenly. "I wish I could smell it where I live."

"You are not on the edge of the desert, so you won't smell it often at home, if ever. We could plant a creosote bush in your yard if you like the scent, and you could go out and smell it after a rain. If we put it near the patio, you might be able to smell it while you sit and read. Maybe we should plant more than one, just to be sure." He smiled and set off down the path. She was beginning to understand why he went on hikes instead of going to church.

The slow uphill climb ended at the foot of the cliffs, where an empty plunge pool lay filled with rocks and boulders. Black desert varnish streaked the light color of the rock wall. "After a rain, if you come up here soon enough, you will see a waterfall. The water then fills these pools as it runs downhill." He pointed to one after another, strung out like beads on a necklace, as they punctuated the dry wash that ran down the arroyo.

"It must be magnificent."

"Water controls life in the desert. So anywhere you see it becomes almost magical. It is like that here when the water is running." He turned to look up the cliff to where the water would come over the lip of rock.

He didn't see her stare at him, stupefied by how poetic he was. She pulled her eyes off him and turned back to see the view. They had gained just enough elevation that the desert lay spread out before them, no sign of humans. It was awe-inspiring. "I love it here. Can we come back sometime after a rain?"

She could almost feel his reaction, in spite of having her back to him. "Of course. I hoped you would want to see it."

They headed back down the trail and hiked to the truck at a leisurely pace. He continued to stop along the way, pointing out things she never would have noticed on her own. Lunch afterwards was pleasant and calm. When he shook her hand and left, she realized how much the day had reminded her of being with Leo. She didn't ponder what that meant.

* * *

Alexander, 10:30am

WHEN HELEN STEPPED out of the bathroom with a towel wrapped around her, it took Alexander's breath away. She was so naturally beautiful, her shiny reddish gold hair framing her delicate face and long, slim legs carrying her across the room like a dancer. She caught him staring and blushed slightly, which he found even more endearing. He continued dressing while she disappeared into the walk-in closet to find her clothes.

Spot and Fido were hanging out on the king-sized bed. It was a relief they were getting along so well. Alexander hadn't been convinced it would work, but he wanted it to. Something told him that Helen needed a pet to shower her love on since Fido was taking his sweet time about accepting her into the family unit. Spot had bonded with Helen immediately, lifting her spirits perceptibly. But something was still wrong, and it wasn't just the attention he got from other women. Did he dare ask what?

He wasn't egotistical, but he felt she'd gained a lot by marrying him. She went from a small condo to a lavish home on the golf course. She was able to quit her menial job at Wal-Mart. She now had unlimited funds for improving her life. He encouraged her to pursue her interests, like writing and yoga. He even made sure she got quality time with her girl friends. Now she had Spot to fill the giant hole left when Sheba died a couple months back. He loved her to distraction, and she seemed to enjoy cooking with him and sharing other activities. They had a great sex life. But since the honeymoon, she had seemed unhappy and distant at times, and her outburst the night of Barbara's party (though he still wasn't sure exactly what it meant) proved he wasn't imagining things. He couldn't overcome the impression that he was the cause of her unhappiness.

The other day when she'd said she wanted to talk, it had never happened. He'd fully intended to, but events intervened and both of them let it slide. She had insisted she was going to make him sit down and talk with her, and part of him was glad to have escaped it, but he knew that trouble was brewing, and it was only going to get worse if he kept ignoring it.

At the risk of blowing it wide open, he decided to speak first. As he stepped into the closet, she was just finishing dressing. Turning to him, she saw the determined look in his eyes and flinched. Another reason he hesitated to force things. She always reacted like a frightened deer when he was forceful, and he hated that. He would never hurt her, and he felt bad that she was afraid of him. "Helen, we need to talk. We got sidetracked the other day. Let's do it now."

She hung her head and followed him as he turned and walked out of the closet. He led her out to the living room and sat on the couch. It seemed a cheerful and comfortable place to talk, the morning sunshine splashing across the room. She sank into the couch next to him, close, but not touching.

She stared wordlessly at him as if he'd called her on the carpet and not the other way around. He felt annoyance creeping in and pushed it back. "You said you wanted to talk to me, that you really needed to. Please tell me what's been bothering you. Ever since the honeymoon, things haven't been right between us, and I have no idea what I did wrong, but somehow it feels like you're mad at me."

She shook her head vehemently, but still said nothing. Tears began to fill her eyes. He reached over and took her hand. "I love you, and I just want us to be happy. Please help me to fix this. You mean everything to me."

She burst into tears and got up to retrieve the box of tissues from a nearby table. Back in her seat, she twisted the Kleenex after blowing her nose and wiping her eyes delicately. Taking a deep breath, she sighed. He couldn't imagine what was causing her such pain.

"I'm sorry. I've been a mess. I can't figure out how to explain what's wrong with me. Every time I go over it in my head, I sound like a total bitch. I feel like you'll hate me if I tell you, that it makes me sound ungrateful and spoiled. I'm afraid that you won't love me anymore. Yet I've been so unhappy, I really wanted to tell you. I'm upset that you think I'm mad at you. I'm just disturbed and restless and unhappy." She paused and began to twist her pants leg. He knew that meant she was nervous. He squeezed her hand to encourage her to continue.

She looked up at him with glistening blue eyes. "What's wrong? In no particular order: I've gained weight since we married, and my clothes are beginning not to fit. You won't want me if I get fat. Fido still doesn't like me. I haven't been able to get back to writing yet, and it's been weeks. I love your house, but it's *your* house, not mine, and I don't feel I fit in. There's so little of *me* here. I never had elegant things, and I feel like I'm living in a model home. It seems too grand. I worry that you'll find out I'm beneath you and get rid of me. I'm jealous about women throwing themselves at you, even in front of me. I'm disturbed that I want to scratch their eyes out, even my own daughter's; I've never been a violent person, and my anger scares me. I'm confused about Lou's betrayal. It seems he's reached out from the grave to hurt me, when I thought I'd finally escaped his toxic influence. My kids are being total asses about you, and I'm ready to tell them off, but I don't want to lose my grandchildren." She took in a deep breath. "I may have forgotten something."

He felt a smile come to his face. It wasn't him after all. "So it isn't me?"

She shook her head and looked down at the floor. "It's all about me. I was just unreasonably upset because you couldn't wave a magic wand and fix it. Because you didn't even seem to realize what was going on with me. I want us to be soul mates. I don't want to have to complain to you." She sniffled slightly.

He was overcome with relief and reached over to stroke her soft hair. "We'll fix it together. There isn't anything we can't do if we put our minds to it."

She sighed. He looked into her damp eyes again. "So let's think what can be done about this list. I know Sheba left a giant hole in your heart. Is Spot filling it, or should we plan to get another cat or dog, or maybe a parrot?"

She grinned at his stab at humor. "We have enough animals in the house as it is. I am really enjoying Spot, but I'm becoming attached to her, and it's stressing me out. I don't want to wish anything bad on Olivia, but if she gets well and comes home, I have to give up Spot. And I don't want to." The creases on her forehead deepened.

"Fair enough. There's not much we can do about that now. But I promise that if you have to return Spot to Olivia, we'll get you a pet you can love and spoil. Any pet you want. We just need to make sure Fido can get along with it. How's that?"

She beamed at him. "Thank you."

It was so easy to please her. Did she have any idea? He plunged into the subject that was most thorny to him. "About the way women act towards me..."

"It's not your fault. I'm mad at myself for feeling jealous and wanting to slug them."

He couldn't help chuckling. "What a nice picture that conjures up. No one's ever fought over me before. I rather like it."

She laughed, the first of the morning. "Don't be silly."

"I'm not being silly. I'm imagining you slugging some pushy woman. Quite an image. My warrior queen."

She giggled again. "OK, I get the point. I know it isn't your fault. But it would be OK with me if you were a bit less polite in turning them away. Your chivalry towards predatory women annoys me." She looked at him apologetically. "I know, I shouldn't feel that way. I've never loved a man before. I can't bear the thought of losing you."

"You aren't going to lose me. I'll be more forceful in repelling advances, if that makes you feel better. It's not like I'm worried about offending anyone. I guess I assumed you knew no one could lure me away from you." He gave her his best smile, and her face lit up.

"I'm sorry about seeming to criticize your beautiful home. It really is amazing. I love the kitchen. But it's just so much more than anything I've ever had...I can't get used to being well off. I tell myself you're the rich one, not me. I don't know why."

"Helen, you're a rich woman. When we have those diamonds appraised, you'll see just how rich you are. You're independently wealthy."

Instead of seeming pleased, she looked at him with fear. "That only makes me feel that something could come between us. I'm so scared of losing you. I don't feel I deserve you," she said miserably.

So that was the basis for everything. "How could you think that? I was living a fairly empty life until you came along and woke me up. Just because I had money and a career didn't mean I felt happy or fulfilled. I love having you in my life. I love cooking with you, sleeping with you, making love with you...how can I convince you?"

"It's up to me, Alexander. I need to learn to settle into being a

129

whole human being. I was in jail for so long that I can't seem to leave the cage. Mary Beth said I don't know how to be happy. She's right. My whole life, I just tried to get by, to keep my head down, to do what's right, but I never thought for one second I would be loved. It's like a dream that I'm afraid of waking up from. I think I'd die if I found out it was only a dream." She reached over and squeezed his hand.

He wondered how he could help get her through this. "We're both adjusting to a new way of being. But we love each other, and that will make it work out. It never occurred to me that you'd feel out of place in this house. I want to give you the world. So if you want to redecorate and make your mark on it and make it our home instead of just mine, we have plenty of money to do that."

She shook her head. Too fast, he thought. "No, I would never waste money that way. Your house is beautiful. That was why I was so upset. I couldn't think of any options that weren't frivolous. What's the point in hiring a decorator and replacing perfectly good furniture?"

"In my opinion, it wouldn't be a waste if it made you feel more at home. I'm sorry it never occurred to me before. It seemed OK to me, so I assumed it was OK for you." He did his best to project his sincerity, but he could still feel a wall between them.

She switched to another subject. "I know we'll need to sell my condo at some point. Mary Beth can't stay there forever. I haven't forgotten that. But most of my stuff is there, and there's no room here for it. I don't want to pay to store it. I guess I can give it to my kids. That would make them happy."

But he could tell it wouldn't make her happy. "Your family is giving you pain. I can't do anything about Lou and his ongoing betrayals, nor about your kids and their selfishness. I'm glad you wrote that letter to the woman in France, but I wish you'd leave Lou buried and get on with our life together now. As for your kids, I know you're afraid of losing access to your grandkids, but I don't think we should let them be rude to us. If they can't be courteous, we should avoid them like the plague. I know it's easy for me to say, and the risk is all on you, but that's how I feel. I won't put up with them mistreating you anymore, and I am tired of overlooking their behavior towards me. We need to agree on some course of action." He hadn't realized how strongly he felt until he started talking about it.

"You're right. I've been hoping they'd change, putting off doing anything rash. But it isn't helping. Sally hardly ever contacts us anymore. Do you suppose she's embarrassed about breaking up with Red?"

Was she kidding? "Sally embarrassed? I don't think she's familiar with that emotion. At least not the receiving end. Red obviously felt bad. He made it clear she jilted him when he proposed, or rather, she told him it would never be more than it was, and he wanted more. He has more integrity than most guys, and I can't figure out what her problem is. She seemed to like him."

Helen sighed again. "Sally's always been a caution. She's never really cared what any of the family thought about her." She stared off into space for a minute, and he just held her hand. "Lou wanted to abort her, but I'd hidden the pregnancy too long for that. He seemed to forgive me after a while. I was so alone and unhappy, she became my miracle baby. I fantasized about how much she'd love me, maybe because no one else in the family did. As it turned out, she never had a focus on anyone but herself. She sort of became the family pet since she came along much later. She was always smart, but a risk-taker and not afraid to make a selfish decision. I think I admired her for it because I wish I could have been more like her.

"Since I found you, I can see how little respect my kids have for me. I kidded myself about Sally for too long. Probably because I thought she was all I had. Now I have you, and I see how little I had with Sally. She always showed up when she needed something, like last summer when she was pregnant and out of work. She asked me to move somewhere we could live together so I could take care of her kid. When I think back to how I struggled to say no, I'm horrified. I would have just perpetuated the life I had before. I'm so grateful for you. In the past, I let myself be used and gave myself approval points for it, because I didn't have love, and useful seemed better than nothing. You make me feel so loved, but I'm not used to it. I don't feel deserving of such treatment."

He was so grateful she'd finally talked to him. "You're the best thing that ever happened to me. I was the walking dead until I found you. If all I had in the whole world was you, I'd be a happy man."

"Even if I'm fat?"

He sputtered. "Where did that come from? You're not fat!" Why did women always worry about that?

Her mouth turned downward. "I'm growing out of my clothes. We eat too well."

"I love our cooking. And you look luscious to me. You were too thin when we met."

"Be that as it may, I don't want to buy a new wardrobe just because I like to eat. I want to look good for you."

This was a losing battle. "Then why don't we get a bit more exercise? We have a dog now. We could take her on long walks. And the Rec Center has some amazing equipment. I like the stationary bikes, but they also have stair masters, treadmills, weights, a running track. What kind of exercise do you like?"

"I love the yoga, but it doesn't burn calories. I think walking Spot would be great. And maybe cycling. I don't like really strenuous exercise, but I've read that weights are good for women my age. It helps with bone density."

"My, aren't you well read! We can sample all the different things and find a routine that keeps us fit. I don't want to quit eating good food. Cooking with you is my second favorite activity."

She looked at him quizzically, then blushed.

"I know we haven't resolved all the troubles that were bothering you, but have we made enough progress that we could talk about my favorite activity?" He flashed her what he hoped was a seductive smile.

"I'd rather *do* your favorite activity." She stood up, pulled him to his feet with surprising strength and dragged him back towards the bedroom. He didn't resist. *I'm a lucky dog.*

* * *

Samantha, 10:40am

NUMBED BY THE NEWS, Samantha hung up the phone. Dad was dead. Even though she'd known it could happen, it was still a shock. He'd never come out of the coma. They tried to make it sound like a blessing, and maybe it was good he didn't linger, but somehow she couldn't imagine him giving up on life so easily.

Yet he'd been talking about dying for years. She'd actually found the talk aggravating. But as long as he was still talking about dying, he was alive. Now he'd never lecture her again. She felt a hole in her life that she knew would never be filled. It wasn't that they'd had a warm, close relationship. But he was Dad, and now he was gone forever. It would be only Mom and her from now on.

Then it hit her all at once. This changed everything. She was supposed to start her new job this week. But how could she?

She went into the living room and sank into the couch, overwhelmed by all the worries flooding her mind. Despite the fact that she hadn't been tested, it was clear that Mom had mild dementia. It was hard to gauge, given her eccentric personality. Living alone wasn't going to be safe for her, but she wouldn't face that. Ethan could keep coming to walk Beau and do heavy lifting, though she was sure Mom wouldn't let him do much. Arthur would do what Samantha asked him to do, but he wasn't the type to volunteer, not that she blamed him. Mom had never taken much of a liking to Arthur, and Samantha didn't blame him for being standoffish with her. But if she worked for Jack, she'd never be able to stop by during the day or have lunch with Mom. What a disaster this was!

There was no time to try and solve all these problems now. She needed to go to Mom. She got her bag and a jacket and hopped into her truck and drove the two miles to Mom's house. Mom answered the door with a dark look on her face. So they'd already called her. "Mom, the hospital just called me."

Mom stepped aside and waved her in. Beau came up quietly to touch her with his nose, almost like he knew what was going on. She patted him distractedly. "Do you have any coffee? Shall I make us a pot?"

Mom seemed to come back to present time. "There's a pot made."

Samantha went into the kitchen and poured herself a mug of Mom's deadly strong coffee and topped up Mom's half-empty cup. Carrying them out to the living room, she put the cups on the coffee table and patted the seat of the couch. "Come sit with me."

133

Mom sat beside her, dazed, not touching the coffee cup. She didn't say a word.

Concerned, Samantha filled the silence to cover her own anxieties about the future. "I'm so sorry, Mom. They said he didn't suffer. Just slipped away. I'll help with the funeral. Daddy showed me where everything is. He paid for it already, so there isn't much to do." She squeezed Mom's hand and noticed how cold it was. Mom didn't react. "Is there anything I can do, Mom?"

Mom's watery blue eyes seemed to finally take her in. "I'm just having a hard time believing it. He always said he'd go first. I figured he was right. But I didn't expect it so soon."

"I know this probably isn't the time to ask, but did you and Dad talk about what you'd do afterwards? He briefed me on finances and kept hammering away at how little you had. Did you two make any plans?"

Mom looked at her like she was an alien. "He never talked to me about anything. I left the money to him. It's not that I'm incompetent, but he liked being in charge of our finances, and I let him. He never spoke to me about what to do after he was gone. I don't even know what financial preparations he's made, other than I know the funeral is paid for, because I had to get involved in that when he bought the plots and made the arrangements." She sighed, then reached for her coffee cup.

So it was even worse than Samantha had imagined. Mom had no clue about living on her own, and Dad hadn't left insurance or much of anything to support her. This was not good. Mom owned the house, but that wasn't going to be enough security. Samantha had a suspicion Mom would spend money faster than it came in, and eventually, that would be a problem. Maybe she needed to look into a reverse mortgage. But it wouldn't solve the main problem, which was that with her osteoporosis and forgetfulness, Mom wasn't really able to live alone in a big place like this. But how could she convince her of that?

Samantha patted Mom's knee in sympathy, all the while feeling a flicker of anger and resentment simmering underneath the sadness and loss. No one was going to appreciate her sacrificing her new job. In fact, Mom would probably insist she take it if she knew what Samantha was thinking. She'd like it if Samantha didn't 'butt in' so much. But there was no way Mom could stay here without a lot of help. And Samantha

was almost sure Mom would choose to stay. Might as well find
out now.

"Mom, I know there's no good time to talk about this. With your
osteoporosis and everything, I think that being alone here is not really
that safe. The doctor said you shouldn't lift more than two pounds. Even
with Ethan coming over, there's so much you can't--or shouldn't--do.
Would you consider either moving in with me and Arthur or maybe
moving to the assisted living area here in Palm Lakes?" She braced
herself for the expected reply.

"There's no reason I can't stay here. Why do you want to make me out
to be incompetent? This is my home."

"Gee, Mom, I don't mean to be difficult, but you aren't even up to
cleaning it, and you won't let me hire someone or do it for you. When
was the last time you dusted, for example?"

Mom paused as if giving it careful thought. "I don't think I ever
have."

Samantha's jaw dropped. But maybe it shouldn't have. The place was
always messy. She just hadn't realized how bad it was. On second
thought, that might explain why on rare occasions, she'd come over and
seen her Dad vacuuming or cleaning a bathroom. She wasn't sure she
should pursue this line of questioning, as it seemed to relate to their
turbulent marriage. "Well, this is a big place, and I know you don't want
my help, so I'd like you to consider options, but we don't have to talk
about it now. I'll do what I can to help. I'm going to Dad's office to find
the documents for the funeral. Would you like me to call and handle the
arrangements?"

"You know how I feel about funerals. I don't want to go."

"You don't have to, Mom. It's OK." She impulsively gave Mom a
gentle hug, ever cautious about her pain. "I'll take care of it. Is there
anything I can do before I leave?"

"I can't think of anything. I'll be all right." Mom looked adrift and
vague. Anything but all right.

Samantha found the documents in Dad's small file cabinet and went
back through the kitchen, checking that no burners were on, then said
goodbye to Mom and headed back home.

On the short drive in the pale wintry sunshine, her thoughts returned to her new job. She needed to decide today. She either went to Jack's Tuesday or went begging for her old job back. She knew what she wanted, but it didn't seem to matter. She couldn't make herself believe that taking this new job was the right thing to do, not with Mom stubbornly on her own and no one else to look after her. She needed to be able to stop by a few times a day if necessary.

She felt ashamed at the resentment that bubbled up and then had to push back tears. She'd finally managed to convince herself the job with Jack was a good idea, and now she was going to have to turn it down. Life seemed so unfair.

Suddenly she realized that Arthur didn't even know Dad had died. When he got back from his tennis game, she needed to talk with him. She was relatively certain he'd see things her way. He didn't really want Mom to move in with them. Only an idiot would. But he knew Mom needed more care than she realized, and it wouldn't occur to him to volunteer to do it in order to save Samantha's job. Mom was her responsibility, after all.

She pulled into the garage and walked into the house feeling smothered by worries. Before she could change her mind, she dialed Jack's home number. At least she was alone and could speak freely. As the phone rang, Samantha fretted that she'd have to leave a message. She really wanted to talk to Jack now while she was alone. Thank heaven he finally answered. "I was afraid you weren't at home. It's me, Samantha."

"Hi, Samantha." His voice took on a sudden tone of worry. "What's going on? You're still coming this week, aren't you?"

"My Dad died."

"Oh, Samantha, I'm so sorry. Is there anything I can do to help?"

"That's the problem. My Mom has osteoporosis and is showing signs of dementia, as I told you, and now she's alone. I just got back from visiting her. I have to take care of the funeral. She can't go to them. She has a phobia. But that's not why I'm calling. She insists she will stay in that house, and I know it isn't safe for her. She can't do what needs to be done and won't allow me to do it, nor will she hire it out, except now and then on the yard work, and grudgingly at that." Samantha heaved a deep sigh. "I need to get her into assisted living, but I'm even wondering if she can afford that, to be honest. I guess if we sell the house...My Dad doesn't appear to have provided well for her. Anyway, she says she won't move, but that means I'll need to be there for her more than ever. I don't see how I can take the job you offered. I need to be able to drop in at her place at a moment's notice. Arthur can't handle her. I'm the only one she has."

She could hear Jack sigh. "Even with the reduced schedule you can't work things out?"

"Your very generous schedule would have worked if Dad were alive. But I'm honestly afraid for Mom. I need to be there, check her often and keep working on her to move or get help. I'll have to do her shopping, her cleaning, anything that involves lifting. And most of all, I need to check in on her and make sure she doesn't burn the house down or do something dangerous. I can't do that as freely if I work for you."

It was quiet on Jack's end. She knew he wasn't going to guilt trip her. "You have to do what you have to do. I'll keep the job open. You never know how things will change. I know you love your Mom, and I think you're amazing to put her first. I want you to work with me. Please, can we stay in touch? If I end up having to hire someone else, I will, but I'll wait as long as I can."

It wasn't enough, but it was more than she could have hoped for. "Thank you, Jack. I can't tell you how much I appreciate you. You know I wanted this job. I really did. And maybe it will work out in the future. I hope so."

"Will you call me and let me know how things are going?"

She knew this was personal, not professional, but she needed a lifeline now more than ever. "Yes, I'll call you. But that's all. Are you really OK with that being all there is between us?"

"For now, it will have to do." He sounded totally resigned, no trace of anger.

"Thanks for not being annoyed at me for pulling out at the last minute."

"How can I blame you? I'm just disappointed. But I refuse to give up. We can really make my business special, and I still want you to work with me to do that."

"Thanks, Jack. I want that, too."

"Would you like me to come to the funeral?"

She was momentarily shocked. Then she recovered, thinking it might be a good idea. Dad didn't have many friends here, and Mom wasn't even coming. But then she was concerned about Arthur. If he laid eyes on Jack, that would be the end of things. She wouldn't be able to hide her feelings for him, even at a funeral. "You better not, but I really appreciate the thought."

"I figured, but I wanted to let you know I'd come if you wanted."

"Thanks, Jack. I promise I'll stay in touch."

"Let me know if I can do anything."

"OK. Bye, Jack."

"Bye." He didn't hang up for a few seconds, and neither did she. She felt like a silly teenager not wanting to hang up, but talking with him had really helped calm her nerves. She finally hung up and then considered her next move.

She needed to contact Julio and get her old job back. Good thing he'd offered. He was a man of his word, so she wasn't worried.

Arthur came in just as she was trying to figure out when to call Julio. She didn't have his home number, and he wouldn't be at work. She turned to Arthur, and he saw the look on her face. "Is it your Dad?"

"Yes," she mumbled. "He died. I've been to Mom's and got the funeral file. I talked briefly with her. She doesn't want to consider moving in with us or going to assisted living." Suddenly, Samantha felt drained. She leaned against the counter.

Arthur came over and awkwardly hugged her. "I'm so sorry. I know your Mom is a real worry to you."

"I called Jack and told him I can't take the job. I decided I need to be closer to Mom since she won't move. She's going to get herself in trouble being alone there, and I need to keep an eye on her and be there for her."

"You think Julio will give you your old job back?"

"He said he would, and I believe him."

"Well, that's lucky. Do you need my help arranging the funeral?"

"No, Dad prepaid and arranged it all."

"OK. Oh, what about your Mom? She going to the funeral?"

"No, you know she won't."

"I figured not. Do you want me to stay with her during the funeral? It might be better for her not to be alone."

Samantha was surprised at his insight. "I hadn't thought about that. You're right. Would you mind very much? It would be a big help."

"No problem. She and I can get along for that."

Samantha saw that meant Jack could come to the funeral. Maybe she'd call him back. He'd like that. It just depended on who else came. She couldn't let word get back to Arthur. Damn. She was planning her Dad's funeral and plotting how to let her would-be boyfriend attend. That was kind of creepy. But it didn't deter her from thinking about it. If she had to give up the job, why couldn't she invite him to the funeral?

* * *

Mary Beth, 12:30pm

MRS. J--CATHERINE--WAS DIGGING INTO THE HOMEMADE RAVIOLI, barely coming up for air. Mary Beth smiled. She liked to cook for an appreciative audience, and Catherine was enthusiastic about anything she put in front of her. Mary Beth suspected it was mainly because she was lonely. Poor dear.

"Catherine. Do you mind me asking if you have any other friends here in Palm Lakes?"

"Oh, no, dear. I don't get out much. As you know. Thanks so much for driving me places. It was beginning to be difficult for me to drive. You are an angel." She continued to munch on the ravioli.

Mary Beth poked at her salad. She wasn't that hungry; she was worried about tonight. "Do you have relatives nearby?"

"No, I'm quite alone in the world, dear. Not that I mind. It's peaceful. And now I have you." Her washed out blue eyes twinkled behind her thick glasses.

Mary Beth marveled at how positive Catherine was. Wasn't she afraid of becoming debilitated or needing long-term care? "I'm here if you need anything, at least for as long as I'm here--that didn't sound right--I hope I get to stay a while, but you never know." A wayward thought surfaced. "Oh, I meant to tell you, I had a serious inquiry about Mom's condo this morning, of all days."

Catherine paused in her efforts to clean every drop of sauce from her bowl. "Tell me all about it."

Mary Beth smiled. "A couple from Canada looked at it. They are thrilled that it's furnished, and they said the price is right. I think they might actually buy it. That will be a relief."

Catherine sighed. "The only bad thing about that is the snow birds don't live here year 'round. It gets pretty thin in the summer. But the Canadians are such nice people...I know you aren't supposed to stereotype, but maybe if it's a positive stereotype, it's OK." She turned to devour the last of her salad, then put her fork down with a satisfied sigh. "You are such a good cook, Mary Beth. I appreciate your inviting me to eat with you."

"It's my pleasure. Mom and I used to make big feasts for special days. She would have liked to welcome in the New Year with us." She halted, fighting back an unexpected urge to cry.

Catherine didn't seem to notice. "I'm too old to stay up drinking on New Year's Eve, so this was just perfect for me. But you're a young person. What are you planning for this evening? Are you going out with that nice young man I've seen visiting?"

Mary Beth felt her neck and face grow hot. Damn, she must be blushing. "First off, Catherine, he's not that young. He's at least 15 years older than I am."

Catherine put up her hand like a traffic cop. "Never you mind. He's a young man to me, and he looked quite nice."

Mary Beth rushed to agree, "Yes, he's very nice. But we aren't dating. At least I don't think so. He's asked me to go out tonight, but I'm not sure why. I like going out, so I said yes. He's very kind and thoughtful, but I'm not sure what he has in mind."

"For tonight or with you in general?"

"Both, really. I didn't ask him where we were going. I just like to go out, and he's very easy to be around. I like him a lot. But he doesn't act like he wants to be my boyfriend. Boyfriend. What a stupid word. I'm 45 and he's 60. We're hardly girl and boy anymore." Mary Beth ran her hand through her thick hair, feeling exasperated. "I wish I knew where it was going."

"Maybe you need to become a bit more aggressive."

Mary Beth felt her jaw drop. "Catherine! I thought you were old-fashioned."

"I don't know what you mean by that, but I will tell you if I'd waited around for my Harold to decide he wanted to marry me, I'd still be waiting." Her eyes took on a dreamy look, then she humphed. "That boy couldn't even make simple decisions. I had to do all the work to make sure he proposed. Maybe your young man is the same. You shouldn't sit around waiting for him to make up his mind. It's obvious he likes you."

"I don't know, Catherine. I'm not even sure I *want* him for a boyfriend. Though I have to say I love being around him. He's so easy to be with. In fact, it just occurred to me he reminds me of my Dad. Maybe I have unresolved Daddy issues." She chuckled and shook her head. "Dad was always so easy-going, attentive and supportive, and there's something very attractive about that. So I think I just like him for who he is."

Catherine got a sharp look in her eyes. "Then what are you waiting for? Do something about it."

"He may not want that kind of relationship."

Catherine shook her head, causing both her chins to jiggle. "Honey, they all want that kind of relationship."

Mary Beth felt her face grow hot again. It was true that she suspected Ethan liked her a lot. She just didn't know what to do about it. "I guess I'm afraid of making another mistake."

"Aren't we all? But you can't live if you worry about making mistakes. Maybe the man is afraid you'll reject him. Men have pride, too, you know. The age difference may matter to him."

"I thought all men wanted trophy wives." Mary Beth took another swallow of wine.

"I'm sure they do. But he sounds like a genuine sweetie, so I don't think that's all he'd want. And he may figure he's not good enough for you."

Mary Beth almost blew wine out her nose, she snorted so hard. "Oh, that's a good one, not that you're the first person to mention it. Samantha speculated the same thing. Look, I have all kinds of bad habits. Though you'll notice I haven't cussed yet today. I finally quit smoking. But I have a low rent job and no prospects. I don't socialize. I'm over the hill. I have wrinkles and flab."

Catherine looked at her hard. "He's got more of that from what I can see. I'm sure you look great to him. Everything is relative. He looks pretty fine from where I'm sitting." She gave Mary Beth a pointed look.

"Then why don't you go after him?"

Catherine cackled. "That's a good one. If I were ten years younger, I might. But I don't think I could ever find anyone I'd love as much as I loved my Harold. It's kept me from seriously looking for another man. Not that I mind. I have my memories." She looked off into the distance dreamily.

"I wish I felt that way about someone. Maybe you're right. I should give it a chance and speak up to him. I'm not getting any younger." She swirled the wine in her glass, thinking about how she'd go about it.

"You do that, honey. Then tell me all about it."

Mary Beth guffawed at the picture of sharing her love life with someone old enough to be her granny. "OK. But it's on you if it blows up in my face. You'll get no more ravioli dinners."

* * *

Helen, 2:30pm

THE HOSPITAL WAS OVERFLOWING with visitors. On the way to Olivia's, Helen glanced in the rooms she passed and saw balloons, flower arrangements and families jammed into small spaces visiting elderly relatives. Almost every patient was a senior due to the many retirement communities nearby. The occasional room was empty of guests, the person in the bed looking forlorn and abandoned. It must be terrible to be in the hospital during the holidays.

As she entered Olivia's room, she was taken aback by how crowded it was. Olivia's roommates' family were visiting her, and Olivia had three women by her bed. A plush stuffed bear sat on her tray table. Helen hesitated to inject herself into what was obviously a family visit, but she did want to tell Olivia that Spot was doing well.

Olivia noticed her standing in the doorway and waved her over. Helen stepped past the crowd visiting the roommate, murmuring apologies, and forced herself to confront Olivia's visitors. She hated meeting new people, but there were times you just had to. She belatedly wished she'd made Alexander come with her, but until they were sure about Spot and Fido, she didn't like leaving them on their own for long.

Olivia's brown eyes danced with merriment. Her bed was angled up into a sitting position, so she looked like an aging queen giving an audience to members of her court. The three women looked at Helen. She was uncomfortable under their appraisal, but Olivia quickly broke the silence to introduce her. "Girls, this is my next door neighbor Helen, who has so kindly taken Spot into her home while I'm here."

A variety of looks crossed the girls' faces. The tallest woman, who had dark hair and eyes and a naturally serious visage, looked pleased. The middle one, who was slightly chunkier and had blue eyes and lighter brown hair streaked with gray, appeared to be weighing what Olivia had said. The shortest, who had bleached blonde hair and blue eyes, and who appeared to be the youngest, smiled widely.

Helen filled the gap. "I'm just glad to help."

Olivia wasn't going to let her off the hook. "Girls, Helen is the one who found me. Spot was barking her head off, and Helen investigated and found me down for the count. No telling how long I could have lain there otherwise. But silly me, I haven't told you my daughters' names. Where are my manners?" Olivia put her hand on her thinning white hair as if trying to collect herself. Pointing to the tallest girl with the dark hair, she said, "This is my oldest girl, Susanna. She lives a ways up the road. Next to her is my second daughter Joanna, who lives even farther away, in Albuquerque. And this is my youngest, Diana, who lives close by." She pointed to the blonde, who was wearing a friendly smile. All of the women nodded and mumbled appropriate greetings. Susanna even held out her hand. Helen shook hands, a bit overwhelmed. "All your girls have variations on the name Anna."

Olivia chuckled. "You noticed. Of course, how could you not, with them all lined up this way. My mother was Anna, and instead of just naming one after her, this way, they all got named after her."

"That's quite ingenious. I never would have thought to do that."

The girls obviously were not as taken with the idea as she was. Diana rolled her eyes conspicuously. Joanna frowned, while Susanna shrugged her shoulders and said, "We used to get kidded about it when we were younger."

"I didn't mean to butt into your visit, but I just wanted to let you know that Spot is doing very well."

Olivia looked relieved. "Thanks so much for taking her in. My daughters couldn't take her, and she'd hate a kennel."

Susanna interjected, "I have two dogs and five cats, and I don't think Spot would do well with me. I wish I could have taken her, though."

A flash of something like annoyance went through Joanna's eyes as she looked at Susanna. "I'm in the same boat. I have a dog already."

Diana seemed more lighthearted about the subject. "I rent an apartment, and we aren't allowed to have dogs."

Helen found herself grateful that she could offer Spot sanctuary. Susanna seemed genuinely sorry for not taking the dog, but the other two were glad not to be bothered; she was sure of it.

"Have you heard from the doctor about your situation, Olivia?"

Olivia looked dejected. "I broke the hip, just as you suspected. Or was it Alexander who said that? Girls, you must meet Alexander. He's like a movie star, he's so handsome. Anyway, I'll be out of here soon."

Helen felt herself blushing at the same time as she tried to shove aside her usual annoyed response. "He is indeed. You're welcome to stop by anytime. We're the house on the east side of your Mom's. To the left if you're standing looking at her house. We'd be happy to have you come by if you'd like to see Spot. Or any time you want to drop in."

Susanna spoke up first. "That's very kind of you. I'd love to see Spot. I don't want to bother you on New Year's eve, but maybe I could come by tomorrow afternoon. I'm spending the night at Mom's. In fact, so is Jo. Di lives so close, she just goes home." The other women nodded in affirmation.

"I'd love to see you tomorrow afternoon. Any time after 1pm should be fine. Just knock on the door. I'll head out now." Olivia was beaming as she walked out. It was nice her daughters were so devoted to her.

Alexander came to greet her as she entered the house. "How's Olivia?" He wrapped her in a big hug. It felt so good not to have bad feelings between them.

"Her three daughters were there when I arrived. Two of them are staying at her house. I invited them to come over tomorrow afternoon if they wanted to see Spot. They'll probably come just to see you. Olivia made a big point about how good-looking you are."

He put on an innocent look as his green eyes twinkled. "It's not my fault. I wasn't even there, officer."

She laughed in spite of herself and reached up to sweep her hand lovingly through his longish gray hair. "You are such a hoot."

He turned and kissed her palm. "What do they say about Olivia?"

"She broke her hip, alright. But she says they're planning to release her soon. I can't imagine her staying alone in her house, but it's none of my business. She has three daughters who can figure it out. And none of them want Spot. Hooray for that!"

"I'm so glad for you." He pulled her closer and kissed her soundly. She lost track of time and all sense of anything but how complete he made her feel.

Just this morning, they'd made love like hormonal youngsters, and she was ready to drag him back to bed again. With the trouble between them out in the open, they'd slipped back into honeymoon mode. Maybe it wouldn't always be this crazy and wild, but she was loving it while it lasted. It was way better than any romance novel she'd ever read. She'd told her friends as much at lunch the other day.

As if he'd read her mind, he paused and looked at her meaningfully. She just laughed out loud. He grinned salaciously as he led her back to the bedroom. She couldn't stop laughing. She was *so* glad they'd had a talk this morning.

* * *

Red, 9:45pm

"It's barely been a week, Lydia." Red gave her what he hoped was a firm look. "What can we possibly do?"

"I don't know, Red. I just hate this waiting. I've heard arguments coming from her condo now and then, but nothing much beyond that. I just feel something bad is going to happen, and I want to stop it." Lydia swirled the scotch in her glass and frowned at it.

"That's the down side of our legal system. You can't act on anything except evidence. And you certainly can't arrest someone based on what they *might* do. In my years on the force, I found that the two biggest reasons cops got dirty were greed and vigilantism. It's hard to be a policeman when you see criminals get off so easily. You convince yourself you know who's guilty and decide to bypass a corrupt or defective system. It doesn't work out well." He sat down next to her, searching her eyes for understanding.

"Oh, I know that. It's just hard. I guess maybe that's why most people don't tap into this ability I have. Why would they?" she grumped.

He patted her hand. "Believe me, I understand the frustration. I can only imagine how I would have felt if I had had your gift while I was still on the force. It would have been so hard not to act on it."

She smiled at his empathy. "I still can't get over you accepting it so easily."

He looked surprised. "Everyone has intuition. Some have more than others. I consider myself very intuitive, and you're just on the extreme end of the spectrum." He leaned towards the coffee table to sample the mixed spiced nuts Lydia had brought to their informal New Year's eve celebration. "These are good! You made them yourself?"

She put on an insulted look. "Of course, I did. I slaved over a hot stove for maybe 30 minutes." Then she grinned. "I'm glad you like them. It isn't anything special."

"Well, it's special for me. I don't like to cook, and I'm glad not to be on my own tonight. I try to avoid drinking too much, but..." He found himself staring off into space, thinking about Sally and how they could have spent tonight. He jerked back to reality, looked embarrassed and said, "You know what's on my mind. I'm getting past it, but times like this are a little hard to take. It's nice that you're here."

Her brown eyes radiated sympathy. "It will get better, Red...So tell me. How did you get the name Red? I've been wondering."

He sighed. It was a question everyone asked when they got to know him. He didn't often tell the story. "You've shared with me, so I'll share with you. It happened a long time ago. My given name is Eric. I worked homicide, and sometimes it's dangerous. One time a crazy perp stabbed me before I could get a shot off. I was covered in blood by the time it was over; mine and his. The guys started calling me "Eric the Red" like the Viking. Cop humor can be pretty dark. Then it got shortened to "Red." I hardly ever go by Eric anymore."

She looked at him with wide eyes. "How awful!" Then her eyes softened. "Do you like the name Eric?"

"Yes, I always did. But everyone started calling me Red, and I didn't bother to correct them."

"Shall I call you Eric?"

Maybe he should say no. He had a hard and fast rule about not getting involved with women in Palm Lakes, and this could be the first step on an icy slope. Instead, he found himself saying, "Sure, why not?"

She smiled as if he'd granted her a boon, and he became concerned. He was lonely, and she was attractive. "Look, Lydia, I don't want to give you the wrong impression. You're a beautiful woman, and I'm feeling lonely, but I don't date women in Palm Lakes. I have a rule about that. And you don't need a rebound romance. They always turn out bad."

Her smile faded, but she sat straighter and feigned indifference. "I was just being friendly, Eric. I'm not trying to lead you into temptation. You don't seem to be having a hard time holding yourself back," she added with a bite.

So he had hurt her feelings. *Damn.* "If we spend much more time together, it *will* get hard (*inner groan*). You just happen to be my type, and I like you."

Fortunately having missed his choice of words, she brightened up. Then came the obvious question. "What about Sally?"

Of course. Sally was Lydia's opposite. Exasperation took over. "Come on, Lydia, I made a typical guy mistake. A pretty 30-year-old blonde throws herself at me, and I catch her. I take responsibility, but it wasn't a decision I made with my brain. Obviously. Besides, the whole thing was unreal; it's almost like it didn't happen. It was more like a hallucination that lasted a couple months." A symphony of emotions washed over him. Embarrassment. Defensiveness. Regret. Sadness.

"I didn't mean to upset you." She looked chastened. Of course she could see everything he was feeling. He began to feel sorry for the guy who'd married her.

Unsure why he felt he needed to explain, he continued, "I'm a three time loser at marriage, and my ex-wives, who were really nice women, all said the same thing. I couldn't leave the job at work. I became obsessed to the point of closing them out. I guess they were right. I've tried to keep a balance since I came to Palm Lakes. I figured it would be easy, you know? What goes on in a retirement community? But then this thing with Owen Schmidt came along, and I became fixated on him. I knew I was getting crazy about it, but I would patrol his street even on my time off, sometimes at night, hoping to catch him at something." He rolled his eyes. "It was a waste of time. I found myself skipping workouts and avoiding relaxing. I promised myself I'd go to Vegas, gamble a bit, find a friendly lady. But I kept putting it off. By the time Sally came along...well, just say I was ready for distraction. In retrospect I know she wasn't for me, but it was like I was having a late life crisis. For some reason it seemed like a last chance of sorts. I don't know how to explain it. Besides, I don't have to with you."

"That's not quite true, Eric. I can see your emotions very clearly. And I see certain personality traits, too, but human motivations are complex, and my gift is not a substitute for honest communication. Friends still need to talk to each other." Her brown eyes searched him hopefully.

"I won't be able to get anything by you, will I?" He knew that wasn't what she wanted to hear, but it was the first thing that came to mind.

"Not very often. And that tends to ruin things." She was uncharacteristically withdrawn, her eyes downcast.

"It won't ruin things with me. Not the way you think. I don't intend to ever lie to you. And from what you're saying, I'm not as open a book as I feared. So there might be some mystery left between us." He put on a brave smile, then remembered she could probably see he was concerned that she might judge him. He looked down into his empty glass. "Time for a refill?"

She gave him a gentle look. "Of course." She held her glass out to him.

At least she was willing to let him off the hook. *She's OK.* He went over to refill their glasses. When he returned, she accepted hers calmly, looking him up and down before he sat next to her. "How do you stay in such good shape?"

He beamed at the change of subject. "I work at it. I don't have the best diet, because I'm not much at cooking, but I exercise a lot. I run at the indoor track over at the Rec center. I do the weight circuit. Sometimes I use the other equipment. I tend to rotate things, because you can't get a full workout with just one method."

"I love doing yoga, but I haven't experimented with anything else. I think I'd like to be more toned, but I just don't know what to do. Do you have any suggestions?"

"Well, do you have any joint issues?"

"No."

"Then you can do about anything you want. Running will mess up your feet and knees eventually if you do too much. But it's good aerobic exercise. The stationary bike is less harmful to joints. Or swimming, but lots of people can't stand the chlorine. Stair master and treadmill have the same strengths and weaknesses as running, more or less. You get a lot of flexibility with yoga, and some of those classes are strenuous from what I've seen."

She raised her eyebrows. "Have you ever taken yoga?"

"No, but I've watched the classes for a few minutes, and it looks kind of interesting. I don't think I could bend like a pretzel, though."

"Would you like to try?"

The icy slope beckoned, but surprisingly, there were no red flags waving at him. Yet. "I might be persuaded. But if I try yoga, you have to do something I do. I'd let you choose what."

She grinned. "That works for me. The next yoga class starts this month. There are men in it. Not many, but you won't be the only one."

"I wouldn't regard it as purgatory to be in a class with scantily clad women." He grinned.

She smacked him on the shoulder. "Cut it out, Eric." Then she looked abashed. "Women our age aren't always a lot to look at, so don't get your hopes up."

A not-so-thinly veiled reference to Sally. He wondered why women always compared themselves with some model of perfection. "Beauty is not restricted to a certain age or shape." He gave her what he hoped was a meaningful look.

The silence was filled by the strains of a Bob Dylan tune in the background. Lydia finally filled the gap with a change of topic. "I had word from my friend Jean who's in the UK. I haven't told you about her, have I? She got divorced recently and went to the UK to see a guy she'd met online. Isn't that romantic? Now they're planning to come back here after they marry. I'm letting them have my second bedroom until they find a place to live."

She seemed real eager to see her friend, so Jean must be someone special. "These condos aren't that big," he said with concern. "You sure she's that good a friend?"

Lydia giggled. "I wouldn't offer just anyone. It will be like living on top of each other, but she's my best friend, and she doesn't have much money right now, so this will help her get started. She won't impose for long."

"Is this friend a shortish blonde? Even shorter than you?"

She looked at him with surprise. "How do you know that?"

He grinned. "I may not be psychic, but I have great powers of observation and a pretty good memory for detail." He waited to see what she'd say. She seemed a bit flustered. When she didn't speak, he went on, "Late in August, I was doing my time-wasting patrol one evening down Owen's street, and a party was being held at Barbara Blackstone's. I was curious, so I circled the neighborhood a few times, watching the partygoers arrive. You were walking arm in arm down the sidewalk with a petite blonde. She gave me a sort of scared look as I cruised by, but you didn't seem to notice me. You were laughing. I had the windows up, because the air conditioning was on, but I remember recognizing you as my neighbor and thinking what a wonderful laugh you had."

Maybe he'd said too much. A different kind of smile crept into her eyes as she looked at him. He wondered what she was seeing. Time to change the subject.

"So this guy she met. She was lucky. He could have been some psycho. What was she thinking to invest in a trip like that to meet a complete unknown?" People didn't get any smarter as they aged.

"I know how it sounds. But it wasn't that unknown." She studied him as she chewed her lower lip. "You say you're intuitive. But you probably find that it comes to you in hits of unbidden helpful information."

He nodded. That was exactly how it worked for him.

"And you said that it's pretty reliable."

Again, he nodded in affirmation.

"But you don't always listen to it. And you don't know how to tap into it on demand."

He smiled sheepishly. "Now you're razzing me about Sally."

She sighed. "So you knew all along that was doomed?"

"Pretty much." He shrugged his shoulders. "It didn't seem real. I couldn't believe it was happening to me. I just let myself be carried along, ignoring the warning signs, waiting to wake up from the dream. I guess I always knew at some level it had to end. Makes me sound foolish."

"We're all fools for love, Eric." She smiled compassionately. "Don't beat yourself up. My point was that most of us don't listen to our intuition. We don't trust it. And even those who do can't tune into it on demand. But, turns out, there is a way to do that. Humans have a natural ability to tap into their intuition. It just isn't acknowledged. My point is that Jean and I are practitioners of this method--it's called dowsing--and between the two of us, we determined Ian was a good risk and compatible with her relationship goals. So I'm not surprised it turned out so well. We knew in advance."

He looked at her calm face with disbelief. "Now you *are* beginning to sound like some psychic. I thought dowsing was about finding water. Or am I mistaken?"

She shrugged. "Dowsing is about finding answers to questions, like 'where's the water?' or 'where are my car keys?' or 'is this guy compatible with me?' I know it's weird, but it works. It's just an intuitive way of getting answers to questions the rational mind can't answer. Some day maybe I'll show you. So are you going to think I'm a flake now?"

Why did she care about his opinion? "I'm just having trouble taking it all in, but I'm willing to remain open-minded. I said I'd try yoga, didn't I? How many guys you know would do that?" He shot her a grin.

She relaxed. "Not anyone I can think of. Helen couldn't get Alexander to join us. Said he was too busy. He works out, too...he looks like a movie star...but you could tell the idea of yoga scared him."

He felt a twinge--it couldn't be jealousy--at her dreamy reference to Alexander. Suppressing it, he said, "Maybe this Ian guy will try yoga. Does Jean do yoga?"

"As a matter of fact, she does, but she's not a resident anymore, so she and Ian wouldn't be able to join a class." Lydia seemed sad to acknowledge that.

"Sorry, I forgot about that."

The conversation stalled. Red was almost ready to suggest a third scotch when Lydia announced, "I never stay up until midnight on New Year's Eve. It doesn't really matter to me. I think I'll go home and get some sleep. But how about we welcome the New Year by having brunch together at my place tomorrow? I was thinking of making eggs benedict and mimosas. Would you consider joining me?"

It sounded a lot better than a bowl of grape-nuts and a hangover. "I'm in. I don't have anything to bring, though."

"I have everything I need." She became businesslike, sitting straighter and addressing him in a schoolteacher tone. "Look, we're both feeling a little lonely. I miss Jean and you just broke up with Sally. I'm not trying to seduce you. It just seemed a nice thing to do. I used to make this brunch every year when I was married, but you need at least two to justify the work. I was hoping you'd accept. We'll have fun."

He hadn't missed the reference to marriage, but somehow it didn't seem threatening. "I'd be a fool not to accept. Thanks for the invite. What time do you want me?"

She did a slight double take--she caught the unintended double entendre--and stood up. "What time do you think you could come over? I don't want to make you get up too early on a holiday."

"I won't be drinking or staying up much longer. Name your time."

"Come over at 9. I won't start cooking until I see you, so if you oversleep, no problem. And don't dress fancy." She turned and headed towards the door without further adieu.

They stopped near the door as he opened the hall closet and handed her wrap to her while pulling a jacket off a hanger. She looked at him and objected. "You don't have to walk me home. I live two doors down, and this isn't exactly a bad neighborhood."

"If you think I'm going to let you walk home alone past a house with a dangerous killer, you've got another think coming. I won't argue about this. I will see you home safely." He braced himself for a sharp reply, as he knew Lydia was independent, so her answer took him by surprise.

"OK." It was said with un-Lydia-like meekness.

He didn't know whether to take her seriously or feel he'd just been ambushed. He slipped into his jacket and opened the door, ushering her out ahead of him. As they walked slowly down the deserted sidewalk, she hugged her wrap around herself, trying to ward off the chill. Without thinking, he reached over and put his arm around her, pulling her close for some body heat. She sure was a short little thing. "You should have worn something more sensible. That's a pretty shawl or whatever you call it, but it doesn't give any warmth. It *is* still winter in spite of how beautiful today was."

"Well, I knew I wouldn't be outside for long, and I was going for elegant rather than sensible."

"Your fashion sense is wasted on me. I wouldn't know elegant if it sat on me."

"Really, Eric, you're too modest. I'm sure you know exactly what elegant looks like."

She was referring to Sally again. This could get old. But he had to admit that each time he thought of Sally, it hurt less. That had to be progress.

They turned up the walk to Lydia's condo, and she fished her keys out of a pocket in her skirt. He reached over and took the keys from her, noting the slight surprise in her face. After unlocking the door, he bowed slightly, handed the keys back and asked, "Would you like me to check the place for intruders?"

She tittered. "You're a hoot, Eric. I'm OK. Thanks for seeing me home."

He saluted and then gave her a peck on the cheek. "Happy New Year, Lydia."

Smiling warmly, she returned the wish. He waited for the sound of the dead bolt and then walked back home, listening for sounds from Tanya's condo, but hearing none. His thoughts again on Owen Schmidt, he realized he'd come full circle this evening. He wasn't sure if that was good or bad. Walking down the street lit in monotones by a waxing moon, he felt like Sam Spade.

What kind of karma did he have that Schmidt had landed next door to him? Time would tell.

* * *

Tanya, 10:00pm

TANYA STARED at her glass of white wine. She'd already gone through the champagne she'd bought for tonight. Her stomach roiled with that out-of-control feeling she hated. The one she used to get with her ex-husband. How had she lost control of Owen?

They'd had a tiff the other day, so he hadn't come over tonight as planned. She didn't dare go to his house. If her ex-husband spotted her, he'd put a detective on her to prove she was violating the agreement, and her alimony would go out the window. She wouldn't mind losing the alimony, but only after Owen proposed and she had him committed to marrying her. She'd felt so close in recent weeks.

Sure, there had been the occasional bump in the road. That was normal. But since Christmas, Owen had been withdrawing from her. While he'd never professed undying love for her, he had told her once that he loved her. She was sure she hadn't imagined that. And even now, she could still see sexual hunger in his eyes. But there was something else. There was judgment. And maybe a hint of danger.

She did love an alpha male. She wouldn't even mind if he got a bit rough with her. It would be such a nice change from her wimp of a ex-husband. But so far, he hadn't gone beyond looking at her in a feral way now and then.

What was she going to do? She just needed a new approach. Sex wasn't as big a lever as she had hoped. She couldn't get him to invite her to his house. Something odd there. She knew it was more than the fact that her ex still lived on that street. Owen wasn't telling her something, and it annoyed her that he had secrets from her.

Draining the wine glass, she refilled it distractedly. She hadn't eaten much all day, and she was beginning to feel tipsy. Maybe she should have a snack. But she couldn't overcome inertia. Maybe later. She just needed to come up with a plan.

He'd yelled at her, telling her she was drinking too much, that he found it unattractive. He was beginning to sound just like her ex. What a bore! Couldn't she find a decent man in this town? Starting over didn't appeal to her. The ratio of women to men was not in her favor. She needed to get Owen married to her before he found any other reasons to say no. He may not be perfect, but he'd do. Once she got him hooked, she could move into his house, sell this dump and live the life she was meant to live.

Perhaps if she approached him submissively. He seemed to like that; it even turned him on. Surely she could play that game long enough to land a wedding proposal? It was just hard to remember to stay in type when she had a few drinks in her. She needed to stay focused. Then it came to her. All she had to do was make sure that when he was around, she didn't drink. He had been spending less time with her lately. That would work to her advantage. It all sounded so easy and reasonable.

Remembering how much he seemed to appreciate apologies, she decided to call him up and put her strategy in motion. He answered the phone after two rings. Had he been waiting to hear from her?

"Darling, it's me. I know you don't want to see me tonight, but I wanted to apologize to you for my behavior. You're right, of course. The stress has been so much since the divorce. I let it get to me. But I know it isn't an excuse for drinking. I'm going to do better. You'll see. I'll cut back." She forced herself to be silent so he could reply.

After what seemed like an hour, he spoke. "If you really mean it..." He sounded like he wanted to forgive her but wasn't sure he could trust her.

"Of course, I really mean it. I can't bear the thought of anything coming between us. I know you need your space, but can't we try again? On whatever terms you say." That cost her a lot, but she instinctively knew that putting the power into his hands would cause him to crumble.

He was slow to respond. "We'll have to take it one day at a time. I'm not going to spend so much time at your place, and you still can't come here, for obvious reasons."

She heard defensiveness in his voice and knew better than to argue. "Whatever you say, Owen. You'll see I've changed. We belong together. It's destiny. I will be so good to you." She said it with her sexiest voice and fancied she could feel him responding.

"This is what I'll do. I'll take you out to dinner on Wednesday. I'll be by at 5pm to pick you up. If you get drunk, we're finished."

155

She purred. "Anything you say, Darling." She blew kisses into the phone. "Until Wednesday."

"OK." He hung up. She knew he liked to be the one to hang up first, and thank God she had the presence of mind to let him. She put the phone down. It was going to be hell, but she was determined to get out of this dump and into his house, and if that meant staying sober for a few weeks, she'd do it.

6
WEDNESDAY, JANUARY 17, 1996

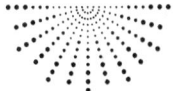

Nora, 10:30am

*N*ora arrived at Barbara's front door, keyed up at the thought of her first Botanica presentation to a non-family member. Barbara opened the door before she even rang the bell and escorted her into the living room, where Nora sat on the edge of the couch and fidgeted with the contents of her overfull canvas bag, thinking she should replace it with something more professional-looking, like one of those little rolling cases. She had decided to economize because Luke was so derogatory about her new venture, but now it seemed a tactical error to have sacrificed looking confident and successful just for the sake of saving a few dollars.

Barbara perched in a chair opposite her, seemingly unaware of Nora's case of nerves. "Can I get you some coffee or tea?"

"Thanks, Barbara. Coffee would be nice." Anything to postpone the inevitable.

Barbara walked into the kitchen and a few minutes later brought back a tray with mugs of steaming coffee, sugar, cream and a plate of pastries. She set it on the coffee table and urged Nora to help herself.

Nora's stomach was roiling so much, she wasn't sure she could even handle coffee. She knew she didn't look confident and professional. Though she had practiced often, she wasn't ready to give this pitch. She didn't want to offend Barbara or lose her as a friend by trying to sell to her. She mostly was terrified that this was going to be the colossal failure Luke was predicting.

Barbara was dressed casually but elegantly as always in slacks, sweater and black leather flats. Her auburn hair was immaculately coiffed and her hands danced around the tray, showing off a recent manicure. The only jewelry she wore were a gold chain and gold earrings shaped like dolphins.

"Thanks for letting me practice on you, Barbara. It means a lot to me." She hoped the quiver in her voice wasn't too obvious.

Barbara poured her a cup and handed it to her. "It's no problem. I'm happy to help."

Nora sighed while adding sugar and creamer. Should she tell Barbara the whole story? Barbara was the nicest person she knew, and she really needed someone to talk to since she couldn't share her concerns with Luke. "I've never done anything like this before, and I really need to make it work--no, I don't want to sound pitiful, although I have to admit that I feel pitiful at times lately. I've been really overwhelmed. Our financial situation is terrible. Right after Christmas--can you believe the timing?--we found out that Luke's pension fund had collapsed. It's our main source of income, and we'd been acting like it would always be there. I can't believe we did that, but there's no going back. We have debt and no real income, and Luke isn't taking it well. No matter what I say, he regards it as his fault."

Barbara's eyes widened for a second, then she leaned closer to Nora, reaching across the gap to touch her hand. "I'm so sorry, Nora. How awful for you!"

"I don't mean to dump on you, and I certainly don't want to appear to be pressuring you for support, but I'm going nuts. I can't sleep, and Luke is so depressed, I have to act strong for him. I desperately want to find a way to get us back on our feet, if that's even possible. My cousin Ellen suggested this Botanica business as better than a menial job, because if I make a go of it, there's no upper limit to income. But I've never done anything like this before, and I'm worried. Luke keeps saying I'm wasting precious time and money on a pyramid scheme and that I need to get a *real* job. I confess it's all I can do not to shout at him that even both of us working at a burger joint isn't going to solve our problems. We're going to lose our house if all we do is get minimum wage jobs. We need something better. It's not that we'd die if we had to move, but if there's a chance I can restore our income with Botanica, it would save our lifestyle and I believe it would help Luke a lot."

"That makes total sense to me, Nora. It must be terribly hard to forge ahead with this when Luke is so skeptical."

"Well, I can't talk to him about my concerns. I have to be brave in front of him. But I'm terrified I won't succeed, then I'll be dragging us down further. I'm embarrassed that I've dumped on you; I just needed someone to be open with, and Luke can't be it at the moment. You've always been so kind and helpful...Anyway, thanks for listening. I needed to get that off my chest. Some part of me isn't sure I can do this, and I don't want to fail. As I told Luke, and as you know, I have no problem opening my mouth. I love to talk to people. It's just that it's so different when it's selling." Nora paused and looked at Barbara apologetically. "Please don't let anything I said influence your decision about Botanica. I need a real, honest test here, and I'm open to any suggestions you have after I finish. Even if you agree with Luke. I need to do whatever it takes to help us get back on our feet. If this can't work, I need to find something that will." She swallowed hard, hoping it wouldn't come to that.

"OK. Don't be nervous about your presentation. I'm looking forward to hearing about these products."

Nora smiled nervously at Barbara and reached for her flip chart and lined up some product samples on the table, then launched into her presentation. She faltered a few times, but managed to press on to the end in fairly good shape. Barbara was an excellent audience, giving her complete attention and not interrupting. When Nora reached the end, she was hesitant to hope for any particular outcome.

Barbara was still smiling, so she must have done all right. "I presented to my daughter a few days ago, but you're my first person in Palm Lakes. Like I said, I'm new to this, but I'm loving the products and I'd be happy to answer any questions you have."

"I'm impressed, Nora. I admit I thought is was going to be one of those MLM schemes, and I don't like them. This is just a shopping club when you get down to it."

Nora was flooded with relief. "Exactly. That's what attracted me, too. I don't have to pay a pile of money up front for a lot of stuff, nor buy from an individual, and the prices are competitive."

Barbara nodded. "Having a computer, I can shop from home, which is a time-saver. I think it's a great concept, and I trust you about the products. I'd be happy to give it a try."

Nora let out a breath she hadn't realized she was holding. "Wonderful!" She reached into her bag for the paperwork. "It won't take long to set things up. I really am loving Botanica, and I'm pretty sure you will, too, but you can quit at any time. And I'm here to answer your questions. I can help you use the products better, too. There are some neat off-label uses I can share with you."

"I was sold after you told me about the spot remover. That and the cleaning products. I don't like using harsh chemicals around my pets. Well, I only have Jack now. But I don't want to use things that could harm him. And that spot remover sounds amazing. I can't wait to try it."

Nora laughed. "That is the product I was most taken with, too. Ellen told me one of the reps does presentations in his home, and he tosses a glass of red wine onto his white carpet and uses the spot remover to impress the audience. I'm sure it's that good, but I wouldn't dream of doing that to anyone's carpet but my own."

They laughed together while Nora helped Barbara fill out the paperwork and make her first order.

When they finished, Barbara smiled while sipping the last of her coffee. "That was pretty easy. What are your plans for introducing these to Palm Lakes?"

Nora bit her lip. "I don't have a plan. I know people in the clubs that we've been in and at church, but I'm not sure what to do next. I hate to say it, but it took a lot of energy for me to work up the nerve to call you, and I dread the thought of doing that over and over."

Barbara smiled and pointed up in the air. "I have an idea. Why don't I throw a little shindig and invite everyone I know so you can do a presentation to a big group? We could have snacks and drinks. Nothing fancy. But people would come, and you can show them about Botanica. By then, I'll have had a little experience myself, so I can share my story, too. What do you say?"

Nora was overwhelmed with gratitude. "That would be so terrific! I'd really appreciate that."

"I think maybe a weekend would be good. The snow birds are still here, and we could send out invitations. What do you think about a week from this Saturday?"

Nora gulped. "Perfect. The sooner the better. I'm nervous, but it's exactly what I want."

"You leave it to me. I'll provide snacks and drinks. It will be fun." Then she giggled. "Maybe you should find a scrap of white carpet so you can do that red wine demo, since my carpet isn't white." She stared at Nora, obviously serious.

"I'm not sure I'm much of a showman, but if I practice, maybe I can do it well enough."

"You can practice with me until you get comfortable. It's always good to have an element of drama."

Fifteen minutes later, Nora left in a daze, thrilled and surprised at the way things were unfolding. Barbara's parties were legendary. People would come. She was on her way.

* * *

Mary Beth 12:30pm

MARY BETH SAT opposite a despondent-looking Samantha at the Chinese restaurant, waiting for a server.

"You look like something the cat dragged in, girl."

Samantha looked up from perusing the menu, her blue-green eyes hooded. "That's how I feel, too." Then she went back to the menu without further explanation.

Mary Beth frowned. "You're not mad at me, are you?"

Samantha's surprised look reassured her. "How could you think that?"

"Damn, girl, you aren't even talking to me. How can I help if you keep everything to yourself?"

Samantha shook her head. "I don't think there's any way you can help me. My life is a total mess and getting worse all the time."

"Damn it all. Tell me what's going on. You think I haven't felt that way? You and your Mom helped me to find a place in this community. I owe you guys, and I'm not going to sit by and do nothing while you flush your life down the toilet." That had come out a bit more forceful than she intended.

Samantha's eyes started to fill. "OK. You asked for it. But I don't see how you can help."

"You didn't seem this upset at the funeral service."

"I don't think it had hit me then. It was so kind of you and Ethan to come. Julio and Jack were amazingly supportive, too. And of course, Helen and Alexander. You know Mom and funerals." A quiet chuckle escaped, in spite of the tears. "She wouldn't even attend her own funeral if she could find a way to get out of it. Arthur said they had a nice quiet time at her house. It was so weird at the funeral, because none of the people really were that close to Dad. He didn't have friends, but he would have liked to hear Julio tell the story at lunch about how Dad designed their yard himself and how impressed Julio was with his design. We know that's high praise. But Jack never met him and the rest of you rarely did more than say hi to him. It was so kind of you to come... I'm repeating myself."

The server came and took their order. Samantha sipped her water and said nothing else.

"Your Dad was always very nice to me. I didn't say too much to him, but he would come over and admire my jewelry. Why didn't your Mom come to lunch after the service?"

"To be honest, she isn't all that high on Julio, and I didn't want her meeting Jack, and she has never been that sweet to Ethan in spite of all he does for her. I felt it would be easier without her. I couldn't have invited Jack if Arthur was there, anyway."

"I figured. I gathered from what Jack said that he's holding the job open for you. Julio didn't seem surprised. In fact, I get the impression he was happy for you, which doesn't make sense."

Samantha smiled for the first time. "Julio really was great to give me my job back without any hassle, and he said something to the effect that he was sorry it hadn't worked out for me. I don't think he has a clue that Jack has any more interest in me than work-related."

"So how's that going?" Mary Beth felt like she was prying, but she was dying with curiosity.

A grim look crossed Samantha's face. "Oh, that. I think God is punishing me for even considering working with Jack. I knew it would be risky. But I convinced myself it was OK and I'd handle it well. Sometimes I feel like my Dad dying was to keep me from making a fool of myself, and then I feel guilty, because it shouldn't cost someone's life to keep me on track." Tears had welled up in her eyes again, and she brushed them away angrily.

"Shit, Samantha, that's all wrong. Your Dad dying had nothing to do with the Jack situation. That's morbid. In addition to being dumb. Quit blaming yourself."

"Oh, I know I'm acting like a drama queen. I'm sorry. I hated giving up that job. And on top of it, Mom really needs to change her living arrangements, and she won't listen to me. And even if she does, her place is a hoarding black hole. It will take me forever to get it ready for sale. She's not financially in good shape, either. Dad didn't leave her enough to live on well, which pisses me off. Partly because we don't have any savings, so I can't be much help. She really needs to sell her house just to have money to live. But nothing I say is moving her. On some level I don't blame her. Why should you have to sell your home just so you can live?"

Mary Beth grimaced. "You're so right. One thing that makes it hard is parents don't see their adult children as adults. My Mom kept a lot from me. She didn't feel it was my business; maybe she was even trying to protect me from worry. I didn't realize how bad her heart condition was for a long time. And I went to her doctor the other day and found out some information that has me going batshit crazy all over again."

Samantha perked up at the change of subject. "What happened?"

"Well, I went to the doc and asked him about my Mom's medication. I made it clear I wasn't looking to sue anyone, but it just seemed to me that she changed in the weeks before her death. I asked him what her meds were and if he had changed any. He said yes."

Samantha's eyes widened. "So you think the meds could have contributed to her death?"

"I'm pretty sure they did. Won't do any fucking good now, though. Pardon my French. You see, she'd been acting really low and weak and unlike herself. So I asked him about this new medication he'd switched her to. He assured me the drug rep had told him how innovative it was. She'd only have to take one pill a day instead of the six she was taking. He thought it would be easier on her. She hated taking pills. And he said sometimes older people are forgetful, though my Mom wasn't. Anyway, I asked him to look into any reports of problems with the meds. I have to give him credit. Not only did he look into it, I got a call a few days later. He told me there were reports of elderly people dying from the medication. Liver failure. Kidney failure. Shit like that. He sounded really upset and guilty. I didn't let him off too easy. He was afraid I'd sue, but what good would that do now?"

"Oh my God, Mary Beth! That's unbelievable!"

"Yeah, those drug reps apparently peddle the drugs without telling the whole story. If the doc had been sharp, he wouldn't have put an elderly woman on a new drug. It's like making her a guinea pig. But there are too many incentives for handing out freebies and writing prescriptions. Maybe he did have her well-being at heart, but I think it was a stupid choice. And I really hate drug companies now. I'm never going to a doctor again if I can avoid it. To have your own doctor kill you with a prescription drug. Of course, he didn't admit it. He said we'd have to exhume her body and do an autopsy to be sure, and even then, cause of death would be hard to prove. He counted on me not wanting to do that. I don't."

"So you're going to leave it be?"

"I don't see what good it would do."

"I agree. Some people might go for the money, but it would seem ghoulish to me."

"If I can't have Mom, it's of no use to me. Though part of me would like to stick it to the drug company."

"I'm so sorry, Mary Beth. This is a warning to me. I'll keep a closer watch on anything my Mom is given. There are just so many things to do when you're dealing with aging parents, it doesn't occur to you to mistrust the doctor's judgment." She shook her head.

"I didn't mean to make this all about me. I just want you to know that doing the jewelry with your Mom has meant a lot to me. I'm glad she still wants to do it. I'll try to offer to do things for her, like shopping or cleaning. Let me know if I can help you with her. She's been so generous with her time, expertise and materials. Plus I got to meet Ethan there."

Between bites of egg roll, Samantha pointed her chopsticks at Mary Beth and gave her a significant glance. "What is going on with you two?"

"How the hell should I know? He doesn't say anything. He's maybe the kindest person I ever met. He helped me through my Mom's death. He asked me out for New Year's eve. Catherine--you know, my neighbor--said I should get more aggressive with him." Mary Beth chuckled, thinking about the elderly woman's attitude. "I told her I would, but I chickened out. Can you imagine me chickening out? But I guess I'm afraid I'll scare him off. And I really like him a lot. I know he isn't as handsome as Alexander, but to me, Ethan is good-looking. And he's become a true friend."

"So he hasn't declared his intentions or made a move? How strange. Maybe he's scared to."

"That's what Catherine said. Though I'm not buying it. Anyway, you, Maddie, Ethan and Helen are my best friends. Helen and I don't spend much time together since she married. That's OK, but I do miss her. And I was thinking you were going to Temple Landscaping, and I was really going to miss you. I know you're sad about staying, but it's good for me. I don't have any other friends my own age. I hope you do get that job, but I won't complain that I got a reprieve."

Samantha grinned weakly. "It's nice to be wanted. My Mom doesn't give me the impression she likes having me around. I feel certain she would have insisted I take the job if she'd known about it. Arthur is rolling with it. He knows I'm not happy, but he's probably relieved I'm not pawning Mom off on him."

Mary Beth guffawed. "Sorry. I'm fine with your Mom, but I can see how dealing with her as a parent could be challenging."

"That's a nice way of putting it." Samantha dug into the platter of food in front of her and scooped some rice onto her plate. After a moment of reverie, she volunteered, "Jack wants me to stay in touch ostensibly to keep track of whether the job is still open. But we both know it's more than that. I told him OK. I won't meet with him, though. It was nice to see him at the funeral. Kind of creepy of me to invite him, wasn't it?"

Mary Beth cocked her head. "Why would you think that? Your Dad dying was the reason you declined the job. It was kind of him to show support."

"I felt a total creep for not telling Arthur."

"You haven't done anything. And you aren't going to. No need to tell Arthur. I mean, you aren't going to do anything, are you?" Mary Beth knew it was none of her business, but couldn't help asking.

"I don't intend to. I told him we won't be meeting. I'll call him now and then. If I take the job, it will be as before, purely professional. Maybe by then I'll be over him." Samantha grunted in disbelief.

"You'd think our love lives would get easier as we get older."

Samantha seemed to remember something. "Speaking of which, I don't mean to be gossiping, but I had an informal appointment with Mom's across-the-street neighbor today. You know, the one who bought Helen's house?"

"Yes, Maddie thinks she's stuck up. I asked about her the last time we did jewelry."

Samantha laughed. "Emma Lightman's really shy. She's very nice. Julio asked me to talk to her, because she has digestive issues and he knows I healed mine using herbs and some holistic doctors. We had a nice chat. I hope she gets the right help and sees progress. But that wasn't what I was going to say. It's about Julio."

Mary Beth's ear perked up. "What about Julio?"

"Emma's seeing Julio. She says they hike on Sundays. It makes sense. I know he loves to hike, and a woman shouldn't go alone on some trails. She downplayed it. But do you think he's acting different lately?"

"I don't get to see him that much. He breezes in and out of the office, speaks to me a little. I can't say I've noticed anything. What are you implying?"

"She was just so determined to convince me it was nothing that I wondered if there was a little romance going on. You know he's made wild comments now and then about having flings with married women in Palm Lakes and all that nonsense about his dark skin looking good next to white skin, etc. Remember that time he was talking about drug dealers in Palm Lakes and wife-swapping orgies?"

Mary Beth laughed out loud. "Yeah, I remember. We both thought he was exaggerating. But let's face it. I wouldn't be surprised some of the women were throwing themselves at him. He's a total hottie. He could definitely be in one of those calendars." Mary Beth sighed as she thought about different poses.

Samantha giggled. "I just can't see him with Emma, not after all that nonsense he spouted. She doesn't seem the type to have a mad fling. Well, it's none of my business." She paused for a second. "You know, maybe I'm imagining things, but with him being so generous about giving me my job back and coming to my Dad's funeral and this latest thing with Emma, I'm beginning to see past his good looks. I never realized I had a tendency to assume handsome men were shallow. I misjudged Jack, and now it looks like I misjudged Julio."

"Well, if they have hidden depths, they're the exception. I'll stick with Ethan. He may not be movie star handsome, but he looks good to me. Maybe more so because he looks like a real person."

"I think he's very nice looking, too."

Mary Beth smiled at the compliment, then realized she was feeling proprietary about Ethan. "Listen to us talk. You'd think in a retirement community there would be deeper topics than who's screwing whom."

Samantha choked and grabbed her teacup. After gulping down some tea, she laughed. "I never would have guessed how much like Peyton Place Palm Lakes is."

"Peyton Place for old farts." Mary Beth snorted. "You and I aren't exactly immune from being included in that description. Peyton Place, I mean, not old farts." She giggled again. "Maybe there's something in the water."

* * *

Maddie, 4:30pm

MARY BETH WAS COMING Saturday for her jewelry-making session, and Maddie wanted to have something good to do with her. Maddie picked through her latest order from the parts catalog. There just wasn't anything good enough for a new project. Maybe Mary Beth would be up for a trip to The Bead Store.

Maddie toyed with the idea of calling Mary Beth and asking her to go with her. She didn't feel like driving across town by herself. Plus Samantha would raise hell if she thought Maddie were going to drive that far. Riding in a car was painful enough without having to drive and fight Samantha, too. Mary Beth *had* offered to do anything Maddie needed. Finally she convinced herself to make the call.

Maddie went for the green address book in the drawer by the oven to find the number. Flipping through the pages, she realized she'd forgotten Mary Beth's last name. Again. Feeling defensive, she paged through the book starting at the back, looking for Mary Beth's neat handwriting. That much she remembered. Mary Beth had written it in the book herself. Finally she found her in the Cs. Costello. That was the name. It figured that she started at the wrong end of the book. Maybe she should get a new book and enter everyone by their first name.

Taking the book with her to the phone, she dialed Mary Beth's number.

"Mary Beth. It's me. Maddie."

"Hi, Maddie. Is everything OK? Are we still on for Saturday?"

"Yes, I was calling because I was thinking about what we could make on Saturday, and I was wondering what you'd say to a trip to The Bead Store on the other side of town? They have lots of great stuff, and we could both pick up materials for our next project."

"Sure. That's fine by me. When would you like to go?"

"I don't mind. It's about an hour away. Would you drive?"

"Of course! How about we get lunch while we're out. Is there anywhere near there to eat?"

Maddie dredged through her foggy memory. "It's been a while since I went there, but it's very built up, so I think we could find something."

"Then let's plan on that. I could come at 10 and we could do our shopping then get a bite before driving back. How does that sound?"

Maddie sighed blissfully. "That would be so nice."

"You'll have to help me pick materials. I don't know good from bad."

"I'll be glad to do that." It made Maddie feel good to have something valuable to contribute. "Think about what you might like to make. Like a necklace for you or a birthday present. It's a long drive, and you probably won't want to make it again soon. It would be wise to get materials for a few projects."

"Thanks, I'll plan on that. What a blast! I'm glad you thought of it."

"You're welcome."

"Is there anything I can pick up for you before then? Groceries? Dog food? Anything?"

"I'm OK for now."

"OK. I'll see you Saturday at 10."

They said goodbye and Maddie hung up reluctantly. Lately, talking on the phone with a friendly person had become a balm to her nerves. She was even tempted to let Mary Beth shop for her just to keep her around longer. But that would give the wrong impression.

She had no sooner hung up the phone than it rang again.

"Hi, Mom. How are you?"

Maddie relaxed, grateful it wasn't a telemarketer. "I just spoke with Mary Beth. She's taking me to The Bead Store Saturday and then to lunch. We're getting materials for our next projects."

"Isn't that great! I'm glad you're getting an outing. Would you like to come over for dinner tonight? I'm making spaghetti."

Maddie frowned. Samantha knew she was addicted to spaghetti and was hoping it would be impossible for her to say no. Sighing at allowing herself to be manipulated, she relented. "OK."

"I'll pick you up in ten minutes. You can bring Beau if you like."

Maddie simmered about being chauffeured. But it would limit the pain. "OK." She didn't want to rubber stamp every suggestion Samantha made, because then Samantha would think she was in charge. But spaghetti without having to cook or clean was too tempting. "See you soon."

Samantha arrived as advertised, though there was a cloud hanging around her which was atypical. "You OK, Samantha?" Samantha shrugged and changed the subject. "I'm so glad you're coming over for dinner. I made your famous spaghetti. It's my favorite, and I know you like it, too."

So she didn't want to share. *Fine.* Beau followed them out of the house and hopped into the car. On the short drive, Maddie tried not to exclaim in pain when Samantha stopped too fast or turned the corner. She didn't need Samantha having any more ammunition about her moving to assisted living. Finally they arrived.

Dinner was perfect, as usual. Maddie felt it was a slap in the face every time she ate over here. Samantha made it look so easy to make fancy meals and then clean up afterwards all by herself. That was why Maddie had always said Samantha was just like her father; he was organized to a fault.

Beau settled himself in as usual, awaiting treats which would be handed out during dinner on a saucer just for him. Maddie accepted the glass of red wine Arthur offered her, musing that Samantha spent too much on wine, as if that would make it taste better. She couldn't say she liked this wine any better than her usual cheap brand, but she was glad to have any wine at this point.

Arthur tried to make conversation in his usual awkward way. "So, Maddie, Samantha tells me you have a new neighbor across the street whom she got to meet today. Does she like your jewelry?"

"Hmmpf. Well, I gave her some to welcome her to the neighborhood. I suspect she's got money. She sent me a thank you card, but she never comes over like Helen used to. She's kind of snooty."

Samantha looked shocked, but then offered, "She seemed nice to me. I think she is really shy. I don't think she's stuck up."

"Well, maybe not. She came over this afternoon asking for your address so she could send a sympathy card. She said she felt bad she hadn't expressed it to you when you were there today. So maybe you're right."

Samantha raised an eyebrow as if surprised to have won the point. "Her yard is really looking lovely."

"I wish she hadn't put up that wall. But it's more of an eyesore for the next door neighbors than for me."

She saw Samantha roll her eyes, but said nothing. At least Samantha's color was improving. Maddie wondered why she was looking a bit off.

Beau accepted his small treat off the saucer when Arthur offered it to him.

Maddie smiled. "Beau has been so good to me. I don't know what I'd do without him."

"Is it bothering you being alone?"

She was sure Samantha was doing more than showing concern. She wanted leverage so she could push the move to assisted living. "You know I don't like being alone, but I feel safe with Beau."

"You wouldn't be alone if you went into the assisted living place or moved in with us."

Bingo. Maddie replied sharply, "They wouldn't let me keep Beau, and I'd have to get rid of most of my possessions. I'm not ready to do that."

Samantha nodded. "I know it would be a big change. Not an easy one. But I wish you'd consider it. Dad didn't leave you much to live on. Your house is your only asset."

"I'm doing fine."

"Well, the offer is there any time. Meanwhile, maybe it wouldn't be a bad idea to get rid of some clutter. You have accumulated a lot of stuff. I could help you sort through it, and we could get rid of things like Dad's clothes and anything you don't want."

It prickled Maddie to give someone else control of her life. She'd just gotten free of Stanley. She didn't want Samantha in charge. But she didn't know how to say it. "Let's wait a little while for that." It was tiring fighting off all these well-meaning people who wanted to run her life.

Arthur attempted to smooth things over. "We're here for you, Maddie. No harm intended."

They silently finished their spaghetti. After dinner, Samantha served homemade pecan pie, Maddie's favorite. With a scoop of vanilla ice cream on top. No further talk about assisted living marred the evening.

LATER, at home, Maddie sat in front of the TV and poured herself a glass of wine. She wasn't tempted to have chips, her usual treat. She was just too full from dinner. She reluctantly admitted it was nice to eat well and not have to clean up. She hated kitchen work almost as much as house work. Not that she was going to give Samantha the satisfaction of admitting that.

Beau lay on the floor beside her as he always did. He was such a comfort. When it got dark, she was jumpy. She didn't even like to let him out at bedtime, because it made her feel at risk. Samantha had suggested a dog door, and Maddie was horrified at the thought. Anyone could crawl into her house through something big enough for Beau.

She leaned over and petted him. "No one's going to take you away from me, boy. We're a team." She leaned back to watch the Duke do his thing on the tube and forgot about her worries for a while.

* * *

Helen, 7:00pm

HELEN LAUGHED at Alexander's joke as she helped dry the remaining pots and pans from dinner. She knew men didn't like to be called beautiful, but Alexander took her breath away. In profile, she didn't get the full force projected by his gemlike green eyes, but his thick silver hair swept back from his brow in a slight wave and grazed just below his collar, making him look intellectual as well as heart-stompingly gorgeous. Stubble was just beginning to show on his jaw. His coloring was light enough he didn't get a five o'clock shadow. She had to be this close to see it. It tempted her to reach out and caress his face. His deft, long-fingered hands rinsed the last pot, and he turned to hand it to her, his perfect teeth framed by a dazzling smile.

Taking the pot wordlessly, she thought for the millionth time how lucky she was to have him. Smiling to herself, she dried the pot and put it away. As she shook out the towel and went to hang it up, he grabbed her arm and pulled her into a warm embrace, making her laugh again.

"I'm glad to hear you laughing."

"I laugh all the time."

"You haven't been laughing as much since we came home. Now you are. You seem more relaxed."

She snuggled against his chest. "I am feeling better. I still have lots to figure out, but I'm not as worried as I was before we talked. I'm sorry I'm so difficult."

"Oh, stop it. You aren't difficult. We are both adjusting to a very new situation. I think we're doing fine." He ran his hand gently over her hair. She loved how he towered over her. At first, it had been intimidating. Now she felt protected.

Spot came into the kitchen and barked once, then sat in the doorway. "I think Spot wants a walk," said Helen.

"She's pretty smart. It hasn't taken her long to see the pattern. Plus she's getting spoiled. Most dogs would settle for one walk a day, but she gets two." Helen heard the playfulness in his voice and knew he didn't mind.

"Well, at least I'm getting a lot of exercise. Between walking her and doing the weight circuit, I'm feeling much more in shape."

"Can't have you looking like a beached whale."

She play punched him and headed for the front door, Spot at her heels.

As they sauntered down the sidewalk towards the next entrance to the golf course, she pulled her jacket around her against the cold. It had been a pretty mild winter, but the chill at night reminded you of the season. The waning crescent moon cast little light, and they were surrounded by total silence.

"It's quiet, isn't it?" She put her arm through Alexander's.

They matched their speed to Spot's inspection of bushes and landmarks. At least she didn't lift a leg and mark things, but she did tug the lead on Alexander's left arm when he didn't walk as fast as she wanted. "That's one of the things I actually like about here. I prefer peace and quiet. I know it creeps some people out, but not me. I wouldn't mind if you and I were the only people on earth. I could be happy."

His words warmed her heart. She felt the same way, though there was a lingering fear of putting too much faith in his love. Why couldn't she overcome this sense that she was unworthy of such a wonderful man? "I feel the same way, but part of me still wonders why me." There. She'd said it.

He stopped in his tracks and turned to her, ignoring the pull of Spot on the leash. "I thought you got past that."

"I don't think it's something you flick a switch on. I'm trying, but it may take some time. Part of me is still waiting for you to wake up and realize you made a mistake marrying me. I know that sounds melodramatic, but..."

He put his arms around her and hugged her close. It was the best answer she could have asked for. She hoped someday she could let all her fears go. Embarrassed, she changed the subject and started walking again. "I meant to tell you about my visit with Olivia today. I got so excited sharing about the labyrinth that I forgot to tell you how Olivia is doing. You know Olivia got an infection, and that's why they didn't release her like they wanted to? She says it seems to be under control now, but they're keeping her for a couple more days. Her youngest daughter Diana was there."

Spot pulled harder on the leash as they turned down the path to the golf course, and Alexander looked at Helen while trying to contain Spot's enthusiasm. "Will she be coming home or does she have to go to rehab?"

"She thinks she's coming home. Diana says she'll be by once a week to help her, but I'm not sure that's enough. And there's something about Diana...she was too much sweetness and light. It didn't seem genuine. In a way, she reminds me of Sally. I get the feeling she isn't totally honest."

"None of us are, especially with strangers."

"I don't mean that. It's hard to describe. She seemed to manipulate Olivia the way Sally does me. I hadn't ever looked at it before. But seeing her do that shed some light on Sally's behavior. Olivia dotes on Diana, but Diana isn't being genuine. She seems to say and do what she thinks Olivia wants, and Olivia soaks it up. Diana left before I did, and Olivia was going on about how wonderful Diana is. It's obvious she's her favorite. She talks about Susanna being so much like her father, and when she says it, it doesn't sound like a compliment. Joanna seems to be odd man out. Olivia doesn't say anything nice about her."

"Don't go getting too involved. I know you like Olivia, but she needs to work things out with her daughters by herself."

"I know, but I remember how bad I felt when my kids were trying to force me to leave here, and I get the sense that her kids are trying to make her do what they want. I don't know if she's up to living alone anymore, but I empathize with her. I'm so glad I didn't end up that way."

"You're a lot younger than Olivia, Helen. She may need her family to do more for her. But I'm glad you didn't go back to Wisconsin, too. I think you would have been miserable."

"I have a life now. I didn't used to. I guess I have a selfish reason for being so involved with Olivia. What if she wants Spot back? She won't want to live in that house all alone. I've grown so attached to Spot. And even Fido seems to like having her around."

"I was surprised at how well they get along, too. We'll just have to play it by ear. If you have to give her back, we'll get you another pet. I know it won't be the same. But that's the best I can promise."

"I wouldn't wish anything bad on Olivia. And I know she loves Spot. It must hurt her to be away from her. I hope she recovers fully, and I guess I need to face that will mean Spot goes back. But since her daughter only comes once a week, I bet she'll let us walk Spot. She's come to love her walks."

Alexander put his arm around her shoulders. "We can certainly do that."

* * *

Lydia, 8:15pm

WHAT? Lydia had been sitting on Eric's couch recounting the events of the day, then suddenly, it was as if someone had stopped time. Eric's trademark crooked grin was plastered on his face. The smell of his aftershave overlay the scent of single malt in her glass. The colors swirled in his energy field. Everything had stopped, because there was a new color. Or at least, she had never noticed it between them until now. The indigo of his intuition, the silver of his integrity, the green of the affection he obviously had come to feel for her. All these she was used to seeing. It was the flicker of orange that had stopped time for her.

"I'm sorry, I forgot what I was saying. Talk about senior moments." She was lying and he must know it, but he said nothing. "Oh, that's right. I'm going to London on Friday. Finally Jean got a date for her wedding.

It's a civil ceremony, and there were details to work out since she's American. They're trying to get hitched as soon as possible, so they can move on to the next phase of getting him a green card. It didn't leave me much notice, but I got a decent flight and a motel near them. I'll only be staying a few days. They'll be leaving on a honeymoon soon after the wedding."

His eyes widened at the news. "Aren't you the world traveler! London! That should be fun."

"I really am looking forward to Jean's wedding. And she was eager to have me there." What she didn't say was that she regretted going away now, just when things seemed to be developing between them. "I'll miss our visits."

His eyebrows raised. "I enjoy them, too. I'm glad you won't be gone for long. I won't say send me a post card, because you'll get back before it does."

She laughed. "I'll bring you a souvenir. What would you like?"

His eyes looked up as he contemplated an answer. "Some nice British beer would be good, but you can't bring that. If you find a decent scotch in duty free that isn't too expensive, I'd like that. I'll reimburse you."

"Nonsense. It would be my pleasure. I'll try to find something exotic and wonderful."

He grinned, knocking her off balance for a few seconds. When she recovered, she went back to describing the labyrinth party at Emma's while a second line of thought ran through her head simultaneously. "The weather was kind to us today. We did a pot luck lunch, and it turned out terrific. It's easy to see Emma is feeling better. Her colors are more clear and strong. She told us she went to Samantha's naturopath and took some of her advice, and it's made a difference."

Eric nodded at her, urging her to continue. Maybe the orange she kept seeing was because he was thinking about someone else, not her. He couldn't have feelings like that for her. "We had a big laugh at your expense about yoga class. They couldn't believe I talked you into it. But they'll be very nice to you, don't worry."

"I would expect no less. Helen's a classy lady, and Barbara is, too. I don't know Emma, but she must be like the rest of you, so I'm not too worried." There it was again. That orange flicker. For some reason, it made her think of his Viking ancestors, strong and lusty. He was physically imposing at 6 ft, and his body was hard, his face chiseled. So alive.

She coughed lightly to bring herself back to present time. "Emma is looking so good. But it's more than what she said about her digestion improving. If I didn't know better, I'd say there was a man in her life." It felt good to have someone to share with, but it hit her that she was treating him like she would a husband. "I shouldn't be telling you what I see. It's become a bad habit. You have to promise to keep it in confidence. I have no one else I can share with. It wouldn't be right to talk about one of the girls to any of the others. I don't mean to be a gossip." She fumbled for how to say it. "I've gotten used to telling you things I don't tell anyone else." She frowned at the inadequacy of her words.

"It's OK, Lydia. I like that you trust me. I don't have anyone close and haven't for some time. Even when Sally and I were together, we didn't share confidences. We didn't have that kind of relationship. Looking back on it, I guess you couldn't really call it a relationship. It lacked a depth of feeling and measure of trust where you share your dreams and fears. I'm not sure I've ever had that with anyone." The colors in his aura heightened in clarity, with green growing stronger. *My God, don't tell me he's falling for me. I'm having enough trouble not falling for him. He doesn't date women in Palm Lakes.*

Suddenly she realized he'd stopped talking and was looking directly at her, his blue eyes boring into hers. She gulped, because she knew that he knew that she knew. *Oh, hell!* She broke contact and looked down at her glass.

He pressed on. "I know I keep saying it, but I'm only now really seeing the full extent of what your visual ability means. I can't hide anything from you. And the funny thing is, I'm beginning to be able to read you, even though I don't see colors around you. Maybe it's a way of leveling the playing field." He grinned boyishly and her heart nearly stopped.

So he was also reading her. He knew how she felt, the things she hadn't even admitted to herself yet. That was nerve-wracking. She hadn't realized how much she liked having the advantage with people.

"Eric, I know you don't date women in Palm Lakes. I'm not trying to make you change your rules." She felt so brave and righteous, but was afraid he would agree. Then what would she do? If he agreed, he might stop seeing her altogether. The thought didn't bear thinking. She had become so attached to having him to talk freely with. Not worrying about hiding her gift. In fact, she was enjoying him so much, she'd begun to worry about how she could admit to using pot, because sooner or later, she'd have to own up to that with him. Maybe now she wouldn't have to.

He reached over and took the glass out of her hand, putting it on the coffee table. "Maybe some rules are meant to be broken. Maybe some rules should never have been made. I've imposed a solitary life on myself, and don't get me wrong, I've done OK. But lately, I see what I miss by doing that. I lost three wives, all decent women. Being with you has helped me see how shallow I was in the past. I've always gotten involved with women first for sex and then on rare occasions it grew into something else, but there was never any depth or breadth to the relationships. And so they didn't hold up under pressure." He grimaced as if judging himself. "I feel stupid that I never wondered why it seemed to always turn out the same way. For so many reasons, I guess it was easier to find women who would treat me as a sex god, if only for a little while."

Lydia suppressed images of Eric naked. She could certainly picture him as a sex god, but didn't want to do it in front of him. Too late. He was picking up on her. The orange flared in his field. She spoke to cover her reaction. "I'm sure you're being too humble. There are plenty who would see you as a sex god."

His left eyebrow raised. "The only person I want to ask about that is you."

So there it was out in the open. "Eric, I have to be honest. I find myself talking to you as if we were...married, or at least lovers. I feel I can share anything with you. It's liberating. It's joyous. It's sexy. But we live practically next door to each other. I can't have a fling with you. I like you too much. I'd get hurt, because it would end sooner or later. Then every time I'd see you, it would pain me." She shut up. How could she explain her reluctance without sounding as if she were rejecting him? She wanted nothing more than to throw herself at him.

His sad look made her regret her words, but instead of retracting them, she stood up. "I think I should go home now." Without offering any further explanation, she headed for the front door, getting her wrap out of the closet on the way, the only thing in her mind to get out before she made a fool of herself.

Eric beat her to the door, putting his hand against it to keep her from leaving. "I didn't mean to scare you. I would never push you to do anything you didn't want."

A gusty sigh escaped from her. "You don't understand, Eric. I do want. But maybe your rule is right. If things went wrong, it would be too painful for both of us. We need to act like adults." She made the mistake of looking up into his eyes and saw the hunger as the bright green and orange licked around his head, the two colors together indicating more than just physical attraction.

She didn't know if she trusted what she saw. It looked a lot like what Helen and Alexander had, and she'd envied them for it. Was she going to turn away from what could be her last chance at happiness?

Tears of frustration pooled in her eyes and she averted her face so he wouldn't see them. Conflicting emotions were tearing her apart. It was as if she could see multiple paths leading into the future and had no idea which way things would go. They all seemed infinitely possible in that moment.

Then he put his arms around her and all but one of the paths disappeared.

* * *

Red, 11:55pm

ERIC LAY in the dark looking at the ceiling in his bedroom. Now he'd done it. He'd broken the prime directive. But somehow, he didn't feel guilty. He should be worried. What if it turned out like it had with Sally? But this felt so real. This was the first time in his life that a relationship had started with friendship instead of sex. Surely that would make a difference? Maybe he was just kidding himself. He was pretty much a loser at relationships.

179

The glimmer of light from the living room, where they'd left lights on in their rush to intimacy, created a silhouette of Lydia's body as she lay on her side facing away from him, sleeping quietly after they'd taken a long time and a lot of effort to wear each other out. Twice. The curves of her body were so beautiful. He reached over and touched her thick, silky hair and caressed the curve of her side as it swelled to her beautiful ass. She stirred, but didn't awaken. He was alert all over again. Oh, yeah. She did something to him. He hadn't wanted to admit to himself how she made him feel, but when he did, it had become overpowering.

He'd only wanted to reassure her. Her tears had cut him like a knife. He had only meant to hug her. The minute they came together, rational thought vanished. He'd swept her into his arms and carried her back to the bed, wanting the first time to be there, though he was hard pressed to maintain the control he needed not to just have her on the floor in the living room. The tears had stopped and she had responded to him with more passion than he'd imagined. And he'd imagined a lot. Her desire for him shook him as much as it gratified him.

Logic said it was too soon after Sally, but this felt right. Somehow they fit together physically as well as they did when they talked and shared confidences. She was a little thing, lush curves in all the right places. He reached for her and she responded, murmuring his name. He loved that she called him Eric. No one else did anymore. It felt intimate and sexy.

She turned to him and her dark brown eyes searched his in the shadows. "Any regrets?" Her voice was sensuous and scratchy, with just a touch of uncertainty.

"Lydia, I think I'm falling in love with you."

"I know. And I with you. I hope that's not a regret." She kissed him and wrapped her body around him. She certainly was strong and flexible. Maybe there was something to this yoga after all. That was the last thought he had for quite some time.

* * *

Owen, Midnight

OWEN CAME into his house through the garage after returning Tanya to her place. She'd wanted to spend the night here, but he'd begged off and driven her home, using her ex-husband being down the road as an excuse. He couldn't remember whose idea it had been to bring her here. It was true she'd been lobbying him for ages, and he'd kept putting it off. Even now, he didn't want her in his sanctuary.

But he'd given in, and he wasn't sorry. He was enjoying replaying the evening in his head. They had come over after dark. He'd led her around the house, watching her reaction. Unlike her place, which was sorely in need of proper cleaning, his house was in order. He'd watched her raise her eyebrows when looking at his alphabetized CDs in the spotless living room. He'd steeled himself for a sly comment about his model train setup, but she'd just admired it and asked him some questions. She'd made appropriate observations in his weight room, complimenting his body as she always did. By the time the tour was over, he could hardly keep his hands off her, but he'd delayed long enough to give her a present.

Tanya was like a little girl when you gave her a gift. Her eyes lit up with joy, and the frown lines that etched her face disappeared almost magically. And the new Tanya was even more submissive and feminine than the post-rehab Tanya he'd first become entangled with. He was loving it. For a while now, he hadn't smelled alcohol on her, and the critical edge was gone from her voice. She'd stopped whining at him to marry her or even to bring her to his house. Maybe that's why he'd done it. He was finding himself doing things he had never planned on doing, and liking it.

As she unwrapped the ribbon and paper and opened the small box to find a gold ankle bracelet, she exclaimed with joy, "Owen, you are so wonderful! I love it!" Then she threw her arms around him. After a brief hug, she looked at him seductively and picked up the small suitcase she called a purse and nodded towards the master suite. "I thought maybe I could change into something more comfortable. May I?"

He swallowed and nodded his head affirmatively, his heart pounding faster and harder. The door shut to the master bathroom. He guessed she must have gotten a new bit of lingerie. She knew he loved it when she dressed scantily. He slipped out of his shoes and began to undress.

As he sat in his shorts on the bed staring at the doorway to his walk-in closet, his blood cooled and he began to worry. She hadn't been too nosy, but he couldn't have her look hard in his closet, because she mustn't find the hatch he'd added in the wall, behind which were his special mementos. It had been so long since he'd visited them, he'd almost forgotten about them. They were like echoes of a former life. Maybe he should get rid of them. But even now, when he rarely looked at them, he couldn't bear the thought. Their very existence defined him.

Just then, the bathroom door opened, dispelling his worries, and she stuck her leg out the doorway, holding it up at a sexy angle to show him the ankle bracelet. She had great legs. But her tits were what drove him crazy. She stepped out wearing little scraps of black lace that didn't begin to cover her. He couldn't wait to tear them off her. He'd had enough of playing the gentleman with her.

The rest of the evening was a blur. He remembered he finally got to fulfill his fantasy of fucking her up against the wall in his bedroom. It seemed to inflame her when he tore the lace off with his teeth and treated her roughly. He'd never seen her so hot. And his speculation of several months ago had been answered long since. She was a screamer, and he loved those animal noises she made while he was pumping her.

Just thinking about the evening had him horny again, but she had wanted him to wait a while before seeing her again. She said she was worried her husband might have someone following her. Maybe he did.

Coming back to present time, he began to think that the only way he could have what he wanted was to give in and marry her. If he did that, he'd have to make some big changes. He wouldn't think about it now.

He got his cleaning supplies and thoroughly cleaned the bathroom, wiping all trace of her from it. Even the scent of her perfume was gone by the time he finished. In the kitchen, he polished the counters. The few things out of place in the living room he quickly restored to order. He stripped the sheets from the bed and threw them in the washer, then remade the bed with clean ones. The only evidence of her visit was the scrap of lingerie he'd asked for as a souvenir, which he put in a small ziploc bag with her name and the date neatly inscribed on it. He went into the closet, removed the hatch and put it next to the other items he'd collected over the years, some of them much more personal than scraps of clothing, each one labeled carefully.

Minutes later, he was in the closet undressing when the withering voice spoke to him. "So now you're bringing your whore into this house." It had been over two months since he'd heard her complaints in his head. He'd prayed she was gone forever. Nausea and anger threatened to overpower him. He ran to the bathroom and threw up in the toilet, then immediately retrieved his cleaning products and started scrubbing with more emphasis than needed. Maybe if he ignored her, she'd go away.

"I'm here to stay, Junior. I'm your mother, and you have to treat me with respect."

"How many times do I have to kill you to get you off my back?" He held his head in his hands. Suddenly it was pounding. He couldn't believe she'd returned. The blessed silence he'd enjoyed since beginning the affair with Tanya was shattered.

"You're a fool if you think that bimbo loves you. There's nothing to love about you. She just pretends you're a man so she can get what she wants."

Fuming, Owen couldn't stick with his commitment to ignore her. "You're wrong. She thinks I'm great." He paused as unpleasant memories returned, threatening to empty his stomach again. "You're jealous. You can't stand that I found a woman who cares about me. You have no right to criticize Tanya. At least she isn't trying to fuck her own son."

The anger seemed to settle the nausea, but he still didn't like to think about how Mother had touched him when he was a teenager. He strode through the house and went into the weight room to escape her. It was the one place she never talked to him, his safe room.

He sat on the bench, panting from anger and fear. She'd been dead for years. He'd shoved her when she came on to him (again) in a drunken state, and she'd fallen down the stairs and broken her neck. Why couldn't she shut the fuck up? He wasn't going to let her ruin his life any more. He wasn't giving up Tanya no matter what Mother said.

7

SUNDAY, JANUARY 21, 1996

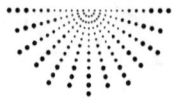

Emma, 12:30pm

*T*he hike had been strenuous today, the weather perfect. It was one of those days that showed the promise of spring. Emma found it hard to imagine spring was just around the corner, but Julio assured her it started in February.

The man in question came out of the bathroom after washing up for lunch and sat at the counter, watching her prepare the meal. His long, wavy dark hair was caught in a leather tie, wisps of hair escaping and framing his face. His bronzed skin was smooth, reminding her of the age difference between them. His hands rested on the counter, a bit restless with nothing to occupy them. She decided to take pity on him. "Would you set the table while I finish with this?" He jumped up and went to the cabinets where he'd seen her get the dinner things previous Sundays and laid them out on the table silently.

Picking up a thread of conversation started on the hike, Emma said, "So I was telling you that I went to see Samantha's naturopathic doctor? And he was very encouraging about helping me improve my digestion and overcome the food allergies. His whole approach was totally different from what conventional doctors do. He uses natural remedies to balance the organs and systems, and instead of just looking at my stomach, because that's what hurts, he looks at other parts of the body that relate to digestion. It was really eye-opening. I want to thank you again for sending Samantha over. She must be going through a lot lately, with her Dad dying."

Julio paused in laying out the silverware. "She was all set to take another job, a good job from the sound of it, but she asked for her old one back so she can take care of her mother. I am glad not to lose her, but she seems sad, and I do not think it is only about her father." He shrugged. "I do not ask, though."

Emma carried the chicken salad over to the table. She went back for a plate on which she'd placed some bread, a nod to Julio's personal preferences. He grinned as he accepted it. After bringing the pitcher of iced tea over, she sat, and he sat after her.

Sometimes his courtliness surprised her; it was a marked contrast to how American men acted, and seemingly strange for a man who made a living working on the land. In spite of not having the benefit of a college education or wealth, he was like a European gentleman. That thought was an inevitable reminder of how he had taken his leave the previous Sunday. Instead of shaking her hand before he left as he usually did, he took it in his hand and then kissed it. Why it seemed so natural, she didn't know, any more than she understood why it made her hand tingle. She wasn't ready to admit she was drawn to him.

She picked at her food as usual, but enjoyed watching him eat with gusto. It was such a pleasure to watch a man enjoy a meal. Leo used to eat like that. She hated cooking for herself alone. Until she resolved her stomach problems, it seemed such a waste of time, cooking when there was no pleasure in eating. Just as she was thinking sadly of eating alone for the next week, he looked up at her with his chocolate eyes, as if he'd heard her thoughts. "This is really good, Emma. Thanks for making such a nice lunch. I do not eat as well when I am on my own. You spoil me." He went back to eating.

"You're welcome. It's more fun to cook for two than for one." True as it was, she hoped she hadn't said too much. She still wasn't sure why he bothered to hang around with her. He never made a pass at her, but he did seem to want to be with her. And she had grown to relish the times they spent together.

"You know, if you got married or found a steady girlfriend like your brothers, you wouldn't have to eat alone." She meant to tease him.

"I grew up in a poor family. My mother worked herself to death. I never wanted to have children. I suppose I think children are a burden. I guess that's why I never married." He went back to his meal with less enthusiasm.

Emma now felt awful for bringing it up, but touched that he would share something so private. "My childhood was a bit of a nightmare. I ran away when I was 16. I practically lived on the street for a long time, taking whatever jobs paid, until I lucked into waitressing at a fancy restaurant. That's where I met Leo. He was a regular, and he started asking to be seated in my section. Eventually, we became friends. Later, he asked me to marry him. It all seems so long ago."

Julio was staring at her. She realized she'd never shared this much with him. He smiled gently, as if in thanks for the trust. "What made you decide to come to Palm Lakes?"

"Leo died, and I had no one in Oregon. I always felt I needed to live somewhere warmer and sunnier. I read about Palm Lakes in some magazine, and here I am. I love it here."

Julio's warm look indicated he may have misinterpreted that last statement, but he said nothing for a minute. "I am glad you love it here. I do, too." He gave her a meaningful look.

"Julio, I don't know why you want to spend time with me. I'm too old for you. We don't have a lot in common. I'm sure you could have any woman you want. You'd do better to invest in someone else. I'm no good for what you want." The truth of it gave Emma a pang of regret for the first time in her life.

Julio stopped eating and gave her his full attention, the way he always did when he wanted to say something important. It must be a cultural thing. Or maybe it was just Julio. "Emma, what do you think I want from you?"

She felt her face burn red. How could she have gotten herself into this position? Now she was accusing him of wanting to sleep with her, when in reality, he had never done anything to hint he was interested. "I apologize. I shouldn't have said that. I didn't mean to imply anything. You're just so young and handsome, and...I don't know what I meant." She was so miserable she couldn't bear to look him in the eyes.

"Emma, I am aware that we are from different cultures and religions. And that you have more money than I do. But we both love the desert. We enjoy hiking through the wild land. We love plants and making landscapes into poetry. We enjoy being quiet together. Maybe that is more in common than you think."

His words wrenched her heart. It was true. She never felt he was pushing her for something she couldn't give. "I'm sorry. I really am. I shouldn't make it seem like sex is the only thing a man and woman can share. I apologize for implying it. I am grateful for the time you spend with me. I just can't understand why you do it. There are others who would give you more." There it was again. Why did she have to keep bringing up sex?

Julio looked at her meaningfully. "I have always loved women. I respect them, too. If you want to know the truth, I don't have to chase them. They chase me. And I know they are just using me. I am just a Mexican to them. They feel good to be with a younger man. But they want nothing more. Which has always been fine with me. I preferred not to get involved. That is why I never spent time with widows or single women. Until you. Lately I feel there must be something more to life. I have not determined what it is, but I am looking."

Emma was stunned. Then she sputtered in laughter. "I'm your mid-life crisis?"

"An interesting way to put it. Perhaps. I am trying to find a path to take into the second half of my life. I do not really want to stay on the one I have been on. It makes me feel...empty."

She looked at him with new respect. "I am also trying to find a new path. With Leo gone, I have wondered what I am meant to do with my life. Maybe that has made me bold enough to spend time with you. I would not have in the past."

His hurt look prompted her to rush to explain. "It's not you. It's me. I can't be around men. I'm not really much better with women, but men scare me, always have. Ever since my uncle. He gave me this." She pointed to the scar on her left cheek. She hadn't intended to ever tell him, but he'd been so kind, she couldn't have him thinking she was a racist. Far better he know she had a phobia.

"What happened?" The gentleness in his voice nearly broke her.

She blurted the whole truth out. Maybe it would chase him away, and perhaps that was for the best. "I'm no good for sex. Not since my uncle. My whole childhood, he..." She saw a flash of violence in Julio's eyes, and his hands clenched on the table top. She couldn't go on. "I ran away as soon as I could. He hit me for resisting one time. He had a big ring on, and it cut me. My mother never believed me."

"That is horrible. I am sorry. But I thought you were married?" Of course it would look that way to Julio.

"Promise you won't ever tell anyone what I've said?"

"Of course not."

"Leo and I were best friends for a long time. He asked me to marry him because he was gay, and being gay in his career was not a good thing. It worked for both of us. I didn't want sex. He needed a wife. We were best friends. I was happy with him. I felt safe."

"You're safe with me."

"I know that." It came out faster than thought. She really did feel safe with Julio. "I hadn't intended to tell you. But you can't expect anything like that from me. I have a phobia about sex, and...I'm sorry. I shouldn't be implying that's what you want from me. It's ludicrous." Embarrassment swamped her again. She'd never told anyone except Leo her story.

"Emma. I will never, ever force you to do anything against your will. You are totally safe with me. But since you have been so honest with me, I want to be honest with you. I would like it if you trusted me enough to let me show you that not all men are monsters, and that being with a man can be very pleasurable."

She swallowed hard, not knowing how to respond. He went back to eating, which gave her a chance to recover.

AFTER THEY FINISHED DOING the dishes (it had surprised her that he was so willing to do 'women's work'), they went into the living room with cups of tea. He sat on the sofa and put his tea on the table, then patted next to him, indicating she should sit by him.

She brought her tea over, abandoning her usual spot in the wing chair, and sat next to him, far enough away to feel safe.

"Do you mind if I ask you a question?"

She shivered in fear. "Go ahead."

"I have noticed you don't shrink from my touch like you used to. You shake hands. You let me take your hand to pull you up on a rock ledge or help you down a steep slope. Does that mean you feel safer with me now?"

"Yes, it does."

"Then things are able to change."

"I wouldn't assume they can change much more." She was feeling pressured now and wished he would leave. But she wasn't afraid he would force her to do anything.

"If I asked to hold your hand now, could you do it?"

"Yes."

He held his hand out to her and waited. She looked at it. She had indeed allowed his touch recently without flinching. It was positive change. He didn't move any closer to her. She knew if she refused, he wouldn't press her further, but she wanted to see if she could do it. She reached out slowly as if watching someone else and touched his hand. It was warm and dry. He didn't move at all, didn't try to grab or hold her. She ran her palm across his, feeling little sparks of something from the friction. She could see a reflection of them in his eyes. Still he didn't move. She wrapped her hand around his and clasped it, feeling powerful, because it was her choice to do so. After a few seconds, his hand responded and gently held hers.

He let go of her hand before she let go of his, and she felt abandoned. But she also felt free. She gave him a smile. "Thank you for your kindness." The tea was totally forgotten.

"Any time." He got up. "I think I better be going."

She was suddenly sad. Had she offended him? "You aren't mad at me?"

He looked at her quizzically. "Why would you think that?"

"Because I'm so difficult." She felt like such a failure as a woman.

"I do not want to overstay my welcome. You have honored me with your trust, and I appreciate it. We can go on a hike next Sunday?"

Her spirits lifted. "Yes, I'd like that."

She followed him to the front door, half wanting him to go so she could ponder the events of the day, and half desperate to make him stay so she could continue to be the object of his warmth.

He slipped into the jacket he'd left in the front closet, then turned to say goodbye. "Would you mind if I gave you a kiss before I leave?"

It didn't occur to her to say no. She just nodded her head, unable to form the words.

He reached over and gently brushed her hair back from her scar and traced it with a finger, then leaned over and kissed it, his hand still touching her cheek.

She inexplicably felt disappointment that must have shown on her face, because he cocked his head to the side in question, then as if reading her mind, he leaned in and gently kissed her lips. The contact electrified her, and she lost all sense of separateness. For some reason, the expected fear never materialized. For the first time in her life, she felt desire as she opened herself to him and their limbs and tongues entwined in a bid to become one instead of two.

The illusion vanished when he broke the kiss, leaving her muzzy-headed and feeling in need of something to support her. "That is probably enough for one day. I will see you next week, Emma." He caressed her face again, turned and left.

Her legs felt ready to give out under her. She closed the door and went and collapsed on the sofa. "Oh, Leo, what have I done? This cannot end well."

* * *

Julio, 1:45pm

JULIO GOT into the truck and drove away from Emma's house without looking back. It had taken all of his strength to walk out of that house. She wanted him. Whether she realized it or not. Yet he didn't feel triumphant. He felt he'd been given a gift, an almost sacred trust. And he wasn't sure where to go from here.

She meant something to him. He wanted her to look at him with love and desire, because from her, that would mean something special, something he had never experienced.

He felt drawn to her magnetically. Yet she was right. They had so little in common. His family would hate her. They'd think she was using him like other women had. Everyone she knew would think he was after her money. Sooner or later his brothers would find out, and there would be hell to pay. But that paled in comparison to his thoughts of how he would feel if he hurt her.

Back at his apartment, he slumped into a chair and stared off into space. He and Emma were in a world of their own. She had no one to turn to but him. He had no one but her. Maybe they needed to turn to each other.

Before he could change his mind, he got up and went to the phone and dialed her number from memory.

"Julio." Her voice sounded hopeful and afraid at the same time. He cringed at being the cause of her fear.

"I called to see how you are feeling. I am sorry I took liberties. Are you OK?" He held his breath hoping for a positive reply.

"Why wouldn't I be?"

"I should not have kissed you. I know you have been hurt in the past. I do not ever want to hurt you."

"I know that, Julio. I'm not sure it's possible for people to promise they will never hurt each other. Maybe letting your guard down means you might get hurt. What matters is we never do it intentionally. I trust you." He could feel her wanting to reveal something to him, but nothing further came out.

"I did not want to leave you. I only left because if I had stayed, I would have had trouble holding back. I want you to have time to decide what you want. I will not rush you, but I have to tell you the truth. I want more than friendship. I will not press you for more, and I will not leave if friendship is all you want, but you need to know." There, it was out in the open now. Maybe she'd reject him and save them both a lot of trouble.

The silence was deafening. He said nothing, waiting for her to pass sentence on him. He realized he'd never put himself in a position of being rejected, and he was scared.

Finally, she spoke. "I didn't want you to leave, either. I'm afraid, Julio. I'm no good at sex. Leo and I tried one time. He knew I wanted a baby, and he liked kids, so we thought why not?" She laughed nervously. "It was a disaster. I wasn't what he wanted or needed that way, and I was terrified of being touched. We laughed about it afterwards, but at the time it was awful. I don't want to repeat that with you." She sighed sadly.

He treasured her honesty. "I have no one to talk with about you. You have no one to talk with about me. All we have is each other. It is important we talk to each other. I am glad I called. I do not want us to have any secrets."

"You're right. If we can't talk to each other, we won't have anything. I'm a little afraid of what will happen between us and a lot afraid of the future. But you've become my best friend here, and I don't want to give that up."

Thank God. "Then may I see you more often?" He hoped she would not feel he was pushing.

"I was afraid of what the neighbors would think at first, but now I laugh at myself for being so silly. We're adults and can do what we please. Neither of us is married. So what if others see us together? Whatever happens, we aren't hurting anyone. We have a right to be friends. And if you're willing to be patient, maybe we can be more. I just can't promise."

"Thank you, Emma. I am grateful for your trust. When can I come over again?"

"Would tomorrow night be too soon?"

"I would come back right now if you asked." Silence greeted him, and he wondered if he'd said too much.

Then she started laughing, so free and relaxed that he felt maybe things would be all right. "I'm not very good at asking. But I'll try to learn. Why don't you come back now and teach me?"

8

TUESDAY, JANUARY 23, 1996

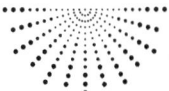

Lydia, 10:25am UK time

*L*ydia clutched her carryon bag and dragged her rolling suitcase as she ran through the automatic doors to the terminal at Heathrow Airport. The freezing wind spit icy rain on her as it blew Jean and Ian into the building behind her. Each was pulling a single, small wheeled bag. Stepping out of the mass of travelers, they paused to get their bearings. Ian peered around, his hazel eyes sharp, and made a decision. "Let's go this way. We need to get you checked in, Lydia. We're all set; we just need to check in at the gate."

He led them to the right, past a long series of airline counters. Lydia couldn't help noticing--not for the first time--that Ian had a nice build. Wide shoulders, narrow waist, thigh muscles stretching the legs of his jeans. They had to run to keep up with his long strides. He was really fit for a man of his age.

In a few minutes, they came to the British Airways section. "You guys don't have to come any farther with me. You need to find your gate."

Jean waved her hand in dismissal. "We're going to get you checked in first and confirm that there hasn't been any change in the flight, and then we'll go most of the way to your gate and visit for a little bit. Our plane doesn't leave for three hours, and your departure is still more than two hours from now."

"Well, I'll take all the time I can get. Just don't cut it too short."

"We have it figured out. There's time before we leave for Florence."

"Don't make me jealous. Florence is such a wonderful place for a honeymoon. Did you see that movie, 'While You Were Sleeping'? I just loved it. In the end, he took her to Florence for their honeymoon."

Jean laughed. "Well, in fact, that was part of the reason I thought to suggest it, though Paris certainly would have been terrific, too. But we wanted to go somewhere neither of us has been, and Ian has been to Paris a number of times."

"Lucky boy," said Lydia. "My time here has flown by. It was so great to be at your wedding."

Jean wrapped Lydia in a hug. "You'll never know how much it meant to me to have you here."

Ian nodded. "Thanks for going to the trouble of coming for such a short time. I'm glad we got to do a few things to make the trip worthwhile."

"It was amazing. I've never seen London before, and I always wanted to. I loved the British Museum. I have to admit I've gotten hooked on Indian food. Your fish and chips are unbelievable, too! I have to warn you, you won't find as good in Palm Lakes." She looked at Ian and Jean, pleased to see the harmony and love in their auras. "It has meant a lot to me to see you guys." The woman at the counter called Lydia forward, and she got her baggage checked.

After checkin, Ian looked at Lydia's boarding pass. "Your gate is this way. We'll only go part way, because we can't follow you through security." They hiked for several minutes before Ian stopped. "This area will do." They found a few seats in a fairly quiet section and sat down.

"It's been good getting to know you better, Ian. And meeting you in person after hearing such nice things from Jean has been a treat."

He shrugged off the compliment. "It's very nice to know another American besides Jean before I make my new home in Palm Lakes."

"I can't imagine how hard it is to give up the country of your birth."

She could see he had a lot going on underneath the surface, but nothing that affected his commitment to be with Jean.

"As you know, I don't have family left here, so that makes it easier. And my current job isn't exactly a career path. I've enjoyed doing it, but I can do the same things anywhere. Which is why Jean and I thought it might be fun to start a business."

"Your experience with computers is going to be indispensable. The worldwide web is becoming quite the thing for small businesses, and although I'm no expert, I think it could be a real asset to have a website."

"My experience isn't as broad as I'd like, but I'm pretty confident I can figure things out. We'll want a website no matter what direction we go in. I don't mind learning the software required to build one. It will save us a lot of money."

Lydia felt excitement building as she pictured their plans. "I'm glad you're doing that part. I'd be totally lost. Jean and I will split up the remaining tasks: marketing, bookkeeping and secretarial stuff. I've been using Quicken for my personal finances for a while, and I could do just about any of the tasks remaining. Jean, do you have a feel for what you'd like to do?"

"I don't know anything about marketing, but I could do correspondence and secretarial stuff. I'm guessing we'd be using email and the computer, and I'm pretty good on correspondence and word processing. I have no experience with financial software, so if that part is OK for you, maybe that should be your baby."

Lydia smiled and spread her hands out. "Looks like we have a lot settled. None of us has selling experience as such, so we can all learn together. I'll see if I can find some courses or books when I get home."

Ian shifted in his seat, looking a little uncomfortable. "It was kind of you to offer to loan the business enough to get started, Lydia. Are you sure it won't be a problem?"

"It's no problem at all. I won't put any more in than I can afford to lose."

Jean eyes widened. "I know you told us you have money, but every time we talk about it, it sounds like more. Are you rich?"

Lydia cringed. "I don't like to label myself. I feel enough like a fringe person without people knowing I come from money. My family accumulated wealth the past couple generations--I'm a trust fund baby and an only child--so I've never been forced to work for a living. I had it pretty easy growing up, at least in terms of money. I got the best education, always had a nice car, lovely clothes. But just as my visual gift seems to cause problems in relationships, so can having a lot of money. And perhaps strangely, I've never cared that much about money. I am happy living as I do. So I tend not to tell anyone unless I have to. Not that I doubted your friendship, Jean." Lydia looked pleadingly at her.

Jean laughed. "Don't worry about it, Lydia. I don't care whether you're rich or poor. You're my best friend. Actually, I like having a best friend who's rich."

Lydia grinned, feeling relief. "I should have told you earlier, but it never came up."

"Why should it? I feel very lucky that you're able to make a loan to our business to get us rolling. We're going to make a go of this and pay you back."

"There's no worries. I'm doing it because I want to. I believe we can succeed, but either way, I want to invest in this venture. Enough about me. Jean, have you and Ian put together a list of places you want to visit once you get to Palm Lakes?"

"We have talked about it, but we don't have a list as such. He definitely wants to see the Grand Canyon and Sedona. I'm so looking forward to showing him around. He's done such a marvelous job of showing me his country."

Ian smiled lovingly at Jean. "I enjoy showing my favorite places to appreciative people. And Jean has allowed me to see them with fresh eyes. It's been a way for me to say goodbye, at least for now. I know we won't be back for a while."

Lydia shook her head. "I am still thinking of all the ways that this is a massive change for you, Ian. You are so courageous."

He smiled disarmingly, his hazel eyes twinkling. "I have to be. Jean was the one who took the biggest risk, and I can do no less than she did. She didn't really know me, hadn't even met me before she came here. She only had one picture of me. I could have been totally different from what she thought. She gave up so much to come here, not knowing it would work out. Now that it's obvious how well matched we are, where we live is a much smaller decision. And I have to admit that I've always fancied living in America. So I feel blessed."

Jean reached over and stroked Ian's arm, then tugged playfully on his ponytail. "It's all worked out perfectly for us, and it will only get better." The caress turned into a hug, then a kiss.

Lydia regarded them snuggling with slight envy. Having had to leave so soon after she became involved with Eric, she was reluctant to mention him to Jean, especially in front of Ian. Now that she was headed back, worry was creeping in. Would he have reconsidered breaking his rule about not dating Palm Lakes women? Would she find that the fireworks between them were a temporary thing? She was almost afraid to go home and find out. Seeing how happy Jean and Ian were made her long for a loving relationship. She sighed and held her secret.

"Sorry, Lyd. Don't mean to be a public spectacle."

"Just envying you two." Lydia smiled at her.

"I hate to say it, but we should probably leave," said Ian, looking at Jean for agreement.

Jean nodded and slowly rose. After a final goodbye with hugs all around, Jean and Ian left.

Lydia sat, unable to find the motivation to trek to the gate. Ever since she'd left two days after her fateful night with Eric, she'd struggled with second guessing and second thoughts. The whirlwind visit with wedding and sightseeing and restaurants had kept the worries at bay. But now that Jean and Ian were gone, her worries rose to the surface like ice floating on water. She rubbed her burning eyes, pushing aside thoughts of how traveling hadn't seemed so tiring when she was younger. Her love life had never been smooth, but you'd think it might get easier as she got older.

She wondered what would happen when she returned. Eric had taken her to the airport and kissed her goodbye like he was really going to miss her, but he'd broken his big rule about not dating women in Palm Lakes, let alone not sleeping with them. And even if he felt the same, would she? She'd been trying not to berate herself for falling into bed with a man who was barely out of another relationship, but her rational mind was saying she was an idiot. How could she trust that this was real? His words about rebound romances haunted her. She didn't want to be just a transitional relationship to him.

She shook her head. Too much analysis. It was so unlike her. But she hadn't had a relationship in years, and seeing Jean and Ian together made her want to be with someone special, to be loved that way.

9

SATURDAY, JANUARY 27, 1996

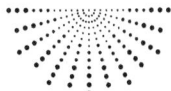

Mary Beth, 9:30am

*M*ary Beth heard the mailman stop out front and then drive off down the road, so she went out into the brilliant sunshine without a jacket to pick up the mail and reveled at the hint of warmth in the air. She loved the way it even smelled like spring was on the way. How could spring have a scent? There were no flowers in bloom, yet the fragrance of life filled the air.

Her new neighbor, Canadian snow bird Irene, came out of Mom's condo--she needed to stop calling it that, but couldn't think of it any other way. Mary Beth waved at her, and Irene came bustling over. "Mary Beth, how are you doing? We surely do love your Mom's condo. It's perfect for us!" Her brown eyes twinkled as she delivered the compliment.

Being about Mary Beth's height, Irene and she were eye to eye, and Mary Beth found herself looking at Irene's earrings and necklace. They were a lovely southwestern design in silver and turquoise that somehow looked perfect with her short, curly white hair. "I love your jewelry."

Irene touched her necklace self-consciously. "I treated myself to this. I wear it a lot, because I love it so much. I don't usually buy jewelry, especially not for myself." She winked.

Across the street, a door opened and Catherine waddled down the walk to her mailbox. She waved at the two women.

"Hi, Catherine! How are you doing?"

"Fine, Mary Beth. And you?"

"Great! Have you met Irene?"

"Yes, I have. You know me, Mary Beth. I'm a nosy old busybody. Hi, Irene. I hope you and Henry are settling in nicely. Isn't this a gorgeous day?" She spread her arms to indicate the sunshine, blue skies and crisp but pleasant temperature.

Irene laughed infectiously. "Toronto is buried in snow as we speak. This is heaven by comparison. I don't even mind when we have colder, gray days. It's always better than winter in Ontario."

After a few more pleasantries, they separated and returned to their respective condos. Mary Beth closed her door and flipped through the stack of envelopes. Mostly it was for her mother, which always depressed her, as it reminded her Mom was gone forever. She rarely got personal mail, which made her feel lonely. Then she came to an envelope addressed to "Occupant." It was from the HOA. Immediately she felt the bottom drop out of her stomach. She ripped the envelope open and scanned the official-looking letter, not really taking it in.

She sank down on the couch. "Son of a bitch!" She forced herself to reread the single page carefully, hoping she had misunderstood the intent. She had not. Some asshole had turned her in. This letter was a copy of one being sent to Helen at her new address (how did they even know that?). The Homeowners' Association was demanding that Mary Beth leave, since she was not within the age limits set out in the covenants. Who the hell had turned her in? She knew it wasn't Catherine.

So soon after losing her Mom and having to move, this was devastating. She had a small nest egg after selling Mom's condo, but she couldn't afford anything this nice. She'd have to find a crummy apartment nearby. For the first time in a while, she felt desperate for a cigarette. She knew how it was when people moved away. She hadn't seen Helen more than a couple times since she married, and Helen used to be such a great friend. If Mary Beth moved, she wouldn't be able to help Catherine or spend time with her. Ethan, Maddie and Samantha all lived in Palm Lakes. She didn't want to leave. But now she had no choice.

She needed to call Helen and warn her, since it was her property and they'd hold her in violation of the covenants. Then she had to find somewhere to live before the HOA did something bad to Helen. Her Mom had told her the covenants gave the HOA the right to stringent measures, including fining and suing people and even putting a lien on a house. She felt a headache coming on.

By midday, Catherine was sitting at the dining room table where Mary Beth and Helen used to drink wine in the evenings and chat. Catherine's sympathy over the latest HOA nonsense had helped Mary Beth calm down, and she didn't want her to leave. "Can I invite you to stay for lunch, Catherine? I'm just having a grilled cheese sandwich, but you're welcome to have one, too."

"My dear, that sounds lovely. I would be pleased to join you." Catherine sipped her coffee pensively. Mary Beth got up to fix the sandwiches. "I'll be very sorry to see you leave."

Mary Beth flinched. "I'm sorry, too. I can still drive you places. I don't intend to go far, but we won't be across the street from each other, and that will mean I won't get to see you as often. Life sucks sometimes. Pardon my French."

"You're so right, dear. It just isn't fair. You are a good citizen and so helpful to me, and I'm sure you will be missed. I wish they'd mind their own damn business."

Mary Beth grinned. "My jewelry mentor Maddie says the same thing."

"She sounds like a smart lady."

Mary Beth put together the sandwiches and turned on the frying pan, her back to Catherine.

"When are you going to speak to your young man about this? Maybe it would get him to do something."

Mary Beth laughed nervously. "I don't want it to appear I'm fishing. I haven't figured out how to tell him, but I'll have to, because I can't tell Maddie and not tell him. I'm going over to Maddie's this afternoon." The smell of melting butter and cheese wafted up from the frying pan. She inhaled the delicious smell to distract herself.

"Do you have enough money?"

She turned and looked at Catherine, who was staring at her owlishly from behind thick lenses. "Thanks for being concerned, Catherine. I got a bit from selling Mom's place. Not enough to own a place of my own, but I can afford to rent an apartment in spite of the low pay I get at Palo Verde. At least for a while. I'll have to figure a budget.

"I've been invited to a Botanica presentation with a friend this afternoon--you know, Maddie's daughter, Samantha, who works with me? Barbara invited her and told her to bring a friend. It sounds like one of those home businesses or an MLM. I might have to consider doing something like that to supplement my income. What pisses me off is I really like my life the way it is right now. I don't want to get another job or move again." She turned back and flipped the sandwiches, trying hard to suppress tears.

"I know it isn't my business, but I think you should tell your young man. He would help."

Mary Beth laughed out loud. "Catherine, you're a hoot. I know Ethan was there for me when Mom died, but I can't expect him to solve this problem, and we aren't even really dating as far as I can tell. I wouldn't dream of trying to wangle a marriage proposal out of him just so I could stay in Palm Lakes."

"Do you love him?"

The question hit Mary Beth hard. It was one that needed asking, but she'd avoided thinking about it for a long time. "I don't know. Maybe. I like being with him. He's so kind and supportive. He acts like I'm special. I think he's smart and handsome. But all we do is dance around the subject like it's dangerous, never really doing anything to move the relationship beyond friendship. It's my fault as much as his, but I have to admit I wonder if it means we aren't suited well.

"He isn't really my type--no, that came out wrong. What I mean is, I'm not sure I can be attracted to nice guys. Jason was flashy, and he acted nice during our courtship, but he wasn't truly nice like Ethan. Jason's niceness was a flamboyant act, while Ethan's niceness is low-key, but genuine. I sometimes think there's a defect in me, that I can only be attracted to assholes. Pardon my French."

She plated the sandwiches and added a handful of potato chips and a dill pickle to each plate. She sat down without the slightest appetite. Everything was so fucked up. She stared at her sandwich, then watched Catherine devour hers with her usual enthusiasm. Mary Beth's coffee had gotten cold. She felt as if everything was turning to shit, but forced herself to pick up her sandwich.

"Just tell him what's going on. Give him a chance to do the right thing."

Mary Beth, in the process of biting into the sandwich, almost choked. "That sounds like a shotgun wedding to me. We haven't yet gotten that far."

Catherine cackled. "It's about time you decide to pee or get off the pot. Talk to him about this situation and see what he says."

Mary Beth laughed. "Well, I intend to tell everyone in a timely fashion. I'll tell him and Maddie today and then on Monday at work, I'll tell Samantha."

* * *

Helen, 10:12am

HELEN PULLED her journal off the shelf and began to write as she glanced out the window to the yard, which was dappled in early morning sunshine.

January 27, 1996

It's been more than two months since I did any real journaling or writing. I used to write before bed, but now that doesn't fit into my schedule.

She paused as she thought about elaborating, then decided not to. Some things she wanted to hug to herself. She was used to sharing her pain with her journals, but ecstasy seemed too private to write about.

To be honest, it wasn't about time. It was about motivation and focus. It was about having something to say. For the longest time I worried that I was never going to write again. I stared at the blank page and had nothing to say. I

203

wondered if now that I have a loving husband, I didn't need an escape anymore, so the motivation was gone. It hasn't been easy.

I went through a period of adjustment. It makes me feel such an ingrate. How could anyone complain that it isn't easy to adjust to being wealthy and loved by a man everyone calls 'movie star handsome'? Mary Beth pointed out I wasn't used to being happy. She was so right. I've never been happy for more than a few hours at a time. How could I have lived most of my life that way? It's like a whole different life now, but part of me is afraid. And another part is confused and wants things as they were before. Why are old patterns so hard to break, even when it's obvious they need to be broken?

I wish we'd never found the box with Lou's secret treasures. It's nice to have my own assets, but for some reason, his betrayal with that woman haunts me. I wrote her and haven't heard back. I probably won't. I need closure, but I feel funny talking with Alexander about it, because he obviously doesn't understand why I feel this way. Honestly, I'm not sure why I feel this way, either.

Olivia recovered from her infection and came home a few days ago. She's lost a lot of weight and is really frail. I go see her every day when we take Spot for her walk. We're only doing one walk a day now that she's gone back to Olivia. I'm so lonely without her. Spot, not Olivia.

Olivia's eldest, Susanna, came by with a very nice bottle of wine and some expensive chocolates to thank us for taking care of Spot while Olivia was hospitalized. She seemed so genuine about being pained as to what would happen to the dog if her Mom died, something her sisters don't seem too worried about. I promised her if it came to that, I'd gladly take Spot. She was immensely relieved. She lives farther away than Diana, but closer than Joanna (the middle sister). I haven't had much time with Joanna, but Susanna strikes me as the most loving and intent on her mother's happiness, though she doesn't seem to get credit for it.

Olivia tells me they are all pressuring her to sell the house and move to assisted living, and though I can see the sense of it, I sympathize with her. It's hard when your kids are trying to force you to do something you don't want to do. She won't be able to take Spot most places; that alone would be enough to make me resist. Maybe eventually Spot will return to us.

Her youngest daughter has been there a few times when I visit. She reminds me of Sally. She's a bright and lovely girl, but there's a forced feeling about the positivity she projects. Like she's never saying what she truly feels about anything. I don't know that I would have noticed if I were not with Alexander. Loving him has opened my eyes to a lot of things. I guess we're all a little blind to the faults of those we love. I had high hopes that Sally and I would grow closer over time, but except for her tapping me for help when she needs it, nothing much has ever developed between us. I rarely see her now, even though she lives close by. The baby is due in two months, and I don't even know if she has a new boyfriend since she broke up with Red. Such a nice man, but he's probably better off without her. What a horrible thing to say about your own daughter!

Lydia would be a good match for Red. She brought him to yoga, and he tried so hard, but he wasn't that flexible. We laughed 'til we almost peed our pants, but he was unfazed by it. I haven't seen a man who was a better sport. He looks at her like he really sees her, the way Alexander looks at me. She hasn't said they're dating, but they seem to be fast friends. Lydia's always seemed the independent sort, but since she told me about her special gift, I've begun to wonder if she lives in self-imposed isolation because of that.

I just got off the phone with Mary Beth, who was notified by the HOA that she must move. I will have a copy of the notice in today's mail, too. This is a sign that it's time for me to sell the condo. I feel so sorry for Mary Beth. She has nowhere to go. Thank heaven she sold her Mom's condo. That should give her a small nest egg at least. It seems another lifetime that she and I used to sit and chat over a glass of wine when I lived next door to her and Serafina. I don't get to see her very often anymore, but I should see her today at Barbara's.

Barbara has invited me to a party this afternoon where her friend Nora, whom Alexander and I know from the cooking club, is presenting about a company that makes environmentally-friendly cleaning products and health-related things like vitamins. I remember when I had to get a job, and I want to support Nora in her venture. Anything is better than a minimum wage job.

As I write, it seems that so much is going on in my life, which is quite the opposite of how it was just six months ago. I can't believe how much has changed. I've been thinking of basing my novel on some of my life experiences and people I've known. Yes, I finally feel like I have a story to tell! If it ever got published, I'd be in trouble with my kids for sure, and maybe a lot of other people who might see themselves in it. Ha! I've always been such a quiet, submissive type. It would be fun to surprise everyone.

* * *

Samantha, 1:00pm

"MOM, I can only stay another 90 minutes at most. Barbara invited me to that Botanica party. Didn't she invite you, too?"

Mom looked up from her jewelry project. "You know I don't like things like that. I said 'no' to the invitation. Plus I thought you wanted to spend as much time as possible getting Dad's stuff out of the house."

Samantha sighed in frustration. She knew she couldn't win. Now Mom was acting like she wanted her to stay and throw things out. *Sheesh.*

Almost as if she could read minds, Mom said, "Don't throw things out without asking me, you hear?"

"Yes, Mom. All I'm doing is going through Dad's clothes and getting a feel for what else is there. I have a garbage bag full already. The master bedroom closet is chock full of things besides clothes. I assume you were using it for storage?"

Mom nodded. "Yes, and don't you throw any of that out without my permission."

"I won't." Samantha went back to the master suite before she said something she'd regret. Pausing in the doorway to the closet, she looked at the contents. Dad wasn't a hoarder, but he'd kept most of his suits and dress shoes, even though she hadn't seen him dressed like that since he retired. His dresser had yielded unopened bags of underwear in addition to those he was using, and in one large drawer in his bathroom, she'd found the mother lode of Band-Aids of all sizes, box after box as if he'd cleaned out the drug store shelf. She'd always known he was a little OCD, but she couldn't understand about the Band-Aids.

She was barely scratching the surface of what would need to be done when the house went up for sale. And so far, Mom was resisting doing that, even though Samantha knew she hated being here alone. At least she had Beau. And what was going to happen to Beau when Mom moved? He wouldn't be welcome at the assisted living place, and she didn't have a fenced yard or the money to put one up, since the covenants required block or wrought iron. She couldn't bear the thought of anything bad happening to Beau, but why did she have to always step into the breech?

As she jammed pairs of neatly-matched socks into a garbage bag, she felt an overwhelming sadness. She should be working for Jack, doing something she loved and being appreciated for it. Instead, she seemed to be spending her life doing things she didn't want to do for ungrateful people. She paused mid-thought, a pair of socks hovering above the mouth of the bag. Who did she sound like? She sounded like her mother. Maddie O'Neill had often let her know just how much she didn't like all the things she had to do as a wife and mother, and that she rarely if ever got to do what she wanted.

The socks fell into the bag. Samantha felt positively deflated. She couldn't be turning into her mother, could she? Then she thought about the separate lives she and Arthur were living, how emotionally distant he was, and it slammed into her that she had created a softer version of her mother's miserable life. No wonder she was unhappy. But what could she do about it? She felt trapped by duty and promises.

One thing was for sure. Mom wouldn't mind at all if Samantha stopped doing all this. She'd probably be thrilled if Samantha took the job with Jack, even if it meant she didn't come over as often. But it wasn't that simple. Mom needed help, whether she admitted it or not, and Ethan might not keep coming over, and even if he did, it was only once a week. Mom needed more help than that, and it was to Samantha's advantage to get the house in shape for being sold, because the more time she spent in it, the longer her estimate became of how long the job would take. It was up to a few months now, and she suspected that estimate was optimistic by half. Or more.

She shoved the last of the socks into the bag and smiled that another drawer was empty. In fact, she had cleared out the whole dresser.

Her troubled thoughts pushed in again. So should she just give up on her life and do her duty? The sad truth was, as big a project as it was, this was a limited engagement. Sooner or later Mom would be somewhere safer, and Samantha would be free to do whatever she wanted. She paused and thought about that. Maybe she was the one procrastinating. Maybe she was afraid to get on with her life. She had to admit she felt threatened by the degree of change that hovered in her future. Working with Jack could turn out to be much more than just a job.

Shaking her head, she went into the closet and began taking suits off the hangers and putting them into the bags. It went faster than she expected. The shoes went into another bag, and when she was done, there was actual space in the closet for the first time since she could remember. Though it felt like plowing through molasses, she had to admit this was more straightforward than figuring out her life. Maybe she should regard this as a vacation. She laughed out loud at the metaphor. She was getting loopy.

Glancing up to the shelf, she saw a red felt hat she'd bought when she was in high school. She hadn't worn it too often. She wondered why she'd bought it. She didn't like wearing colors that drew attention to her. It had a floppy brim and was very feminine. A layer of dust covered the surface. Something like that needed to be in a hat box. The real question was why had Mom kept Samantha's hat through two moves? Mom never wore it. Did she think Samantha would eventually come back to claim it? Until now, Samantha hadn't even been aware that Mom had the hat. She shook her head thinking of all the things Mom had kept that she would eventually have to throw away or cart to Goodwill.

She dragged the bags out and threw them in the back of the pickup, then went inside and washed her hands. It felt good to have the dresser empty and some space in the closet and bathroom cabinets. It was a fraction of what needed doing, but every little bit would help.

She sat down at the table next to Mom and looked at what she was making. It was a beautiful amethyst chip necklace. The original strings of amethyst chips sat to the side, many of them loose on a white cloth. Mom was grading the sizes so that the chips became progressively smaller on the necklace as they climbed to the back of the neck. It was painstaking work, but beautiful. "That's lovely, Mom. You are so talented."

Mom stopped and looked at her with shining pale blue eyes, and for once didn't deflect the sincere compliment. "I'm rather pleased with how it's turning out."

"I'm at a good stopping point, so I'm going to quit for today. I cleared out the dresser and part of the closet and some of the bathroom. I'll try to come back next weekend for some more. How about I plan to do a bit of housecleaning then?"

"No need for you to do that."

"But Mom, everything is covered in dust."

Mom looked speculatively off into the distance. After several seconds, she said, "It's clean under the dust." Then she went back to her jewelry, not noticing that Samantha's jaw had dropped. Well, she could fight that battle another day. "I'm going to go home and rest a bit before coming back to Barbara's party. After that, Arthur and I are going out with Christine and her husband. She's the client I told you about who moved here from California, and they're both really nice. I haven't had friends here."

"You have Mary Beth. She'll be by soon. She said she could only stay for about an hour, because she's invited to that party, too. But she's your friend."

"Yes, but she isn't really a legal resident of Palm Lakes. I think of her as a work friend. We see each other every day at work, and we go out to lunch a couple times a week." Samantha leaned over and kissed Mom's cheek. "I'm not sure I can call tonight, because I don't know when we'll be back from dinner, and I don't want to startle you by calling late. Is that OK?"

Mom waved her hand dismissively. "You don't have to call me every night. I'll be fine."

"OK, then I'll see you later. Ethan's coming today, isn't he?"

"I suppose he is. Not that I need him to."

Samantha vacated the place before she got into an argument. As she pulled up to the stop sign at the intersection, she made a sudden decision. She turned the opposite direction to the way home. When she arrived at the Rec Center, she parked and went to the secluded pay phone and called Jack. She no longer needed to carry a card with his number on it; it was etched in her mind. Calling him had become her way of rewarding herself for doing her duty. She was informed he had gone home with a cold, so she called his home number.

Jack answered on the third ring. "It's me, Samantha. They said you have a cold. Are you OK?"

"Yeah, I just haven't been sleeping well, and it hit me harder than it should. What's up with you?"

"I just got finished a round of cleaning up at my Mom's house. It always leaves me out of sorts. She fights anything I want to do. She won't clean house, but doesn't want me to. She won't throw junk out, but doesn't let me. I was lucky she let me take a few bags of Dad's clothes. It made a small dent in the Augean Stables. I dread how much work it will be to get that house ready for sale once she either moves out or dies. But enough of me complaining. How's work going?"

"Same old stuff. I don't mind listening about what you're doing. It makes me realize that you didn't really have much choice about the job."

For some reason, that made the tears come. She swept a hand across her eyes. "Thanks for understanding. I'm so concerned about her. She doesn't think ahead. Like what can I do with Beau when the time comes she can't have him anymore? I don't have a fenced yard, and I can't count on Arthur to walk him. He doesn't like animals, which is why we have no pets now. I can't bear the thought of taking him to the pound. I'd like to have Beau, but..."

"I'll take him. I always wanted a dog. You said he was a big yellow Lab, right?"

"You're a good listener. Yes, he is. And smart and sweet and a great watchdog, too. I love him, but I don't think Arthur would like it, and without a fenced yard, it would be awfully hard. Are you serious?"

"I own a business where I'm outside most of the time. He can come to work with me. He minds, doesn't he? Labs are usually smart."

"He learned all the basic obedience stuff, though he still pulls on a leash. If you're serious, I would be so glad. It would take a weight off me knowing he would have a loving home."

"It would be my pleasure."

Then, as it always did, the conversation seemed to trail off. It wasn't that there wasn't anything to talk about. Samantha didn't want to go there, and Jack respected her wishes.

"I'm doing my best to convince her she should be somewhere she would be safer, where there would be no need of doing anything that could damage her bones, but it's a slow process. Sooner or later, she'll see the sense of it, but all I can say is I hope it's before something bad happens. I'm embarrassed to admit I'm glad she's so adamant about not living with us. I don't think I could manage it. Our house is too small for the both of us." She felt guilty just saying it, but it was true.

"Maybe she just needs time to adjust to your Dad being gone. You said she isn't in great financial shape. Eventually, something will help her make her mind up. I think you're pretty amazing to give her as much latitude as you do."

"I don't see that there's a lot of choice. She's not sharp mentally anymore, but she's far from incompetent, and I just have to trust that the angels or someone will watch over her and keep her from harm while she comes around to seeing she can't stay there. She doesn't drive the car anymore, thank God. I just need to get her to see the sense of being in the assisted living place. She's actually a terrific candidate for their independent living section. I'm sorry to dump on you. Arthur has heard it all a hundred times, and he's sick of it. He and Mom were never best friends. Thanks for letting me bitch about it."

"You're not bitching. You're concerned. I think you're a great daughter."

The tears came again. "You're just flattering me so I'll call again."

"I'm holding your job. I'll keep holding it for as long as I can. I want you, not someone else."

The double entendre didn't slip past her. "Thanks for waiting for me. I feel so sorry for myself sometimes when I think how I could be working with you. If Mom goes into assisted living, or even if, God forbid, she accepts our offer of a place to live, I think I can take the job. I just don't want to wish something bad on her to make that happen."

"It will all work out, Samantha."

She pictured him lounging on a couch, talking to her on the phone, his long legs stretched out in front of him. He was probably wearing black. It was his favorite color. Tight-fitting black jeans and T-shirt. His long, raven-black hair might be loose, though maybe not. She hadn't spent any time with him that wasn't work-related. She had no idea how he relaxed.

"Are you still there? It got awful quiet."

"Sorry. I drifted off. I was thinking about you." She spent a lot of time doing that.

"Good, because I think a lot about you."

"I better get going. I have two more engagements today."

"Well, aren't you the social butterfly?"

She laughed. It felt good. "Thanks for making me laugh. I'd almost forgotten how. I'll call you again when I can."

"Do that."

Samantha waited for him to hang up after saying goodbye, but he did the same to her. Finally, she put the phone down and broke the connection. It felt like cutting off a life line every time she did it.

* * *

Nora, 3:00pm

NORA STOOD in Barbara's powder room assessing her appearance. She wasn't beautiful by anyone's standards, but she kept herself well. Her weight was appropriate for her height. She had nice skin and attractive hazel eyes. Her short gray hair was sensible as well as stylish (she hoped she could soon afford to go back to her old hairdresser, who was a real artist) and her clothes were classy and understated. She'd been coached by her cousin Ellen about what to wear to this presentation, and she felt she was well-prepared, but it didn't stop the butterflies from flapping in her stomach.

She wished she could be more relaxed, and she desperately wanted to feel more rested. She hadn't had a full night's sleep in a month, as the smudges under her eyes showed. At least she was able to cover them up, but the anxiety was wearing her down. Her eyes lacked a spark, and she had to force herself to smile, but it didn't look genuine.

What if Luke was right, and she couldn't get this business off the ground? She'd had a few enrollees, but nothing spectacular. Sometimes she was afraid he was correct; other times she suspected he was envious that she wasn't working with him at the burger joint. She did feel guilty that he was having to work such an awful job. Mostly she doubted the wisdom of her choice. Wouldn't she be better off bringing home a regular paycheck? He seemed to think so, and it was hard to buck him; after all, he was the money expert.

Everything she did was taking her further from the man she loved. All that would satisfy him was money in the bank. If this did pan out, it wouldn't happen overnight. Plus, there were no guarantees all her efforts would pay off. It pained her to think she might have to give up later and get a menial job. If that happened, she'd have to listen to a lot of 'I told you so's', and that would be the least negative outcome. The worst didn't bear thinking about.

She sighed deeply, then looked in the mirror. "I will create a successful business, and Luke will become a part of it." She smiled at the thought of success, and there was a hint of warmth in it. That's what this whole thing was about. So she and Luke could be happy and live the life they wanted to live. If all they did was both get menial jobs, they'd lose their house and lifestyle for sure. She was beginning to worry they might even lose their marriage.

She joined Barbara in the kitchen, watching her dance around the platters and dishes in her typically efficient fashion. "I can't thank you enough for doing this, Barbara. I really need to make a go of it. Poor Luke is hating the burger joint. Who wouldn't? That's no way to spend your retirement."

Barbara stopped and regarded her with sympathetic brown eyes. "Nora, it's my pleasure to help. I love the products, and that's going to be the whole key to success for you. Botanica is about great products at a good price. No MLM frills. I'll be happy to give a testimonial today if you like."

"Oh, that would be so wonderful. I'll do my presentation and then ask you to share whatever you want to."

"It looks like we should have about 25 people, and I think most of them are good prospects. In any case, you're sure to get enrollments today. We'll have Luke working as your bookkeeper before you know it."

"That's the plan." Nora smiled at the thought of being able to tell Luke he could quit his job. That would bring them back together. "What can I do to help?"

Barbara pointed at the counter. "Why don't you put the dishes, utensils and napkins at that end while I finish putting out the food? We'll let them come in, greet each other, settle with food and eat a bit before you start. How does that sound?"

"It sounds perfect to me."

Just then the first guest arrived, and Barbara went to the door. She was followed back by Lydia, but never made it to the kitchen before the doorbell rang again. It all became a blur after that. Nora did her best to remember the names of the new people but was grateful she had name tags for them. Everyone was amenable to wearing them, and that made her job easier. The food and drink drew everyone to the counter, and voices kept adding to the din as more people arrived.

Before she knew it, she had made her presentation, telling people her story and why she liked the products. It helped that she knew some of the people in the crowd, like Helen from the cooking class. The samples and some catalogs were circulating as she offered to enroll people for $1 instead of the usual fee. The red wine demo elicited gasps and laughter, even a little applause at the end when the carpet was restored to perfectly white. An unexpected swell of people moved in her direction when she finished, and she spent the next hour helping people fill out forms and choose products. It tickled her to think that she'd introduced all these people to such wonderful ways to improve their lives. She hadn't expected it to be so much fun to have a home business. Not to mention the commissions she'd get in her next check.

After everyone had left and Barbara was gathering dishes, she went through the stack of paperwork. Lydia had been the first to join. She said the products just glowed, and she couldn't wait to try them. What a nice thing to say! She also said her friends Jean and Ian might join when they came back to the US next month, so Nora had made a note in her appointment book to contact her later on. The two younger women, Mary Beth and Samantha, had both made good-sized orders. Mary Beth expressed some interest in the business side of it, but Nora wasn't sure it was serious. Helen had also enrolled and thanked her for taking the time to share with them. The stack of enrollments totaled 18. Her sponsor was going to be amazed. And it was all because of Barbara.

"Barbara, let me help with the cleanup."

"There really isn't a lot to it. I'm just going to throw it all out the window."

Nora stopped in her tracks and looked at Barbara in shock.

"Just kidding. I'm going to put it in the dishwasher and use some of the Botanica liquid. I'm pleased with how well it cleans."

Nora was so glad to hear Barbara liked the products. "You know, they told me you can use the glass cleaner as a rinse aid. Just use the concentrate as is. I find it works really well."

"What a great idea! The fewer nasty chemicals I use, the better. I can't believe I've never heard of Botanica before."

"I hadn't, either. It seems many of your friends hadn't, too. Thankfully."

Barbara stopped stacking dishes. "I'm glad so many enrolled. Even Emma did. I wouldn't have bet on that. I just had a feeling she cared about the environment and liked healthy products. Just goes to show you shouldn't prejudge anyone."

"This went so well that I think I'll do a party and invite people from my church to come. You are an inspiration to me."

"Oh, Nora, it wasn't anything. I like getting people together and think it's a service to let them know about things that could improve their lives. You just have to make it painless for them and convince them there will be no pressure. I'm sure your church friends will be as impressed as I've been with Botanica."

"I hope so. My cousin who sponsored me tells me that to really make a decent income, I'll need to enroll others who are interested in doing the business, and I haven't come to grips with that yet."

"One step at a time. Seems to me that you aren't the only person who is living on a tight budget for one reason or another. I would think that all of the retirement communities around here would be fertile fields for finding business partners. I know a lot of people won't join if they're on fixed incomes, but on the other hand, that can motivate people to get on board with the business. Seems to me it would be worthwhile, if only to get their products for free. Did Mary Beth make noises like she was interested?"

"Yes, she did. She was the only one today who seemed interested, although Lydia said she and her friends might be starting a business that could incorporate the products somehow. I didn't get the feeling either were desperate for a job, just that they were open to the possibility. I'll follow up with them and see what develops." She started packing her rolling bag. By the time she was done, Barbara had finished loading the dishwasher.

They walked together to the front door. Barbara followed her out to the car. "You tell Luke about the nice check coming next month. Keep the momentum going. This could be a really good thing for you." She hugged Nora, then went back inside.

On the drive home, Nora dreamed about how great it would be to tell Luke he could quit his job.

* * *

Emma, 4:55pm

EMMA STARED AT THE CLOCK, willing it to reach 5pm. Julio was never late, but she couldn't relax until he arrived. Even going to Barbara's little party hadn't helped the day pass fast enough. The only part of the day she enjoyed was when he was with her.

When had that happened? She used to love to walk her labyrinth, do yoga and stick her nose in a good novel, letting the day unfold however it wanted to. Lately she found she was too distracted most of the time to read or watch TV or even listen to music. She paced a lot. She thought a lot. She worried. Like she was doing now.

Julio had come back last Sunday like a shot. She was shaking when he arrived, affected by the new feelings coursing through her. He'd sat with her while she had a cup of chamomile tea. That's when it finally registered. He was serious about her. A young, handsome man was pursuing her. She felt both flattered and foolish.

He was coming for dinner tonight. She wondered why it had never occurred to her to suggest that. The poor man ate alone most evenings, just like she did. It made sense for them to have a meal together more often than just on Sunday. At least that's what she told herself.

The doorbell startled her out of her reverie. She ushered him in and was rewarded with his brilliant, white-toothed smile. She didn't flinch as he leaned over and pecked her on the cheek.

"How was your day, Julio?"

"We are getting ready for the spring planting. New shipments of plants coming in. Lots to do. You would not know it today, but soon it will be spring."

"I can't believe it. February seems too early for spring." She led him into the kitchen, where she checked the roast in the oven.

"It smells delicious."

She smiled at the compliment. "We have peas and mashed potatoes and gravy to go with it. I hope you're hungry."

"I am always hungry when I am with you." She suppressed a grin, knowing exactly what he was hinting at.

"If spring is coming soon, I should start thinking about my garden. I reserved a plot in the community garden, and I have to do all the work myself. They only supply hookups to water for irrigation. Could I pick your brain for ideas? I'm totally clueless." She was almost flirting with him, and it didn't feel forced.

His easy smile made her weak in the knees. "I can do better than that. I will help you plant the garden. Raised beds would be good. I have plenty of materials we could use. Do you know what you want to plant?"

"I'd like some herbs, tomatoes, peppers, things like that. I need you to tell me what varieties and what to plant and not to plant. I don't know the climate here."

A wrinkle appeared on his normally smooth brow as he considered her question. "I do not usually plant a garden, but I have some ideas. I think you would like a vertical garden here on the patio for herbs instead of planting them in the community garden. Most of them will not take full sun, and that way they can be close to the kitchen."

She clapped her hands in delight. "Oh, that sounds excellent. What is a vertical garden?"

"We mount a metal frame that goes from ground to patio cover, providing slots for putting plant pots in. We can even add irrigation if you do not want to have to water it daily. It takes up very little space and looks nice, too."

"Oh, my, yes, I want that for sure. What else do you suggest?"

"I know we need to plant early tomatoes. It will seem strange, but varieties like they plant in Alaska work best here, due to the short growing season. It gets too hot by mid-summer. I will have to do some research on other plants. We can go to the plot and lay it out and plan and prepare the soil in February."

She impulsively threw her arms around him and hugged him. He looked stunned, but said nothing. She pulled back, apologizing. "I didn't mean to be overwhelming."

"Please, overwhelm me any time." His eyes flashed with warmth and affection.

The meal and cleanup afterwards felt so normal to Emma, she wished they could have dinner every night, but she refrained from saying so. She hadn't realized how lonely she was. They settled in the living room for tea after the meal.

He looked at her over his mug. "You seem to be eating with more enthusiasm."

"You noticed. I am feeling better all the time. It's slow progress, but measurable. I look forward to our meals together." She paused, struggling to express her true feelings. "I don't mean to put anything on you, but I like it much better when you're here. I'm nervous about the future when I think about it, but one thing I know for sure is I am so grateful that you want to spend time with me."

He reached over and touched her hand. She didn't pull away. "I am grateful, too. If this is what a midlife crisis is, I am happy to be having one."

She laughed at his joke, but couldn't put aside concerns about where it was going. "Has anyone said anything to you about us?"

"No. I have not told anyone, and so far, no one seems to know. It will not last. I am sure your neighbors have noticed, and people talk. Eventually my brothers will find out."

"And they won't be happy." She didn't ask. She knew.

"They disapproved when I 'dated' women in Palm Lakes who were married. Obviously, they were concerned about hurting the business. But they never worried that I was serious about any of those women. They will know this is different. And the differences are what cause people to judge. Just like your friends will tell you I am after your money, my family will say you are toying with me. But in the end, I fear we will find my family to be the more prejudiced."

She sighed and put her mug on the coffee table. "Why can't we just have our own private universe?"

He grinned. "That would be perfect. We can, you know." He lifted his right arm out and she went over to sit next to him as she had become accustomed to. He held her and stroked her hair. Being touched was becoming soothing.

The man who had once seemed simply a talented young gardener was revealing himself to be a person of rare depth and sensitivity. She kept reminding herself that guaranteed nothing, but the more she knew him, the better she liked him. The problem was, 'like' didn't even begin to describe her feelings for him anymore. She closed her eyes and immersed herself in the moment, brushing away troubling thoughts. Her head lay against his chest, where his heart beat in rhythm with her own.

"Julio, I want you to show me if you still want to..."

His arm tightened around her. "Querida, I have been waiting to hear that."

She reluctantly extracted herself from his arms and stood, then walked towards the bedroom, his soft footsteps echoing behind her. She felt trepidation, but curiosity and desire trumped fear.

* * *

Samantha, 5:15pm

THE CHINESE RESTAURANT WAS BUZZING, Saturday night being one of its busiest times. Samantha was enjoying being out with another couple for the first time in ages. The husbands didn't know each other and had little in common, but they were both nice guys. Jerome was a retired banker, and although he was dressed formally for the desert (he was actually wearing a sports jacket), his manner was gentle and easygoing. Arthur seemed relaxed, though he hadn't participated much in the conversation.

"Jerome and I are just loving those dwarf bottlebrush you suggested for around the patio. The rabbits aren't eating them, and the hummingbirds love them. Of course, we are familiar with bottlebrush trees and bushes, but I'd never heard of a dwarf variety."

Samantha basked in the praise. "They're one of my favorite plants for all those reasons. People like you who live on the golf course have the most trouble with rabbits, and there are so few plants rabbits won't eat, and putting wire cages around them is an eyesore."

Christine nodded. "Absolutely. I wish we could outlaw them. They look so tacky."

Samantha was surprised at what seemed like an extreme opinion, one

219

that was not really practical. "Well, I sympathize with the whole looks thing, but without caging, there are so many plants that would never make it. They're a necessary evil. At least that's my opinion."

Christine seemed unfazed. "You're the plant expert, Samantha, so I have to go by what you say."

Pleased that she had helped bring clarity to the situation, Samantha smiled and continued eating her salad.

Christine finished her salad and pushed the bowl to the side. Her alert brown eyes scanned the room. "I hope we don't have to wait too long. They're really busy tonight." She patted her short gray hair in place as she dabbed the corner of her mouth with the cloth napkin. "Samantha, I just had a great idea. I was wondering if you would mind giving a presentation to a group I'm in. It's a sort of sorority. We meet monthly and love to have educational or entertaining presentations. I was thinking maybe you could talk about desert landscaping and how to avoid common problems, like choosing the wrong plants. Then you could give out your cards at the end, and maybe you'd get some business."

Samantha was charmed with the offer, even though it would mean no financial gain to her. It felt good to have the trust such an invitation showed. "I would be pleased to do that. Just email me some times. I would need a little preparation to put together a good talk. But it's one of my favorite topics."

Arthur broke his silence. "Jerome, what do you like to do here in Palm Lakes? Play any tennis?"

Jerome looked up, seemingly surprised at being spoken to. "No, my sport is golf. I have never played tennis."

Arthur smiled as if adrift. "Well, then, I won't invite you to play tennis with me. And I don't play golf. So I guess that settles that." Samantha grimaced at what sounded like a dismissal, but probably wasn't meant to be. Jerome didn't seem to have taken offense.

"I'm getting too slow and old to even consider something like tennis," said Jerome, shaking his head in a self-deprecating way.

Samantha looked at Jerome and realized for the first time that although he couldn't be more than ten years older than Arthur, ten years at that age made a big difference in a person's health and mobility. She frowned at how out of place she felt with the Palm Lakes crowd. It didn't even occur to her to feel old. At least not yet.

Christine jumped in. "Jerome and I both love to play golf, always have. It's a nice course we have here."

Samantha smiled, but wasn't sure what to say. "It certainly is lovely to look at, though I've never played golf and wouldn't know what a good course should look like." Samantha always felt out of water when the topic turned to all the activities in Palm Lakes. She never had free time for any of that. "Someday I hope to get involved in one or more of the clubs here. I just don't have the time now."

"You have your parents here, don't you?"

Samantha had told Christine several weeks ago, when she was doing her first job for her. It was before Dad had died. "My Dad died suddenly a few weeks ago, but I still have my Mom, and she needs a lot of help."

Christine looked shocked, even embarrassed. "I'm so sorry for your loss."

Samantha shook her head. "At least it was quick and painless. But enough of that kind of talk. What other activities are you in besides golf?"

"I'm on the board of the HOA. I belong to that sorority, CSL. We have chapters all over the US. I was a longtime member in California; we raise funds for women's college scholarships. And I do various volunteer things. It keeps me busy."

The conversation seemed destined to be limited to Christine and Samantha. Maybe this was a mistake. Just as she was considering never accepting an invitation like this again, Christine spoke up. "Samantha, Jerome and I are members of the Botanical Gardens. Are you and Arthur?"

"Oh, yes, we're members, too."

"I got a notice that said they're having that big art exhibit there in March, you know, the one with the large glass sculptures? How would you like to go together? It sounds really interesting."

Samantha wasn't sure how to respond. She'd like nothing better, but Arthur would probably like to avoid closer fraternization. He hadn't warmed to the Sommers at all. "I would really love to, but I'm not sure if I will be free. I have so much to do with my Mom. But let me know when you plan to go, and we can see if we're free." She really wanted to spend more time with Christine, but she might not be able to do it with Arthur.

Arthur unexpectedly spoke up. "What's it like being on the HOA, Christine? The covenants are pretty extensive, and enforcement seems problematic. Is the board of one mind about the topic of enforcing them?" Samantha was shocked that Arthur would bring that subject up. He knew Mary Beth was illegal here. Or maybe he was feeling out Christine for Samantha.

"The board members are not in total agreement, though for the most part, we are in favor of enforcing the rules strictly. People don't seem to realize that the covenants are what keep the property values high. If we get slack, we lose the look and feel of Palm Lakes, and the property values will drop. I was in favor of incentivizing reporting infractions, but we couldn't agree on it, so it didn't happen." She started scooping rice onto her dinner plate.

Samantha was shocked. She didn't like how strict the covenants were, but she went along to keep peace. Having signed them, she had no real choice. But she was seeing Christine with new eyes. Christine had always impressed her as someone who had it all together and was tremendously organized and a born leader, someone she wanted to be like, but she hadn't seen this aspect of her personality. "How harsh do you think the HOA should be about enforcement?"

Christine frowned. "I know there have been accusations and references to Nazism, but I think that we should not feel guilty about enforcing the covenants. Homeowners sign them. They are a contract. It's really pretty straightforward, as I see it." She began serving herself some General Tso's chicken.

Arthur gave Samantha a pointed look that neither Jerome nor Christine saw, and then he began to serve himself his dinner. Samantha wasn't sure what to think. At least she was forewarned not to talk about Mary Beth with Christine.

Christine continued, "I once suggested we use the Posse to report violations. They have so little to do, what with crime being so low. But they weren't willing to do that. So myself and a few volunteers keep our eyes open for violations and report them. I believe we're doing a good job staying ahead of things." She started eating her meal.

The rest of the evening went swiftly and innocuously in spite of the detour to the subject of the HOA. Jerome and Christine gave warm goodbyes to Arthur and Samantha, promising they would get together soon, and Christine reminded Samantha of her commitment to give a presentation to the ladies of the local CSL chapter.

BACK HOME, Arthur didn't wait long before commenting about the evening. "So did you know Christine was on the HOA board?"

"Hell, no."

"She seems a bit extreme about it."

"She's passionate about what she believes. I don't agree with her viewpoint, but I admire her a lot."

Arthur's brows raised, but he said nothing.

"What?"

"She just doesn't seem to have a lot in common with you."

"Who does in Palm Lakes? I'm almost 20 years younger than the average resident. I count myself lucky she invited me to do anything. No one else does."

Arthur looked injured. "Don't attack me. I had no idea you felt that way. Aren't you happy here? You were the one who suggested we move here."

"No, actually, I wasn't. The first time we came here to visit, you said you wouldn't mind living here. I was thrilled at the time, because I do love the desert and living here was a dream I had. I'm not saying I don't like it, but it hasn't turned out exactly as I would have liked. You may notice that I work full time and spend a lot of the remaining time with my parents--my Mom now. I don't have time for clubs and activities and sports. I don't really even have time to go on a field trip to the Botanical Gardens, but I would like to have a friend here. A legal, female friend. And even though I disagree with some of Christine's opinions, I like her."

"Don't get all huffy. I didn't know you were so dissatisfied with living here. Maybe if you had stayed with the other landscaping job, you'd feel better."

"I'm sure I would. It was a great job and had many benefits. Jack did say he'd hold it open for a while, but it's possible it will be filled before I'm available to take it."

"Is that what's bothering you?" His brown eyes gazed at her. She felt he was really looking at her for the first time in ages. She didn't know what to say, afraid to reveal too much.

"I'm upset with Mom. Big surprise there. She's impossible. And I wish I could have taken the job at Temple Landscaping. It's just that I never seem to have time for myself, time to relax."

"Then why don't we plan on going to the Botanical Gardens with Jerome and Christine?"

Samantha was floored. "You don't care for the Gardens that much, and you didn't seem to be that taken with them."

"You need a break. I know how hard it is with your Mom, and I appreciate you not involving me. Call Christine and accept her invitation if you want. I'll go along and be a good boy."

Samantha wasn't sure what to do. She wanted to pursue the friendship, at least give it a chance, since it was the only one on the horizon. There was no one like her here. It seemed necessary to compromise with people, considering the age difference. And with Arthur being supportive, it might actually work. But she felt guilty letting him do something for her. Was her marriage already doomed by her fatal attraction to Jack, even though nothing had come of it? She forced a smile. "Thanks. I really appreciate it. I'll call her tomorrow and thank her for the evening and say we'll go."

* * *

Lydia, 5:30pm

LYDIA STIRRED the beef stew in the crock pot on Eric's kitchen counter. She'd felt an awkwardness since returning and had pleaded exhaustion when he picked her up at the airport Wednesday, which was totally true. She'd slept most of Thursday. But Friday she spent alone in her condo dithering about how things would be between them now, afraid to find out that maybe it had all been an illusion. Well, today she would find out.

She heard the garage door go up, and Eric came in a few minutes later, dropped his gun and holster on a table and then came out to the kitchen. He accepted the glass of red wine she handed to him. "It smells great! You didn't have any problem finding what you needed?"

"No. Your place is obscenely organized." She grinned at him shyly. "The key worked fine, and all I needed was an electrical outlet for the crock pot and a corkscrew for the wine. I did all the preparation at my place. There's nothing like homemade beef stew on a winter's day."

He chuckled. "It didn't feel much like winter around midday. I was actually sweating in my car, even without a jacket. Though I have to admit when the sun gets low, you can feel the nip of winter. But it sure isn't Minnesota. Are you all rested up from your trip? How was it?"

"I'm sorry I crashed. It was such a whirlwind, I was really beat. But I had a marvelous time, and I'm glad I went. Jean was a lovely bride. She and Ian are so cute together, and I got a chance to know him better, which is nice since they'll be living at my place soon. They took me to a few sights in London, and I had some amazing meals. The Indian food there is out of this world. And the fish and chips--we don't have anything to compare."

"I'm glad you were able to go, and it makes sense that you get a chance to know Ian. But I missed you." Sincerity pulsed through his aura, reassuring her.

"I missed you, too. I confess I've been feeling funny, because the trip interrupted the natural flow of what was going on with us, and now I feel I've been plopped into a play and don't know my lines."

He laughed and put his glass down. "Leave it to you to be so honest. I've been having the same concerns. Why don't we just start again?"

"Sounds like a plan to me." She could see he meant every word he said. Finally, she began to relax.

He leaned past her to sniff the stew. "I don't want you to think I'm comparing you to anyone, because I'm not, but this is new to me. I've never had a woman over to my place; I've never dated anyone in Palm Lakes; I've never really had a woman friend before. I hadn't thought about it much until now, but I wonder if I was protecting myself, putting up walls. I've never shared with anyone what I've share with you."

"It's the same for me. I find myself wanting to tell you what I 'saw' today. I've never been able to do that with anyone. It makes me feel less alone."

"So what did you 'see' today?" He grinned at her. Did he have any idea the effect he had on her? Tall, broad shouldered and boyishly handsome, he distracted her so easily. She almost forgot what his question was. "Oh, today, yes...well, the presentation at Barbara's was really good. I signed up for a membership in the shopping club for Botanica. Nora, the presenter, brought samples, and you should see how they glowed. I might not have told you, but I can see energies around a lot of things besides people. Anyway, Nora fell on hard times when her husband's pension fund collapsed, and she's doing this home business, and I feel good being able to help her and also get good products."

"How many people were there?"

"I think there were more than 20. It was pretty crowded." Now would be a good time to broach the subject she'd been avoiding. "Being in crowds that long has an effect on me, not a good one. I can't turn off what I see, and I try not to soak up the energies, but I end up taking them on just the same. I feel all their emotions, and most of the time, it isn't pleasant. People are generally pretty stressed. It's very unsettling and not good for my health. That's why I avoid doing things like that too often. But I've found that I can clear myself and rebalance my energies." She paused, unsure how to proceed.

His eyes were fixed on her, and she made a snap decision. "You've been so understanding about who I am and what I do. I've never known a man like you. I don't want to ruin it, but I also don't want us to have secrets." She felt herself losing her nerve.

He put his glass down and reached out for her free hand. "Lydia, you can tell me anything. I'm not going to judge you."

She laughed weakly. "I'm not sure of that. Maybe it's one of life's little ironies that the only man I've ever known who might accept me for who I am is a cop."

"Retired cop, Lydia. I'd hardly call the Posse a police force. I just volunteer my services."

"I love being able to tell you things like today Emma was at the presentation, and I'd swear there's a man in her life. Her colors were much warmer and more balanced, plus it looks like she's healthier. Her colors were always pale and weak and to the blues. Now there's a bit of orange and warmth and brightness there. I couldn't tell anyone else something like that, and I couldn't wait to see you to share it. But I don't want to have to filter what I tell you." She knew she was just playing for time, but she hated to tell him.

"Then don't." There was a glimmer in his eye as if he knew what she was going to say. But how could he?

"I honestly don't think I could be in crowds for long with this so-called gift unless I had a coping strategy, and I found one some years ago that works for me. But it isn't totally legal."

"So you're finally going to tell me you smoke pot?" He smiled smugly.

Her jaw dropped. "How did you know that?"

"I can smell it on you, Lydia."

Her breath caught. "You're kidding!"

"Nope. Any kind of smoke gets in your hair and clothes. My nose is pretty good."

She searched his eyes, worrying what came next. "You don't mind?"

"Lydia, I..."

A scream pierced the bubble of their heart-to-heart. It seemed to be coming from Tanya's place. When another blood-curdling scream confirmed it, Eric ran for his gun. "Call 911. Stay here."

Racing back through the kitchen, he pushed open the sliding glass door and headed for Tanya's across the back yard as Lydia grabbed and dialed the phone. She stared out the open door as she waited for an answer. More screams added to the tension. She was scared for Eric to go up against the man with the black aura, even though he had a gun. Then she heard two gunshots and felt as if they had slammed into her. She dropped the phone.

* * *

Owen, 5:55pm

THE GIFT-WRAPPED ring box in Owen's hand was as forgotten as last week's garbage. He'd come intending to propose, but things had taken an unexpected turn. Tanya had obviously been drinking. A lot. His hand gripped the small box so hard it hurt.

"I told you she was a drunken whore." His mother's voice raked the inside of his head like sharp fingernails drawing blood on sensitive skin.

"Shut. The. Fuck. Up." He couldn't deal with both of them at one time. Tanya had just turned her back on him and headed for the kitchen, skewering him with a final insult about his small stature, implying she was also referring to his dick.

His head was spinning in confusion. He'd come in through the garage door, which she'd left unlocked. They were supposed to have dinner tonight. He'd decided he would propose right away because he couldn't wait to see her face. He knew she'd been wanting this for a long time, and he'd finally overcome his reservations.

Now he felt he'd walked into a nightmare, and he wished he could just leave, but anger at her taunts was building, threatening to sweep aside his confusion. He was caught in the maelstrom of conflicting emotions.

Following her across the living room, still trying to understand what had caused her to go off on him the moment he entered the condo, he asked, "What's going on? You quit drinking. Things were going so well."

Instead of responding positively, she launched a more scathing attack. "What are you whining about? I'm not supposed to ask you to marry me, I'm not allowed to ask you to take me to your house, and I shouldn't ask you to do anything, but you get to whine to me?" As the venom flowed from her mouth, she swayed and poked her index finger at him to punctuate her points. Her vicious words lacked crispness, and her focus seemed to wander. She was like a fire hose out of control, spewing all over the place.

In spite of the rage he could feel blossoming inside him, Owen was turned on by her raw sexuality. Her bare feet had sexy red toenails. Her tanned, firm legs peeked out occasionally as her red silk wrapper slipped open to reveal them, also giving him glimpses of her stunning tits. She was glorious when she was naked, drunk or not.

The anger seeped out of him like air out of a balloon. He sagged into a chair and put his head in his hands. Tanya stood in the doorway to the kitchen, looking at him contemptuously, one hand on her hip, the other gripping the doorway for support.

Mother railed at him. "You're a fool, Junior. Is that how a woman looks at the man she loves? How could you think she loved you? You were going to ask her to marry you? You are such a loser."

He twisted and turned and shook his head trying to get the harpy's voice to shut up. Tanya looked at him with a question in her faded blue eyes, but lacked the clarity to voice it.

"Shut up!" he said to the voice in his head.

Tanya's eyes flared in rage. "How dare you talk to me that way!"

"Not you." Owen couldn't tell her about Mother. He just wanted Mother to go away. Or at least shut up.

"Who else is here? What do you take me for? You've had your merry way with me for weeks and weeks now, and it's obvious you never intend to do right by me. Now you tell *me* to shut up? I hate you, you miserable *little* man."

He could barely control himself. Mother had always harped on his size when she wanted to criticize him. Now he had both of them on him.

"Well, Junior. It seems she's got your number, even if she is a drunken whore."

The voices inside and outside his head had merged to become one hateful diatribe. Unable to shut them out, he felt the pressure building inside again. It wasn't the kind of pressure he used to feel when he was on the hunt, looking to find a woman to punish. It was way bigger. The pressure sang to him, saying if he would just give in to it, he would finally prove how powerful he was once and for all, and he would have peace.

He stood up, no longer hearing individual words as the voices droned on, bathed in a red haze of anger. He walked towards Tanya, and in her pale blue eyes he saw fear. Like a prey animal, she realized what was coming. The pressure grew and grew, pushing him to follow her as she retreated into the kitchen, where she pressed herself back against the counter, her wrapper slipping open further, revealing her naked body. She reached a hand out defensively. He pulled the biggest knife from the block that sat nearby, looking at its edge as if assessing it for a job. Tanya's eyes widened in panic. Her fear poured electrically through him in a way that was more powerful than sex. It was time to judge her. Somehow, he had known it would always come to this.

The ring box fell out of his left hand, bounced across the floor and hit the wall. Tanya's eyes were glued to him, so she never saw it. A faint whimpering began to emanate from her, stoking his anger. He saw his power reflected in her eyes. The more fearful she became, the larger and more powerful he was. Small? He was huge. She would learn the error of her ways.

He raked her with the knife, cutting across her beautiful tits. It was like marking his property, and it made him feel powerful. Blood flowed from the wound, spilling a darker red onto her wrap, and Tanya finally found the energy to scream. It had no effect on him. He wasn't hearing much of anything except a dull roar inside his head, his own blood pounding as it flowed through him, proving how powerful he was. No woman could stop him.

Tanya screamed again and again quite loudly, but he easily knocked her hands aside and swept the blade across her neck, cutting deeply. She fell to the ground gurgling as blood pumped out onto the floor, making a lake on the white tile.

Owen gazed at her, thinking she had never looked more beautiful, a feeling like sexual ecstasy flowing through him. Gunshots and the sound of breaking glass in the next room affected him like a distant alarm, wrenching his focus from his handiwork.

* * *

Red, 6:10pm

RED FELT the adrenaline pour through him as he frantically rattled the handle of the sliding glass door on Tanya's patio. It was locked. He couldn't wait for backup. He shot the glass twice in quick succession, and it dissolved into myriad tiny pieces that clattered on the tile. He tried to see as he threaded himself through the hole he'd made, but it seemed dim after the bright sunshine. His heart pounded in fear. He knew he could easily walk into something bad, but if he didn't act, it would surely be too late for Tanya.

Once inside the living room, he could see with dismay he was too late. Tanya's feet were visible on the kitchen floor, surrounded by a growing pool of blood. Keeping his gun at ready, he stepped cautiously into the room. It looked bad. Real bad. He scanned the area carefully, worried that Owen was waiting to jump on him from the other doorway, but everything was quiet. He managed to reach for Tanya's ravaged neck to check for a pulse. The pulse was almost nonexistent, and she looked beyond help. Casting about for something to try and stop the horrific bleeding, he briefly took his attention off the doorway he'd entered through, and Owen slipped in behind him and buried a large knife in his right shoulder. Pain radiated through his body, and he dropped his gun. As it clattered to the floor and Red struggled to remain standing, Owen yanked the blade out and prepared to deliver a coup de grace.

Knowing he had few seconds left to make his move, Red dropped to the floor, grabbed for his gun and rolled to the side while shooting Owen until the hammer clicked on an empty chamber. It was impossible for him to miss at that range in spite of the pain in his arm, and he had the satisfaction of seeing Owen's shocked look as he fell to the floor, his chest already bleeding from multiple holes.

He needed to find something to put on Tanya's neck to stop the bleeding, if it was even possible. But there was no energy left to get up off the floor as the pain weighed on him, blood pouring from his shoulder wound.

The sound of feet crunching on broken glass pushed through the waves of pain, and he turned his head to see Lydia coming towards him.

"Get back, Lydia. Owen may still be alive."

"He's dead. No colors around him. Tanya's gone, too. I heard the shots and couldn't wait anymore. Help is on the way." She pressed something against his shoulder wound. "Can you lean against the counter? I need to unlock the front door for the police and EMTs."

All he could do was nod. He backed up to the counter and tried to press the cloth into his injured shoulder, but the pain started shrinking his field of vision, so he stopped. Lydia was soon back and applying pressure. He tried to thank her, but he couldn't find his voice, then everything went black.

10

TUESDAY, FEBRUARY 6, 1996

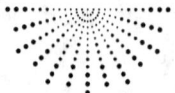

Helen, 11:45am

*E*ven with the limited lighting in the closet, Helen was amazed at how sparkly the gemstones were. She sifted them back and forth from one palm to another, entranced by how alive they looked. She wasn't even thinking about their monetary value. Maybe that was how people became obsessed with gold and jewels; it was mesmerizing. Somewhat regretfully, she poured the diamonds back into the velvet bag, wondering for the millionth time how Lou had gotten them. She would never know, and she was surprised to find that unsolved mysteries didn't set well with her. Especially those involving her abusive dead spouse. *Damn him.*

Anger was a new feeling for her. She'd buried it her whole life. Scared, victimized, depressed...all of them she was intimately familiar with. But anger, not so much. It was so *big*. And being big made it scary, as if she might not be able to control it if she ever let it loose. She let the feeling prowl around inside her, sensing its power and heat. Like the diamonds' sparkle, it was seductive, but there was no target for it. She wondered if Alexander would understand her, or if he would think she was dwelling in the past, or worse yet, if he might judge her.

The thought of Alexander reminded her she really should be helping him get lunch, but she'd been drawn back to the closet where she kept her jewelry boxes as if the diamonds had been singing a siren song to her. Closing the box, she marched out to the kitchen to see what she could do to help.

"There you are, my lovely wife. We're almost ready to eat. Come and taste this and see if I need to adjust any seasonings." He stepped aside, pointing at the dish on the counter.

"Is this what I think it is?" Helen's mouth began to water. He'd made this once before, and she loved it.

"Yes, it's my famous curried tuna salad. It's fast. It's easy. It's tasty. I got swallowed doing a chapter this morning and almost forgot lunch. I see you've been writing, too." She saw the question in his eyes.

She stepped up and dipped the spoon into the salad and tasted it. "Yum. It's as good as I remembered, or maybe even better. And yes, I am finally writing. Who would have guessed?" She laughed. "I was afraid I was never going to get started, and now it's pouring out as if I were a broken water main."

He put his arms around her, and she laid her head against his chest, listening to his heart beat, feeling the warmth, enjoying his scent. "You've made some remarkable changes in your life. I'd say taking several weeks to sort things out is actually pretty fast work." He kissed her neck, and she felt like suggesting they skip lunch, but they'd never get anything done that way.

She hugged him hard. "I love you so much."

He stroked her back. "I love you, too. Shall we eat?"

She looked up into his glittering eyes and saw he'd been just as tempted as she was. "It's my second choice of things to do, but I guess we ought to. I'd like to get 1000 words done today, and I need my wits about me to do that. But I happen to be free this evening."

He tossed her a dazzling smile. "OK, boss, that's a date for later. Let's eat."

Helen enjoyed using lunch time to catch up on things. It was something she'd never had before, and it felt like a bonding ritual every time. "I meant to tell you that we're trying to drag things out a bit on the sale of my condo to give Mary Beth time to find somewhere to live. I've contacted the HOA and told them I'm putting it on the market, and that Mary Beth is leaving. They seemed satisfied with that, but they'll no doubt check to see if I follow through. I don't know how long I've got, but I told Shari to take her time listing it. I need to figure out what to do with the furniture. I don't want to pile it up in the garage, but I don't intend to sell it. I haven't spoken to Sally yet, but I was thinking of offering it to her. Lena and Warren don't need it, and they live so far away." She sighed. "It doesn't matter what I do, someone will be mad at me."

Alexander chuckled. "Who cares? That's their natural state anyway. Try not to let it bother you."

"You're right. I shouldn't let them upset me. It's my stuff to give away as I wish. Sally needs it more than anyone, and she's here, so I'm going to give her first refusal on all of it. If anything's left, the others can fight over it."

Alexander chewed his salad with a thoughtful look on his face. "Is there anything you'd like to keep?"

Helen gave him a mock glare. "You read me too well. There are a couple pieces I'd like to keep, but we don't have room for them here."

"We'll make room. You shouldn't give away anything you love."

"I tell myself it's just stuff, and I don't need it. But there is a nice dresser I had as a child..."

"Keep it. What else do you want to hold on to?"

"There's a floor lamp supposedly made from some part of the *Leviathan*. The ocean liner. I don't know the entire story, but I always liked it. Nothing else, really."

"I don't see why we can't make room for those pieces."

"Thank you, Alexander. I do need to be pushed sometimes to do things just for me."

"You're welcome. We can get those pieces as soon as Mary Beth moves out and then let Sally collect the rest. My bet is she'll take it all." He had a glint in his eyes.

"I won't take that bet." She smiled back at him, well aware of Sally's acquisitive nature.

After lunch, they were cleaning up the kitchen when Helen remembered she hadn't told Alexander the most important news. "I can't believe I'm so forgetful. I didn't want to disturb you this morning when Olivia called. I hope you'll think it's good news. Well, it's good news for me, kind of sad news for Olivia."

Alexander had stopped loading the dishwasher and was staring at her. "What is it?"

"Olivia told me that suddenly yesterday she just decided it was time to move to assisted living. She didn't give me any clear reason why. But they won't let her take Spot, and her daughters don't have a place for Spot, so she asked if we would take her." Helen held her breath.

"You do know this is a big commitment? Spot is a young dog."

"I want her. I felt she belonged with me from the first. And even Fido accepts her. As long as you say OK, I want to keep her."

"OK by me. Two animals aren't that much harder to care for than one. We have one to board when we travel, and maybe this way, if they're together somewhere, they'll be happier. Or we might even consider getting a house sitter when we travel."

"You say that like we'll be doing it a lot."

"I forgot to tell you that my publisher is talking about having me do a book on the South of France. You know, travel through the area, staying at small bed and breakfast places, eating at local restaurants. Then doing a book that has recipes from the region and photos and stories. Would you like to go to France this summer and do some research?"

Helen was gobsmacked. "Are you kidding? I'd love to go. I can go with you?"

"You don't think I'd leave you alone in Palm Lakes for weeks at a time, do you? Some guy would come along and carry you off. Besides, I need you as my muse. I love watching you have new experiences. It gives me a perspective that adds wonder, which is very important in writing about this sort of thing. I've gotten a bit jaded, and you restore my sense of fun."

Helen smiled shyly. She was almost getting used to his extravagant compliments. "I think my summer calendar is totally free," she said coyly.

"I'm going to have to brush up on my French. I'm not fluent, but I have enough to get by. Although one of my teachers once said they don't speak French in the South of France. She was from Paris."

Helen giggled but wasn't sure she really got the joke. "Will you teach me? I don't want to be a total idiot in a foreign country."

"It would be my pleasure. Want your first lesson?" He had an unmistakable look in his eye.

Helen considered. What the heck. She'd write 2000 words tomorrow.

* * *

Mary Beth, 12:15pm

"THANKS FOR OFFERING to take me to lunch, Samantha. I'm all over the place right now. I should have expected it, but the HOA's letter took me by surprise. I've come to feel I belong here. Isn't that weird?

"I think it's great you feel good here, Mary Beth. I feel bad you're going through this now. Have you found a place to stay?"

"Not yet. Catherine, my across-the-street neighbor, offered me her couch for a while. She only has one bedroom. It's a kind offer, but it would be too crowded. Helen wanted to offer her guest casita, but she's concerned the HOA is focused on her since she owns the condo I'm staying in. I think it wise for me to avoid being seen on her property." Mary Beth bit into her spring roll and chewed thoughtfully. "I could get an apartment, but if I live outside Palm Lakes, I won't be back much. I really enjoy Catherine and doing jewelry with your Mom, and I'd miss Ethan."

Samantha's left eyebrow shot up. "So what about Ethan? How has this development changed things between you?"

Mary Beth let out a frustrated sigh. "Not at all. He offered to help me move. I didn't want him throw his back out, so I declined. He said he'd be glad to take me to look at apartments, but I'm not ready to do that quite yet. If I get big expenses, my tiny nest egg will be gone before I know it. I'm not making enough at Palo Verde to live anywhere nice."

Samantha gave her a sympathetic look. "I was kind of hoping you'd say this shook him out of his torpor, and he proposed something." She flashed a grin at Mary Beth.

Mary Beth mirrored her smile. "I wish. Catherine says I should get aggressive, but I just can't. He has yet to indicate he has more than platonic interest in me, and I really like our friendship and worry about ruining it if I throw myself at him."

"Most men would gladly catch a pretty woman your age. Here in Palm Lakes, you're a real catch."

Mary Beth snorted. "Ethan doesn't seem to think so. Or maybe he's just unaware." She shook her head and piled rice and kung pao chicken on her plate. "I have a little time to figure it out."

Samantha seemed to weigh something, then spoke softly. "We have a spare bedroom. I know it wouldn't be as nice as Helen's condo, but you could stay with us for a while."

"Arthur wouldn't mind?"

"I asked him, and he seems open to it."

"I'll keep it in mind. It's my best offer so far. I still need to create a permanent solution. I can't leech off of friends forever. I'm thinking I need more income. I was wondering about doing Botanica as a business."

Samantha chewed slowly, seeming to consider it. "I really like the products. I'm not much on selling things, though. Which may sound strange considering what I do, but I think of myself more as a design consultant. I wouldn't enjoy cold-calling and that sort of thing."

"I'm not worried about that with my big mouth." Mary Beth grinned. "My biggest problem is I don't have a large family or lots of friends, and that seems to be the best way to kick start a business."

Samantha nodded. "I'd be in the same boat. Did you talk to Nora?"

"Yeah, she was really open about it. She wants to help me if I'm serious, but she agrees it may be slow going if I don't have contacts I can speak to."

"Is it possible someone you know has a large circle of influence? I was thinking Nora benefited from Barbara's social circle."

"Ethan has a pretty large family, but I'd feel funny imposing on him. Not to change the subject, but your Mom has been encouraging about how well I'm learning from her. She says my designs are really good now. We talked about selling jewelry as another stream of income for me. She mentioned a couple consignment shops where I could put my pieces. It might take a lot of work, but if I found good places to put my jewelry, maybe I could make enough money to finance a nice place. The problem is, it wouldn't be here." Mary Beth took a sip of tea. "Enough about me. Tell me what's going on with you."

Samantha shrugged her shoulders. "Same old stuff. My Mom hates being alone, but won't leave her house. She's getting more forgetful all the time. Last week I happened to stop by when she was writing checks, and I offered to put envelopes in the mail box for her, and there was one for the Posse. I asked was she donating--she has so little of her own--and she said yes, and I mentioned that I thought she'd already given them some money recently. She was surprised and said she thought they mailed annually. I told her they mail more often than that. She was just going to mail them a check any time they asked for money. That's the kind of thing that happens to elderly people. She won't let me help her with her bills, and I worry she's going to overdraw her account. I still can't believe my Dad left her in such bad shape." With a disgusted look, Samantha stabbed at her food with her chopsticks.

"I think Stanley dying was a shock to her. She hasn't recovered. Maybe she never will. But she's so much brighter than the average person. Hopefully that means she has farther to fall than most before it gets bad."

Samantha grimaced as she chewed. Then she shook her head and swallowed. "She isn't ready to leave the house, but she needs to have more help. She thinks she's independent, but if Ethan and you and I stopped doing for her, she'd never make it. That's why I turned down the job with Jack."

"So are you still in touch with Jack?"

"I phone him now and then and tell him how things are with Mom. If I could get her into assisted living, I'd feel it was safe to take that job. But as things stand now, I don't see how I can. Even if she decided to move tomorrow, just getting the house cleaned up and ready for sale would be an enormous project. I keep revising my estimate upward every time I spend an afternoon there trying to clean things out. I'm up to four months now." She frowned as she scraped the last of the food from her plate.

"She is a bit of a hoarder." Mary Beth grinned at the understatement, hoping to make Samantha laugh.

"Ya think?" Samantha laughed out loud. "I wish things were different, but I love my Mom and want to do right by her, and there's no way I can budge her until she's ready. I just keep hoping she'll realize it before she burns the house down or something terrible happens. I call her every night. I worry about what might happen if she falls and can't get up. No one would hear her call for help. She doesn't imagine something like that could happen, but with her osteoporosis, it's possible."

"Helen told me that happened to the widow who lives next door to her. If her dog hadn't kept barking, she could have lain on the floor for days...maybe more. I'll keep offering to help out when I'm there on Saturdays. If you need help cleaning the house or moving her, let me know."

Samantha smiled. "Thanks. I hate moving, so I know how you must feel moving so often in the past year. I'd be happy to help you when the time comes."

"I appreciate the offer. You know, it's hard to believe at times like this, but things are going to change for both of us. I'll eventually find a place to live long term, and at some point, you're going to take that job with Jack. We just don't know how or when."

Samantha looked at her wistfully. "I hope you're right...Of course, you're right. Things can't go on like this forever."

* * *

Maddie, 6:30pm

MADDIE SAT SIPPING wine and munching on potato chips, watching an old John Wayne movie on the VCR. She'd seen this one so often, she had it memorized. Her attention kept drifting to what Mary Beth had told her on Saturday. The damn HOA was forcing her out of her condo, or rather, Helen's condo. Simply because she was under 55. Poor Mary Beth! It hadn't been that long since she lost her mother. She'd been forced to sell her Mom's place, and now she was being thrown out of Helen's. Maddie couldn't imagine living with so little security.

Mary Beth had been given offers of temporary shelter from various people, but she didn't want to accept any of them for various reasons. When she'd left after Saturday's jewelry session, she'd been more down than Maddie had ever seen her. She had dark smudges under her lovely green eyes, and she was frowning way too much.

The shoot-'em-up was taking place loudly on the TV, but Maddie hardly heard it, because she'd just had a brainstorm. Why hadn't she thought of it before? With Stanley gone, she had a spare room. Mary Beth could come stay with her. Maybe that would solve both her problem and Mary Beth's. If Maddie had a live-in companion, maybe Samantha would quit lobbying for her to move to assisted living. She could possibly even get a bit of rent from Mary Beth to supplement her meager income. And she'd never be alone at night anymore. Staying alone at night was her biggest problem.

Mary Beth was such a respectful girl and so easy to get along with, Maddie was certain it would work out fine for them both. She'd still be illegal, but she'd have a place while she was figuring out her future plans. And it would buy Maddie precious time. She couldn't wait to tell her. She ignored the pain in her bones as she got up to search for the phone.

* * *

Emma, 7:00pm

EMMA SLOUCHED onto the sofa beside Julio, too tired and achy to drink her tea. "I'm sore in places I didn't know I had muscles."

He grinned at her and patted her back. "You just aren't used to it."

She rolled her eyes. "I don't need you reminding me of my age."

His dark brown eyes became serious. "I was referring to the fact that you are not accustomed to manual labor. That has nothing to do with age."

She slanted a look his way, her blue eyes envious. "You don't look the least bit done in."

"Well, even though design is my focus, I do a lot of manual labor. Gardening is new for you. Most of my life, I made a living by manual labor."

Emma sighed and laid her head back against the top of the couch. "If

I'd realized how much work it was going to be, I might not have suggested this."

His laugh washed over her like a balm. "I think it is good that we have this project together. When the plants begin to bear, you will feel differently, I promise."

"I hope you're right. We've only just begun. I hadn't realized how much work a vegetable garden was."

"If it were easy, everyone would do it. You will see a big difference between what you grow and what you buy at the store. I will be here to help."

His last statement cut to the core of her. She had to admit, she wasn't sure she believed it. He'd never lied to her, but some part of her still wondered why he bothered with her. She didn't dare ask again. He must be tired of her incredulity. She was torn between being fully honest with him and being afraid of annoying him with her insecurity. She didn't want him to infer she mistrusted him, when it was herself she didn't trust to make this work. Which led to a topic she had to voice.

"I'm sorry about how things have been going." Her voice had dropped to a whisper. It was as if she didn't want to broach the subject. Well, that was true. Part of her thought he'd flee if she did the wrong thing. And she felt most of what she did was wrong.

He put his arm around her and pulled her against him. She noticed it felt natural to her. If only the rest had gone so smoothly. "It takes time to heal. Instead of healing, you buried the past. Now we are taking it out of the place you hid it and forcing you to look at it. I cannot imagine how hard it is for you. I think you are very brave."

She let the tension drain out of her body and relaxed into his warmth. "Thank you for being so patient. I had no idea how I would react. I was pushing myself. Maybe I just wanted to get past it."

"Emma, this is not something you 'get past,' like bad-tasting medicine. I am sorry you have to face the fear all over again. If I could take it away from you, I would. But I am here for you. If or when you are ready, you will feel it. When you are ready, you won't be able to stop it from happening, but it will not be forced on you. Maybe that is what you are afraid of. Losing control. But you will always have control with me. Whatever you say is what I will do."

His voice was like a lifeline keeping her from drowning. Did he have any idea? Tears of gratitude welled up in her eyes, but no words came to her.

He pretended not to notice. "When I was a child, I was bitten by an angry dog. You can still see the scars on this arm, where I tried to protect myself. See?" He held it out to her and pulled his sleeve up. The scars were lighter than the rich coffee tones of the surrounding skin. She reached over and stroked it, feeling the hard knotting of the scar tissue under the surface. He became quiet, and she could see a pulsing in the side of his neck.

Taking a deep breath, he continued. "I was very young and after that, all dogs scared me. My mother was still alive then. She was the one who helped me to see that not all dogs bite. I knew in my head that she was right, but it took a long time for me to overcome my fears. But I eventually did."

Emma sat back and looked at him with new eyes. "I could tell you empathized with me, but I couldn't imagine why or how. It never occurred to me that my problem was like any other phobia. It's obvious I can't just push past it with raw will, but I can also tell that I am doing better." She cast her eyes downward in embarrassment. "I used to be afraid of you a little bit."

"You seem to be afraid I will get mad and leave or hurt you if I do not get what I want. That would not be me. That would be your uncle. I am not him. You can always say no to me, and I will listen."

His kindness was a debt she didn't know how to repay. She knew she wanted to please him physically, but it wasn't something she could do yet, not the way he wanted. At the very least, she could be open with him. So she vowed to herself she would overcome her shyness and speak to him in ways that would show her trust and respect for him.

"You said something a few days ago about how we only had each other. You're right. I like my women friends, but somehow I can't bring myself to tell them about what happened when I was little. Maybe I still feel ashamed. Or I want them to like me, and I'm afraid they will look at me like I'm damaged or dirty. You don't treat me like I'm broken."

She paused and wiped tears from her eyes, pausing only briefly as he reached for her hand. "I have spent my whole life avoiding sex. I cut it out of my life quite successfully. Even thinking about sex only reminded me about my uncle, so it was easiest to just avoid it. But I realize now that I know next to nothing about the subject. I feel like an idiot. I don't know what to expect, what is normal." She felt drained from admitting how naive she was.

"What about love?"

"There are many kinds of love, and I concentrated on the ones that didn't involve sex. I did love Leo. He was such a great man, so kind and compassionate and loyal."

"What about romance?"

She laughed. "I pretty much refused to believe in it. I think I deadened the part of my heart that relates to romantic love and sexual attraction." Her voice went to a whisper again. "I'm afraid I won't be able to find it. Not this late in life."

"It is never too late for anything, Emma."

"I just don't think I can go back to the bedroom with you again yet. The minute we got there, I froze. It triggered too many bad memories."

"Then we shall go more slowly. I will learn to awaken your heart."

"I think you've already begun. When you kiss me, I feel like a different person. A whole person. For the first time in my life. I just wish I could do better."

"You must learn to be happy about the good things and not look at what has not changed. I will help you. I think kissing is a good place to start."

That was the end of talk for the evening.

* * *

Red, 11:45pm

RED KNEW *what was going to happen next, but he felt powerless to change it. He tried to lunge for the knife in Owen's hand to stop him from slashing Tanya, who stood paralyzed in fear, her hands up in a mute gesture of defense that Red knew would be useless. Red struggled mightily, but his body didn't respond the way it should. Instead, he was trapped like a fly in fast-setting amber. The harder he tried to move his arms and legs, the slower he moved. He watched as*

243

Owen, his eyes filled with glee and rage, swept the butcher knife across Tanya's neck, cutting it deeply. Blood sprayed everywhere, even on him, and within seconds her red silk bathrobe had turned a darker shade as she fell to the floor, hands still up. Blood poured from her onto the tile, creating a lake of red on the white. She gurgled as she tried to draw breath. All the while, he tried to scream for help, to distract Owen, but he couldn't make his voice work. Until it did.

He bolted upright, covered in sweat, his heart pounding like he'd run a marathon. The stabbing pain in his shoulder woke him up like a bucket of ice water. He looked around wildly as Lydia's voice soothed him, "Eric. It was a dream. You're OK." Her soft hand caressed him back into a horizontal position.

Embarrassed that he'd awakened her, he said in a strangled voice, "I've been having the same dream every night in the hospital. I'm sorry. I thought maybe now that I was home, things would get back to normal."

"Eric, you've been through a terrible trauma and were injured seriously. These things take time."

"Somehow, it's worse than when it actually happened. I feel responsible. If only I'd stayed more focused on Owen, maybe I could have saved her." He rubbed his hand across his face as if trying to wipe the memory away. "There was so much blood."

"I know. It was terrible. But it isn't your fault. There was nothing either of us could have done. This is what I was trying to explain to you. Sometimes seeing more than others see is a curse instead of a blessing."

He sighed and turned to her, burying his head against her shoulder. "I wish I could forget."

"Are you in pain?"

"Yes, but I don't like to take pain pills. I can handle it." For some reason he felt like pushing her away; he felt guilty for wanting space.

"Nonsense. I'm going to do some work on you."

"Lydia, it's almost midnight. You need your sleep."

She looked at him pointedly.

"What do you see?"

"You don't need any special powers to know what I know. I see a very stubborn man who is in rather a lot of pain. I understand you don't want to take the pills, but at least let me try to help."

"Seems you're more stubborn than I am."

"Does that mean you don't mind if I try?"

He sighed and pulled the pillow under his chest so he could lie face down and let her work on him. "I deeply appreciate how you are taking care of me." Yet some part of him was irked at his need and didn't want her to see it.

He could hear the grin in her voice when she said, "It's your place, Eric, and you're letting me stay here. The least I can do is help you feel better."

She slipped out of bed and crossed the darkened room to the dresser, where she had left her sack of crystals and other whatnots. He was hurting badly enough and was disturbed enough by the recurring nightmare that he hoped she could do some magic.

She padded back to the bed, leaving the lights off, and laid a few crystals on top of the covers. He couldn't see well enough to tell what colors they were. "So this healing with rocks. Does it really work?"

He couldn't see her face clearly, but he imagined the raised eyebrows. "Everything I do 'works.' It's just that you can't dictate exact results. I know that sounds like an evasion, but each person is unique, and what they do with the energy is very dependent on a lot of factors I cannot control. Think of energy healing as gentle and natural, working with your own energy, while drugs are a like a hammer that overpower your body and force an outcome. My way is slower, more natural and not as predictable, but has no side effects. What I can promise is that you will feel more calm and probably less pain, and that your wound will heal faster if you let me do this for you every day for the next couple weeks."

"I'm willing to try anything. Especially if the nightmares go away. They're worse than the pain."

"I've chosen some crystals--rocks--that feel appropriate to me for what we're trying to do here. Hold this one in your left hand. There. And this one in your right hand. OK. Now I'm going to lay a third on the bandage over your wound. I'll be quiet for a little while, then you'll hear me chanting. You just rest."

Eric couldn't feel anything happening at first. After a minute, Lydia began some kind of chant. It was low and hypnotic, lulling him back to sleep. Then his hands began to buzz and heat up around the crystals. After another minute, he could feel his wound in painful detail. Then a warmth invaded it as well, soothing it, singing it to sleep like him. His heart had slowed to a normal pace, and the tension in his muscles drained away. She continued for several more minutes, doing a simple chant in her marvelous, sexy voice. Tangentially, he wondered if she knew how sexy her voice was. He started to drift off and caught himself in time to realize the pain was much less than it had been. "This is amazing," he stuttered. "I never would have guessed..."

"Hush now. Let it work. Allow the pain to drain out of you and feel yourself filled with a golden, healing light."

Some time later--it could have been minutes or hours--she stopped. Red felt better than he had since before the murder. "Thank you. I feel much better."

"Try to get some sleep." She took the stones from his hands and went back to the dresser, then returned and gently stroked his back, murmuring soothing words to him. Sleep stole him away.

11

THURSDAY, FEBRUARY 22, 1996

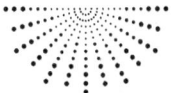

Lydia, 9:57am

*J*ean and Ian had arrived three days ago and were obviously thrilled to be in Palm Lakes. But the condo was just too crowded for three people, so Lydia was spending most of her time at Eric's place.

Eric had left a little while ago for his shift with the Posse. She knew he needed to get back to a normal schedule, but he wasn't healed yet, in spite of all the work she'd done on him. His aura had blank spots in it, and the nightmares continued to plague him. She was concerned about him going back to work so soon, but she knew he needed to do something. The only way he knew how to be whole was to act whole, and she didn't object to that logic as long as it didn't set his healing back.

Eric was fine with her sleeping at his place, but things had never gotten back to how they were before the murder. A distance had grown between them that made her feel like his guest instead of his partner. Since the incident with Owen, Eric hadn't been as affectionate and open. Like a wounded Viking, he struggled with not being at full potency, and everything she did only reminded him of his infirmity. He was not a man who liked being in a weakened state. He'd been acting like a injured bear, with nearly the same unpleasant and dangerous attitude.

His lack of interest in sex was understandable at first, but she was beginning to fret that his experience had shifted how he felt about her. She knew he was healed enough, but he seemed to be avoiding physical intimacy.

It would be so easy to blame herself. She was never any good at relationships. They always imploded, so why not just give up on this one? She and Eric were so different, and now he seemed to have gone off her. But when she ignored her own fears and tuned in to her heart, she felt that this man really cared for her, and she wasn't willing to let him go. He just needed to heal more. And she had an idea how to accomplish that. But she wasn't sure that Eric would agree to it. However, she was so certain it was the right path that she wasn't going to ask him.

Picking up the phone, she dialed Digger's number.

"Hi, Digger. Lydia here. Could we meet up?"

"Sure, girl. The usual place at 11?"

"Sounds good to me. I'll be there."

After hanging up, she prepared to meet Digger at the local McDonald's, where many of the Palm Lakes residents gathered for morning coffee and gossip. It was the perfect place for a drug buy if the parties were senior citizens.

She set out for the McD's under a bright spring sky, cloudless and hinting of the warmth of a low desert spring. When she entered the restaurant, it was easy to spot him in the far back corner. His faded, long red hair was a beacon, even though he was beginning to bald, as if he were wearing a long red wig that had slipped back on his head. After getting a cup of coffee, she slid into the bench seat opposite him and looked into his pale blue eyes. As usual, he was smiling. She'd never seen him in a bad mood, but she'd always attributed it to his weed habit more than his personality. He was munching on an Egg McMuffin.

"You want anything to eat, Lydia? I wasn't sure if you'd had breakfast."

"I already ate. Thanks. Coffee will do me." She smiled, reflecting that Digger always seemed to have the munchies, though he never gained weight from it.

"What can I do you for?" His eyes twinkled at his own humor.

"I have an unusual request. I'm thinking about making a herbal extract. Have you ever done that with our herb?"

Digger's eyes became thoughtful as he pondered the coded question. "You know, I never have. But there's no reason not to. It won't work as fast as some delivery methods, but it should still work. At least that's what I think. Why are you making an extract?"

"It's not for me. It's for someone else. For my...boyfriend? Do women my age have boyfriends?" She laughed at the absurdity of it. "My lover. But you see, he doesn't smoke, and he's a retired cop. So I thought the extract would be best. Oh, let me start at the beginning. Did you read about the murder in Palm Lakes?"

Digger's eyes widened. "Yes."

"It was next door to me. Eric's on the Posse, and he and I both were concerned about the people in the condo between our two. The guy was creepy. Finally, one day he snapped. Eric ran over when he heard the screams, but it was too late. It was really messy."

A light dawned on Digger's face. "He has post traumatic stress?"

"Yup."

"You and I both know this herb is good for that. In fact, that's how I got started using it. I had some demons hanging on after 'Nam, and the herb chased them away. It's just the ticket for your man. But is he one of those righteous types? You need to make sure he doesn't bust me." Digger's voice cracked with anxiety.

"We've talked about it a little, and he knows I smoke, and he's fine with that. He was homicide, not narcotics, and he doesn't have a negative attitude. But I can't be sure he'll try it. I just think my best bet is to make an extract for him. It's easy and safe to store, and there's no smell, and he won't have to smoke it. What do you think?

"I think it would work. Just please don't tell him about me. I don't want to get picked up and have them sweat people's names out of me. I'm not that brave, and I don't want to betray my clients."

Lydia reached over and patted his hand. "I won't put you in danger, Digger." She noted that his skin still had pink irritated areas like eczema. His aura was a blue as faded as his eyes. He'd never been the healthiest person. But there was silver threaded through the blue.

Digger might be a 'drug dealer,' but he was an honest person, and she trusted him. "I know you aren't really in business. I appreciate that you sell to me. I need some help with the stress of crowds, seeing what I do."

"You'll need a bit more than usual if you're making an extract."

"I didn't want to say on the phone. How much do you have?"

"Something told me to bring extra. I have enough for what you want to do. Four ounces. If it works out and he needs more, just give me a call and work the number of ounces you want into the conversation."

"Is it the usual price?"

"Yep."

She rummaged through her large purse and extracted the exact amount of cash and slid it nonchalantly across the table to him. At the same time, he slid a large baggie of herb her way after scanning the area to make sure no one was watching. Lucky for her that her purse was so large. The transaction took place amid the background murmurs of a dozen conversations and the kitchen noises from the door next to them. "Thanks, Digger. You're a life saver."

BACK HOME, she started the herb soaking in the alcohol solution in a darkened cabinet of her kitchen. She'd need to shake it daily. Maybe she should take it to Eric's place. But she wanted to tell him about it and be sure she had his permission to have it there. He'd freak if something happened and it were revealed that a Posse officer had weed in his condo. She decided she'd tell him today when he got home.

Jean walked into the kitchen, her hair mussed, looking weary but happy in sweats and a t-shirt. "Still jet-lagged, Jean?"

Jean stifled a yawn. "No, but I'm having trouble catching up on my sleep. I'll be OK soon." She looked at the coffeemaker longingly and sighed with relief that there was fresh coffee available. "Just what I need to kick start my day. Do you mind if I grab a cup for me and Ian?"

Lydia grinned. "Of course not. That's why I made a big pot." She looked at Jean's aura as she poured coffee. Bright, swirling colors created a kaleidoscope effect. The greens and oranges were predominant and everything was bright and clear. "You look good."

Jean turned and stared at her, registering what she meant. "Do I look different?"

Lydia looked at her longer blonde hair, clear blue eyes and lovely skin. "You look great."

"But do I look different energetically?"

"Very, but all in a good way."

"How do I look?"

"Your colors are brighter, stronger and more clear. There is more green and more orange, both signs of a loving relationship. I'm so glad to see you so balanced and happy."

Jean sighed. "It's great, isn't it? If I could see colors around you, I bet I'd see the same." She gave Lydia a meaningful look.

Lydia was surprised to find herself blushing. "Maybe. I'm afraid to hope. It's never been like this for me. I still can't believe he accepts me as I am."

"He's a keeper, Lyd. You deserve someone who will love you as you are. You're a wonderful person. We've both been scraping by for too many years on less than enough to be happy, telling ourselves it was all right."

"You've changed, Jean. You're more confident now. Ian suits you. And he's a handsome devil. Oh, and that accent. You'll have to warn him about women throwing themselves at him because of that gorgeous British accent. If I weren't with Eric, I'd be swooning over him."

Jean rolled her eyes. "I know. I still melt just listening to him talk. He can say anything with that accent, and he'll have my full attention." Jean poured the coffee and added sugar and creamer, then left Lydia to ponder how to tell Eric about her plan.

THE HOURS DRAGGED by as she waited in Eric's condo, but finally she heard the garage door go up and the car pull in. Moments later, Eric came into the living room. She was already standing, and she threw her arms around him. "How was your day?"

He pulled his head back and searched her eyes. "You really need to ask?" There was an element of mischief in his voice, which heartened her. He hadn't been playful lately.

"Yes, I need to hear from you how your day is. My abilities don't preclude communication, as you know." She was feeling defensive, knowing what she was going to tell him, and she silently chastised herself for being difficult. It wasn't going to help her case. She suddenly realized she was afraid of how he would react. Somewhat chagrined, she decided she had to explain her plan to him now. But by then, he was answering her question.

"Well, it was a routine day here at Palm Lakes. Mostly I drove around. I told one person to put their garage door down. There have been a rash of burglaries lately, the common element being that in all cases, the residents had forgotten to put their garage doors down. Fortunately, nothing major was stolen, since most people don't store valuables in their garages. Maybe kids, maybe drug addicts looking for something to fence. But in spite of keeping my eyes peeled, I saw nothing suspicious. I'm guessing it happens more often at night, so I was thinking of taking a night shift. Would you mind?"

Lydia's knee jerk reaction was shock that he'd do that. He was newly back to work and not yet healed, but then she understood. He thought to avoid the nightmares by working at night. Part of her pushed aside a fear that he was trying to distance himself from her. "I'd miss you, but you have to do what you think is best."

A look of surprise lit his blue eyes as he pulled her into a tight embrace. "No one has ever said that to me and meant it. I believe you do." He kissed her, and she was grateful she hadn't expressed the disappointment she'd felt when he told her. All the more reason to tell him her plan.

"I know that you think work is a balm for what ails you, and I'm sorry that what I've done hasn't chased away the nightmares, but I believe I have a way to do that, if you're willing to trust me."

He took her hand and dragged her over to the couch and sat down, pulling her after him. "I'm all ears."

It was easier to talk to him when he wasn't looming over her, but Lydia still found herself bracing for possible judgment. "You probably could guess that anything I suggest will be highly unconventional."

He chuckled. "Of course. And don't put down all you've done for me. The doctor said I healed much faster than he expected, and the pain was always significantly less after you worked on me with those rocks." His steel blue stare was laced with humor. She knew he was calling her crystals 'rocks' just to gig her. She wasn't going to take the bait.

"I'm glad you feel that way, but this may be a stretch for you. I'm making a herbal extract. You soak the herb in alcohol and it leeches out the healing bits. Herbal extracts have been used practically forever in healing."

"That sounds good. I like alcohol and I like plants." The laugh lines around his eyes were crinkled. "But I can tell there's something else."

"Yes, there is. How observant of you. The herb in question isn't entirely legal to use, but it's well known anecdotally to be helpful in cases of post traumatic stress, which is what a doctor would call what's causing your nightmares. The person I obtained the herb from has personal experience. In fact, that's why he uses it. I have the extract 'cooking' at my place, but if you agree to use it, I'll bring it here, since I'm here more often now. I just didn't want to involve you in something illegal without warning you. It won't look or smell like pot. That's why I made the extract. You can take it with impunity. It will just involve one or two droppersful a few times a day. I'll figure out the dosage if you agree to use it." She held her breath waiting for his reaction, not wanting to upset the balance in their relationship, half expecting this would be the thing that drove him away from her.

She was afraid to look at him, because she knew she'd see the truth right away, and she wasn't sure she could take it, but she forced her eyes up to engage his. With a shock of surprise, she saw his aura was shot through with gold, uncommon in adults, as it represented wonder and awe. The greens were deep, dark and rich and entwined the gold. She released her breath in a sigh. *He loves me! He really does! But does he even realize it?* She vaguely registered annoyance with herself for her lack of trust in him.

When he spoke, his voice was uneven, as if he were overcome with emotion. "No one has ever cared as much about me as you do. You constantly amaze me. I've never been a stickler about weed. I don't really consider it a problem like other drugs. It still surprises me you can obtain it so easily here, but don't tell me how you get it. It's better I stay ignorant of that part of the deal."

"So you don't mind having the solution here? I won't label it, and it doesn't look like anything bad."

"Bring it over anytime. We just have to agree not to tell anyone else about this, not even your friends. OK? I can't risk it getting out. There could be repercussions."

"I'm fine with that. It's our secret. You get to decide who to tell, if anyone. I won't even tell Jean."

Eric was staring at her as if seeing her for the first time, and it warmed her all over to know he actually respected and valued her. Loved her. She was almost ready to admit to herself that this was the real thing.

* * *

Jean, 10:20am

JEAN NUDGED the bedroom door open with her hip, watching that the coffee didn't spill, then pushed it nearly closed once she got fully into the room. Sun was streaming from behind the closed curtains, but Ian was still snuggled deep in the covers. She loved to watch him sleep, though she'd rather see his hazel eyes looking at her like she was something special. She couldn't remember ever having that with Richard.

Strange how thinking about her ex-husband no longer evoked a twinge of pain and guilt. Not that she had done anything wrong, but her refusal to gossip about the cause of their breakup no doubt made her look responsible for it, and she was certain Richard took advantage of her discretion to deflect any appearance of blame on his part. *Well, who cares?*

She put the mugs down on the night stand on her side of the bed and sank into the mattress. The only people she'd told about Richard's porn addiction were her best friends Lydia, Helen and Barbara, and they were sworn to secrecy. Richard still had to live in Palm Lakes, and she saw no reason to make his life more miserable than it already was. He hadn't dealt with the divorce badly, but he hadn't been gracious, either. Maybe he was on tenterhooks waiting to see if she'd tell everyone about his addiction.

No, she wasn't feeling that twinge of guilt for leaving him anymore. She knew in her heart it had been the best, though hardest, decision she'd ever made. Richard and she had grown apart so much over the years, and at best he only tolerated her interests and never participated in what mattered to her. She'd thought she could live that way, but then his porn addiction had surfaced, and he wasn't willing or able to kick it, and that was the last straw.

Sighing, she leaned over and stroked Ian's stubbly face, watching his eyes open slowly, focus and blink at her. "Good morning." His voice was scratchy and low, and he cleared it a couple times before going on. "What time is it?" She still couldn't get over hearing a British accent in bed in the morning. It was terribly sexy.

"It's almost 10:30, sleepy head. I brought you some coffee. We need to adapt to this time zone, and I figured it was OK to roust you out of bed now."

"Sure, give me a second to wake up." He didn't wake up instantly like she did. Instead, he needed time to swim up from the well of sleep. She continued to stroke him.

"I'm sorry my beard is rough. I'll shave today."

"It doesn't bother me. I just like to touch you."

He gave her a sleepy smile with his eyes shut and reached for her, stroking her arm. "I like to touch you, too." There was a warmth in his tone and meaning in his touch, and her first thought was that the coffee was going to get cold. She wasn't used to having a man reach for her in the morning with sex on his mind, and it was taking some getting used to, since they hadn't had a normal courtship. On the other hand, it felt perfectly natural. She didn't know how to explain it, but she felt like they'd known each other for years, been married for years, and she loved it. She'd never felt this way with Richard. Like she belonged with him.

She sank into the covers and gave herself over to his sleepy kisses as his warm hands caressed her, promising her much more than just a cuddle. She sighed again, enjoying the moment.

· · ·

MUCH LATER, Jean pushed herself to a sitting position and reached over and shook Ian's shoulder. "It's really time to get up now. Aren't you hungry?"

"Yes, I am. But before, I was only hungry for you."

"You silver-tongued devil. Come on, get up." Jean slipped out of bed and picked up her clothes, which were strewn across the bed and floor, then dressed quickly. This whole situation with Ian was like something out of a movie. Find your soul mate on the internet, and he lives in another country, and you get divorced, go to meet him and marry him and bring him back? Who did that kind of thing? She had never thought of herself as brave or a risk-taker, but she couldn't deny her courage now.

In retrospect, what made success possible was her willingness to rely on her intuition, rather than just doing what seemed logical. And she never would have done that in the past. Only since she'd started training herself to listen to her Inner Voice through the use of dowsing had she come to trust and even rely on her intuition. This had been a real test, and she felt she had passed with flying colors. She would never ignore her intuition again.

She was dressed before he'd even sat up, but she knew from experience he wasn't going back to sleep now, so she grabbed the still-full mugs and went out to the kitchen to get refills, glad that Lydia wasn't there to tease her about not getting around to drinking it. They really needed to find their own place so they could have more privacy and not impose on Lydia.

Jean made a pot of coffee, standing by, musing about their future as the brown liquid dripped through noisily, when Ian stepped into the kitchen. His long gray hair was sexy and uncombed, and he was dressed in jeans and an old black t-shirt he'd gotten at a Pink Floyd concert. He ran his fingers through his hair as he looked at the coffeepot longingly. "I really need a cup of coffee. This move threw me for a loop. I'm more exhausted than I would have expected." He padded across the kitchen on bare feet and gave Jean a hug. She practically melted, still unused to the attention and affection, even after months with him.

"Of course you're exhausted. This is the biggest thing you've ever done. You'll get adjusted soon." She wondered how long it would take for her to feel blasé about having such a great husband. She hoped never.

* * *

Alexander, 1:10pm

"I KNOW you want to go back to work now that we're done with lunch, but I thought a glass of wine would be nice. There are some things we ought to discuss." Alexander held a glass of white wine out for Helen and they walked into the living room. Sunlight streamed through the picture windows. Golfers were scurrying around the course, enjoying the early spring weather. The sliding glass door was partially open, letting a warm breeze float in through the screen door.

Helen sank into the sofa, and Alexander sat next to her. He reached over to the envelope that lay on the coffee table. "I see you got this back today." The letter she had written to the woman in France had obviously traveled far. It had several messages in French stamped on it and had been returned as not deliverable. "Are you OK?"

She reached over and took the battered letter from him, sadness etched on her face. "We knew it was a long shot. She hadn't written him in ages. She either moved or died, or both. This is the end of it. And I am ready to be done with the mystery and accept that you don't always get answers to questions about life." She looked up at him, her eyes brimming with tears. "Of course, it would have been nice to find out, but as with the diamonds, there's no one left to ask. Life isn't like a mystery novel. Things don't always get neatly tied up at the end of the story. Lou took his secrets to the grave, and I'm tired of letting that bother me."

He put his arm around her shoulders. "At least you tried. And the good news is that the diamonds are now yours. Think of it as Lou paying for the bad things he did. He didn't get to enjoy them. Now you will. It all works out even in the end, in spite of the mystery."

Her laugh was forced, but she seemed to be throwing off the sadness. Wiping her eyes and sighing, she said, "That wasn't all you wanted to talk about, was it?"

"You must be psychic. I have a couple other things. Where are we at with selling the condo?" He was a little afraid to ask, still uncertain she was willing to let it go. She hadn't redecorated the house in spite of his offer, but she hadn't been acting upset with him lately. He didn't like to bring up subjects that could escalate to a confrontation, but the condo needed to be sold.

Pushing a strand of her shiny reddish gold hair back from her face, Helen answered calmly, "I've been thinking about an unconventional solution." Her green-flecked blue eyes sought his out. "Jean and Ian are looking for a place. She has some money from her settlement, but it isn't enough to buy a condo. I was thinking what if we let them rent-to-own? We could ask for a down payment of whatever they can afford, then let them pay us monthly until they own it."

"You know that's a risky proposition, even moreso between friends. What if they can't pay at some point?"

She sighed and began to twist leg of her pants. "I know. They don't have steady jobs, and they're considering starting a business, which of course means no guaranteed income. It's just that they're my friends, and I'd like to help them get started. They're legal, and it would take the expenses off us. We'd make sure they paid more than enough for insurance, taxes, HOA fees, utilities, etc." Her eyes pleaded with him.

"I don't want to say no. We can afford the risk. But if they get to the point they can't pay, we'd have to ask them to leave and sell it outright. Do you agree to that? I know it could put a strain on the friendship to ask them to vacate, but it would be even worse if we had to pay for their home."

"They wouldn't want a free ride, Alexander. They're friends, but they're very independent."

"That's fine with me, then. We need to go to a lawyer and have it all in writing. I don't want any misunderstandings."

"They wouldn't, either." She smiled shyly. "Thanks for being open to that."

"Why wouldn't I be? We don't really need the money. I just don't want to jeopardize your friendships, nor do I want us to be embroiled in a problem down the road. But I'm willing to give it a try."

Helen threw her arms around him. He loved when she was like this. She was the least jaded woman he'd ever known, and her sweetness made her delectable.

"Now to an even more interesting subject, how are things with Sally? You went out baby shopping yesterday, right?"

Helen's face clouded as she frowned and reached for her wineglass. "I can't believe how blind I've been about that girl all these years." Alexander waited for her to continue, thinking nothing would surprise him. But he was wrong. "She hasn't prepared for the baby. She has two bedrooms in her apartment, but she hasn't made one into a nursery. There was no baby furniture, nothing. And she's got a new boyfriend who was hanging out there in the middle of the day."

Alexander couldn't stop his left eyebrow from raising. She saw it and punched him on the shoulder. "Don't even go there. I know what you're thinking. She's found herself another guy to wrap around her little finger."

"When you got it, flaunt it," he said drily.

"He's some kind of musician, thus doesn't work days. He looked like her usual type: long hair, grubby, tattoos and probably on drugs. Plus he was smoking in the apartment. I think he's living there. I tried not to be judgmental, but it was the empty nursery that got to me. She makes good money, but she isn't preparing for the baby. So I went and bought furniture for the room. Don't be mad at me." Her voice had shrunk to a whisper, and she looked concerned.

"You're not confusing me with that asshole you were married to before, I hope. You're independently wealthy. You get to do whatever you want. Why would I complain?"

She let out a gusty sigh. "I can't help it. Habit, I guess. It was a fair amount of money. And partly, I'm annoyed with Sally, because I think she set it up so I'd do that. I didn't used to notice her manipulation. She seems only to value me as a source of help or money."

Sally's antics made Alexander fume, but he kept it to himself. Helen reacted badly to anger in any form, and he didn't want to scare her. "It's your grandchild, and I'm glad you got the basics for her. But we probably ought to consider distancing ourself from her. She hasn't exactly been attentive to you, and I don't like seeing you taken advantage of." He reached over and took her hand and kissed it. "You deserve respect and love, and I hate to sit by watching your kids mistreat you. I'm sure they learned that by watching their father, but that's an explanation, not an excuse. They still could choose to treat you better."

"You're right. I haven't minded backing off from Lena and Warren, but it's taken me a while to accept that Sally is no different. You're right," she repeated, as if trying to convince herself.

"You have me, Helen, and you always will. You're not alone anymore." He put his arms around her, and she leaned into his shoulder. He was encouraged when she didn't cry. She was getting stronger. "You know, I'm really excited that you're finally writing. I can't wait to read your novel when it's done."

"Masterful change of subject, mister." She pushed back and smiled at him with shining eyes. "I don't know how good it is, but it feels great to get it out on paper. It's like creating something out of nothing. I enjoy going back into that world and seeing what happens each time I sit at my desk. It's almost like it writes itself. Isn't that weird?"

He was pleased she'd moved on from the Sally problem. "I don't think that's so weird. It sure seems to be a sign that you were meant to write. Isn't it wonderful being together and writing like this? It isn't like work at all."

"That's how I feel, too. I'm getting used to living in your house."

"*Our* house," he interjected.

"Our house. But I hope you don't mind me saying that I keep remembering our honeymoon."

He was bombarded with images of them in bed. "I do, too."

Her blue-green eyes glinted with mock judgment. "I didn't mean *that*. I was referring to living in a tropical paradise surrounded by turquoise seas filled with a rainbow of fish, palms swaying in the breeze, the pace so gentle and easy. I wish we could live like that." As she described it, her face became even more beautiful, lit up as if she were seeing a heavenly vision.

It made him want to give her dream to her. "Do you like that better than living in the desert?"

She looked at him quizzically. "I hadn't thought of it that way." She paused thoughtfully, then looked directly into his eyes. "Yes, I believe I do. How about you?"

"I could live anywhere as long as I'm with you. I have to say that I've always been drawn to the idea of living on a tropical island."

She stared at him as if evaluating his honesty. "Really? You're not just saying that?"

"Really. I just never had the motivation to go beyond daydreaming about it."

She said nothing for a while, but went back to twisting the fabric of her pants nervously. He placed his hand over hers. "You don't need to be nervous. It's good to share how you feel. I am a whole different person than I was when I moved to Palm Lakes. So are you. Together, we're something new and even more different. Maybe we should consider whether we really want to stay here permanently. We have the ability to live almost anywhere."

Her eyes met his again, and he could see the excitement in them. "So maybe we could look at places that would meet both our dreams?" She seemed to be holding her breath as she caught her lower lip between her teeth.

"Of course we can! Let's both do some research and compare notes and see what options we can come up with. Best idea wins a prize."

She reached over, picked up her wineglass and raised it as if for a toast. Doing the same, he waited for her to speak. "To us and our next adventure."

* * *

Nora, 5:30pm

NORA OPENED the wine and checked the chicken biryani. The naan bread was made and warming in the oven, and Luke should be home momentarily. She closed the sliding glass door to the patio. The sun was low enough that the warmth had fled from the air. She heard the garage door go up and rushed back to the kitchen to finish preparing dinner.

Luke entered through the door to the garage and paused briefly, sniffing the air dramatically. "What's that I smell?" Blue eyes twinkled. He knew she'd made his favorite.

"Your favorite meal to celebrate my big check!"

Instantly his humor faded. "How big is big?"

She felt a twinge of annoyance that he was acting skeptical, even though she knew it was because he was sick of his minimum wage job.

261

She looked hard at him, staring down his attitude, then answered. "I made over $500 in the last month."

He stopped as if he'd hit a wall. "You got how much?"

"Over $500. And that's just the first month. I'm going to make more. You'll see."

Pushing his glasses back up on his nose, he shook his head. "I can't believe it."

"Believe it. This is a good business, and I'm going to rock and roll."

His eyes lit up, then the light faded. "How do you keep it going?"

She was encouraged. It was the first time he'd asked a serious question about her Botanica business. "Well, obviously, I need to keep enrolling shoppers to buy the products monthly, but since they are all products everyone needs, it's a pretty easy sell. The trick to a big paycheck, though, is to find others who also want to do the business. You grow much faster and stand to make serious money that way."

"Have you found anyone?"

She smiled that he was finally getting with the program. "Yes, I have. I know we need more than $500 each month, and I've been working my ass off, so it's more like a 60-hr-a-week job, but it's going to pay off. The idea is to enroll business builders and get them to do the same. Just duplicate and scale up."

"How many does it take?"

"It depends on how much you want to make. I figure if I can get 10 good ones, we'll have a good income, and more than that will give us a better lifestyle than we can imagine."

He came over and hugged her. He smelled of stale grease and sweat, the signature of his job at the fast food place. The hug felt desperate, like he was a drowning man. She hugged him back, giving him time to take it all in.

"You said a while back that maybe I could join you. You still think that?" His hangdog look meant more to her than an apology.

She gave him a mock measuring gaze. "There's a place for you at the top of my organization." She laughed with relief when he smiled at her joke. "It's getting harder to keep track of things. My goal was to have a bigger check next month and have you quit your job at the burger place and join me. Let's see how the next three weeks go. If I can get some good business builders, I believe we can do it."

Luke put his arms around her and nuzzled her neck. "That sounds good. Can we eat my favorite meal to celebrate now?"

She kissed him hard and looked him straight in the eyes. "You bet. You pour the wine. I'll tell you all about my plan for world domination." She prayed this meant he was on board. She was determined to pull them out of this hole they were in.

"I like how you think. Maybe we can stay in this house after all. I sure would like to do that."

He hadn't been that positive in weeks. She smiled. "You and me both. That's the plan. Things are looking up enough that I bought us tickets to the cooking club dinner next month. Let's plan to have you on board by then."

Relief washed over his face. "That works for me."

* * *

Mary Beth, 6:15pm

MARY BETH SAT at the table with Maddie, working on her latest jewelry project, a necklace of graded turquoise beads with gold findings. It was simple but quite striking in her opinion. "It's so nice to be able to do this any time I like."

Maddie kept her eyes focused on the beads she was stringing, the tip of her tongue sticking out. Then she blinked and turned to Mary Beth. "Just like I told you. This is great. I don't think anyone will turn you in. My neighbors feel sorry for me losing Stanley. They'll be glad to know I have some live-in help." She went back to the beading.

Mary Beth couldn't resist commenting. "I'm happy to be of assistance. But as I've told you, I can't stay here permanently. Sooner or later I need to find a place that's legal for me." She gathered her courage to continue. "And you need more help than I can provide. You aren't letting me do as much as I'd like to, and I'm not here to make sure you're OK during workdays."

Maddie stopped and put the string of beads down. "You're here nights. That's the hardest time for me. I can handle anything else." She gave a weak but stubborn smile.

"What about that pan you left on the stovetop this morning? If I hadn't found it, you could have had a fire here. I don't mean to be disrespectful, but living alone in a big house with a yard is a lot of work, and you've said that you have limited income, plus you have osteoporosis and the doctors said not to lift more than two pounds. Don't you think you'd be safer in assisted living?"

Maddie's frown was tinged with anger, and her voice stabbed at Mary Beth aggressively. "I've lived here for a long time, and I know what I'm doing. I'll leave when I'm damn well ready. Did Samantha put you up to this?"

Cringing at the violence of Maddie's response, Mary Beth said with some regret, "No, she didn't ask me to speak with you. I'm telling you how I feel based on what I see. But we both care about you very much, and we worry that a slip of memory or a physical fall could be quite serious with you living alone. I'm sorry if you think I spoke out of line. You have to make your own decision. I just worry about you." She went back to stringing beads, hoping Maddie would accept her apology.

Instead, Maddie just got silent and continued to string beads, biting the tip of her tongue again. Well, that was better than fighting.

Mary Beth wanted to change the mood, so she changed the subject. "I've been looking for ways to supplement my income, and I'm not sure I can do the Botanica business. But I'm really interested in trying to sell my jewelry. I went to those consignment places you mentioned, and they're willing to put my stuff in their displays. Then I got a brainstorm and went to the three fanciest resorts nearby and pitched to them, showing them my best pieces. Two of them said they'd give me space in their shops."

Maddie had apparently forgiven her, because she looked up with a big smile, her pale blue eyes twinkling. "I told you that you had talent. I'm glad you did that. There are other resorts if you don't mind driving. Or maybe you want to offer exclusive deals to a few, but if you do that, you should get a bigger commission on sales."

"I haven't thought it out very clearly. You're right. I need to get a strategy for making the most income, because it will take time and effort to do this, plus there's a lot of overhead involved. And all the paperwork."

Maddie mumbled as she went back to her beading. "That's the part I wouldn't like. That, and I don't like to drive anymore."

"I'm happy to drive you anywhere, anytime. I'm not going to be here forever, but as long as I'm here, I hope you'll let me help out."

"I wouldn't mind you making spaghetti like you did tonight. I could eat that every day. I don't care to cook."

"We can have all kinds of Italian food. Do you like lasagna? I make a mean lasagna."

"I like any Italian food."

"Then you're in luck. I'm a veritable cornucopia of Italian recipes. Do you mind if I invite Ethan to dine with us one night? I'll make the meal."

Maddie gave her a shrewd look. "What's going on with you two? He's old enough to be your father."

Mary Beth sighed. "I know how old he is, but wasn't Stanley a good bit older than you?"

"Yeah, and look how that turned out."

Mary Beth was floored at Maddie's candor. She'd never said much about her marriage. "Were you unhappy?"

"Enough about me. I just think he's too old for you. But if you want, he can come to dinner. It would be a way to pay him back for all he does here. Not that I need his help."

Discretion being the better part of valor, Mary Beth didn't comment.

Emma, 7:25pm

EMMA SIPPED her after-dinner tea thoughtfully, regarding Julio out of the corner of her eye. Why was he acting different? He'd come over after work at about 3:30 and they'd gone to the community garden on the other side of Palm Lakes and spent a couple hours doing hard labor to get her plot finished and ready for planting. The raised beds were beautiful, the soil amended and the irrigation in place. He'd put a small rabbit fence around her plot, which he warned her wasn't going to be enough, but it would deter them a little. There was even a gate in it. He had an amazing gift for making it all seem easy. Now all that was left was planting. She was exhausted and sore, but happy. She didn't want to contemplate how guilty it made her feel that he had put in a full day's work before he came to help her. Was he annoyed with her? Did she dare ask? As if aware of her scrutiny, he looked directly at her, and his warm smile dispelled any worries she had about him being out of sorts with her.

"Emma, I have a suggestion, but you do not have to do it." He bit his lip as a worried look crossed his face. "It is just that you have been saying how sore your muscles are after all the hard work in the garden, and I had an idea..."

So she'd been right. He had something on his mind, but it wasn't anything bad. She sighed in relief. "What's your idea?"

"Well, I have been sore myself. I tried some of that Ben-Gay you can rub on sore muscles, and it helped a little, but not a lot. I started thinking about how people get massages when they have sore muscles. It is expensive, and I have never had one, but it does not seem that hard to do. So I went to a store and talked with a girl there, and she sold me some massage oil that she said would help relieve muscle pain. She said it is really easy to use. I wondered if you would let me do that for you. You do not have to say yes." He looked down as if afraid of her response.

She was speechless. It sounded heavenly. She'd never had a massage, either. She had never been keen on anyone handling her body for any purpose. But her shoulders were aching something awful, and surely it would be OK for him to loosen up the knots. "I'd like that."

"You will need to remove clothing so I can do this properly, but you can lie face down on the bed and not turn over. Just undress above the waist. Call me when you are ready. I promise not to do anything to scare you."

Her heart was hammering away, and she felt nervous, but it wasn't because she thought he'd hurt her or try to take advantage. It was because it would be a step towards greater intimacy that didn't involve sex. "I'll holler when I'm ready."

"Give me a couple minutes to get the oil from my truck." He disappeared out the front door.

She walked slowly back to the bedroom, remembering the debacle from the other week. She knew he wasn't going to push her, but as she looked at the bed, she found fear nibbling at her extremities. This time, she told herself she could manage. It didn't take her long to strip her shirt and bra off, stick them in a drawer and lay face down on the bed. She felt exposed, but determined. She heard the front door open and shut. "I'm ready, Julio."

She heard him stride down the hall and pause in the doorway. She held her breath and said nothing. She knew he was looking at her bare back. She urged herself to relax. He wasn't seeing as much as he would at a beach. It was just that she felt his eyes on her.

She heard him set the bottle down on the night stand. "Emma, would you mind sliding over a bit so I have somewhere to put my knee?" She slid over as requested. "My hands might be a little cold. I will try to warm them up first." She heard him rubbing his hands together. "I am going to put some oil in my hands, then rub it on your shoulders. I will do my best to work the knots out of your muscles. You can tell me where it hurts. Do not let me push too hard." She heard the cap flip up and then shortly after, his warm hands spread oil across her upper back and shoulders.

She found it difficult to speak. "My right shoulder and neck are hurting the most." He rubbed oil evenly everywhere, then began to squeeze and rub her muscles. On the right side, there was pain, but it was a welcome kind of pain, as if the knots were being teased into unwinding. He seemed to instinctively know just how much pressure to use. He rubbed her neck, shoulders and upper back. The oil sent heat into her muscles, relaxing them further. "What's in the oil?"

"It has mint, camphor, manzanilla and something else. She said it was perfect for sore muscles."

"Mmmm. It's warming and very nice. You seem to know what you're doing."

"I have never done this before. I have never had anyone massage me, either, but I know where I am sore, so I am just trying to loosen the same places on you."

He'd never touched a woman this way? His big hands were gentle but strong, and his touch was soothing, but also filled with affection. Or so it felt to her. She suddenly realized she was fantasizing about him touching her lovingly, wanting him to continue, wanting it to be more than just a massage. She got a tightening in her heart.

"Emma, just relax. I am not going to do anything you do not want."

He sure did read her, but this time, he hadn't read it right. "It wasn't that. I know you won't." She wasn't sure she could tell him what she'd been thinking. It would sound like she was leading him on, and what if she couldn't follow through, like the other day?

As he continued to work the oil into her body, she found herself floating off into a warm, comfortable place as his hands moved up and down her spine, kneading muscles from shoulder to lower back. She almost drifted off.

"Is that OK?" His hands had stopped, but were still on her.

"Yes, that was pure heaven. I could let you do that all night."

"Do not tempt me." She could hear the smile in his voice.

"What about you? You said you never had a massage. Would you like one? I wouldn't be as good as you are, but I'm willing to try. I feel practically boneless I'm so relaxed. This was a wonderful idea."

"I would like that. I will go out into the living room. Call me when you are dressed." He got up from the bed and walked out of the room, shutting the door behind him.

She sighed in pleasure, not really wanting to get up, but if she lingered, she knew she'd fall asleep. She pushed herself up and got her shirt out of the drawer. She slipped it on and opened the door. "Come on back."

He walked in looking as if he were trying to be small and unthreatening. As if he could ever not fill any space he was standing in. It was charming that he was trying so hard not to scare her. "Take off your shirt and go lie down where I was."

He nodded, then pulled the shirt off in one very masculine motion, revealing a breathtaking chest and six-pack abs. Tossing the shirt on the floor (well, he was a typical guy that way, at least), he lay on the bed exactly where she had just been. Something about it sent a tingle through her. Tonight she'd sleep right where he was now lying. Shaking off the image, she went to the oil bottle. "I'll rub my hands together like you did.

Mine tend to be cold. I apologize in advance." After rubbing them together, she poured oil in her palm. Then she found herself staring at his bare back unsure about touching him as the oil started to drip between her fingers. Unable to delay without making a mess, she put her hands on his back.

His skin was warm and smooth, and as she rubbed the oil on his shoulders, adding some more because it wasn't quite enough (he had broad shoulders), she tried to picture the muscles and how to rub them to release the tension. It required her to feel his musculature, get to know his body so she could do it right. It was like being given permission to touch him as much as she liked without him doing anything to her. The effect was electrifying.

Although she tried to stay focused on just helping relieve pain, she found herself enjoying the warmth and texture of his skin, the coffee color of it, the feel of his muscles just under the skin, the scent of the oils. This was something else she could do all night, though she knew her hands weren't strong enough to keep it up for long.

Being allowed to be so close to someone was humbling in a way. It came to her like a thunderclap that he felt the same way about her. When he was rubbing her, she could feel in his hands what she was feeling for him now. Which meant he could feel what was pouring through her fingers as she kneaded his shoulder muscles and back. It was frightening in a way to be so exposed to someone. Almost as scary as being shirtless with him.

"That is so good, Emma." The sincerity of the words warmed her heart.

She continued to knead, rub and apply pressure until her hands and wrists were yelling at her in discomfort. "I'm not used to doing this. I need to develop muscles in my hands. I'm afraid that's as much as I can do today."

He sighed deeply. "That was wonderful. I feel so much better. I could let you do that all night."

"I know exactly what you mean."

She stood up and rubbed her hands together, wondering where to wipe the excess oil, when he turned over and shot into a sitting position, taking her breath away. God Almighty, he was beautiful! She sensed his awareness of her admiring glance and felt flustered, averting her gaze. "I didn't mean to stare. You are just so..."

"Look all you like."

She dragged her eyes up and looked at him full-on. Not an ounce of fat on him. Muscles in all the right places, but not too many. She didn't like a musclebound man. Maybe it made her think of being attacked. Julio was just right. She turned and grabbed his shirt off the floor and handed it to him wordlessly. It was too intimate a moment, totally new in her experience. It suddenly occurred to her she was alone in her bedroom with a half-naked man who was looking at her with desire in his eyes, and she felt no fear.

Wanting to leave while things were still positive, she walked to the door. "Join me in the living room when you're dressed. I'll make us a nice cup of tea."

A few minutes later, they sat side by side on the couch sipping hot chamomile tea, saying very little. Finally, she decided to put it out there. "I liked that a lot. I'd like to do it again. But we're mostly done the hard part about the gardening."

"You do not need an excuse for that sort of thing, Emma. It is a wonderful way to relax with someone you feel close to. I have never had that sort of closeness before. I like it. I would like to do it again, too."

"The only problem is whoever gets the last massage will feel like falling asleep. Maybe we could take turns going first." The next words came out of her mouth before she even gave them thought. "I wish you didn't have to leave."

His eyes, always intensely dark, became even darker. No one had ever looked at her that way. Was it passion? Whatever it was, it was quickly replaced by regret. "Tomorrow is a work day. I have to be at work early. I do not have a change of clothes or toothbrush."

She nodded, slightly embarrassed and maybe a bit relieved at his declining to stay.

"Maybe Saturday. I do not work Sundays. I could come prepared to spend the night if you wish."

Suddenly overcome by a chill, Emma felt a need to clarify. "I'm not promising sex. I just mean I like being with you and tonight was special, and I feel so alone when you leave. I know it would be asking a lot, but maybe we could just hold each other and sleep?" Feeling stupid, she cursed herself for putting the poor man in yet another unpleasant position. Why did he put up with her at all?

"That is fine. Perhaps I should pull my car into your garage when I come. It would not do to have the neighbors see it out front all night."

"You're right. They'll probably know anyway, but no need to rub their noses in it. Call me before you head over, and I'll have the garage door up. We can have a nice dinner and maybe watch a movie and then if you like, we could give each other a massage before bed." She felt her natural shyness urging her to take it back. She felt so exposed. Until she looked at his face.

He looked like a kid who'd been given his wish for Christmas.

12
THURSDAY, MARCH 14TH

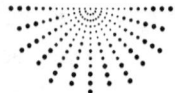

Maddie, 10:05am

Maddie sat on the patio with a cup of coffee, reveling in the spring weather. Since she didn't drive anymore, she hadn't had a chance to see the profusion of wildflowers in the desert. She used to love just driving around to look at the carpets of colorful blooms. Samantha had brought her a large bouquet of wildflowers she'd picked from the roadside, and it was beautiful, with penstemon, Indian paintbrush, desert marigolds, globe mallow and a little purple flower she couldn't remember the name of. She liked flowers, but not the kind you paid for; what a waste of money they were.

The warmer, longer days had stimulated new growth on all the plants in her yard...soon she'd need to get someone to prune them, and she ground her teeth at the expense. Her mood shifted like a switch had been thrown, her focus back on problems she had no solutions for. There was never enough money to do what needed doing, and she was annoyed that there was no discretionary income at all. She'd stopped ordering from the jewelry supply place for the first time since she began the hobby.

After Stanley had died, she thought she could stay in her home. It was where she was comfortable. She really wanted to stay in spite of the pain and struggle physically, and she'd thought maybe Mary Beth would make a difference, but there just wasn't enough money to do everything, even with Mary Beth contributing some 'rent' money.

She lifted her mug to take a sip, only to find out that the coffee had gone cold while she was pondering her future. She spit the coffee back into the mug and set it down, muttering about how unfair life was.

In spite of her protests to her daughter, she wondered how she was going to manage to stay afloat. No matter how she ran the figures, it didn't seem she had enough to make it work here. HOA fees were going up, the car was a drain on resources, yet she didn't like to drive it because of the pain, and the cost of having it sit in the garage was ridiculous. But if she sold it, she'd be totally dependent on Samantha and others. Without the car, she didn't see how she could stay in her home.

Mary Beth was a nice girl. She helped clean and cook, doing whatever she thought needed to be done, but at times Maddie felt annoyed because all the help implied she needed it. She was beginning to feel she was in assisted living now, even though it didn't look like it. Between Mary Beth, Samantha and Ethan, she wasn't doing things her way. She was being waited on, and that galled her. It felt as if they were rubbing her nose in her physical frailty, even though she knew it wasn't intended. She could only imagine what they'd do if they knew about the hallucinations. Shaking her head, she muttered under her breath some more, but no answers came to her.

With great difficulty, she stood up and ignored the pain in her joints as she went back into the house, mug in hand. She put it on the counter by the sink as she passed through and went to her work table. Doing the jewelry soothed her nerves. She could immerse herself in a project for hours. She always felt resentful when she had to pull her attention away from her creative endeavor and do something mundane like eat or sleep.

She desperately needed an escape, but as she stared at her project in its half-finished state, she didn't feel her usual sense of eagerness to dive in. She felt depressed. She had no one to share her feelings with. She never had. Stanley wasn't one to understand feelings, especially hers, and she'd learned early on not to bother him with what he termed 'bitching.'

She had to resolve this on her own. But she couldn't see any good resolution. She pushed her chair back and stood up slowly, mind churning with troubled thoughts and no easy answers. She drifted into the kitchen, vaguely aware that it might be good to see what she had on hand for dinner tonight. As she grabbed the handle of the refrigerator, a flash of insight came to her, passing through her like electricity.

It was time to go. As if someone had inserted a new awareness into her brain, she realized in that moment that she wasn't living independently anymore. That time was gone. A brief rush of sadness filled her heart. As much as she hated to admit it, maybe Samantha was right. Mary Beth wasn't going to be here forever. Maddie had painted a picture in her mind of Mary Beth being her companion, helping her remain independent indefinitely, but she suddenly knew that Mary Beth would be leaving before long. And the money wasn't there. Even if she could find a live-in helper (she wouldn't be likely to find someone who paid her like Mary Beth did), she just didn't have the money to stay here. Damn Stanley for leaving her in this mess! It was unkind to think he had done it on purpose, but she suspected he had.

Sighing deeply, she turned and went into the living room and sat gingerly on the couch. If she did what Samantha wanted and moved to assisted living, she'd have money from the sale of the house, perhaps even some discretionary funds. She could sell the car, too, as they had transportation for residents. It was expensive to live there, but with the house sold, she would have enough to last a good long while. The way she'd been feeling, it didn't seem likely she'd last too many years. Her body seemed to be disintegrating on her.

Another wave of disappointment passed through her. If only she were more healthy. If only she had more money. If only she were younger. But none of those were things she could change.

Samantha was at work. Tonight, Maddie would tell her she'd decided to move to assisted living. It vexed her to think how glad everyone would be. They didn't seem to be aware of the cost to her of such a decision. All they cared about was feeling she was 'safe.' She humphed to herself. They wanted to feel good about where she was, but they didn't care how she felt. To Maddie it would be like living in a jail, and although the cage would be gilded, it would bring her one step closer to the grave, and she hated to admit it, but that scared her.

This was a momentous decision. She felt tears filling her eyes. Doing this would be like obliterating her Self, becoming a husk taking up space until she left the earth. The shrinking feeling crowded in on her, pressing the tears from her eyes. No one understood.

* * *

Julio, 10:45am

JULIO STOOD by his truck in the parking lot at Palo Verde Landscaping, talking to his older brother Sergio. "It is not like that, Serge." Julio skewered Sergio with a sharp look.

Sergio paid no more attention than he usually did to Julio's protestations about his women. "You are putting our business at risk playing these games. We have warned you many times. It's one thing having an occasional one night stand, but you're spending too much time at that woman's house. We don't need that kind of scandal." His handsome face was creased with worry and judgment.

"It is not what it looks like," Julio maintained stubbornly.

"It isn't you spending the night at that gringa's house all the time? Do you have any idea how that could affect our business' reputation? This has to stop. You need to put our family ahead of your reckless idea of fun." His dark eyes flashed with judgment.

"I am not doing anything wrong. She is a widow. I am single. We have a right to spend time together." He didn't tell Sergio he wasn't even having sex with Emma. He wouldn't have believed that, even though it was true.

"Julio, the family has been very tolerant of your activities, but this is too much. You have to make a choice. You can't keep seeing her this way without hurting our business. Those people are not going to look kindly on you having an affair with a woman old enough to be your mother."

Julio ground his teeth. "She has a name. Her name is Emma."

"Whatever."

He shot back a retort without even thinking. "What if I am serious about her?"

Sergio practically choked. "She's taking advantage of you because you're young, Mexican and good-looking. She's treating you like a gigolo. The family won't accept her. She's old. She's white. She isn't Catholic."

He'd known it was going to be like this, but he'd hoped he was wrong. He loved his family dearly, but he wasn't going to give up Emma. "Are you saying I am fired if I keep seeing her? That I will be thrown out of the family and our business?"

Sergio looked hard at him. "Don't test us. This is serious. Drop her now." He turned on his heel and marched up the steps to the office, slamming the flimsy door after him.

Julio needed to talk to Emma. He'd only hinted about the family drama their relationship was stirring up, afraid she would withdraw from him, but he couldn't put it off any longer.

MINUTES LATER, she answered her door with a surprised and happy look that changed when she saw how tense he was. "What's wrong, Julio? You look upset." As he came into the house, she touched him on the arm with encouragement. "I'll make you a cup of tea."

He followed her into the kitchen and watched her making tea, wondering how to tell her. Suddenly, he was afraid she was going to turn on him, too. What if she wasn't serious about him? Could Sergio be right?

"Did something bad happen?" She turned and looked at him over her shoulder. When he didn't answer, she stopped what she was doing and gave him her full attention. "Tell me." In that moment she reminded him of his dead mother, her voice stern and loving at the same time.

"My brother has given me an ultimatum."

Her look of worry turned to fear. "What do you mean?"

"He told me to stop seeing you or I am no longer part of the family or business." There, it was out in the open.

Her mouth was open in disbelief. "You're kidding! They wouldn't do that. You haven't done anything wrong!"

"They are concerned about the reputation of the company, because I am spending so much time with you. They think they will lose business. And the family does not feel you are an appropriate match for me. You will not be invited to any family function. They're putting pressure on me, because it means I'd have to choose between them and you on any given holiday."

Her crystalline blue eyes filled with pain. "I'm so sorry. This is all my fault." She touched the scar on her cheek self-consciously. "You can't sacrifice your family and your career for me. They mean too much to you. I never meant for this to happen."

He went over and took her hand. "Please come to the couch. I need to talk with you." He led her to the living room, hurting for the tears that were filling her eyes, angry with his brothers and himself that it had come to this.

Sitting down, he took both her hands in his and looked intently into her blue eyes. "Emma, I have seen this coming. I have thought about options. I need to ask you now. Are you as serious about me as I am about you?"

Her jaw dropped open again. "How serious *are* you?"

"You do not know? I love you. I want us to be together. I do not feel I can ask you to marry me. Everyone would say I am after your money. But you must know how I feel about you."

She looked dazed. The silence stretched out painfully, and he wondered if she was going to reject him. "After my money? Are they nuts? I always assumed people would think I was taking advantage of you because you're young and handsome."

"Well, that is exactly how my family feels, but here in Palm Lakes, it will be the other way." He grinned crookedly and shrugged a shoulder.

"You said you had options? I'm eager to hear them."

He straightened up his shoulders. "I can start my own company. They will have to give me something for my part of the family business. There is a need for some services in Palm Lakes that Palo Verde is not providing. I can offer yard watching for snow birds and those who travel. I could do redesigns and maintenance as well. Palo Verde wants the big jobs. I can send those to my brothers and demand a referral fee."

She looked stunned. "You'd do that for me? But what about your family? Even if you can start your own company, I know how close you are to them. I can't ask you to choose between me and them."

"You did not. They did. And I do not want to stop seeing you. If you want us to be together, that is what matters most to me. Maybe one day, they will come around. Maybe not. But that is for them to decide." He felt better now that it was out in the open.

She looked down at her hands, her straight, raven-black hair half obscuring her face. He reached over and raised her chin to look her in the eyes. "Please be honest with me, Emma. This is important. I told you once that I wanted to live my life differently. I have come to really enjoy the life I am living now, and I do not want to go back."

"Would it be better if you didn't come to my house? If I came to your place instead, would they drop their objections?"

It was his turn to be shocked. He knew this was her refuge. "My place is not nearly as nice as yours. It would stop the rumors in Palm Lakes and might satisfy their concerns about the reputation of our business, but my family would not be satisfied. You would still not be welcome."

She frowned and shook her head. "This is so wrong. You haven't done anything, but I understand their concerns. I know I'm too old for you. But it's not like you asked me to marry you. If they think I'm taking advantage, why don't they wait for me to tire of you? Why are they acting like it's serious if they think I'm merely toying with you?"

"Because when they confronted me, they assumed I was doing what I did in the past. They were hoping I would reassure them that even though I had been seeing you for a while, it meant nothing; that I would drop you. I could not lie, Emma, even though it might have bought me some time. This happened because I told them the truth. I told them that I love you and I am not going to give you up. You can send me away, but if you do not..."

"You love me? You'd give up everything for me?" She looked confused.

"I am sorry I waited until now to say it, but you need to know it is true. And as for giving things up, I already have. You can send me away, but I made my choice, and I am happy with it. But I would like to know how you feel. It is your choice, too."

"This is too much. You can't do this. You'll regret it. I can't give you children. I don't fit in with your family. No wonder they want you to dump me. I don't blame them. If things don't work out between us, you've gambled everything and lost. I can't be responsible for that. I've already made your life difficult enough with my problems."

"I know this is hard, Emma, and I am sorry. I did not want it to come to this. Please just think about what I said. I have already given them my decision. But you are not obligated. If you want to back out, you can. I am going to go to my place and give you some time to think."

He stood up reluctantly. He hated to leave her when she was leaning towards giving him up from some false sense of honor. But he knew his presence was too much pressure. He'd said what he wanted to. Now it was up to her.

As she followed him to the door, the fear returned to her eyes. "Will you call me?"

"Of course. Think about what I said. If I do not hear from you today, I will call you tomorrow. This is a big decision. I have had a lot of time to consider it, and I am happy with my choice. You have to decide what you want."

He kissed her on the cheek and left before he started to beg. He was so worried she was going to cave in to the pressure from his family and her own insecurities.

Back at his place, he got a soda from the refrigerator and slumped on the couch, unwilling to face work. Maybe he should have prepared her more. He hadn't want to put other pressures on her. Things had been going so well. She was like a late-blooming, exotic flower. Spending time with her was like being in high school again, which certainly had its frustrations, but it had given him something he had never had, a chance to create a relationship with a woman that wasn't all about sex. He had to take it slowly and allow her to discover her sexuality and power. She was a deeply passionate, loving woman, and he knew they could be happy together. But she had unresolved fears and doubts, and this problem with his family was going to challenge the strength of what they'd built together.

His sense of certainty began to weaken as he thought about the fear he'd seen in her eyes. He wondered if she trusted him enough to get through this. He also wondered if she was ready to choose happiness at such a price. If she thought about it long enough, she'd start seeing how being with him would cause her problems with her friends. Sure, he was young and good-looking, but what else could he offer her that was worth all the trouble? Maybe he was being selfish, wanting her in his life. He was willing to pay the price, but was it fair to ask her to do the same?

* * *

Emma, 11:05am

EMMA SAT on the couch staring into space. Her whole world had disintegrated. She was angry with Julio's family, mad at the whole world for its mean-spirited ways. It was so unfair. They weren't hurting anyone. She was just getting used to feeling special. She was thinking maybe she could be loved and love in return. Now it was spoiled.

Tears started to flow, blurring her vision. Julio had become such a big part of her life. What had she been thinking? Did she think he was going to marry her, a woman more than ten years his senior?

Then it struck her. He'd said he loved her. He wanted to be with her. He wasn't going to ask to marry her, because he was afraid how it would look. Maybe he was even afraid she'd reject him.

Yet it was a terrible choice. She couldn't bear the thought of separating him from his family. He was so close to them. Was there any chance they would accept her later on? Maybe. But she couldn't assume that. She had to act on the assumption it would not change.

It kept going back to the age difference. He claimed it didn't matter, but he'd have no children if he stayed with her. He might lose his family altogether. And he'd have to start a new business. It really would be just the two of them. No one had ever sacrificed so much for her, and she didn't feel worthy of it.

She glanced out to the patio, where the nearly-finished vertical herb garden and her Christmas cactus were mute reminders of the many things they enjoyed doing together. Everywhere she turned and everything she did reminded her of him. Somehow, without her being aware of it, he had become an important part of her life.

If they stayed together, he couldn't move in with her, because unless they were married, he'd be illegal in Palm Lakes. And she'd heard from Helen that she'd gotten a letter telling her to evict Mary Beth because she was under the age limit. They could live together somewhere else, but she liked it here. She had finally created the perfect sanctuary. Even if they married, how would the community react?

As the arguments raged inside her head, something happened. Like fog clearing, the objections were swept aside by a sense of peace, a brightness and clarity. He had said he loved her. He wanted to be with her. What more did she need? Why was she thinking about what others thought? The only two people who mattered were him and her. If she had to leave Palm Lakes, she'd do it. It's not like she was so blended into this community. What mattered to her was him. She suddenly realized she couldn't give him up. She'd marry him if he wanted. She wasn't sure it would be a good idea for him, especially considering her unresolved issues with sex, but she knew him well enough now to know how good it would be for her.

She went over to the phone and dialed his number before she lost her nerve.

* * *

Red, 12:30pm

ERIC ROLLED AROUND in bed restlessly. He'd collapsed into it shortly after 7am, when he'd returned from his shift. He hated to admit it, but sleeping alone didn't do it for him anymore. He missed Lydia's warm, sexy body. At least the nightmares had become rarer. That herb stuff worked.

Throwing off the covers, he stepped over to the chair he'd put his clothes on last night and dressed. He'd shower later. Splashing water on his face to try and wake up fully, he stared at himself in the bathroom mirror. The dark circles under his eyes had gone away, but he still wasn't looking healthy.

Striding out into the kitchen, he found Lydia at the dining table reading a book. "Hey, beautiful." He went to the coffee pot and poured himself some liquid energy. "Thanks for having the coffee made."

She looked at him, and he knew she was reading him. "You haven't been in bed long. Are you really rested?"

"As much as I can be."

She humphed. "Night shift is terrible on the body. I don't like to tell you what to do, but I hope you decide to get back on day shift soon. Did you have any nightmares?" She pierced him with her brown eyes.

"No, I was restless, but no nightmares."

Her face lightened. "That's five nights in a row now. Progress."

"Yes, I think so."

"It will take time, but I believe if you let me keep working on you and you take the herb, things will get balanced again. You never forget such trauma, but it doesn't have to define you or ruin your life." She made a show of going back to reading, but he knew she wasn't.

"I know you're worried about me, and I appreciate your concern. I am also grateful you didn't argue with my decision to work nights. I think it's helped to distract me. But I miss my bedmate. It isn't the same sleeping alone."

She snorted and continued to look at her book, but said nothing. He stared at her, able to do so unobserved for a change. Her curly dark hair cascaded to her shoulders, partially obscuring his view of her face. The blouse she had on was delightfully low cut, showing her cleavage. He went to stand behind her and put his hands on her shoulders. "Thanks for not abandoning me. No one has ever stuck by me like you have."

She looked up at him quizzically over her shoulder. "What kind of women have you been hanging out with? Why should I abandon you as if you'd done something wrong?"

He shrugged his shoulders. "It doesn't always matter. I've never been good about expressing feelings. I try harder with you than I ever did before, but I know I'm still too much of a loner."

"Look, my Viking warrior, you matter to me. Sure, I want to share your bed. I wish we could spend more time together. But you have to do what you have to do. I'd like to make this work." She looked back up at him, and he detected vulnerability in her eyes. "I'm not that great at relationships, either. But I'm not giving up. Things were going well with us before the murder, but Owen was what brought us together, so I can hardly complain about the temporary glitch. It isn't easy to watch you suffer, but I can tell you're feeling better. I believe you'll continue to see progress. I want to be a part of your life, if you'll have me."

Her words made him feel all gooey inside, and he knew she could see that, but what he didn't want to share was his unwillingness to saddle her with a psych case. He began to massage her shoulders while he thought, and she went back to looking at her book. Until he was normal again, he couldn't contemplate moving forward in this relationship, even though he could tell his distant behavior was paining her.

He hadn't told her how nervous he was on patrol, how his hands sometimes shook when he thought about having to face a perp of any kind. He couldn't have her tied to someone who was scared of his own shadow. Yet he couldn't bear to tell her how bad it was. He just hoped it would fade, like the nightmares had.

"I know you're standing behind me so I can't read you," she said accusingly, but without rancor.

"I feel I've been under a microscope these past weeks, and I find it uncomfortable." He knew it was inadequate, but he couldn't bring himself to tell her the whole truth.

She sighed, and he could tell she wasn't buying it. He knew if he opened up, she'd brush off his concerns, but they were serious. He had to get well before he asked her to marry him. He hoped she didn't get tired of waiting.

* * *

Jean, 2:45pm

"Where's Eric, Lydia?" Jean looked behind Lydia as she walked through the front door.

"He's at home. He still hasn't recovered from last night's shift. He said to tell you both 'hi'." Lydia shut the door and followed Jean out into her kitchen, where Ian sat at the table in the breakfast nook drinking a cup of coffee.

"Hello, Lydia. You look lovely today, as always." His hazel eyes twinkled, and Jean noticed Lydia's reaction to the accent. She was going to have to get used to that. It was potent. Maybe they could find a way to use it to advantage in their business.

Jean handed a mug of coffee to Lydia, and they migrated to the table, where a stack of papers, file folders and a plastic binder were stacked precariously.

Lydia took it all in. "You've been busy!"

"It took us longer to get rested up and settled in than I would have thought, but we're ready now to get started on our business. Ian and I wanted to go through all the things you gathered for us, but I guess what we most need to talk with you about is the whole concept of our business. Knowing what you now know, what do you think we should do? Is it a viable plan? We really need to be able to pay our way. We aren't going to impose on you for much longer."

Lydia's brown eyes warmed. "You can stay as long as you need. It isn't a problem. I'm at Eric's most of the time now, anyway."

Jean was bursting to tell Lydia the news and couldn't hold back any longer. "We have a place."

Now it was Lydia's turn to look surprised. "I could tell you had some big news, but I never would have guessed. Tell me everything."

Jean looked at Ian and reached over to squeeze his hand. Lydia smiled at the gesture. Jean knew she was seeing good things in their energy fields. "Well, you know Helen is selling her condo, right?"

"Oh, yes. Poor Mary Beth got notice that she had to leave, and that was the only reason Helen was delaying the sale." Lydia looked at Jean speculatively. "Are you buying it?"

"Better than that, Lyd! Helen is accepting a down payment and letting us rent-to-own. She did the yard so beautifully, and we both love it. There are two bedrooms, so we can turn one into a home office. This allows us to keep a nest egg to help us while we grow the business." Jean felt worry edge in. "That is, if you really think we can make a go of this."

"As I mentioned before, the covenants won't let you run a business from home, in the sense that you cannot have clients show up. Of course, if you kept it low key, you could probably get away with it. I'm not ruling that out as a possibility, because the overhead for having a real office would be much higher. But if you want people to take you seriously, you are better off having a storefront. I checked into options, and what we are talking about doing doesn't really go along with chiropractic. I'd been thinking about how massage therapists and healers often rent space from chiropractors or in healing centers, but we wanted to offer intuitive readings as well, and I don't think that would work with a chiropractor. They wouldn't want to be seen as advertising divination services." Lydia paused as if working up her courage. "I found us a potential office for rent in the strip mall just down the road. If we intend to have Palm Lakes be our market, it's ideal. It's not too expensive for what it is. However, it wouldn't necessarily be ideal if we want a broader market, but the other places I looked at outside of Palm Lakes were not very affordable."

Jean was excited to hear there was a nearby place for rent. "What do you think about the market?"

"That's the big question, isn't it? I wish I could be sure. The market for energy healing like Reiki and services like tarot and psychic-type readings--though I hate using the term 'psychic'--is solid nationally. We would have to be very cautious about how we advertise the energy healing, or we could run into trouble with conventional doctors, but I've thought about that, and I think we can do fine. The 900 number thing is looking very successful for psychics. I've been thinking, and it's just thinking, mind you, because I know little to nothing about what's involved, but my feeling is that if we only go for the local market, we may struggle a lot. Palm Lakes is older folks, many of whom are not open to what we offer. But if we could find a bigger market, we could make it work. It would mean advertising, having a website and having a toll-free number or whatnot. I haven't looked into details. But when you consider the two things we offer: readings and energy healing services, both work fine long distance. Those who want them would have no compunction about ordering them long distance. It would raise our overhead, unless we wanted to solely do business that way, in which case our overhead would be much lower. What I'm saying is don't emphasize the local market. Go national."

Everyone sipped coffee, digesting the idea. Finally, Jean broke the silence. "If we can get a short lease, maybe we could do both and see how it goes?"

Lydia nodded. "I was leaning that way. Ian, what do you feel about the options?"

He smiled crookedly. "I don't know. I can't get a feel for it. I'm sorry. I think I'm adjusting to living in a new country, and I haven't gotten fully grounded yet." He shrugged.

"That's OK. It takes time," Jean said. "I know there's a lot to decide, but it looks like we're doing this, so my next question is what shall we call our business?"

Jean searched Ian's hazel eyes and Lydia's dark brown ones. "I was doing some reading on naming your business, plus I looked at business names of existing businesses like ours. I have to admit there aren't a lot of New Age-y ones out there. And some of those names I found seemed so dumb. They don't describe the business. I think we need something that says what we offer, but since we're doing both healing work and readings, I'm not sure what would work." She'd been thinking about it a lot, and she knew what she didn't like, but she hadn't thought of anything she did like. She hoped one of them had a good idea.

Lydia looked lost in thought. "I've given it some thought as well, and I couldn't come up with anything I liked. At first I was going off in the la-la direction you're talking about, then when I pulled my head out of the ozone, I couldn't come up with anything practical that sounded sexy enough."

Ian finally spoke. "It makes it hard that we are offering two types of services. I think we need to have a name that can cover any type of service, the in-person and the distant, intuitive stuff, just in case we expand in the future. What about something like 'Sixth Sense Consulting'?"

Jean and Lydia shrieked at the same time. "That's perfect!" "How wonderful! Exactly what we need!"

Ian smiled in satisfaction. "I guess we are going to have a business."

They all raised their coffee mugs for a toast.

* * *

Mary Beth, 4:00pm

SHIT, fuck and damn! Mary Beth cursed and then apologized silently to no one as she pushed the vintage vacuum across the carpet in Maddie's master bedroom. Apparently, Stanley had used this bedroom, and Maddie felt more comfortable in the guest bedroom, so this room had become hers. The master suite was spacious and had its own bath and a walk-in closet, which in spite of hours of work on Samantha's part, was still overloaded with junk. At least there was space to hang her clothes.

Samantha had moved on to cleaning out the two-car garage when Mary Beth moved in. It was so packed, it was a miracle one car would fit in it. Mary Beth's car was parked on the driveway. She wished she could get it out of sight, but Maddie was adamant that no one would turn her in. The house desperately needed cleaning, but Maddie was stubborn about not doing it. And she didn't want Mary Beth to do it, either. It apparently hadn't been vacuumed since before Stanley died. Mary Beth was afraid to ask why Stanley was the one who did the vacuuming, as housework seemed to be a touchy subject.

If only Mom could see her now. She chuckled at the irony. Here she was, forcing her cleaning services on Maddie, when Mom had done all the cleaning at their place and berated her for not helping. Mom had probably thought she was a lazy parasite, but Mary Beth had never been able to beat Mom to the cleaning. It was also ironic that Maddie didn't appreciate Mary Beth's efforts. Mary Beth couldn't help it. She couldn't live in the midst of such a mess. Was she turning into her Mom? Jesus, she hoped not. She loved her, but she'd been such an obsessive cleaner.

She finished the carpet in her bedroom and began on the hall. She dreaded getting within sight of Maddie, who was working on a jewelry project at the dining table, because she knew she'd get a dirty look for her efforts. Was she doomed to be judged no matter what she did? On top of everything else, Maddie had been acting weird today. She wondered what was going on.

Shit. Fuck. Damn. And to hell with apologizing. Why was life so complicated? At first sight, living temporarily with Maddie had seemed brilliant. Maddie was eccentric, but the most generous person she'd ever met, and she seemed to genuinely like Mary Beth. Mary Beth had thought it would be simple being here, but every attempt to help Maddie created discord. She just couldn't accept help. Yet she needed it so badly.

On top of the tension that hummed beneath the surface all the time now (it was almost as if Maddie had adopted Mary Beth, because she was treating her like Mom used to), Mary Beth was confused and fuming about her non-relationship with Ethan.

The one dinner she'd invited him to last month had been stilted, not at all like when they'd eaten at her place, so after that, she only saw him away from Maddie, but Maddie was terribly nosy about how she spent her spare time. She wanted Ethan to insist on more time together, but instead, he was patience personified, making himself scarce, only seeing her maybe once a week outside of Saturday afternoons. For some reason, that made her mad. Didn't he want more from her? Was she that undesirable? She knew she still carried some extra weight. On the plus side, she'd quit smoking. She still cussed like crazy, but he'd never objected to that. Why didn't he want her?

The ringing barely pierced the roar of the vacuum, and Mary Beth shut off the antiquated monster and ran for the phone, knowing Maddie hadn't heard it. "Hello, O'Neill residence."

"Mary Beth."

"Ethan." She felt guilty, as if he'd heard her angry musings.

"Are you totally settled in now?"

"Yes, I've taken up housework. Maddie doesn't want me to, but the place needs a good once over. Or maybe a twice over." She chided herself for blathering on about meaningless crap.

"Would you have time to go out for dinner and a movie or something like that?"

"I could really use a break. Thanks for offering to have dinner out. It's more fun than if we do it here under Maddie's watchful eye." She cringed at the unintended double entendre, then blundered through, lowering her voice, hoping Maddie couldn't hear. (Seemed she was deaf only in certain registers.) "I don't think I could bear that again."

"Is 5 too early?"

"Hell, no. I'll be ready."

"Great!" He sounded cheerful, but tentative. She wondered what that was about.

. . .

LATER, over lasagna at the Italian place (seemed like Italian was all she ate anymore, not that she minded), Ethan was getting more personal than he ever had. Mary Beth was both pleased and a little scared.

She sipped her wine as he pressed on with his revelation. "So you see, I haven't had the courage to say much before now, but I started feeling like I might lose you. When you were saying you had to leave Palm Lakes, it made me frantic. I wanted to offer you a place to stay, but I didn't know how you felt about me, and I didn't want to presume. Plus, it would mess up your reputation to be at my place, us not married and all."

Mary Beth almost blew wine out her nose. "Don't talk like that. What do I care what people think about me? I care what you think. Or do *you* care what people think?"

"I'm a lot older than you, Mary Beth, old enough to be your father. It looks like I'm trying to be your sugar daddy. People would talk. You deserve better. Besides, I have a pretty big extended family, and they wouldn't like it, either, if I were living in sin. Not that I'm implying there would be any sinning." He looked at her sheepishly, his gray eyes pained.

Emotions washed through Mary Beth. She was touched at his kindness, but annoyed at his concern about what people would think. "So what is this confession about, anyway? You're just apologizing for not offering me a room? You don't owe me anything."

His face creased with worry, exaggerating the wrinkles around his eyes. "I'm not saying it well. I was never good at this sort of thing. I think it's great that you're with Maddie, but it's temporary. You'll either be asked to leave again, or she'll finally realize she needs to go to assisted living. I don't want to sit back anymore and take a chance on losing you." He reached for his wineglass and nervously gulped some red wine.

"Losing me? You don't have me." *Damn, that didn't come out right.* "I mean, what do you want?"

"Want? What I want and what I can have are two different things. I wish I were younger. If I were even ten years younger, I'd ask you to marry me. But you don't need to be saddled with someone my age. I'm OK now, but in ten years, I could be a burden. You deserve a husband who's young and strong. And there are other things." A shadow crossed his face. It looked like embarrassment.

Mary Beth's eyes widened. "Are you talking about sex?"

"You don't have to shout it." He pouted as he glanced around the room in embarrassment.

"I wasn't shouting. I just want clarification."

He looked down at his plate and took another swig of wine. "I haven't been with a woman that way for years. My wife was sick for a long time, you know. I'm not sure I have it in me anymore. You're young and beautiful, and you deserve someone who can satisfy you. I'm not sure I can." The sadness in his voice stabbed Mary Beth in the heart. She suddenly realized just how much she loved him.

"Shit, Ethan. Pardon my French. You should have told me all this a long time ago. Now I don't have a place of my own, and you don't want to go to your house. What are we gonna do? I guess we'll just need to go to a hotel. I'm going to have to show you the error of your thinking. Maybe not about me being young and beautiful. I'll accept that." She grinned at the idea that anyone would think she was young and beautiful. "You're the one I want to be with. I really care for you. If you care for me, things can work out. I'm not concerned about the age difference, and there are many ways to express love and affection, so don't narrow it down to just one thing." She could see hope dawning in his gray eyes. "So what do you say? Are you willing to take a chance on me?"

She could see his adam's apple bounce as he gulped. "Let's get the check." A cautious eagerness filled his silvery eyes.

She reached for her purse. *I'm going to have to listen to Catherine say, "I told you so."*

* * *

Samantha, 5:15pm

THE PHONE RANG, displaying Mom's number on the Caller ID. Samantha simultaneously tried to guess why Mom was calling, push away a sense of panic about all the scary scenarios she could imagine, and answer the phone.

"Hello?"

"Hi, it's me." Uh-oh, Mom sounded down.

"Hi, Mom. Is everything OK?" Samantha's heart started pounding. Had she had an accident or started a kitchen fire? Mary Beth had told her about the near miss a while back. She lived in constant fear that even with Mary Beth living there, Mom would burn the house down. She was so easily distracted.

"Everything's fine." Mom's voice sounded anything but fine. Samantha waited to see what Mom would say, anxious and a little irritated that she was taking so long. "I made a decision."

This was the last thing Samantha expected to hear. It sounded important, and she didn't dare to wish that Mom had seen the light and decided to move to assisted living. "What decision is that, Mom?"

"The one you've been wanting me to make for a couple months. I'm ready to move. When can we get it done?"

Samantha was unable to process this sudden reversal in Mom's intentions. Mom had categorically stated she wasn't going to move. What had happened to change that? "What caused this?"

"I don't know. I was just opening the refrigerator and it hit me that I can't stay here. Even with all the help I have, there isn't enough money, and if I sell the car, that's only going to make me more dependent on you. I might as well go to the assisted living place. I'll have some money if I do that, right?"

Samantha's mind raced. How was she going to get the house ready for sale? And what would they use for funds to get Mom accepted until the house sold? If only Mom had allowed her to do more before now. But sudden reversals in direction were commonplace with Mom, and she knew she couldn't delay. The longer she waited, the more likely it was that Mom would reverse again. "I'll get the process in motion. You should get a good price for the house. It's paid for. I know a good realtor, the one Mary Beth used. I would think you would have more money to spend if you do that, though you'd need to save, because it would be how you're paying the fees at the assisted living place. But yes, you'd be

291

better off financially." In her mind she silently said, 'if you don't live too many years.' Though it was a guilty thought, she couldn't suppress it.

Mom sighed. "Then let's do it. Will you find out what I need to do?"

"Sure, Mom. I'll take tomorrow off and get things sorted. Then I'll come talk to you about what will be involved. We need to get the house sold fast, but for the best price, and that means doing a lot of work to prepare it. I'll do my best to see it gets done quickly." Relief flooded her in spite of the enormity of the job she faced. "I know you don't want to leave the house you've lived in for so long, and I know it will be hard to scale down, but the independent living section here in Palm Lakes will give you more freedom than you'd think. You might be surprised to find that you like it there." Not that she thought there was a chance in hell of that happening.

"It doesn't matter. I can't stay here anymore." The depression in Mom's voice pained Samantha. "You know you'll have to take Beau. I won't be able to have him there, and I won't put him in the pound." Defiance had crept into her voice.

"I'll do everything I can to make it as easy as possible, Mom. We'll take Beau. He's a great dog. I'd never let him be harmed." She'd tell her later on about Jack taking him.

"I know that. I'm going to say goodbye now. I'm feeling tired."

"I'll come by tomorrow after I get all the information we need." Samantha hung up the phone as her mind raced about the tasks for the next day. She had a contact at the assisted living place--she hadn't told Mom she'd gone by and toured the place to check it out shortly after Dad died; thank heaven she'd done that, as it gave her a good picture of the next step. She'd go see what rooms were available. God, she hoped a nice one was open. If they had to delay, Mom might change her mind. She'd make an appointment with Shari Lopez, the realtor. And she needed to get a game plan for cleaning up the house and scaling down the amount of stuff that would be moved. She didn't relish the thought of being under pressure to get it done fast. She hoped Mom wouldn't resist or obstruct.

Suddenly, another thought entered her mind, chasing away the worry and anxiety. If she got Mom into assisted living, she could take the job with Jack. The knowledge both thrilled and scared her. She might be able to take it soon if there was a place Mom could move into. If he allowed her the flexible, short work schedule, she could use afternoons and weekends to clean Mom's place up for sale. Maybe she could start at Jack's in a couple weeks. The extra money would be useful for helping Mom during the transition. It would be the beginning of a whole new chapter in her life, no matter what happened. She couldn't call Jack and tell him now, but tomorrow, after talking with Mom, she'd ring him and tell him the good news.

Arthur would be glad to hear that Mom had decided to move, but he wasn't too keen on the work involved, not that he would help much. She brushed aside annoyance. She might as well tell him now and get it over with.

* * *

Helen, 6:00pm

THE LIGHTS WERE ROMANTICALLY low in the large dining room at the Rec Center. Floor-to-ceiling windows looked out onto the golf course and lakes, burnished gold by the setting sun. Inside, candles, fine silverware and white linen tablecloths added to the elegance of the occasion.

The dining room, an extension of the kitchen classroom used by the International Gourmet Cooking Club, was the venue for the annual club dinner tonight, and the lushly carpeted room was packed in spite of the hefty charge for what was being billed as a 'five-star, five course meal' that was being served by a prestigious valley caterer.

Helen and Alexander had grabbed seats at one of the large round tables nearest the windows that gave an unimpeded view over the golf course. Out to the right, they could even see a bit of the purple mountains in the distance.

Spring was in full swing, and the weather was fine, so Helen and Alexander were wearing what amounted to summer clothing, though it was 'desert formal' (what everyone called the casual wear accepted at formal occasions here in the desert). There were no tuxedos or evening gowns. Very few of the men had on jackets or ties other than bolo ties.

Some of the women were decked out in Native American jewelry and some wore long skirts, but few were wearing high heels.

Nora and Luke had claimed seats next to Helen, with Nora sitting beside Helen so they could chat. Next to Alexander sat Ray and Alan, a gay couple who were the most entertaining guys Helen had ever met. They always kept the cooking class in stitches with their impressions and impromptu skits.

The other tables were filling up fast, and the chatter in the dining room was making it hard to converse. Although the classes rarely had more than 20 students, the membership of the club ran to at least 200, and it looked like most of them had turned out for the annual dinner, a chance to eat great food prepared by someone else and mingle with others who loved to cook. The soft background music had been drowned out some time ago as the room filled. Helen was grateful that the seats were padded, because she knew they would be here a long time for a five course meal. Wine would be served with most of the courses, and waiters were moving from table to table filling water glasses and offering iced tea to guests.

The theme was French for this meal, and as the pumpkin soup with truffle cream was being brought out, Helen turned to Nora. "It's been a while since I've seen you. How are things going with your business?" Nora looked marvelous tonight, not nearly as stressed as she'd seemed last time Helen had seen her.

Nora smiled, hazel eyes aglow. "Everything is going well. I can't believe how much has happened this year! You know, the Botanica business is going to save us financially, and it might just have saved our marriage."

Helen's jaw dropped. Recovering her wits, she replied, "I'm so glad you're happy with the results of the business. I love the products, but I don't think I could do it as a business. I'm much too shy and don't know whom I could even approach. How do you do something like that?"

Nora shrugged. "It wasn't all that hard once I got over my fear of selling. I have a lot of family and plenty of friends around Palm Lakes, and I do love to talk to people. You know, it's simply a matter of offering to tell them about something that could be useful for them. I don't worry anymore about being turned down, because I figure they're able to decide whether it's in their best interests. Maybe that's why I so often get affirmative answers. I haven't figured it all out yet, but it's working well." Her eyes flashed with enthusiasm and she dropped her voice a notch. "I've been able to get Luke out of that awful minimum-wage job at the burger place. He's going to be my accountant, scheduler and organizer. He's perfect for the job; I was beginning to be overwhelmed by all the tasks. For a while there, I was worried what was going to happen to us. Now, the sky's the limit." Nora was beaming, and Helen was thrilled to hear of her success.

"I know what you mean. I have had so many life changes in the past year, it's hard to imagine. I went from feeling totally lost and alone and concerned about my finances to being married to a wonderful man who is a successful author and lives in a beautiful house. Kind of like a fairy tale for me."

Nora patted Helen's hand. "I'm so happy for us both, dear. We deserve it."

Helen smiled in agreement. "I have other good news. I just became a grandmother again. My daughter Sally had her baby a little early, but Mama and daughter are doing fine."

"We're going to have to toast that once we get some wine."

Nora leaned over to say something to Luke, and Helen looked at Alexander, who was carrying on a conversation with both Ray and Alan, who didn't look as bright and jolly as they usually did. Helen wondered if something was wrong. She hoped not. Ray and Alan were so much fun and so kind and generous to her in the cooking class. Everyone loved them. But Helen couldn't hear their conversation over the dull roar of the crowd, so she set about eating her soup.

The food was incredible, but by the time the final course was finished, Helen was ready to go home. She was full and had run out of things to chat about with Nora and Luke. And it was impossible to talk to anyone across the broad expanse of the big round table. She caught Alexander's eye, and he reached under the table and squeezed her hand. His emerald eyes questioned her, and she smiled and said, "I'm fine. Just feeling tired for some reason. You almost ready to head home?" He smiled and nodded.

· · ·

295

THEY ARRIVED home to the enthusiastic greeting of Spot and the non-greeting of Fido, who tended to punish them when they went out and left him alone with the dog. "I guess we better take Spot for at least a short walk," Alexander mentioned.

Helen kicked off her shoes. "Yes, we'd better. Let me change into walking shoes. I wish we had a fence around the yard, but given what we've been discussing, that would be a waste of money." She went into the master bedroom and came back with her sneakers on.

Thirty minutes later, she and Alexander were laying back on the couch, shoeless feet up on the coffee table. "Would you like anything to drink?"

Helen sighed. "I have no room for anything else, but thanks for asking."

Alexander took her hand and threaded his fingers through hers. "Did you enjoy the club dinner? It's your first one."

"Yes, very much. But it was hard to talk to anyone except the people right next to you. I wish I could have talked with more people. Nora was telling me about how well her business is doing. I'm so happy for her and Luke. What was going on with Ray and Alan? They're usually so upbeat, and they looked down."

Alexander sighed. "They're having a family crisis. I feel so sorry for them. Bottom line is that Ray, who was married for a short while as a young man, has a grandchild, and the child is now an orphan, because her mother died in a car accident, and the father, who ran off soon after she was born, is in the wind. Even if he could be found--and he never paid child support or showed an interest in his child--he wouldn't be a likely candidate to raise the girl. Ray's ex died of cancer some years back, and there's no one else. Ray doesn't want the child in a foster home. You know how bad that can be."

"Oh, what a terrible situation! Was he in contact with his grandchild before?"

Alexander shook his head. "No, Ray's ex-wife was bitter about Ray coming out and divorcing her, and she didn't allow him to be a part of his daughter's life. Now she's gone, and he's never met his grandchild, but he's the closest thing she has to family. A distant cousin called him. No one else wants the kid."

Helen suddenly realized what it meant. "Oh, no! They can't stay here if they take the child, and raising a child is a big thing. What does Alan say?"

Alexander shrugged. "I'm not sure. He was pretty quiet at dinner. He's not happy, but he obviously wants to support Ray. I didn't get a feel for whether he's on board with having a kid to raise. Not even Ray seems that sure of what to do. I am so glad we aren't in a position like that."

Helen nodded. "No wonder they looked depressed. We'll have to stay in touch and see if there's anything we can do to help. It's a difficult thing to be facing at this time of life when you were looking forward to just taking it easy and doing what you like. I can't imagine going back to raising a daughter... school work, teenage problems, dating. Oh my God! Those poor men. Do you think it could break up their relationship?"

Alexander grimaced. "It is the sort of thing that can drive a wedge in even the best relationship. I guess time will tell. We just need to be there for them."

"I'll call tomorrow and see what, if anything, we can do."

"They'll like that."

Helen paused, reflecting on how lucky she was to have the life she had. "I should say it more often. I feel so blessed to have you and our life together. It's made all the difference in my life."

His smile warmed her. "I feel the same way."

"Well, I'm sorry for Ray and Alan, and I hope things work out for them. It must have taken the edge off your dinner when you heard all that. I would have lost my appetite. I thought the food was amazing! How did it compare to past dinners?"

"I think it was one of the better ones they've done. But you can't go wrong with French food. Speaking of which, this trip is going to be so much fun. I can't wait to show you around France and let you taste all the marvelous flavors the country has to offer. And the scenery...it's divine."

"I'm looking forward to it, too. I've never been out of the country before we went on our honeymoon. I feel like I'm becoming a real globetrotter." Helen closed her eyes and relaxed at the thought of spending time in France. Then a guilty feeling stabbed her. "We still need to figure out what to do with Fido and Spot. I hate leaving them alone for long, but I'm leaning towards the idea of having a house sitter. I was considering offering the job to Mary Beth. She could use some money, and it wouldn't be illegal to hire her as a house sitter. I don't know if she'd say yes. What do you think?"

"I think it's a good idea. We want someone trustworthy and kind to animals. I like Mary Beth."

"I'll ask her tomorrow."

"Speaking of globetrotting, I've been wanting to talk to you more about our research into where to live. Have you made progress in the past few weeks?"

"I'm learning to expand my horizons. I have looked at the library, but also online. It's amazing what you can find out there." Helen leaned back and closed her eyes.

"And have you gotten any ideas?"

She opened her eyes and regarded him with suspicion. His green eyes were flashing. "You have an idea. You're just baiting me."

He laughed out loud. "Yes, I do. But I wanted to let you go first. Have you got any place that grabbed your attention?"

"I know we said we'd move wherever, but as I began to search it just seemed smarter to stay in the US and its territories. And that doesn't leave us a lot of choice if we're looking for a tropical island to live on. Hawaii, the Virgin Islands, American Samoa. That's about it, I think."

"That's what I thought. American Samoa would really put a lot of distance between you and your family. You probably wouldn't want to be quite that far away."

"I was thinking the same thing. I'd be glad to have some space, but that would be too much. I'd never see my grandkids again." She felt excitement building. They were obviously on the same wavelength.

"Hawaii is amazingly beautiful. But it's also quite distant from the mainland. Very expensive for folks to visit."

"The same thought occurred to me." She leaned towards him in anticipation.

"The Virgin Islands are a bit more accessible. The waters of the Caribbean are warm and turquoise, much like those in the South Pacific. There are three islands to choose from, each very different."

She suspected they were coming to the same conclusion. "I've done some reading, and I also felt the Virgin Islands would work for us. Considering our interests, hobbies and personalities, I think one island is better suited than the others."

Alexander looked at her sharply. "I agree. Which island did you pick?"

Helen hesitated, enjoying his complete attention.

He stared at her like he'd caught on to her game. "Come on, woman, which island? I'll tell you if I agree."

It occurred to Helen that in the past, she wouldn't have had the courage to speak up in a situation like this, because her opinion had never mattered to anyone. So much had changed. "I like St. Croix."

The smile that made her knees weak lit up his face. "Just as I thought. We are in accord." He slid closer to her on the couch and planted a searing kiss on her lips.

Her brain overloaded, just like it always did when he kissed her. She came up for air. "So that means we're moving to the Virgin Islands?"

He wrapped his arms around her and pulled her closer, nibbling her ear and whispered, "Let's go to bed and discuss it."

NEVER TOO LATE: A PREVIEW

Tuesday, March 19, 1996
Eric, 2:30am

At the first sight of blood, Eric felt a powerful, unseen force begin to suck him into the past. *Not again.* Cold sweat bloomed on his skin despite the warmth of the night. He clenched the steering wheel and stared fixedly ahead at the darkened parking lot to avoid seeing the tiny, nearly black rivulet inch along the back of his hand, but in spite of his efforts, he was transported back to the murder scene, where his neighbor Tanya was bleeding out.

Her life's blood pooled around her in an expanding scarlet lake on the white kitchen tiles, the coppery smell assailing his nostrils. Her red silk bathrobe was gruesomely two-toned and soaking wet. The panic in her blue eyes waned as her life poured out onto the floor. He applied pressure to the vicious knife wound on her throat, but he only succeeded in soaking his hands with warm, sticky blood. Her gagging mocked his powerlessness. So much blood...his heart pounded in response to the carnage, but also with the knowledge that he was about to be stabbed in the back by the man who had done this.

Then suddenly, he was back in present time. He let out the breath he'd been holding and raggedly sucked in air. It was over. For now. He took several more deep breaths, willing his heart to calm and prying his hands off the steering wheel one finger at a time, as if they belonged to someone else. He turned his hands this way and that, almost surprised that they weren't drenched in blood.

He reached into his pocket and pulled out a handkerchief, blotting the trickle of blood that had triggered the flashback. Then he examined the hand for the source of the blood. A minuscule crack had opened at the cuticle end of the nail of his index finger. It was so damn dry in the desert, he often developed these insidious cracks in his skin. They were tiny, but they hurt, and when they opened, they bled, which was not good for him right now. That was an understatement. Lydia was always going on about moisturizing. If only the solution were that simple.

His water bottle and the Tupperware container with homemade cookies sat untouched on the passenger seat. He'd pulled into the parking lot at Desert Breezes, the assisted living place in Palm Lakes Senior Community, and parked under a street light so he could have a snack halfway through his night shift with the Posse, the community's security force. He sucked another deep breath in, then let it out gustily. He was still shaking and felt a little weak. Not to mention foolish.

He hadn't told Lydia that the sight of blood made him return to the time of the murder, when he was stabbed by Owen Schmidt, Palm Lakes' own serial killer. With her help, he'd gotten to the point where he rarely had nightmares about the incident anymore, so she thought he was improving. But he hadn't told her about the flashbacks. He couldn't understand why he'd developed this pattern of freaking out when he saw blood. Prior to retiring, he'd seen plenty of blood as a homicide detective, and he'd never had an adverse reaction. Hell, his nickname 'Red' referred to a bloody incident with a perp. If he didn't overcome this problem...it didn't bear thinking about.

Leaving the cookies untouched, he guzzled the water, then, feeling better, he piloted his Posse cruiser through the deserted streets of Palm Lakes, windows down, letting the mild breeze flow over him, no music on to cover the night sounds, not that he expected much in the way of noise. Bedtime came early for most residents.

The new moon guaranteed a spectacular showing of stars in the cloudless sky. He paused when he reached the next stop sign, marveling at how many stars he could see and how bright they were. Anything to distract himself from what had just happened.

He'd been patrolling for hours, and the only vehicle he'd seen was the other Posse car when he'd met his partner to choose which portions to cruise at the beginning of the shift. But there was plenty of nonhuman nightlife, thanks to the undeveloped desert that bordered Palm Lakes on the east and north. Disturbingly large bats danced around street lights, no doubt feeding on the insects attracted there. A coyote had slunk across the road as he passed the golf course, and the occasional cottontail sprinted across the lane in front of him, testing his alertness.

It was easy to get lost in the winding streets of Palm Lakes if you weren't familiar with them, but after serving with the Posse for nearly two years, Eric could navigate them in his sleep. He was patrolling the half of Palm Lakes to the south and west of the central golf course, while his partner cruised the other half. This route would take him by his own condo several times, where Lydia slept, awaiting his return when the shift ended at 7am. The graveyard shift was a boring, routine task, but for now, it suited him to be up while everyone else slept. Sleep had become problematic after what had happened eight weeks ago.

He turned onto Sunset Drive, the road he lived on which ran parallel to the 6-ft block wall that formed the boundary of Palm Lakes. It was these homes with the outside world on the other side of the wall that had the highest level of property crimes. He crawled down the street, nodding his head as if to greet Lydia as he passed by his condo, looking into the back yards across the street which had the boundary wall. Recently, there had been some thefts from garages where homeowners had forgotten to put the garage door down, a frighteningly common occurrence in this community of seniors. He hadn't found any doors up so far tonight, so maybe it would stay quiet.

As he cruised down the road enjoying the silence, he mulled over his present situation. Lydia had expressed a hope that he'd get off night shift. It made sense, because their schedules currently had little overlap, but she hadn't pushed him. She knew he was struggling to get back to how things were before January 27th. She saw so much, and she didn't agree with his choices, but she didn't complain. He'd never had a relationship where he was given so much support, and it pained him to keep things from her, but she didn't need to know how much trouble he was still experiencing. He had to sort it out before he'd know if they had a future, and he wanted one. The problem was, he had no idea how to resolve the issue himself, but telling her about it didn't seem the way to go. He was already leaning on her far too much.

He crossed the main road that exited the gated community south of the intersection. On this side of the four-way stop were a strip mall and some other businesses, then it graded back into single family homes. He'd just gotten back into residential when he thought he spotted movement near a house up ahead on the right. The shadows were too tall to be coyotes, and it was unlikely a homeowner was creeping around at nearly 3am. He killed his lights and eased the car over to the curb at the house next door and peered into the darkness. Sure enough, the garage door was up. Maybe he should radio his partner for help. By the time he got here, though, it would all be over. Mostly, it was kids doing this kind of shit; nothing to be afraid of. In spite of that, he felt tension pluck his nerves and anxiety fog his mind like poison gas. Unsure whether he was overcompensating or merely being reasonable, he decided to handle it alone. He grabbed the flashlight that lay on the passenger seat, slipped out of the car as quietly as possible, clicked the door shut and put the flashlight in the loop of his belt. When they heard him, they would probably run off. Unless it was some drug-crazed loony. He paused and reconsidered calling for backup, then dismissed it.

This was an older section of town, and a mature olive tree dominated the front yard of the home, blocking his view of the garage next door. He ducked around the tree, crunching on the gravel as little as possible-- almost all of the homes in Palm Lakes had gravel instead of grass--and slipped closer to the open garage, which was on this end of the neighboring house. He hadn't seen anyone since the earlier shadows and wondered if they were gone. He hoped so. His heart was hammering in his ears, and his hands were sweaty. He'd been in much worse situations and kept his cool, but that was before January 27th. He pressed on anyway.

Just as he arrived at the corner of the house, two people raced out of the garage, nearly running into him. He grabbed the smaller one--it was only a kid. "Posse! Stop right there and put your hands up."

Neither one obeyed him, and he wondered if they understood English, as even in the dark he could see they were Hispanic. He had a grip on the younger one's shirt, and the boy wasn't struggling much. It was obvious he was in shock. The older one--he might have been late teens--pulled a knife and menaced Eric. "Let him go now or I'll cut you, viejo," he said with bravado. *Well, at least one of them speaks English.*

The drumbeat of Eric's heart turned into a roar as he looked at the knife. It was a wicked-looking military blade, and the kid held it like he knew how to use it. Eric put his hand on the butt of his gun, wondering if he could make himself shoot a boy, as darkness began to fill his peripheral vision, shrinking his field of view to only the knife and the hand wielding it. He felt faint. Glad he had the kid to lean on. He didn't have the strength to draw his gun, even if he could commit to shooting it.

The knife-wielder was a good ten feet away from him, backing up as if he intended to run into the back yard and jump the wall to get out of Palm Lakes. Not wanting to be abandoned with the lawman, his younger companion struggled to free himself from Eric's grip, but Eric tightened up, taking a handful of shoulder so the kid couldn't rip out of the shirt and escape.

Keeping his eyes on the older one and his hand on his holstered gun, Eric stood silently but shakily and let the other kid run away. Still leaning partially on the boy, he bent over to catch his breath, glad that his normal vision was slowly returning. The boy had stopped squirming and stood like a rock, probably terrified of what was going to happen next.

Eric dragged the boy to the front door of the house and rang the bell. After a few minutes, the door opened. A groggy elderly man with thinning white hair squinted at Eric. "What's wrong, Officer?"

"Sir, your garage is open, and I found some kids in it. I don't know if anything is missing, but we'll need you to check it out first thing tomorrow and file a report if you believe anything was stolen."

The old geezer stared at the boy next to Eric. "Is that pipsqueak a thief?" he asked incredulously.

"He was with an older kid, maybe 18 or so. I didn't see them take anything, but both were in the garage. Will you let us know first thing tomorrow?"

"Sure thing, Officer. Thanks for the help."

"And sir? Please put your garage door down before you go back to bed."

"Oh, right." The old man shut the door, and Eric waited for the garage door to go down before heading back to his car, young would-be thief in tow.

When they got to the vehicle, Eric stopped and looked hard at the kid for the first time. He didn't look very old. Dark hair hanging into his equally dark eyes, gangly body, a face that radiated innocence. "So, kid, what am I going to do with you? Last thing I need is a lot of paperwork in the middle of the night. But your friend was pretty scary, pulling a knife on a police officer."

The boy drew himself up to his full height. "He wasn't scared of you, and I ain't, either."

"Well, you ought to be. How old are you, anyway?"

The kid looked like he was unsure whether telling the truth was a good idea. "I'm almost 12."

"What would your parents think about you being out at night stealing?"

"I didn't steal nothing. I just came along for the fun. I never did this before." He looked down at his feet and shuffled them. "I don't think I'll ever do it again."

"That's the smartest thing you've said so far. I'm going to take you home. Where do you live?"

The kid's dark eyes filled with fear. "I can walk."

"Sure you can, but I want to talk to your folks."

"I don't have any folks. I have foster parents."

Eric felt bad for the boy, but it didn't change the plan. "I still have to take you home, talk to them and verify your name and age in case this man lodges a complaint. You better hope he doesn't." Eric opened the rear passenger door. "Get in nicely and I won't cuff you." As if his cuffs would be any restraint for such small wrists.

The boy looked at him as if gauging whether he meant it, then scrambled into the back seat. Eric shut the door, went round to the driver's side, got in and pushed the button to lock the back doors so the kid couldn't escape. Last thing he needed was the boy falling out and hurting himself.

Ten minutes later, following the child's halting directions, he pulled up in front of the boy's home in a modest, well-kept neighborhood not far from Palm Lakes. By now, the kid was deflated and scared, but he didn't attempt to run away. He got out and went with Eric to the door and waited stiffly after Eric rang the doorbell, as if in anticipation of trouble to come. The door opened on a sleepy-eyed woman of about 40. Her dark hair was in a single braid, and like the boy, she was Hispanic. "What?" she said when she saw the boy. "Miguel, what is this?" Eric could feel the boy shrinking, but the child remained silent.

"Ma'am, I found him in Palm Lakes with an older boy in the garage of a resident. I'm not sure what he was doing, but it wasn't good. At the very least, it's trespassing. Are you his mother?"

She shook her head as if still trying to process the information. "Foster mother. We have several children we foster, and Miguel is the oldest. He isn't supposed to be out at night. I thought he was in bed."

"If it turns out anything is missing, the homeowner will be filing a complaint tomorrow. I will be back tomorrow afternoon and let you know either way. Will you be home after lunch?"

"Yes, I can be here all afternoon."

"I'll see you then and let you know what is going to happen. Keep him inside at night from now on." Eric turned and walked to his car without looking back. He made a decision and reached for his radio. "Nick, you there?"

A burst of static preceded the answer. "Sure, Red. Whatcha need?"

"I had a little tussle on Sunset drive with two hoods in someone's open garage. One got away, and I just took the other one home. Do you think you can take the shift for the rest of the night? I'm feeling like I need to go home." He didn't have to say why. It was common knowledge what had happened on January 27th.

"Sure, Red. You go on home. Nothing else gonna happen tonight. I've got it."

"Thanks. Johnson out." He drove the two miles back home, reaching for the garage door opener as he turned into the driveway. Lydia would probably hear the garage door and wonder why he was home early. Not much chance of slipping in unnoticed. He sighed, resigning himself to having to explain to her.

As the garage door closed behind him, he breathed deeply a few times and let the tension slip away as much as he could. He shook himself, then got out of the car, taking his water bottle, the uneaten cookies and his flashlight with him. He got all the way into the kitchen before Lydia caught him.

"What's wrong? Or did you just stop to refill your water bottle?" She yawned and stretched as she stood in the doorway, her thick, curly hair a dark curtain around her face. She had on a thin cotton nightgown that wasn't meant to be sexy, but the way her curves filled it out, it was. He felt a stirring of arousal and was pleased. At least something was returning to normal.

He smiled at her, knowing that she was reading him and there was no point lying. Not that lying was his style; well at least, not outright lying. He just wasn't telling her everything.

"I had to deal with an incident--nothing terrible--and I asked Nick to take the rest of the shift on his own. I caught some kids messing in a guy's garage. He'd forgotten to put the door down. I only managed to hold on to the small one. Damn, but they start young these days. He wasn't even 12. But I don't think they stole anything. The man will let us know tomorrow morning...this morning."

She stared at him, and he knew what she was going to say. "What else happened?"

"The bigger kid pulled a knife on me, one of those fancy military ones, probably a KA-BAR." He drew in a deep breath, then sighed heavily. "I had a flashback. I didn't black out, but if the kid had wanted to take me, he could have. I didn't have the strength to pull my gun; I could barely stand. I'm lucky he ran." He shook his head and dropped into the chair by the kitchen table, setting his burdens down on the table as he did.

Lydia said nothing, but walked over to him and put her hands on his shoulders. She was good that way, no, great that way. She always seemed to know what to do or say. "I'm so grateful you're OK." She began to massage his shoulders, and it felt heavenly. "How about a hit of herbal remedy?"

"Yeah, I could use that for sure."

She stopped what she was doing and went to the cupboard and pulled out a quart-sized brown glass bottle. She squirted a couple droppersful of liquid into a drinking glass, then added some water and handed it to him. "Bottoms up!"

He smiled weakly. "Thanks." He drained the glass in one big swallow, then sputtered a little. "It would be nice if it tasted better."

She grinned at him. "Quit your bitchin'. It isn't even technically legal, but it works."

"Damn right it works. My woman is a genius with weed." He regarded the empty glass with distaste. "No one would suspect this is marijuana."

"Has it really been helping with the nightmares?"

It was hard to take her scrutiny. "Yes, I rarely have nightmares anymore, but apparently, when put in the position of being threatened with a knife, I get incapacitated." He looked down at the empty glass. "I was hoping it was getting better." He wasn't about to tell her about the flashbacks when he saw blood. This was bad enough.

She looked at him quizzically. "Of course, it's better. It just isn't cured. It takes time. Why are you so pessimistic?" She studied him with dark brown eyes as she stroked his shoulder.

"I know you're reading me."

She nodded. "And I know you're keeping something from me. It would be nice if you trusted me enough to tell me."

"It isn't a matter of trust." He frowned, because he hated her thinking that. "I'm frustrated at my lack of progress. Grateful for all you've done for me, because I know without all you've done, I would be far worse off. Thanks to you, I was able to get back on patrol. But after tonight, I have to admit I'm a liability to the Posse. Me, a guy who worked homicide in St. Paul for years can't handle a teenager trying to fake me out with a knife." He wasn't sure what he was going to do with his life now. And unless he recovered completely, he couldn't ask Lydia to marry him. He couldn't saddle her with a psych case. He knew she could tell he was holding out on her, and he hoped she didn't think it was anything to do with her. He balled his hands in frustration.

"At least until you feel you're back to normal, it might be a wise decision. But don't regard it as permanent. You've made more progress than you seem to realize. Why not take a leave of absence and focus on allowing yourself to heal?"

It made good sense, yet seemed a bleak future. "You're right."

She started kneading his shoulder muscles again. "Would you like a scotch before you go to bed?"

"You read my mind."

She kept massaging him for a couple minutes, then fetched him a double. "You had a rough night. But, it was just an opportunity to see where you are in your healing process. You aren't up to facing an armed subject yet. And if I were given a vote, you would never face one again, but I do believe that with time, you will get your old confidence back. Just be kind to yourself."

He gulped down the scotch instead of sipping it like he usually did. "You're right again. I'm lucky to have you be the voice of reason for me. I can't stand feeling broken."

"Don't talk like that. You aren't broken. Being stabbed is traumatic. Anyone would be affected. Most would still be trying to heal physically. Speaking of which, do you have any pain?"

"Occasionally, but not bad."

She sat down in the adjacent chair and reached over to stroke his cheek. "I'm grateful to have you home at a time when we can sleep together."

A spike of fear flashed through him. He wasn't up for sex, in spite of noticing how delectable she looked. He tried to hide his fear, but she'd seen it. "I can't hide anything from your X-ray vision."

She smirked at him. "Then don't try. I'm not trying to seduce you. I know you've had a shock and sex is the last thing on your mind. Come to bed and get some sleep. I meant it would be nice to wake up next to you in the morning."

He gave her a sheepish grin. "That sounds good."

ABOUT THE AUTHOR

Maggie McPhee is a writer of contemporary 'boomer' women's fiction. The *Autumn In The Desert* series is based on life in a fictitious retirement community in the desert Southwest of the US. She also writes nonfiction under her real name, Maggie Percy.